The Last
Real Hobo

The Last Real Hobo

by
Terry A. Albritton

Tuleburg Press
Stockton, California
www.tuleburgpress.com

TULEBURG PRESS

The Last Real Hobo

Published by
Tuleburg Press
Stockton, California

www.tuleburgpress.com

Dedication

Dedicated with admiration and gratitude to the steadfast settlers and polished transients of the Central Valley who keep the California grizzly growling.

Table of Contents

The Last Real Hobo

Siberius Griffin was a Kansas boy who left the Dust Bowl in 1935 after his mother died on Black Sunday. He caught out on the rails, ending up in Chicago, where he learned the hobo signs and lingo; worked as a pearl diver, a sewer hog, and a splinter belly and messed with the whores at the Dill Pickle Club. None of these jobs: dishwashing, ditch digging, or carpentry kept him from reciting poems by Robert Frost in Bughouse Square. His fellow travelers gave him the moniker Kid Sisco, but by the time he headed out for California, he had begun to lose the "Kid" part and to follow the first commandment of the Hobo Code: "Decide your own life; don't let another person run or rule you."

Terry A. Albritton

The Body

Sisco and Choo-choo Blue snaked up the valley from Bakersfield on an Espee—a Southern Pacific freight loaded with tomatoes, corn, and squash. From the top of the boxcar, they saw the Oakies, Wops, Portugee, Chinks, and Spics working the fields in red, green, and white bandanas wrapped on their heads topped off with straw hats that looked like lampshades. The bugs were so bad that even the speed of the hog and the grit of the steam couldn't keep down the flies and gnats. The air was heavy with the smell of hay, alfalfa, and manure.

At the water tower in Hayden, they sprung it to cool off and to raid the grub box before catching out north to fish and to pick up a stake with the apple knockers. Sisco had no idea that a valley jerkwater would keep him in a place for two years—longer than he'd stayed put at one time since hitting the road at fifteen. Already there and jungled up behind the tower were Memphis Shorty, Camelback Curly, and Georgia Peach.

"We got here yesterday," said Peach in his thick southern speech. He sat on a crate with his stomach pushing out behind his overalls. He wore his usual dirty baseball cap with letters so faded you couldn't read them. He liked to cover up his bald head so he didn't look as old as he was.

"What ya got to drink here?" asked Blue, who didn't much care for Peach or the boy Spic who traveled with him. Carlos didn't seem to be around, and Sisco wanted to ask after him, but decided to wait until Peach was by himself.

"Help yourself to the dago red in the grub box," offered Memphis Shorty. "The mulligan's ready. Let's eat!" With his good arm, Shorty stirred the stew one more time and served it out in tin cans. There was a sweet smell

3

of dill weed, basil, and oregano that Peach always added to the potatoes, carrots, and meat for extra flavor.

"Where's your crummy at?" demanded Blue as he chugged the wine.

Peach didn't answer; he seemed kind of jumpy. He didn't much care for Blue either.

"Probably off with some cute Spic gal," said Curly, who leaned against the oak tree next to the access road. He wore his trademark flannel shirt with long sleeves. He thought it hid his hunchback. No matter how mean the heat, he always wore that faded shirt full of holes.

Nobody laughed at Curly's joke. They all knew that Carlos wouldn't go far without Peach, and he sure wouldn't go muff diving.

"Mulligan's mighty tasty," said Shorty as he offered Curly a can of stew. "You better get some, too, Peach, before it's all gone."

"Hey," mumbled Blue, "this here mulligan's only for fellas that work. Don't look to me like the Georgia boy done any of that lately. Too busy crying over his punk."

Blue always pushed things. Some kind of mess was chasing him. It could have been he was on the run from a chain gang in Louisiana or trying to beat a rap in some local calaboose. With dark, scarred up skin, he looked like a Negro without the smashed nose and lips. He claimed Cherokee blood and decked a rattler faster than any of the hobos. He knew a lot about riding the top of fast-moving trains—when to get on and when to jump off. Still, the fellows didn't like traveling with him because he drank too much and was always ready for a fight.

"Cut him some slack, Blue," said Sisco. "He done more work than you or me in the last week."

"Betcha' life I have," belched Peach who had downed his can full of stew. "Y'all look here at this pack of Camels that Carlos went to buy. Found 'em 'long side me on the ground next to our bedroll. Somethin' ain't right."

Beads of sweat dripped down his cheeks. The light from the fire made them shine as they streaked over the dirt on his face. They started up faster; Peach was crying.

The 'bos were quiet. Blue had sense enough to keep his mouth shut.

Finally, Shorty stood up and moved over to put a hand on Peach's shoulder. "Don't ya think he mighta gone into town for some decent Spic food? This Hooverville used to have a good cook from Old Mexico at the greasy spoon. Carlos prob'ly wanted some real grub—not them canned turds and tamales we eat."

"So why'd he go into town to eat last night when he never done it before? And why didn't he come back to me last night? I know somethin' ain't right."

"Don't ya think Carlos gits tired of us? He don't talk the same lingo, and we can't understand most of his jabber in Mexican. Ya know he misses his kinfolk in Old Mexico. Carries that picture of his mama everywhere."

Shorty was the one who always tried to make things better. He was the oldest of the hobos, probably somewhere in his fifties. When he was younger, he had a bad accident when a bull dick threw him off a train on the milk and honey route in Utah. A Mormon lady paid for an operation on his shoulder and took care of him until he got better.

"So, if ya ain't got no use for 'em Camels," said Curly, "how 'bout passin' 'em round?"

Peach stood up. He was having a hard time, and his belly moved in and out like he couldn't get any breath. "These here smokes is the last thing Carlos gave me. Nobody touches 'em till he gits back." He went behind the jungle across the access road toward the RICO Milk Plant where there was a bench.

Even as the crickets clicked and the frogs croaked, Peach's sobs cut into the night music. The moon was up now; it looked like the last slice of a melon after somebody had his way with the rest of it. The stars flashed signals to each other as if they knew a secret code and wanted to tell the folks below. What if those sparklers could telegraph each other like the boomers signaled back and forth about the trains? Near Lodi, a hog blew to let the station agent know that she'd be pulling into Hayden soon.

"Ya know, fellas," said Shorty, "I been thinkin' to go north up Washington way with the apple knockers." He moved over next to Curly to roll some cigarettes so they'd have fags to smoke.

"That's where Sisco and me was headed," said Blue, who chugged the wine but hadn't touched the mulligan beside him.

"Say, how 'bout a swig of that sterno?" asked Curly. "Looks like we ain't gittin' any of Peach's smokes, so we might as well git some sterno before ya finish it."

"I'll give ya some when I'm good and ready," laughed Blue. "What did ya expect from a pretty boy like Peach? Ya can't trust them jockers sweet on double-cheeked fruit!"

Sisco sidled up to Blue, grabbed the jug of dago, and handed him the can of mulligan. "Eat this can of stew, bum! Ya ain't left anybody 'nough hooch to matter."

Blue grumbled, threw the spoon into the dirt, and drank the mulligan.

"Don't choke on the 'taters," teased Curly.

With his words all mushed up, Blue said, "Yeah, I ain't used to havin' somebody else's wiener in my mouth like other folks I know."

He was ready to pass out which was a good thing because he was drunk and mean.

From a distance down the track, the hog approached, blinking her yellow white light. They felt her thunder beneath them. Shorty hurried to cover the fire with a pail of dirt. Sisco scuffled behind the oaks away from the view of the big beam, and walked across the access road to find Peach seated on a bench with his head in his hands. He sat down next to him but said nothing.

The hog screeched her way to a loud stop. The fire bin opened upstairs, and the engineer shoveled rocks of coal into the boiler while she took on water. With a nightstick in hand, the conductor showed up from the opposite side of the tracks. He peered inside two open boxcars and waited for some unsuspecting hobo to spring from the guts of the creature stopped to water itself.

Peach didn't seem to notice the noisy rattler. He wasn't looking for Carlos to hop off because it made no sense that the punk would have gone south and turned around to come north again ... unless he had started for Old Mexico, changed his mind, and then highballed it back. Carlos was a chicken, and never left Peach's side except to buy smokes from the home guard near the tracks. He always stayed in sight of the rails ... and of his jocker.

"All aboard," yelled the conductor, who hadn't found any hobos to beat on. He waved to the hogger, who blew the whistle twice and cranked up. The heavy breath of the engine steamed the night air and carried off the bugs for a moment. As she picked up speed, her heave became regular, and the coal smell of her black and white fog eased into the dark.

Peach took off his cap and ran his hand over his head. "He ain't here, is he, Sisco? Somethin's happened to my crummy. I know it! Gimme an answer!"

"Dunno, but I think we should bed down for the night and see if he comes back. If he don't, we'll look for him— ask a few questions in town."

"Ya gotta level with me. Do ya think he had an accident, or somebody did him bad?"

Peach's shirt was soaking wet. He started to cry again with deep sobs and gasps like the hog that struggled to get her wind as she left the water tower.

"Look," whispered Sisco. "It's too hot to sleep. Let's take a gander over at the station. Maybe the night fella there saw him."

Peach got on his feet, ran his palm over his head, put on his cap, and took off near running toward the depot a hundred or so yards down the tracks past the Catholic church. Sisco followed and caught up with him at the station.

"Ya know, if Carlos don't come back, I'm goin' down to Old Mexico to see his kin. Maybe I'll just stay there and wait till he comes home. I learned some Mexican talk. Could git by if I had to." He spat and blew a noisy snot into the brush.

Sisco patted him on the back, thinking there was no way he'd ever find Carlos' people in Old Mexico. If, by some chance, he did, how would he ever explain who he was, or had been, in his punk's life? He let that go and motioned for Peach to be quiet so they could see who was inside the depot.

Through a side window, they saw the night fellow seated at the desk with his back to them. He was on the telephone and pushing a pencil like he was taking down information. Except for the lamp on the desk, the station was dark. He was probably an old geezer left over from the blackout days when you couldn't turn on any lights.

"We'll wait till he gets off the phone," Sisco whispered. "If we go in now, he might call up the town clowns."

They stood next to the station in the shadows. The stars were still sending messages to someplace with their flickering flash code. To the east, a long-tailed serpent cloud hovered near the slice of melon moon as if ready to snatch it up.

Nudging Peach, Sisco pointed west. "Over there by Thornton and the two rivers, folks see strange things in the sky. Once when I was jungled up with Shorty and Blue, we saw a string of lights move 'round like they was hooked to each other. As we watched 'em, they disappeared together."

Peach shook his head, shrugged his shoulders, and peered through the window. "Reckon we can go in now. The fella's off the phone."

They walked around to the front. With Peach close behind him, Sisco opened the door quietly. The night agent looked up and jumped to his feet. He was a tall, skinny guy; his face was hidden by a green visor and the dim light.

"What ya fellas want? No cash in here," he said in a shaky voice.

Peach walked over to the desk, took off his cap, rubbed his head, and blurted out, "Don't mean no harm, mister. My pal and me just lookin' for one of our boys who's been gone a night and a day. Thought ya mighta seen him. Short, got black hair and brown eyes and not too much fuzz on his face."

Before he could finish, the operator sat down, put one hand on the telephone, and took off his visor with the other. He was just a young fellow—probably a boomer who rotated through the stations.

"No need to call the town clowns," said Sisco. "Just wanna know if ya seen a Spic boy. Mighta been with some others like him who talk Mexican."

"Can't help ya. Why you guys so interested in some Spic kid?" He opened the top drawer of the desk and pulled out a pack of Wrigley's. He took a stick for himself and held the pack out to the 'bos.

9

"Care for some Juicy Fruit? This fella in trouble with the law?"

"Hell, no!" chimed the Peach as he took a stick of gum and stuffed it into the pocket of his overalls. Since he had no teeth himself, he decided to save it for Carlos. "He's uh, uh, uh, kinda like a son to me. He don't speak 'nough American to git by on his own, and I sorta look after him. Just worried, that's all." His voice cracked.

"Plenty of his kind in these towns," said the boomer. "Last night the Catholics put on a big shindig at the church. Some wailing band from Stockton played music from Old Mexico till after midnight. Your friend mighta gone to the dance with all them other Spics. Seems like you guys woulda heard the ruckus if ya was camped out near the tower."

"I wasn't here yet," Sisco said and turned to the Peach. "Didn't ya fellas hear the music?"

"Guess not," he answered with his head lowered. "Shorty had two jugs of stiff sterno, and we drank 'em both. Last thing I recollect was Carlos sayin' he was goin' for smokes at the place 'cross the tracks."

With a move toward the door, Sisco waved to the boomer, saying, "Mighty obliged to ya, sir. We'll look round more in the morning."

Peach put on his cap, nodded to the station agent, and followed. Once outside, he grabbed Sisco's arm. "If I hadn't pulled my caper with the hooch last night, I coulda gone with him, or stopped him from goin'." He broke into sobs.

The night air was cool with a Delta breeze that Nature sends in the summer to fan things and relieve the heat. As they walked on the tracks toward the jungle, the ground began to rumble and roll—slowly at first and then faster with the whistle close behind to signal that a rattler was headed into Hayden. His head down like he was walking in his sleep, Peach lagged behind. With a quick turn, Sisco pulled him off to the side so he wouldn't take the Westbound before it was his time. The train thundered past them without stopping. He didn't seem to notice; he was worried sick about his punk.

Of all of the hobos, Peach was the most sentimental. Whenever he talked about his mother, he cried. Growing up in Georgia without brothers or sisters, he lived with her in the house of rich folks who treated her poorly and paid him no attention as long as he stayed out of the way. Although he wasn't sure who his father was, he suspected that it was the man who owned the farm where they lived. Since nobody cared if he went to school, he stayed home with his ma or wandered down the road to play with the nigger kids who didn't go to school either. He had no prejudice against any of them because they were kind to him. The niggers ate better than he and his mother did as white folks. Sometimes he snuck a piece of their homemade cornbread home to his ma. At thirteen, he lost her to the flu, which also took the lady of the house. He stayed around long enough to watch his mother buried in a plain wooden box next to the railroad tracks. Then he took off on the rails and never went back.

At the jungle, Sisco gave Peach a few tokes on some loco weed to help him fall asleep before they searched again in the morning. Then he took a hit, lay down on his bedroll and watched the blink, blink lights in the sky. He thought about something a smart-ass boomer in San Bernardino had said: "The stars are suns, but they're so far off they look small and each one of those little lights might have a whole world behind it with real people." Hard to figure.

When Sisco woke up, the others were still snoring up a storm, and a hint of morning had appeared in the eastern sky. Over to the west by Thornton and the rivers, a bright beam moved above the trees. At first, he thought it was a searchlight like the ones during the war near San Francisco where the Navy ships were docked. As it came closer, it took the shape of a giant baseball field without home plate. A long streak of white light came out of the thing and pointed down at the tracks. Then it moved closer to catch the brick tower of the Catholic church. A flock of pigeons, bats, or some kind of winged flyers burst out everywhere and off into the palm trees. He wondered if the loco weed still had him under its spell. Shaking his head and rubbing his eyes, he saw that the beam just sat there above the tower of the church. Then a big flash blinded him; and when it was gone, the triangle light had disappeared, leaving no sign of itself.

Now Sisco had seen some mighty peculiar things from the top of a boxcar where there aren't any fake lights to blur the view: black, elephant-like thunderheads across the sky, bumping into each other until they let loose with rain to pee themselves out; white, upside-down saucers over Mt. Shasta hovering at the top before they dissolved into pink, cotton candy clouds ready to eat. But he'd never seen the likes of that white triangle in the dawning sky. Now wide awake, he stood up and threw on his Yankee jacket. There was a whiff of something in the air; it smelled like brussel sprouts and cabbage mixed with the smoke of high iron and tar. He gagged, covered his mouth with a handkerchief, and started to the church, wondering if something was on fire or dying.

Inside the churchyard, he looked for animal droppings or something fallen from above. The smell eased off; nothing seemed disturbed. One lit bulb hung over the front door. The Catholics had fallen on hard times because the flower beds next to the steps were full of weeds and the grass around them was dry. Sisco leaned over to touch the ground, thinking it might feel different after the big beam from the sky, but it was just the usual warm earth after days and nights of heat in the valley.

To the side of the church where folks parked their automobiles for Sunday Mass, bright scraps of colored paper littered the asphalt and the sidewalk. At the back were long wooden picnic tables with square card tables squeezed between them. Sisco figured it was all left over from the big dance the station agent had mentioned. It struck him as kind of peculiar that the Christmas lights strung over the tables were still lit. They moved back and forth like dancing fireflies in the early morning Delta breeze. He figured that the clean-up fellows must have had too much tequila at the Friday night shindig and had forgotten to cut off the lights.

He reckoned that Carlos had heard the Spic music and wandered over to the Catholic church where some guy or gal had bought him a shot or two. Peach was always after him not to drink tequila because it made him crazy lovey-dovey.

He'd say, "Now don't git loco on me, Crummy!"

The punk would throw his arms around him and smooch him all over his face.

"Git off me, ya wetback pansy!" Peach would holler, but you could tell he really liked it.

If Carlos had drunk a little sterno on Friday, there was no telling who he might have gone home with. He had talked about a sweet *señorita* in Old Mexico and said he'd go back to marry her when he saved up some money. Peach made sure he never had enough dough to get home.

Sisco walked around to the other side of the church and back toward the front as a big black Caddy pulled into the parking area. The automobile stopped but the headlights stayed on. He figured he'd been spotted and would end up in the local jug for trespassing unless the fella happened to be the local galway getting ready for services. The best

13

thing seemed to pretend that he was headed into the church to pray or confess his sins. Even hobos have a right to some spiritual things.

It was dark inside except for the early morning sun lending a little color as it peeked through the yellow glass windows. Candles lit at the front showed where to go if you wanted to kneel down to pray. He looked for the confessionals with the curtains. In the back to his left were two of them—one with a curtain and the other with a door. He didn't want to make any noise so he ducked behind the curtain. For a minute everything was still; then the sound of footsteps on the wood floor came closer and closer. Someone lifted the curtain. Sisco mumbled "Amen" and began to pray, "Our Father who art in …"

"C'mon outta there, young fella," said a voice.

Stepping out of the confessional into the shadows, he saw a man wearing a decent dress-up hat and holding a satchel in one hand.

Coughing hard, Sisco said, "Morning."

"Morning," answered the man as he set the grip down beside him and took off his hat. "Little early for a confession." He took out a pocket watch. "Just now quarter past six. The priest don't get here till seven."

"Oh, I'll just come back then."

"You new in town?"

"Yeah," mumbled Sisco, staring at the floor. "Been through here plenty a times before and thought to get off and look for some work this time."

"Far as I know, you're in the wrong place to look for work. And for sure, you was in the wrong place to confess your sins. You was on the priest's side. This here's where you're s'posed to go." He opened the door, and there was the body.

Right away Sisco knew it was Carlos. With the striped *serape* thrown over his shoulder and Peach's Dodger cap

14

on backward to show his face, Carlos' body drooped to one side like he was sleeping.

"What the hell?" shouted the man, kicking the corpse's limp leg. "Another drunk Spic in the confessional. Hey, *hombre*, wake up! Looks like this wetback had a lot to confess."

The man laughed as the body fell forward.

Staring at Carlos, all Sisco could think of was how Peach might go crazy when he saw his crummy. There was no blood, but the eyes bugged out like an animal slaughtered for meat. The head looked loose at the neck and dangled like it was barely attached to the rest of the body.

"Never seen a dead guy before, tramp? I woulda thought you'd seen plenty of bums get their summons to ... wherever. Ya know this wetback?"

"Yeah. He's one of us 'bos. Came in day before yesterday and disappeared."

"Well, ya need to get him outta here *pronto, pronto*! I gotta clean up before Father Martinez comes in. Damn Spics made a big mess outside."

Gently, Sisco lifted the body up over his shoulder. Carlos' *serape* fell on the floor. The man snatched it up, walked to the door and tossed it out onto the front steps.

"Much obliged, mister," he mumbled as he strained to grab it up and make his way to the sidewalk.

He started toward the jungle. Carlos felt smaller and lighter than he should have. Sisco recalled how easy it had been to have him on the road because he never complained, didn't eat a lot, or take up much space. There were a few times when the hobos almost lost him because he dragged his leg trying to catch on or jump off the rattlers. He never really got the hang of that part of the rails, but he was the best worker in the fields. Most of all, though, he kept the Peach's nerves calmed down.

Nearing the jungle, he smelled the last of the mulligan and knew that his stomach had to be hungry, but his insides told him something different. He hoped there'd be a pot of coffee brewed to give him a jolt so he and the others could figure out what to do next. He spotted Peach standing off from the fire circle close to the tracks, lifting his cap on and off with one hand and holding a can of java with the other. Seconds later, he saw him drop the coffee and rush toward his lifeless punk.

"Carlos, my crummy, what happened to ya?" he wailed as he lifted the body off Sisco's shoulder and cradled it in his arms.

"He's gone. Found him in the secrets box at the Catholic."

Without another word, Peach turned around with the body, walked into the jungle and sat down on a crate near the fire. Shorty and Blue had been eating Mulligan. They stopped when they saw the corpse. Curly wasn't around just yet.

A rattler blew close by, and the bells at the church began to ring. Nobody paid any mind. Peach sat with the body over his knees and the head in his arms. His wails were deep and loud with gasps from way down in his chest.

The noise of the hog as she filled her belly outdid the blubbering just long enough for Sisco to find a pint of Early Times in his bindle. After a long taste of the bourbon, he handed the bottle to Peach, who gulped down a big swig and then tried to give some to Carlos like he was feeding a baby. The hooch spilled out of the punk's mouth down his chin.

"Lemme hold the bottle, please!" pleaded Sisco. "Your crummy's dead. He can't drink anymore."

Peach handed up the bottle and started to rub the spilled bourbon on Carlos' bruised, red neck. Just then, Curly wandered into the jungle. He backed himself up against the oak tree, lit a smoke, and asked what had happened.

"Dunno. Found him at the Catholic. The crumb boss, or somebody in charge over there, drove up as I was snoopin' round outside. I went into the church and pretended to pray in the secrets box when the fella caught me. We found Carlos slumped over on the other side."

"What we gonna do with the body? We can't take it with us on the road," asked Shorty, who always thought on the practical side of problems.

"Bury it, I guess," answered Curly after a long swig of hooch.

"That's not gonna be easy with the ground so hard and dry. No shovel we got here can break up this earth right now."

Peach was listening to them; he spoke up loud and clear. "Nobody's gonna put my crummy into the ground till he has last rites."

Blue shook his head but had the sense to keep quiet. He grabbed the Early Times bottle, which was almost empty.

"I think he already had his last rites," piped up Shorty. "He was in church, wasn't he?"

"That don't count! He was in there to confess all 'em bad things I made him do with his dick—all that evil shit to shoot my wad while he just put up with everything and thought on his sweet *señorita* in Old Mexico. He prob'ly got killed 'cause he told sins that no galway can forgive!"

Blue shook his head again and mumbled to himself while he finished up the bottle and pitched it into a pile of cans at the edge of the jungle. "You guys got one helluva of a mess on your hands, but I ain't stickin' here to see how ya figure it out. I'm on the first rattler outta this jerkwater to Washington. Ya with me, Camelback?"

"I reckon so," answered Curly, who hung out by the oaks and rolled a smoke. "You fellas can handle this thing without us. Right?"

Sisco looked at Shorty, who had sat down near Peach to share a fag with him.

"Ya always got an answer. What ya think we should do?"

"Ya ain't doin' a thing with my crummy till he has last rites! He was Catholic, and no one's gonna keep him from Heaven, even though I done my best to send him to Hell when he was alive. Y'all hear that?"

"Lookee here, ya dumb bum!" yelled Shorty, losing his patience. "I was brought up Catholic, too. Ya git last rites *before* ya take the Westbound, not after! Carlos most likely had his last rites in the church when he was confessin'."

He looked over at Sisco and winked.

Peach was thinking straighter now. He stood up with the body cradled in his arms and bellowed, "Somethin' ain't right here! How can somebody confess in the secrets box when they been choked to death? Carlos ain't had any last rites, and you fellas damn well know it! If what you're talkin' was true, it woulda been the galway who done him in, and we know that ain't right." He sat down again as the head flopped loosely over his arm.

Shorty paced back and forth between the two oaks. He'd stick around to help bury the body. He was savvy about a lot of things and had pulled some capers but had never landed in the calaboose. "Lookee here, Peach. We gotta git Carlos over to one of 'em rivers that runs all over this place. Nice soft dirt to dig a grave on the bank under the trees. No bone polishers to bother the body."

"Ya gotta give Carlos some rest from all that weepin' and wailin'," counseled Sisco. "Give him some peace so he can go to the angels. You're holdin' him back here. He was a good boy. He's headed straight to Heaven if you'll just him let go. I'll bring ya some water to wash him up for the ground."

The hobos' words must have finally made sense to Peach. After another sniffle or two, he began to wash the body with water from a milk can. Shorty came up with a rag from the clothes line—somebody's snot catcher—and handed it to him.

Blue and Curly gathered up their bindles to deck the next rattler headed north. They planned to jungle up in Dunsmuir to fish for a few days before they headed to Washington and the apple knockers. Shorty said the other fellas would follow after they took care of Carlos.

"I'm gonna mosey into town to see if I can find a decent fella who'll carry us to the river," offered Sisco. As the youngest and best-looking of the hobos, he figured he had the best chance of sweet-talking the lady of the house into having her husband help out. Of course, he'd never before asked anyone to get rid of a dead body.

Terry A. Albritton

Jerkwater

Across the tracks, Claire Lewis, a first grade teacher at Hayden Grammar School, served a plate of bacon, eggs and coffee to Leonard Sutter, principal of Hayden High School. Len had gone fishing that morning when he had promised to take her to church.

"As principal, aren't you *expected* to attend *some* religious service?" she said as she sat down across from him at the kitchen table. "It doesn't seem to matter which denomination."

"There's a certain amount of forgiveness in these small towns, Claire, *if* you understand the local mentality."

He lit up the last of the Luckys in the pack while his breakfast got cold.

"Is that supposed to mean that you have license to sleep with me because you're one of the town's respected elders and I'm just a single schoolmarm?"

"It always comes back to the same subject, doesn't it? Look, I haven't tarnished your reputation. If anything, I've improved it because I've never spent the night here ... and we haven't made love."

Len liked a beautiful woman with spirit, and Claire had both good looks and brains; but she was colder than the fish he hadn't snagged at the river that morning. After a year of chasing her, he'd had to find a not-so-smart, knockout dame who wasn't such a prick teaser.

"I'm sorry about church. I expected to be here in time, but Pluto took off after a bird, and I had to wait until he came back."

"You promise so many things, Len. You have time for your dog, your cronies at the 241, activities at the high, and there's nothing left for me."

She began to weep and grabbed a handful of paper napkins from the holder on the table. "I really don't care about church. I just want to be able to tell Mother and Daddy that I am seeing an honest Christian man."

Len still hadn't touched his breakfast. He pulled out another pack of Luckys and lit two, offering one to Claire. He knew she was having a hard time away from her folks for the first time; but at thirty-one years old, she was still hanging onto the apron strings like she was eighteen. He began to regret the favor he'd done old John Lewis by hiring his only child for her first job.

"I think your mother is intelligent enough to know that I'm not a church person even though I was raised by a family of Methodists. I think she also may know that I'm not even a good Christian. If you want, I'll call her again later, make small talk, and convince her one more time that my intentions are honorable—with regard to you, anyway."

As her eyes filled with tears, Claire said, "But that's just it, Len. Your intentions are *not* honorable, and you know it as well as I do!"

Len saw no reason to continue their talk. He sent Claire to take a bath and promised to clean up himself, so they could go to dinner later in Lodi. After a few brandy old fashioneds and a good meal, they'd both feel better. They'd come back to the house early, do some innocent smooching on the couch, and he'd leave her early enough for a little whoopee with the blonde dance teacher whose husband was out of town on a business trip.

§§§§§

While Leonard Sutter planned the rest of his Sunday, Sisco crossed the tracks into town. Hayden had no particular appeal to the hobos except as a place to ask for a handout or an odd job in the tomatoes, asparagus, or corn. He and Shorty had come into town once before when they hankered for rice, beans, and tortillas with some of that hot *salsa* that the Spics pour all over everything. They had found a greasy spoon next to the tracks just north of the water tower. After the chow, they walked around the corner to the 241 Club. The townies at the bar were nice enough to them while they all drank beer and listened to Buck Owens on the juke box. So on that stifling day in August of '49, Hayden seemed as good a place as any to ask for help with a dead body.

He surveyed the houses on F Street which were most likely built in a hurry during the war. Small white boxes, they had three steps up to the front door with neat beds of red geraniums planted next to the walls. Each house had a shade tree in the yard near the sidewalk, but there were no picket fences in front where a hobo might leave a sign with a piece of chalk or coal to signal other hobos about a friendly lady with a handout.

Sisco had almost given up spotting a mark when he noticed a narrow alley off F Street. It led behind some houses and over to E Street. He saw a '49 Ford parked square in the middle where it blocked the alley from both sides. The automobile was new but filthy dirty, like somebody had driven it into a mud hole. Curious, he walked over to the Ford and looked inside. The windows were all open with a fishing rod propped on the front seat and a tackle box sitting on the back seat. There was as much dirt on the inside as on the outside.

He stopped to think how much dirt was on him. He hadn't washed or shaved for better than two weeks. "A tow-headed grizzly bear" one fella in Chicago had called him when he'd landed there on the Main Stem where the 'bos hung out after weeks on the road. He suddenly wondered why the crumb boss at the Catholic church hadn't called in the local bulls to carry him off to the calaboose and Carlos off to the dump.

Then he saw the cat—a smiling, two-legged critter sketched with a piece of coal on the corner of a half-tall fence between the back wall of the house and the garage. No mistaking the cat; it was a sign left by a hungry hobo who wanted others to know that a kind-hearted Mrs. lived there. If the Ford belonged to her husband who liked to fish, the automobile could carry them to the river with Carlos. He hoped that the Mister had a kind heart, too, and a mind to help with the body.

He opened the gate that led up a walkway to the back steps and a door. When he knocked, there was a loud barking inside. To his right was a window; the blinds flicked while the yowling continued. A man looked out, shook his head, and lowered the blinds. Sisco figured that someone had marked this house wrong—no hobo sign to warn about a barking dog, which always meant a bad-tempered owner. He had just decided to leave when the door opened, and there stood the man from the window. He was a real handsome fellow—tall and thin with slicked-back black hair and a thin mustache. He had the looks of a movie star or a band leader married to a movie queen. He wasn't dressed like high society, though. He wore dirty jeans and a long-sleeved shirt that once might have been white. He had to be the owner of the Ford. Next to him was a brown dog with short hair and uneven white spots sprinkled all over his body. He was dirty, too, but now he wagged his tail.

"Sorry about Pluto," apologized the man. "He's a hunting dog when he puts his mind to it. Barks a lot, but doesn't bite. You looking for a handout?"

"Wouldn't mind one," Sisco answered as he walked back up the steps. "But I really came here for some help. Some of us 'bos in a kinda mess. We wanna do what's right, ya know?"

The man opened the screen door partway and reached out to shake the hobo's hand. "Name's Sutter, Leonard Sutter. Just call me Len."

"Pleased to meet ya. Siberius Griffin. Everybody calls me Kid Sisco or just plain Sisco."

"Come on in. Let's see what the lady of the house has in the way of a handout. She's indisposed at the moment."

They walked through the washroom and into a bright kitchen with a metal table and four silver chairs with red linoleum seats. In the center of the table was a blue bowl filled with apples, oranges, and pears.

"Them apples look like they been polished."

"The lady of the house likes them shiny. Makes no sense to me. They get eaten anyway. Help yourself."

Sisco couldn't bring himself to take an apple. His hands were dirty; he tried to keep them off the table so the gent wouldn't notice.

"I'm a country boy myself," Sutter said. "Born and raised up the road in Woodland. My great, great uncle was John Augustus Sutter, the fella who had the mill where gold was discovered in 1848. How about you?"

"I'm from Kansas. Came to California out of the Dust Bowl with detours through Chicago and other citified places. Never looked back, and prob'ly never will. Your golden state is like heaven for me."

"It's the place of everyone's hopes and dreams," said Len as he offered Sisco a Lucky Strike and took one for himself. "No other state comes close in its geography, natural resources, and just plain beauty. Endless opportunity here now—no wonder the population has doubled since the end of World War II.

"Ya sure don't seem like a country boy to me. Lots of book learnin', huh?"

"I've had my fair share of education, I guess. Put myself through school only to find out that you can never get enough knowledge. By the time you think you're smart, everything has changed. Just remember that knowledge and truth are different. Knowledge walks, talks, thinks, and speaks. Truth is silent, strong, and eternal. She needs no voice. She just is!"

"Ya think the truth is a lady?"

"Absolutely," Sutter answered while he put out one smoke and lit up another. "A woman is loyal, constant, steadfast … and forgiving. A man is arrogant, fickle, and jealous—a changeling beast suited to bull his way through the world banging his balls against whatever gets in his way. All generalizations, of course, because there are exceptions in both genders."

Sisco wanted to ask where he got his ideas, but something moved in the corner of his eye. He turned toward the hallway off the kitchen. A woman in a long, blue housecoat stood there as if waiting for an invitation to the table. To say that she looked like a glamorous movie star would not be a lie. She had the smallest waist he had ever seen. Her long, brown hair fell softly on her shoulders. Her eyes looked too green to be real. When she opened her mouth to talk, the words came out soft and smooth like a long piece of silk that floated toward him to wrap around his neck.

"Excuse me, Len. Is this a private conversation?"

"Come on over, honey. Let me introduce you to Mr. Griffin."

Sisco stood up and sputtered some words as she came toward the table.

"Pleased to make your acquaintance, ma'am. Just call me Sisco. Can't shake properlike 'cause of my dirty hands."

"Never mind, Mr. Griffin. My name is Claire. Claire Lewis. Happy to meet you, too."

A smell of ginger and jasmine floated through the air. He felt the silk scarf tighten and backed away from the table as Claire walked to Len's side and put her hand on his shoulder.

"Ya folks been real hospitable," he choked, "but I got a problem, and I need to find help now."

Len snuffed out his cigarette in the ashtray and put his arm around Claire just above the round of her hips. "What seems to be your trouble?"

Sisco swallowed hard and hoped they hadn't noticed how uncomfortable he was. "Well, we ...we got us a dead body in the jungle on the other side of the tracks. Ain't no way for us to bury him."

"How did he die?" asked Claire, moving closer to Len.

"Dunno. Waited for him two nights. Just disappeared from the jungle. I found him this morning at the Catholic."

Len backed his arm off Claire and lit another Lucky Strike. She moved over to the sink and some dirty dishes.

"You found him in the churchyard?"

"Naw. Inside in the secrets box all slumped over. Bruises on his neck like he'd been choked."

Sutter got up, walked to the sink, and gave Claire a pat on her behind. "I'll be gone for a little while, hon. Call your mother, as usual, and tell her I'm helping out a friend. Give her my regards."

In a quick turn, she stared him down with her arms folded across her chest, pushing her breasts together under the bathrobe. Sisco felt a stir in his overalls.

"This is Sunday, Len, and you promised we'd spend it together. You know how much Mother likes to talk to you. Once a week is all I ask!" She turned back to the sink.

"Look, honey," he said. "Just tell her I'm outside cleaning the fish, and I don't want to smell up the house. Just say I'm taking you out to dinner tonight in Lodi. That will satisfy her."

Claire turned on the water faucet full blast and began to wash dishes.

"I won't be gone long. I might have to go back to the fishing camp to take care of this. Listen to some Benny

Goodman or the Dorseys. There are two good records in there that we've hardly played. Save me a dance."

He picked up the pack of Luckys, leaving an ashtray full of butts on the table.

Her angry voice followed them out the back door. "And take that mongrel with you! You two brought in half the dirt from the river. I'm tired of your messes!"

"Sure thing, hon. I'll be back before you know it."

Sisco didn't say good-bye to Claire. He figured he had offended her already by busting up the plans she and Sutter had made for Sunday afternoon. She might never speak to him again, but he couldn't stop thinking of her anyway. She was like a fairy princess from the storybook his mother had read to him. What was she doing in a jerkwater like Hayden next to the tracks and hitched to a man who didn't take her seriously?

"Come on, Sisco, get in," Len said, opening the passenger-side door of his Ford. Pluto bounded in as if the front seat belonged to him.

"No, thanks. I'll just walk 'cross the tracks to show ya where the 'bos are. Ya can drive in close."

"Suit yourself."

The sun was high now, baking the asphalt with wavy lines on the ground. Sisco wished he had eaten one of the shiny apples on Claire's table. He would just have to settle for any mulligan left over from last night. He hoped that Shorty had been able to get some down Peach, who had to be plenty hungry by now.

On the other side of the tracks, Len steered the Ford behind the oaks and pulled up like he'd been on the access road before. When he opened the door, Pluto jumped over him, raced past Sisco, made a beeline for the space between the two trees and disappeared. Next things they heard were screaming, cursing, and barking.

"Pluto!" yelled Len. "Get your chicken-shit ass back here! Come! Now!"

He whistled long and loud while he followed Sisco through an open space into the jungle.

Shorty was on top of a crate with a shovel in his hand ready to defend himself. Peach stood with his arms spread out, ready to tackle anything that came near Carlos. The body was swinging back and forth in the hammock strung up between two trees. Pluto posed in the middle of everything with a bone from the mulligan in his mouth, his tail dancing to beat the band.

"At ease, fellas." said Len. "Pluto's harmless. He's a hunting dog. Sniffs out the birds and, once in a while, a deer. I see he found somebody's lunch."

"What do ya mean?" yelled Shorty. "Took it right outta my hand!"

He stepped off the crate and put the shovel on the ground next to the fire pit. Peach had gone behind a tree to relieve himself.

Len walked over to Shorty to shake his hand and offer him a smoke. "Name's Sutter. Leonard Sutter. Just call me Len."

Shorty wiped his hand on an old towel to shake. "Glad to know ya. They call me Shorty, Memphis Shorty. Real name's John Henry Curtis. I hail original from Tennessee. Your mutt here did me a big favor."

"How's that?"

"Peach hadn't made a move all morning—just stood there, rockin' his punk in the hammock, singin' to him. Your dog scared his ass into action. He's still pissin' back there—prob'ly for the first time all day."

Len nodded and smiled. "Glad he's good for something once in a while. Scared the hell out of the fish this morning. If it's OK, I'm going to take a look at your friend."

He walked over to the hammock where the body had stopped swinging. At first, he didn't touch it. After looking it over from top to bottom, Len lifted one arm and pulled up the sleeve. Gently, he raised the arm. Just then, Peach came out of the bushes in a hurry and with a fury.

"What the hell ya think you're doin'?" he screamed as he made for Len, who turned around just in time to throw a punch that sent him backward into Shorty's arms.

"I hope Mr. Sutter knocked some sense into ya," scolded Sisco. "'Nough is 'nough! Here's this guy come to help us with your crummy, and ya wanna fight him."

Peach sputtered and spit. "I don't want nobody strange touchin' Carlos," he wailed and then started to bawl.

Len walked away from the hammock, waved Shorty to turn Peach loose, and pulled the pack of Luckys out of his pocket. He lit one, offering it to a dazed Peach, who just stared at the smoke like it was something he'd never seen before. Finally, he took the cigarette and mumbled something about saving it for Carlos.

The hobos looked at each other. They had never seen the punk smoke. Recalling the wasted bourbon earlier in the day, they hoped the Lucky wouldn't end up in the corpse's mouth. It didn't. Peach snuffed out the fag and tucked it into Carlos' shirt pocket. He began to push the hammock back and forth. As it swayed to and fro, he hummed a lullaby.

For a while, everything was peaceful in the jungle. It was past noon, and down Lodi way, a hogger blew. With all that had happened that morning, the hobos hadn't paid attention to the rattlers passing through Hayden. Curly and Blue had decked an earlier train and were well on their way to the fish in the river at Dunsmuir.

Sisco felt kind of dizzy as he tried to remember things after he found Carlos' body. The green-eyed princess kept floating through his mind. As he thought about her, he watched Len, who had sat down on a crate and looked right at home in the jungle. Truth be told, he could have been a hobo or a tramp himself, as dirty as his clothes were. The coal black hair matted in strands over his forehead didn't seem to matter. He would have fit in fine with men in search of work or a fast buck on the Main Stem in Chicago. What made him different was his smooth way of talking.

While it was quiet, Sutter got up and went over to the hammock for a second look at the body. With a hand on Peach's shoulder, he whispered in his ear. The jocker turned full around from his rocking and said, "It *is* my fault. If I hada been 'wake, I never woulda let him go by hisself to the dance or anywhere else. He didn't know nobody in this burg. Why'd he leave?"

"We'll never be sure," answered Len like they knew each other well. "He wasn't running away. Of that I am certain. Something outside your camp caught his attention, and he left thinking he'd be back soon. He might have gone out to investigate a noise or a smell—maybe a skunk or a coon in search of water this time of year."

His voice was sing-song sweet, and Peach nodded his head. Then came the hard part. "Now, what I can also say for sure after a glance at Carlos' wrists is that he was tied up tight. You care to look?"

Peach had tears running down his cheeks mingled with drops of sweat. "Can't do it," he sobbed. "Let Shorty and Sisco look for me."

"See here," said Len quietly as the 'bos came close to the hammock. "These are burns from a rope or cord tied real tight."

He held up Carlos' arms for them to see deep red marks at the wrists. "Above on the forearms are some old scars—made by a knife or razor, I think."

31

When he heard mention of the scars, Peach turned toward the body, picked up the punk's left arm, and rolled the sleeve halfway to the shoulder.

"Got more up here," he choked. "Told me one of his kin cut him up regular when he was a little tyke to make him … to make him do things he didn't wanna." He stepped away from the hammock and back into the bushes to cry.

They watched Len go over the body with a fine-tooth comb. He stayed calm as he lifted Carlos' head to separate the thick black hair so he could look at the scalp. He turned the body from one side to the other and took off Carlos' sandals to see the feet and ankles. Carlos was never without his *huarachis*, even at night. His feet were bumpy muscles with the toes a full shade darker from the sun and years of work outside.

"Take a glance at these ankles, fellas. Your *amigo* was tied up at the feet, too."

Deep red marks showed around the ankles. Somebody had sure gone to a lot of trouble to keep Carlos from moving.

"There's one more place I'd like to see," said Len, who spoke up louder and wiped his hands on the white shirt that got dirtier by the minute. "I know Peach will object if I look at the crack. But if he will allow me to, I may be able to figure some things out."

Sure enough, the jocker heard the last part and came out of the bushes with his face all streaked with tears and snot. "I can't see why ya need to know 'bout that!"

"Just for future reference in case there's ever an investigation or if this sort of thing happens again here."

Shorty was pissed. "Seems to me ya plan to tell the local bulls 'bout the Spic. Don't strike me as likely they'll investigate much. They'll just throw us in the hoosegow. It won't matter that we tried to do the decent thing with Carlos."

Len lit another Lucky and offered one to each of the 'bos. "I have no intention of telling anyone anything. I just want to understand what kind of crime this was."

"If ya ever find the sonabitch who did this, I'll kill him with my bare hands," Peach said as he shook his fists in Len's face.

"Easy now," said Sisco, pulling the jocker back. "He's only tryin' to help your crummy get a decent burial. Why don't ya let him have a quick look?"

Peach shook his head but then changed his mind. "Aw right, ya can see my crummy's private place, but no messin' with him. No disrespect to him! Y'all hear that? And make it quick!" He stepped back and wept.

Len motioned for help to turn the body and hold it steady. Shorty moved to the other side of the hammock. Sisco stood next to Len to brace Carlos and watched as he loosened the pants and pulled them down below the crack. He pried the cheeks apart with his hands. Sisco didn't want to look but couldn't help himself; he caught an eyeful and a whiff. The Spic was torn up bad. There were cuts from his crack into the flesh of his cheeks. You couldn't tell where one slice began and the next one ended. Shit and blood were all caked up in the wounds, and the smell overpowered them. Shorty caught a whiff, too, and turned his head.

"What d'ya see?" asked Peach as he inched closer.

Len steered him over to a seat on one of the crates. In a voice just loud enough for the hobos to hear, he said, "You've been through a lot in your life, haven't you? This isn't the first time you've lost somebody close. It's never easy, but you know how to handle it. All you guys have seen fellas lose arms, legs, and become crippled for life. Right?"

33

Peach nodded his head and looked ready to bawl again. Sisco caught the drift of where Len was heading and said, "Ya shore wouldna wanted that for your crummy, would ya? Carlos got poked with somethin' sharp. That's it. Let's put him to rest while we have Sutter here to lend us a hand. His missus 'cross the tracks ain't too happy 'bout givin' him up on a Sunday afternoon when they had plans."

With mention of a wife, Peach got moving. While Len helped him settle into the back seat of the Ford with the body cradled in his arms, Shorty and Sisco tidied up the jungle. They rinsed the pots and put them in one of the crates. Shorty spooned some ashes from the dying fire into a can. Sisco emptied the morning's coffee grounds into another can. That's how the hobos passed things along from one group to the next. They poured the cooking water onto the last embers of the fire. It sputtered and smoked like a tired hog at the end of the line. They gathered up the rest of the gear—the Kelly stick for agitatin' boiled up laundry, the spoons and cans—and stacked them in a crate.

Len grabbed the shovel next to the fire pit, used it to sprinkle loose dirt on the ashes, and threw it in the trunk of his automobile. "You fellas have any of Carlos' blankets, bedroll, or something to wrap around him?"

Sisco nodded that they did and went behind the oak where one of the guys had stacked the punk's blankets—two thick ones from Old Mexico. The dark brown blanket had a huge tiger head with pointed yellow teeth and black broom-stick whiskers. The other one was bright blue and showed a rooster all puffed up with orange, red, and green feathers. The hobos used to poke fun at Carlos about sleeping between a cat and a cock. He laughed until he spilled his coffee. Nobody was sure that he understood what they said, but he was a good sport and seemed to enjoy the attention.

The blankets smelled like cigarettes, dirt, and Oxydol. Carlos had been crazy to keep his things clean. He washed and beat the big blankets until he broke more than one Kelly stick. Peach was the same way about most things, although the cigarette smell didn't seem to bother him. When he first brought his punk on the road with them, Peach went over him with a fine-tooth comb to find the crumbs. Carlos was lousy with those little critters and their nits in his thick black hair, under his arms, and through his private parts. After that head and hide clean-up, the hobos got to calling him Crummy. At first, Peach was mad; he said it was disrespectful. But after a few trips on the road with Carlos bringing up the rear, Peach said it was OK to call him Crummy as long as everybody remembered it was a nickname for being in back, like the caboose.

They put the blankets in the back seat next to the jocker, who looked peaceful enough with his punk in his arms. Sisco had planned to go in the back seat, too; but Shorty got there first so he wouldn't have to sit next to Pluto, who had planted himself on the front seat when Len opened the door. They rode over the tracks onto Fourth Street and pulled up in front of the drugstore. Two bald men in overalls and straw hats stood on the sidewalk, jabbering full speed until they saw the Ford stop at the curb. They quit talking and turned to watch Sutter get out.

He greeted them and offered each twin a smoke. "Morning, Jack, Joe. You fellas been following the Yankees?"

"Yeah, sure 'nough, we have, Len," they said at the same time. Then one asked, "What you up to with all them tramps in your automobile?"

"Oh, I'm taking these boys out to the river and the fishing camp. They're going to help me build a little lean-to for my gear. Get tired of carrying the stuff back and forth, you know? I'll take you guys out there one of these days when it cools off."

The twins looked at each other like the idea seemed fine to them. Len waved and went through a door next to the drugstore. In a few minutes, he was back with a jug of dago red and another shovel from his room. "Thought we might need a little holy water for the ... construction work," he laughed and pushed Pluto over to the middle of the front seat. He handed the wine and shovel to Sisco, who rested it on the floor between his legs.

"Ya got a place in this jerkwater that sells hooch on Sunday?" asked Shorty from the back.

"Naw," Len answered with a smoke in his mouth. He pulled the choke and started the motor. "I have a little stash for emergencies upstairs in my room. Never hurts to be prepared."

On their way to the river, Sisco didn't hear much of the conversation because he couldn't get past the idea of Leonard Sutter staying in a room over the drugstore. Maybe he wasn't hitched to Claire. Funny kind of deal—whatever it was. He bit his tongue, nodded his head, and tried to listen as Memphis and Len carried on their blabber about ranching, trout fishing, and deer hunting. Later on, when Shorty asked him what he thought about Len being the principal of Hayden High School, he pretended he had guessed something like that because of the way Sutter talked.

After a bumpy ride over a dirt road, they pulled up at the edge of a river. There was no sign of a camp, but the spot was pleasant with willows, elders, aspens, all different oak trees close to the shore, and a green carpet of tule reeds and wild grasses between them and the water. Len got out, opened the back door, and lifted the body off Peach's lap. With Carlos in his arms, he walked to a level patch of grass and asked in a loud voice, "What do you think, fellas? Isn't this a swell spot to take a nice, long *siesta*?"

Peach stumbled out of the Ford with the blankets and looked around. He didn't seem in any hurry to have the body back and laid the two big covers on the grass. He walked to the river, felt the water, and patted the mud on the shore. Then he went behind the bushes and disappeared.

Len wasted no time setting Carlos down on the tiger blanket. Shorty gave him a hand while Pluto sniffed the wet earth. The sun had warmed things up; but near the water, a Delta breeze licked the lingering late summer leaves. In the distance, a hogger blew. Soon the rattler would slither over the trestle above the fishing camp. Carlos would have a perfect place to hear the trains while his cock and cat friends on the blankets kept him warm.

Sutter handed Sisco the keys to the Ford and asked him to get the shovel out of the trunk. Len already had started to poke the ground on the bank with his shovel. Above, the rattler hit the trestle with the hog, blowing her stack. The engineer must have seen them below and figured they were enjoying a picnic by the water with Carlos laid out on the blanket asleep or drunk.

Len began to dig. To no one in particular, he said, "Too wet here. With the first big rain, our friend will be on his way to the Bay. Let's try up there by the trees where Peach went."

He headed up the bank with a shovel in one hand and the jug of wine in the other. Pluto stayed close to him while Sisco followed with the second shovel. Shorty brought up the rear. They came upon Peach seated on a fallen tree trunk and singing a hymn.

"Seems like the funeral service already started," whispered Len, as he took a big swig of the dago. "How about bringing the body up here for the viewing while we prepare the grave site?"

Shorty and Sisco took their cue and walked back to the river. They gently lifted the body wrapped in blankets and carried it to the trees where Len waited to offer them up some "holy water."

"You see, Peach, Carlos will be just fine. He's taken the Westbound. Look at him so peaceful. Don't you worry. We'll make him comfortable in his final resting place."

"How'd you know 'bout the Westbound?" asked Shorty. "Don't tell me you been a bum, too?"

While he dug, Len talked. "I rode some rails when I was younger. You fellas have seen that big yard in Woodland. Met plenty of hobos there before the war. Got drunk with them. They always treated me fine. Never saw a real bum—a guy who didn't want to work. Far as I know, there were only tramps and hobos trying to find work. I can't fault anybody for wanting to make a living and doing whatever it takes."

Peach wasn't listening. He had moved off the log onto the tiger blanket next to his punk. He broke out into a real hymn—full throttle as he rocked himself back and forth. He even sounded like the Negro folks who had raised him. His voice was strong and full of life, but he was dying inside.

Sutter nodded to the hobos like things were going just the way he had planned. He sweated something fierce; Sisco spelled him on the diggin'. The earth was soft, and they'd had enough wine to make the job easy. Pluto seemed to think the whole thing was a game and kept jumping into the grave to dig his own hole. Len hollered at him to get out, that he'd get dirty; but that was the biggest hoot of all since he already was covered with mud.

"I figured Pluto to be a bone polisher when he barked at me from inside Claire's house."

"Well, Pluto has a lot of bad habits, but he's not a biter. He's protective of Claire even though she doesn't like him much. He rolls around in horse shit—probably because

I found him in the dead of winter in a cow pasture near Thornton. He was one cold pup! I think he had been rolling around in the manure to stay warm."

Pluto kept up the dig and barked like he was enjoying himself. He was an ugly mutt with a long, pointed snout and one ear bigger than the other that made him look lopsided. His eyes followed his master's every move.

When the hole was long enough for the body, they deepened her to protect Carlos from the river critters. The dirt was soft and sweet, smelling of the river's edge—the wild berries, primal grasses, and stink worms.

"I think she's ready," said Len, up to his waist in the hole. "Peach, you need to say good-bye, roll Carlos up in the blankets, and tuck him in."

Instead of rolling up the corpse, Peach began to turn his punk over and over, searching the body. On his hands and knees, he whispered to Carlos, "Where is it, Crummy? Where'd ya put it so God knows ya been a good Catholic and lets ya into Heaven?"

Shorty looked at Sisco, who shrugged his shoulders.

"What ya up to there, Peach?" he asked.

With desperate sobs, he answered, "His cross! He musta lost it. Can't bury him without his cross!"

Len shook his head like he wondered if they'd ever get the job done. Sisco nodded to Shorty in the hope that he'd take charge one more time. He came through. Squatting next to Peach and his punk, he said in a strong voice, "Listen to me! We spent the whole damn day tryin' to do the right thing by Carlos. We even get a first-class citizen, a high school principal, to lend us a hand. This here restin' place is ready, and it's as fine as any Spic ever had. Ya gonna help to bury him or just watch while we finish the job?"

After that, things went smoothly. They rolled Carlos up in the blankets from Old Mexico. Peach did help to shovel the dirt, though he was slow. Len brought a large, flat rock from the river to mark the grave, and they stood around the stone to say the Lord's Prayer. It was the only verse they all knew even if Peach stopped short of the end. Then, they finished up the dago, piled into the Ford, and headed for town.

It was almost dark when they pulled up to the drugstore. Pluto jumped out, wagged his tail, and went straight for the stairs.

"You fellas moving out tonight?"

Shorty spoke up. "Reckon Ole Georgia here and I'll deck the next rattler headed north. See if we can grab an open boxcar and get some shut-eye."

Peach had sat down on the curb and looked to be half asleep already.

"What about you, Sisco?" asked Len.

"Dunno yet. Kinda thought I might stick 'round to look for work."

"Well, if you're still here tomorrow, come on over to the high school. The custodian is looking for help before classes start after Labor Day. I'll put in a good word for you."

With that encouragement, Sisco Griffin got off the rails to follow the fourth commandment of The Hobo Code: "Always try to find work, even if temporary, and always seek out jobs nobody wants."

A Stake

Sisco decided to take Sutter up on his offer because he couldn't get Claire out of his head. Every time he thought of her, he had a vision of a princess in a blue housecoat looking at him with her green eyes. From the beginning, he wanted her, but he saw that she was sweet on the high school principal. It was puzzling that they hadn't hitched up, but maybe Len didn't care one way or another. That's how he had acted on Sunday at the river, taking his time to help the hobos bury Carlos, drink red wine and shoot the shit with them. From his many capers with the ladies, Sisco felt Claire required lots of kind, gentle attention which she didn't seem to be getting. He wondered whether he could give her what she needed and if he had a chance.

Alone in the jungle, he recalled some advice from Shorty before he caught out with Peach for Dunsmuir. "Don't git in over your head here, Sisco. Them purty young things at the high school is nothin' but jail bait. When ya get washed and shaved up, ya look younger and plenty presentable to a bobby soxer. Ya might even pass for a halfway decent fella."

Sisco felt uneasy. Was it because of Claire, or was it on account of what had happened to the Peach? Maybe it had to do with staying put in a place where he didn't know if he could trust anybody. He wished his mind was as clear as the cloudless night over Hayden. Of course, there were always clouds somewhere—maybe just east over the Sierra. This time of year saw jackhammer lightning in the mountains; made quite a show from the top of a boxcar over Donner Pass, coming down into Truckee. The sight of a lit-up sky with the peaks pointed to the heavens made a fellow wonder about signs from up there. Maybe those flashes were a warning to folks not to get too caught up with things on the ground like the wheat farmers had done in Kansas. They never thought how they were messing with the grasses so bad on earth that the land couldn't breathe and the dust and dirt blew hard enough to black out Heaven.

The hobos didn't miss many of the pictures in the night sky. Unless there was bad weather or the railroad dicks were hanging around, they preferred to ride on top of the trains to take in the view. Many of them had religion in their own way and believed the Old Master Painter intended people to be awake at night just as much as during the day. Why else would He darken up the ground and light up the sky? You have to lie down to see that world up there; if you go to sleep, you miss it.

Sisco knew that if he hadn't been looking at the stars, he never would have seen the light pointed to the church where Carlos was. If the crumb boss or some other townie had found the body, he probably would have thrown it into the river or the dump. If his pigs were hungry, he might have used it for feed. After all, Carlos had been only a Spic tramp and somebody's punk. Before he fell off to dreamland, Sisco thought about Len one more time. Though he didn't seem to take much care of Claire, he was a decent sort. How many high school principals would have gone to the trouble to help out a bunch of hobos with a dead guy?

He woke up with the white-hot sun making its way through the oak trees to warn that the heat was on its way to cook everything in the valley. He tidied up his bedroll and went to the piece of mirror hung off the trunk of a dead cottonwood. In the glass, he saw the face of a twenty-eight-year-old man with wild yellow hair, too much color on his forehead, and a heavy beard that made him the likeness of a stew bum on the Main Stem of Chicago. When his hair got long and curly, it didn't even sport a cap, and he ended up with frizz everywhere. He couldn't recall his last visit to the barber, but something rang true about the 'bos last shear-up in Leadville, Colorado. That was two or more months ago. He shivered to think that if his ma had lived to see the growth on his head and face, she would have died of fright. He still missed her; and he knew that if she hadn't died on Black Sunday, he'd be farming with her in Kansas. Their luck would have improved because the rains had finally come to the prairie in the '40s.

Now he had the chance to make a new life in a town where he couldn't be sure of anything. If he were to get a job at the high school, he'd have to pass muster with the head janitor—'an old geezer,' Sutter had said. Where would he bunk in Hayden? It wouldn't do for him to live in the jungle with no water for a daily clean-up. He recalled that Len had mentioned a room for rent next to him over the drugstore. He'd have to impress the owner that he was a decent young man who wanted to work and would pay what he owed every week. If he stayed, he'd first have to get shaved and sheared.

He decided to head into town. Hayden was like all the old Central Valley burgs—built close to the tracks near the depot and the water tower. The streets ran parallel and at right angles to one another, all numbers and letters. Nobody figured that the place would ever get big enough to imagine different names. The townies seldom mentioned the proper names anyway. Everybody knew where everything was, and even newcomers found what they needed without much trouble.

Sisco spotted the telltale trademark of the local barbershop. A red, white, and blue barber pole hung next door to the 241 Club where he and Shorty had chugged a few beers two years ago after they chowed down at the Spic's greasy spoon. In the window of the barber shop, a sign said Open, but the place was locked up tight. Through the door of the 241, loud, familiar music boomed from the juke box. He recognized one of the Guthrie boys belting out "The Oklahoma Hills." He wished his pa had lived to hear the words from the chorus: "in the Oklahoma Hills where I was born." His father was an Okie and always had wanted to go back to the place of his birth.

Sisco walked into the club. It was too early for hooch, but he hoped to pick up a swig or two of hot coffee while he waited for the barbershop to open. Although it was dark and smoky inside, he made out some men seated at the bar. A bald guy in a short white coat faced the door with a cup in his hand. The other guy with his back to the door wore a suit. A couple of empty old- fashioned glasses sat on the bar in front of him. The man in the suit turned around. It was Sutter with his necktie loose like he had already put in a full day's work.

"Hey, look who's here—my friend, Sisco!" he said, slapping him on the back. "Come in for a cool one? Let me buy you a drink. Here, have a smoke."

"Morning, Len. Thanks for the Lucky. I'll take ya up some other time on the drink. I'm looking for the barber to get decent for the talk with your crumb boss 'bout a job."

The bald guy in the white coat jumped off the stool to reach out and shake Sisco's hand. "You come to the right place, son," he shouted over the juke box. "I'm Jonah Sturgeon, otherwise known as the best barber south of the Capitol. Pleased to serve you if you'd be good enough to follow me next door." With a nod toward Len, he laughed and said, "Better get over to the high school so them wiseacre kids don't get a head start on you."

The principal finished his drink, crushed his cigarette in the ashtray, and reached into his pocket for some loose bills. "Don't know why everybody's in such a hurry. I'm just fueling up the engine after a big weekend." He winked at Sisco. "After Joe here takes care of you, come on over to the high school so I can introduce you to Skidmore."

Sisco nodded and followed the barber to the shop next door. Jonah Sturgeon draped him up with two white sheets and got busy.

"Been awhile since you had a shave and a haircut, son," he mumbled. "Fix ya up in no time. First order of business is to check for that 'white dandruff' you knights of the road travel with. It's gonna be extra if I find any on account of they're the devil to get rid of."

Where the lice were concerned, Sisco had always been lucky. He had given a home to those critters only a few times on the rails. Probably his light yellow hair was not to their taste because those seam squirrels seemed to like the dark fur best. Now the crabs were a different story; they don't care one way or another so long as they have a warm, damp place to get into.

When the barber didn't find any crumbs, he gave the hobo a good wash and moved him to a chair in front of the mirror. With scissors in one hand and a razor in the other, he asked how much of the mop to shear off.

"Take it all, Mr. Jonah. I gotta be presentable. I'll make it worth your while. Ain't no charity case. Got some jack saved up for just this occasion."

The barber began to chop and cut while he jawed about nothing in particular. He said he missed the hobos and tramps who used to come into town after they had fought in the war. Sisco replied that he had ridden with plenty of them and that most of the veterans were real decent guys in search of a stake. He liked to listen to their adventures of Spitfire planes, Kraut tanks, and Jap kamikaze fighters. Jonah said that he had heard some doozy stories, too.

"You're settling in here at a good time, son. Won't be long before the diesel engines replace the steam locomotives, and them big, modern hogs don't need water. It's gonna be harder to get on and get off when the trains don't stop at the tower."

45

He came around to the front of the chair to look at his shear-up. With one gray, bushy eyebrow lifted higher than the other, he said, "Just remember this is a small town. It ain't like the big cities you been to on the road. If ya stick around, everybody in Hayden will know your business, and you'll know theirs."

"I been on the trains a long time, and I'm tired of not knowin' where I'll flop or when I'm gonna get the next handout. I didn't grow up like this, and I miss the regular things. So far, I've had no trouble with the law, and I aim to keep it that way. If Mr. Sutter and the janitor fella agree to give me a job, I'll settle in here for awhile. I know how to work."

Jonah had trimmed up one side and started on the other. He stopped again and stared in the mirror. "Just how you come to know Len, son?"

Sisco knew that he had to think up some story to keep Len out of the mess with Carlos. He told the barber that he had knocked on Claire's door in search of a handout. Some hobo before him had drawn a cat on her fence in the alley, so he knew that a kindhearted lady lived there. Len had opened up the back door to invite him inside and asked if he wanted to go out to the fishing camp to catch a real meal.

The barber listened, nodded his head, and chimed in with his own story about the Hayden High principal. "Sounds just like him. He'd rather be out in the country any day. Just a farm boy at heart, but turned out to be a good teacher. After a few years in the classroom, talked his way into the head fella's job after convincing the trustees to fire the guy who was there. Got them kids in line and learning their lessons, which is what their folks send them to school for. More students headed to college than ever. Since Len was the first in his family to go to college, he's a good example to the kids at the high school."

Sisco paid close attention to Jonah's talk hoping he'd mention Claire. When he didn't, he asked if she was a local girl.

Before answering, Jonah cocked the other bushy eyebrow and came around to the front of the chair. "Hell, no! Surprised ya couldn't see that yourself. She's from somewhere near San Francisco though her folks hail original from these parts. Came to Hayden engaged to some fella she met at the university. That ended after she started up with Len. A mighty good looker, ain't she?"

Sisco tried to sound casual when he said he caught a glimpse of her dressed in a housecoat. He started to sweat, and Jonah plugged in the fan next to the barber chair. Hair, fuzz, and whiskers blew all over the place.

"Sorry, son. Just couldn't turn her on while I was shearing ya. Too much wind. No, Claire's not from a ranch by any means. I don't think she's much suited to this life herself. Good with them little kids, though. They love her, and so do their folks."

Sisco squirmed in the chair as drops of water dripped from his face. He felt like he wanted to get up and run. The barber didn't seem to notice as he lifted the sheets and let the yellow locks fly like chaff to the floor.

"We ain't finished yet, son. You can finally see your ears, but ya still need a good shave."

Sisco hoped the barber hadn't seen how nervous he was when the conversation turned to Claire. He wanted to change the subject, so he asked about the janitor boss at the high.

"Old Skidmore is the head custodian and honorary deputy police chief. Len got him those titles and he takes his jobs plenty serious. Keeps a close watch on everybody. Your best bet is to work hard and mind your own business. Don't go sweet on any of the gals at school."

Taking his time with the shave, Jonah talked on about the town. He gave Sisco directions to the high school, which the townies fondly called The Grand Old Lady; advised him to see Myrtle McFadden, who owned the drugstore and might have a room to rent upstairs; offered his services to any hobos who might wander in to look for work; said he hoped Sisco would stick around and come back the next time he needed to get decent.

§ § § § §

The Grand Old Lady was easy to find. She was the tallest building in Hayden. Made of brick with a bell tower, she looked like a church and a prison all in one. The tower reminded him of the missions he had seen in San Diego, Santa Barbara, San Luis Obispo, and San Francisco. The Catholics always liked those noisy bells to call everybody to Mass, so they must have held some sway with the folks who built the high school. The two-story brick building also could have been any lock-up joint east or west of Chicago. He guessed that the parents must have had their say, too, so the kids couldn't make an easy escape once they were inside.

As he climbed the front steps, he heard a radio broadcasting baseball. The big wooden door was wide open, leading down a long hallway. On the right side was an office with a glass door, also open, and a counter behind. Inside, a ceiling fan was whirring at full speed, but the office was full of smoke anyway. Seated behind the counter were Sutter and another man in overalls with a long-sleeved shirt rolled up to the elbows. They smoked while they listened to the game.

"Come on in," invited Len, who had lost his necktie somewhere between the 241 and his office. His shirt was unbuttoned, and his feet were propped up on a desk where two ashtrays were full of butts. "Ole T. Williams just hit a homer to put the Sox out in front again."

As he stood in the doorway and stared at the other man, Sisco knew there was something familiar about him.

"Don't be bashful. Come on in and meet Clarence Eugene Skidmore, head custodian of Hayden High School."

"And deputy police chief," added Skidmore from his seat next to the principal. "Pleased to meet you, boy." He reached out his hand to shake. "I hear you're a good candidate to be my helper. Got any experience with clean-up, set-up, and paint-up?"

"Worked all my life, sir," Sisco yelled over the radio announcer. "I ain't lazy and don't mind extra work when it's needed."

Len got up to turn down the radio. "Between innings, anyway," he explained. "We don't listen to the games when the kids are here."

As he studied Skidmore, Sisco knew by his build and his voice that he was the guy at the Catholic church who had sent him packing with Carlos' body. He waited for the janitor to say something, but Skidmore walked to the outer office to bring in a chair.

"Sit down, boy. You come recommended by our principal here. Where you from anyway?"

"Kansas," he answered, folding his arms over his chest so he had a place to put his hands. Maybe the guy hadn't recognized him all shaved and sheared.

"Kansas, huh? What part?"

"Pa had a small piece near Liberal, southwest of Dodge City. Got eat up by the dust. Took out on my own when I was fifteen."

"Well, since Len here recommends you, I guess ya got the job." He looked at Len, who nodded his head.

Terry A. Albritton

"Mighty grateful to … ya … both," Sisco chewed at the words, wondering which one of these two was his boss and how much they already had talked about him. One thing was for certain: they had worked together for a while and seemed to know each other's thoughts.

Len jumped out of his chair to turn up the radio just as the announcer shouted, "Bye, bye, bye, bye, baby!" to a homer by Big Joe DiMaggio.

"Shit!" he yelled. "Time for the Sox to put in a relief pitcher."

Sisco saw his chance for a quick getaway, waved to his bosses and nearly fell down the front steps of the high school. For a moment he was tempted to catch the first flyer through Hayden headed north. On the bank of the Sacramento River at Dunsmuir, he'd find the other hobos jungled up with plenty of fresh trout. He could almost taste the tender white fish. If the fishing was good, he might even stay into the fall when the heat burns a pure pine smell through the trees and the autumn light turns things orange and gold. On his back in the wild grasses by the water, he'd watch the pink and white fingers of a gentle sky monster reach out to the shadows of the black mountaintops. It was the picture show at dusk that came quick and disappeared as fast, leaving a silent darkness to cover the river.

To get out of that jerkwater would have been the smart thing to do. Much as he wanted to stay and cast his lot for Claire, he knew that the chance for more than a friendship was a gamble. He knew he wanted her, but he had had it all before with other women. The ladies in Chicago showed him an adventure with a quick beginning and a faster ending. Even Betty, his regular joylady, never spent any extra time when they made love. He could count on her moves—the same trembling of her breasts and hardened nipples, the same cries of 'Oh, sooo good!' and the same sighs of relief—all rehearsed and repeated. He never knew

50

if he had hit her sweet spot or if she was just glad to be done with one more tramp.

Betty was older, and that was a reason to like her. She wasn't interested in tying him down; her special squeeze was one of the older hobos, a fellow named Fleet Foot Frank. He'd lost a leg on the Missouri, Kansas, and Texas Railroad—the old "Katy" line—in the dead of winter when he couldn't get help after a bad jump off a train. Good guy, ole Fleet, and he treated Betty like a queen, never minding that she earned her living from the night trade.

'You got possibilities, Kid,' Betty would say when they had finished their dance in the sack. 'You can read and write. Get off the trains, and make something of yourself. This life is a dead end for you.'

She was right, although Chicago had a lot to offer a guy of eighteen before the war. Hobohemia was everything he'd never seen or ever imagined in Kansas. On West Madison Street near the river was the slave market where "man catchers" waited to help hobos find jobs. Most guys in search of work wanted to head for places like California. Arriving in Chicago, Sisco had hoped to stay just long enough to pick up a stake and move on. But there was too much to see and experience on the Main Stem, and he ended up in the big city for almost six years.

Working as a cook and dishwasher on State Street, he settled into a flophouse where some older 'bos lived. The home guard tramps adopted him because the younger fellows mostly kept on the move, steering clear of the guys they called the "bummery." The home guard treated him fine and always watched his back. Once when he was drunk and some jack roller stole his wages, the bummery searched in an alley behind Van Buren and found the yegg. They had their way with him and recouped what was left of the stolen poke. After that, the snipe disappeared.

51

On State Street, Sisco saw his first burlesque show and fell in love with a younger gal named Etta. The guys called her "Netta Etta." She had dark eyes, wavy black hair down to her waist, and the longest gams he'd ever seen. She was taller than he was; and when she danced in those black net stockings, she looked like a spider spinning a web. She waved a pink scarf up and down, back and forth through her legs, around her neck, and over her head. He had trouble keeping his pecker in his pants and knew he had to have her.

Etta was the best roll in the hay he'd ever had. He asked her to take off everything except those black stockings hitched up to the garter belt. With those long legs wrapped around him, she became his black widow spider, and he was her prey trapped in a silk mesh web. It turned out to be a one-night stand because he knew she would never have him again. He had dumped his wad all over her and ruined her stockings with his sticky mess. He gave her some extra dough to replace everything.

On State Street, Sisco had his first shave and haircut from a lady barber. She was a bulldike named Lucy and the best barber in Hobohemia. She had red hair styled in a perfect pageboy that looked like a wig. With a nose that hooked upward, she had thick lips painted with heavy purple lipstick. Her arms matched any wrestler's, but her hands and fingers were normal and moved so fast with the scissors and razor that you got a headache watching her work. Lucy had a young gal named Tracy who helped her sweep up the floor, wash up the combs and scissors, and just keep things in order. Tracy's answer to everything was "You betcha!" Sometimes Lucy got mad, kicked the barber chair, and shouted, "Stop actin' like one of them dumb whores! Can't ya say anything except 'You betcha?'" Tracy would answer loud as she could, "You betcha!" But they were a team, and Sisco liked to imagine Tracy all snuggled up under Lucy's big arm in a bed too small for them both, listening to the radio while those fast fingers and big lips moved their way through all sorts of wet places.

At Lucy's place, he heard about the Dill Pickle Club in a brick building on Tooker Alley just off Bughouse Square. To get inside, you had to pass through a line of garbage cans that led to an opening like the entrance to a dark cave. Lit up by a green light, a sign said, "Step high, Stoop low, Leave your dignity outside." Then you walked down a long hall with rooms on both sides and walls gaily painted in all colors and decorated with cartoon drawings, posters, and news clips.

The Dill Pickle was a show that never quit. There were speeches, sermons, plays at all hours of the day and night. Celebrated men like Carl Sandburg, Ring Lardner, and that lawyer Darrow gave talks on the main stage. It was there that Sisco learned to recite poems by Robert Frost, who seemed to know a lot about the hard life. He took a real shine to that poet after he read "The Death of a Hired Man," with the line, "Home is the place, where, when you have to go there ... They have to take you in."

It wasn't just the smart guys who liked the Pickle. Jockers, prostitutes, tramps, queers, and every stripe of person came there to do things that their trade might not allow. Whores sat in a room off the hall with their knitting needles jumping every which way. One night, some wise asshole made a rude remark: "Hey, Mazie, ya gonna put a sweater on his pecker before ya fuck him?" Another whore nearby stood up, walked to the door, and stuck a needle into the man's gut. He ran screaming down the hall and out the door.

Chicago was quite a town up to the war. Sisco went through there last in '42. He thought he might enlist in Chicago since it was the closest place to home he had.

During his physical, the croakers found something wrong with the reflexes in his knees; they said it most likely came from jumping on and off the trains. They gave him a 4F classification and told him to look for a job in a factory where he could stand up or sit down. He couldn't picture himself cooped up like a chicken, so he stuffed the 4F in his pocket and went back to work in a greasy spoon.

With the war on, the Main Stem still crackled, but not like before. It was easy enough to get a job even without identification, but the recruiters hunted you down if they thought you could serve. Some of the fellows started acting sick or loco so they wouldn't be drafted. After Pearl Harbor, with the country at full-throttle war, the mood changed because the Main Stem was shut up and dark. No more capers with the ladies of the night. Most of the whores moved to shift work in the factories to help the cause, so they were too busy or too tired to turn tricks.

Sisco had heard that after the war, things changed again. The 'bos who had been back to Chicago said that Hobohemia wasn't the same because automobiles and airplanes had taken over travel. Just to keep up, the trains had turned to diesel. With everything moving faster, there were more bad accidents—hobos losing arms, legs, and other parts. The GI's had come back in search of jobs, so it was rough for the tramps to get a steady stake. Lots of them just gave up and became part of the real bummery on Skid Row.

§§§§

Hayden was no Chicago; that was for sure. As he walked down C Street, Sisco realized that he hadn't made up his mind about this jerkwater. If he got off the trains for good, what would he miss the most? First and last would be the hobos, the regular fellows he'd caught out with for years and learned to trust with his life. Memphis Shorty and the

Georgia Peach would be at the top of the list. Others, like Choo-choo Blue and Camelback Curly, figured up there, too, but they always pushed a shady caper along the cinder trail. It was risky to travel with those two. After the 'bos, he would most miss the mongee they ate at some stops on the road. If you made a good impression on the lady of the house, she gave you the same grub as the family got—all fresh and home-cooked. Even a sandwich made by a kindhearted woman might have slices of ham or roast beef with mustard and mayonnaise on home-baked bread. Sisco knew he managed to get the best handouts because he had a way with the ladies. His good looks and charm were often rewarded with a special "dessert," too.

With his thoughts on food, he realized that he was hungry. Recalling the Spic restaurant nearby on Fourth Street, he walked toward it.

"You're moving like a man on a mission," said a voice from a slow automobile close to the curb. "Where are you going, Sisco? Hop in, and I'll give you a lift."

Len leaned his head halfway out the window as the ashes from his smoke blew back into his face. He rubbed his eyes and stopped the Ford.

"Reckon I'm goin' back to the jungle for my bindle."

"Good! I'll take you over there and then to McFadden's so we can talk to Myrtle about the room upstairs next to mine. I'll spot you the money until payday. Climb in."

Even with the window rolled down, the black leather seat on the passenger side was hot. Sisco sweated, and his shirt stuck to his skin. Nervous, he struggled to get his breath, wondering why he still had doubts about Sutter, Skidmore, and the job.

"Truth is, not so sure I'm gonna stick 'round Hayden. You deserve a straight answer after the favor ya did us yesterday."

Len didn't say anything as he steered the automobile across the tracks and parked next to the jungle. As they got out, Sisco went straight for two crates behind the oak trees. Len grabbed one to take a seat with a smoke in his mouth ready to light. He held out the pack of Luckys for the hobo, who took one and sat down himself. The whistle at the milk plant blew to signal a change of shift. It wouldn't be long before the next northbound came through. Neither of them had said a word.

Finally, Sutter broke the silence. "Suit yourself about the job. You have the brains to do more than hop freights the rest of your life. Do you have a high school diploma?"

"No. I promised my ma that I would finish twelve grades. When she died, I had no way to do it."

Len got up, opened the trunk of the Ford, and pulled out a flask. He seemed to have hooch stashed everywhere. He unscrewed the top, took a long swig, and handed it to Sisco. "You won't go far in this economy without a diploma. The work force is better educated than ever before with the GI's in school on the government's dime. You need job training to get into most factories now. Demand for consumer goods is high, but you have to meet certain standards to get employment, one of which is graduation from high school."

Just down the tracks, the Northbound blew as she neared Hayden to take on water. Sisco figured he could deck her as she slowed down and never see any of these townies again. But, in his heart, he knew that Len was right about what he said. Now, while he was still young and his brains worked, he should get himself a diploma in a place where there was help to do it.

"You can stay around long enough to finish twelve grades, like your mother wanted. I'll lend you a hand, and so will Claire. She has more patience than any teacher I know."

Nothing came out of Sisco's mouth, but he nodded his head. He choked back the tears and forced a cough so that Len wouldn't know he was about to cry. Finally, he whispered, "Only one thing ya need to know. It was Mr. Skidmore who came upon me in the church when I found Carlos. It was still dark inside. I can't tell if he recognized me today without all my locks and whiskers."

Len didn't act surprised. "Let me handle Skiddy. He owes me, and I don't think he will make a big deal out of Carlos even if he knows. He's a schemer and, strange as it sounds, a 'devout Catholic.' Just don't get him riled up on anything related to the church or his religion."

Now Sisco didn't hold back and reached out to give Sutter a firm handshake. Truth be told, he felt funny taking a job that would put him closer to Claire, but he couldn't help how he felt. To think about her giving him lessons made his heart beat faster and his skin tingle.

"So, do we have a deal?"

"Yeah, we got a deal! Guess I'd better go with ya to rent that room."

The rattler took on water, slithered forward to the depot, and continued on toward Roseville.

As they pulled out of the jungle toward C Street and McFadden's, Len said, "Now, you can do me a big favor. Have to go to Woodland for a few days to take care of some business at my mother's ranch before school starts. Stop in to check on Claire while I'm gone. Just tell her I sent you."

Terry A. Albritton

School

All of a sudden, Sisco had no doubt about Hayden as his new home—at least for a while. Len drove him over the tracks to Fourth Street and parked in front of McFadden's drugstore. He felt familiar with the place as soon as he walked through the door. The counter and stools at the soda fountain looked just like the ones in Sublette, where his pa often dropped him off when he had business at the Rodeo Bar down the alley. He used to sit for hours on the high stool, drinking bubbly lemon phosphates and creamy chocolate milkshakes. If Pa had left enough money with Mr. Kelsey, the proprietor, he even got to eat a grilled cheese sandwich or a thick hamburger. Kelsey was a jolly, bald fellow with a thick black mustache and hair all over his ears, who talked a mile a minute and often lost track of how many drinks he had served from the fountain, but he never charged more than Pa had paid him. The drugstore in Kansas meant a satisfied stomach and a safe place to talk with friendly folks who treated him to penny candies from the colored jars on the apothecary side. He felt right at home at McFadden's.

Myrtle McFadden was a tall, thin woman with gray hair pulled back under a net. Her face showed the lines of hard work, but Sisco thought she was still decent-looking in her own way. She was busy with three gals who guzzled Coca Colas at the counter. When she saw Len, she smiled, and her bright blue eyes danced with excitement. "What you doing here, you handsome devil? Thought you'd gone over to Woodland."

"I'm headed that way, Myrtle. Told you I'd bring my friend, Sisco, by to check out the room upstairs."

She nodded her head, wiped her hands, and came out from behind the counter. "Any friend of Len Sutter's is a friend of mine … and my husband's. If you think you can bunk in the room next to this character, then I'm glad for you to have it. Have to share the toilet and tub with him, though. He's not the neatest guy."

She laughed and winked at them.

Len pulled out a fistful of bills and stuffed them into a big pocket on Mrs. McFadden's apron. "Here you go, Myrtle, the first four weeks' rent. Sisco's just been hired on as Skidmore's helper. Soon be making his own dough."

"I've got towels and sheets in the storeroom, son. You're welcome to use them unless you've got some of your own."

Sisco mushed up his words because he didn't know how to thank them. "Sure ... sure do 'preciate the help, ma'am ... and Len. I'll take ya up on the linens. Just couldn't carry my own with me this trip," he laughed.

"Don't fret about work clothes either," she said. I have a closet full of my son's that he doesn't wear. Moved to Truckee with his gal and needs warmer duds up there in the mountains. He's about your size."

She signaled to the counter where two more young gals had sat down. Calling them by name, she excused herself to fix their ice cream sodas. Len walked over to their stools and shook their hands with a big smile and said he'd see them the next week at the high. Then he went back to Sisco. "Glad to have you upstairs. Hope it's not too tough sleeping in a bed again. See you in a few days."

He blew a kiss to Myrtle and left.

When she finished at the fountain, Mrs. McFadden took her new boarder upstairs to a room that overlooked Fourth Street onto the railroad tracks. The only window was open, but there still wasn't much breeze. The room was sweet enough with a single bed, a chest of drawers, a small table, and a lamp. The toilet was at the other end of the hall; he knew he'd have to pass Len's room to go there. He wondered just how much time the principal spent sleeping over the drug- store.

That night, he tried to rest in his new spot. Although the bed wasn't too bad, the room didn't cool down much from the heat of the August day. He heard the blow of the hogs all night long, and wished he had bunked in the jungle. Close to morning, he dozed off until the siren sounded for the first shift at the milk plant. He got up and took a big bath towel down the hall to the tub where Mrs. Mac had left a white bar of Ivory on the edge. He ran the hot water halfway up the sides and added some cold. Once he got into the tub, it wasn't long before the water turned brown with all the soot, coal dust, mud and dirt that had settled on his body during the past weeks. He figured that his last full soaking had been in San Bernardino when the 'bos spent a night in the whorehouse. One of the ladies had insisted on giving him a good bath. By the time she finished, he had come three or four times and fell on the bed to sleep through until morning.

As he recalled San Bernardino, Sisco took care of business himself and then dried his private parts with the big, fluffy towel. He watched the brown, soapy water gurgle its way down the drain. The water disappeared, leaving a thick, black ring around the sides of the tub. He vowed to find some Dutch Cleanser to clean the tub later.

Dressed in his only decent overalls and a blue denim shirt that needed to be washed, he walked down Fourth Street and headed east on C Street to the high. He hoped to be early on his first day of the new job. The sun had just appeared over the mountains as he sat down on the front steps to wait for Skidmore.

"Won't get any work done like that, boy," said a voice behind him. He turned around, and there was his boss in starched overalls and pressed shirt. He had a broom in one hand and a mop in the other. Sisco stood up and took the broom so he could shake the janitor's hand. Skidmore ignored the hand and led his new helper into the building.

All morning long, they marched up and down the stairs between the first and second floors of the high. The classrooms on both levels looked clean and ready for students, but the super said that each one needed a quick once-over before the first day. He explained that the brooms and mops were kept in the boiler room closet behind the gymnasium on the bottom floor. The gymnasium also needed a wax before next Tuesday, when everyone would gather there to open the school year. It was lunchtime when Skiddy told Sisco that he also was assigned to work at the primary two or three afternoons a week. "That suit ya, boy?"

"Oh, it suits me fine," Sisco answered as he bit off a bite of the bologna sandwich the janitor had brought him. With his heart beating faster, he stammered, "Just met only one teacher over there—Miss Lewis."

"Well, you'll meet 'em all soon enough. Claire's good as any. Don't have any Commie ideas though she went to the big university in Berkeley. It's a pity she got hooked up with Len 'cause he's got plenty of crazy Commie notions."

He folded the piece of waxed paper from his sandwich and poured the last cup of iced tea from his thermos.

"I don't plan to get mixed up in any Commie ideas," said Sisco as he handed over his waxed paper. "Much obliged for the sandwich, Mr. Skidmore. I'll bring my own tomorrow."

As they worked side-by-side during the week before classes, the head custodian and his new helper became more at ease with each other. Skiddy said that he had come from the Oklahoma Panhandle near Boise City right in the middle of No Man's Land. His folks had gone there from Missouri in 1908 when he was ten years old. Some shyster speculators had promised free fertile land that grew anything. Boy City they named it because boy meant tree in French.

"Wasn't no trees anywhere," he said. "Them fellas that invented the place got sent up to the pen for fraud. And the fools that went there to farm had no way to move back where they came from, so they stayed. My ma and pa tried to make a go of it in that desert. For a few years, they did grow a wheat crop.

"We lived in a soddie. Went to school in one, too. Had to ride four miles each way by horse. I was always late and had to put up with a scolding or whipping if I tried to explain that Pa didn't want me to come. He said that book learning wouldn't grow us any wheat.

"Didn't mind the farming. Just saw it as a dead end. One day, I had enough of scorpions, tarantulas, and the stench of cow manure. Took the train to Oklahoma City and never went back."

Though he was already gone from Oklahoma by the time the dusters came, Skiddy knew how hard the Panhandle had been hit. His folks died trying to hang on.

Sisco said that his ma and pa had lost their lives in the storms, too. He had left Kansas because he had no way to survive there anymore.

On Thursday before Labor Day weekend, Skiddy suggested that they walk over to the primary school to find out what the teachers needed. He said that the faculty there was a strong, independent group of six women led by Ruth Jamieson, the teaching principal and the only one who was married. She liked to run her school without interference from Len, her supervisor, or the board of trustees.

"This bunch of old maids is pretty handy in keeping up their classrooms. You shouldn't have a lot to do over here, but ya gotta check in regular anyway."

Sisco wondered how anybody could think of Claire Lewis as an old maid, but he didn't want Skidmore to know how he felt about her. He began to sweat as they neared her room. He took off his cap and wiped his brow, wishing he weren't so dirty and smelly from the wax at the high.

"Claire, this here's Sisco Griffin, my new helper."

She looked startled at first, and then smiled at him. "Oh! I met you last Sunday—with Len."

"Glad to see you 'gain, ma'am." He took out his handkerchief to wipe his sweaty palm. "Seems like I have dirty hands every time I wanna shake with ya."

She wore a pale green sundress decorated with yellow and white daisies. Thin white straps showed off her shoulders and neck tanned from the summer sun. Her hair was tied up in back with a green ribbon. As far as he was concerned, she could have been Goldilocks wandering through a forest of little wooden desks, tables, and chairs, only Claire was much prettier. She led him from the blackboard to the sink to the storage closet, pointing out things that needed to be fixed.

"My helper here will get to what he can before Tuesday, Claire. I'll be tied up at the high all day tomorrow and next week what with kids comin' in. Gotta run a check myself on all the bells. Don't worry, though. What doesn't get done here tomorrow, he'll take care of next week."

"Thank you. There's really no hurry on any of this, but the sooner the better. I hope to see you here tomorrow, Sisco."

She nodded to them both and disappeared into the storage closet.

On their way back to the high, Skidmore told his assistant that he was not comfortable at the primary. He said that he knew about all the kids and their folks: how the youngsters were treated at home—if they had enough to eat; how often they got whopped with a belt, a strap, or a horse whip; whether they slept alone or with brothers and sisters. It bothered him that some of the smallest kids were expected to do the work of grown-ups and came to school with only two slices of bread for their midday meal. He said that it hurt him a lot to watch the Johanssen boys eyeball everybody else's lunch box and grab a peanut butter sandwich or an apple from some little boy who wasn't watching.

"There's folks have many young'uns just to keep more hands on the ranch, and then there's others don't lie together to keep from havin' more mouths to feed. Never had kids myself and figured that any I mighta had was better off not bein' born."

Skiddy said he was a widower; his wife had passed on in '39 of influenza. He was some fifty years old, but it was hard to tell because he still had sand-colored hair without any gray. He had some creases in his cheeks like he might have had a pox as a little boy. His muscles were firm and strong without any fat.

On Friday morning, Sisco finished the wax job on the floors in Len's office and the main entrance to the high. The heat was fierce, and by noontime, he had sweated through his shirt and overalls. Skiddy was dry as a bone because he had spent the whole morning testing the bells. It took him so long because he kept stepping outside to greet students and their folks who had come in from the ranches to find out about the first day of school. He didn't allow anybody to come in through the front door, but he stood on the front steps to make small talk with them. Through the open windows, Sisco heard their words and felt their excitement.

"Hey, Joe, you and me got that pretty algebra teacher. Hurray!"

"What about it, Sue? Sit next to me in study hall?"

"Yeah, I bet the General is hiding inside to plan his battle strategy for the year."

Many of the kids mentioned the General and asked the head custodian where he was. Skiddy acted like the question bothered him, answering, "All I know is that he ain't here yet. Reckon he'll be back on Tuesday."

By noontime, Sisco's head rang like the bells. He was hungry, and the smell of wax with the midday heat made him sick to his stomach. He wanted to get over to the primary, but he needed to clean up first. With Skidmore still on the front steps shooting the breeze with some ranchers, he asked if he could head over to the other school in the afternoon.

"Ya done good this week, son," Skiddy answered in a voice loud enough for the farmers to hear, too. "Take your lunch now, and then walk over to the primary with that new hinge for Miss Lewis's door."

At the drugstore, Sisco cleaned up as best he could and took a seat at the counter to wait for the grilled cheese sandwiches Mrs. Mac was fixing him. At the other end of the fountain, two young girls giggled and pretended not to look his way.

Mrs. Mac took it all in as she flipped the sandwiches on the grill. When the girls had gone and she had served him his lunch, she sat down at the counter to offer some advice. "Watch out for these young girls with ants in their pants. Last fella who worked for Mr. Skidmore got run off 'cause he was caught in a compromising position behind the gymnasium. Skiddy never bothered to take the guy to Len. He just hightailed him out of town. The girl shoulda known better—ended up in a family way. Folks hid her some place in Texas to have the baby."

"No need to worry 'bout me, Mrs. Mac. I don't get mixed up with schoolgirls. Headed over to the primary now. Thanks for the sandwiches."

After checking in with Mrs. Jamieson at the office, Sisco went straight to Claire's room. Her door was open; he paused so he wouldn't scare her. She was walking in and out of the rows to place a little book on each desk. She wore a pink sundress that fit close to her breasts. Her hair hung loose over her shoulders.

"'Scuse me, ma'am," he apologized. "Got hung up waxin' floors at the high. Smelled so bad that I had to go back to my room to wash up."

She looked up and smiled. "The high always takes priority. It's a good thing we can handle things pretty well ourselves over here. Still, I appreciate any extra help I can get."

Sisco saw that every child's desk had a card with a name printed in big black letters: "Walter," "Margaret," "Judy," "Wanda," "Richard," "Joey". He recited them out loud as he walked up and down the rows.

Claire heard him and said, "One of the first motivators to learn to read is recognition of your name. Most of these children have never seen their own name in printed letters, or if they have, they don't recognize it."

He answered that his mother had taught him to print his name before he went to school. She had always tried to keep him ahead of the other kids because she never knew when his father would make him stay home to work or when the dust would cancel classes. "These kids are lucky to have a teacher like you, ma'am. I mean it!"

"It is every teacher's dream to have a child like you were, Sisco—a student who comes to school prepared to learn and supported by a parent who values education. That's a problem here. Not many children have encouragement from their families. Don't you agree?"

Sisco knew he should get to work on the door, but the hair on the back of his neck was standing up, and he had to say his piece even though Claire's emerald eyes dared him to answer her. He put the toolbox on the floor and took a chance. "With all due respect, ma'am, every family's gotta survive best it can. When I was a little tyke, Pa kept me home to work in the wheat 'cause he had nobody else to help. He argued plenty with Ma 'bout me and school. I don't blame him, and I don't blame her. They done the best they could with the dust and all."

She walked over to her desk and began to shift papers all around. "I hope we can talk more about this, but I think it's time for us both to get back to work." She sat down and began to cut bold letters from red construction paper.

§ § § § §

Claire was uncomfortable. She wasn't used to hearing disagreement with her views on education. At least she and Len never argued about how kids learned and what they needed from their folks to stay in school. Maybe she should sleep with Len—just get on with it so they could get married.

During the past week she had had plenty of time to think. She wondered if she had handled Leonard Sutter all wrong. If she agreed to sleep with him, would he be patient and teach her what to do? If she got pregnant, would he marry her? She'd be fine if they eloped to Reno, but her parents would have a fit because they had wanted the formal wedding fuss planned before she broke her engagement to Bob.

A big problem was that she couldn't tell them that Len had been married before to some socialite from San Francisco. It wouldn't do, either, for her folks to know that she had started seeing him while he was still married, although separated. Claire believed him when he said that the whole romance was a college infatuation encouraged by his fraternity brothers and her sorority sisters. He said that it was important to know if a fella and a gal were good together before they tied the knot. When she asked him what he meant, he told her that his marriage had failed because his wife didn't like sex.

She thought about her folks and how they seemed to get on just fine even though they never kissed or touched each other in front of her. They talked about everything— Daddy's job, Harry "Give 'em Hell" Truman, General MacArthur, the Republican Party, and their own family problems with relatives in the valley. They seemed comfortable together. She questioned Len on how this figured in a marriage. He answered that he wasn't sure since his father had died when he was only eight, and he couldn't remember much of his parents together. He guessed that good communication was important, but a married couple needed more than words to make a go of things.

Why was she thinking about this now with Skidmore's new helper replacing the rusted hinge? She had to admit that she liked his spirit and his manners. He possessed an innocence that made her want to educate him. And she liked his appearance now that he was all cleaned up, no longer looking like a hobo. Earlier in the week, she had noticed his blue-gray eyes and wavy blonde hair. He had a rough, rugged look like a mountain man, with broad shoulders and firm muscles that showed he knew how to work his body. She tried hard not to stare at the bulge below his waist as he screwed on the hinge. On the one hand, she wanted him to finish the job and leave so she could go to the teacher bathroom and urinate. On the other hand, she wanted him to stay so they might continue talking. Her classroom was not really the place for the kind of conversation she wanted to have with him. Besides, Mrs. Jamieson, who was all business, might walk in the door at any minute and see that she was socializing with the janitor's helper. Claire gathered up the letters she had cut and walked over to the bulletin board to pin them up.

§ § § § §

"WELCOME TO FIRST GRADE!" read Sisco. "Nice letters, ma'am, but what good are they if the kids can't read?"

"Will you please stop calling me ma'am? Didn't we just agree that motivation creates a desire to learn? To know what these strange red characters say is an incentive to read."

"Sorry, ma'am—I mean, Claire. I don't have much education, so please excuse me if I offended ya. I fixed the hinge, but I'll have to come back next week for a leak in your faucet."

She shook her head like she didn't want an apology and surprised them both when she invited him to the house later for a glass of iced tea. When he accepted, she smiled and headed to the bathroom.

Sisco ran back to the high, where he found Skiddy in the principal's office seated in Len's chair with his feet on the desk.

"So how's things goin' with Claire? Is she pinin' away for old Len this week?"

"Can't say, Mr. Skidmore. Fixed the hinge, but have to go back next week for a leaky faucet. It's near five o'clock. Ya think I can leave now?"

Skiddy sat up in the chair, put his feet on the floor and snuffed out a smoke in the ashtray. As he stood up, he smoothed out his overalls where some ashes had been scattered by the fan overhead. "You done as good your first week as any I've had, son. Keep ya long as ya work hard and stay outta trouble with the gals. Come in early on Tuesday, and don't forget to go to church on Sunday. Oh, and remind Myrtle—Mrs. Mac—to fly her flag on Labor Day!"

Sisco waved and darted out of the office down the front steps. The whistle at the milk plant blew five o'clock, quitting time. He figured Skiddy would be looking for him at church on Sunday, but he planned to explain that he'd been raised up Methodist and he'd join that congregation once he got settled in. He already had spotted the Methodist church ... and the Episcopal ... and the Presbyterian. Like the Catholic church, they were built close to the railroad tracks on purpose to capture the attention of passengers who got off at the station when the trains used to make regular stops at the depot. The idea was to get the folks before they wandered down C Street to another congregation or, worse yet, to one of the local bars that had been in town as long as the churches.

He changed into a shirt less stained by sweat from a long day's hard work. Walking down Fourth Street over to F, he felt a Delta breeze pick up and hoped he wouldn't embarrass himself by soaking through a second shirt. At the fence in the alley behind Claire's, he went through the gate and up the steps to the back door. When there was no answer to his first knock, he rapped harder; the door opened. Claire stood there looking like Rita Hayworth or Lauren Bacall. She wore white shorts and a top that tied low in the front to show her breasts. With her thick brown hair piled on her head in a red scarf, she looked taller. She was as pretty as any pin-up picture he'd ever seen.

"Come in," she greeted him, holding the screen door open. "I have a pitcher of iced tea in the kitchen. If you will carry it out for me, we can sit in the backyard where it's cooler."

He took the tray outside to a small table between two wooden lawn chairs on the grass. She motioned him to sit down while she leaned over to pick up a trowel next to the steps. Her back was to him as she bent over; her shorts rode right up her ass. He saw her white panties underneath

71

hugging her cheeks as firm and dainty as you please. When she turned around, he looked away, hoping she wouldn't see the bulge in his pants. With trowel in hand, she walked over to the far corner of the backyard to scoop up a pile of dry dog shit that she threw over the fence into the alley.

"Len always misses at least one mess when he brings Pluto. Now, we can relax and have some tea. Let me pour you a glass. Tell me about your first week in Hayden."

He set the glass on the arm of the lawn chair and took a deep breath. "It's been fine, I reckon. Mr. Skidmore treats me decent, and so far, I ain't had a problem with anybody."

"You mean you haven't had a problem. Try not to use the word 'ain't' around teachers, Sisco. We do have a problem with that word."

"I know better. Been 'round hobos too long. Ya pick up a lot of bad habits on the road."

She took a sip of her tea. Her red lipstick left its mark on the glass. She had been sitting forward in her chair; now, she relaxed and leaned back to cross one leg over the other. He tried hard not to stare at her gams tanned from the summer sun.

"You seem to fit in well, Sisco. Not everyone can adjust to Hayden. There's a lot of pettiness here."

"Hayden's nice 'nough. Pretty much the same as all the other burgs in this valley."

"Oh?" she asked and uncrossed her legs to lean forward. "You know that I'm not from one of these small towns. After two years, I'm still having a hard time adjusting."

She planted her feet on the grass with her legs spread apart just far enough for him to imagine the dark patch under her panties. He took the glass of cold tea and rested it in his lap to calm down. "Ya coulda fooled me," he lied. "From the little I know, you have a lotta respect in this town."

She blushed, took a swig of tea, and looked down at the lawn. When she lifted her head, there were tears in her eyes.

"Oh, Claire, I'm sorry. Didn't mean to make ya cry. What I said was s'posed to make ya feel better."

How he wanted to hold her in his arms, feel her tears on his face, and smell her sweetness as close to him as possible. When she choked up and coughed, he took a paper napkin off the tray and offered it to her. She pulled it from his hand and got ahold of herself.

"What you said didn't make me cry," she whispered and leaned back into the chair.

"I reckon ya been kinda lonely this week without Len in town."

"Oh, I miss him, but we've spoken every day on the phone. I've actually talked to him more this past week than I do when he's in town."

That struck Sisco as strange because Len didn't seem too busy at the high—when he was actually there. Of course, school hadn't started yet, so there was no way to know just how much work the principal did with classes in session. Len seemed like a man who would pretty much make his own hours.

"He's always got some project that keeps him occupied and away … from me. He helps out some of the poorer families on the ranches near Hayden. And, of course, he looks after his mother in Yolo. This week, he's been supervising the construction of temporary housing for the *braceros* who work on her property. Everyone thinks he's crazy to take that on just to house some Mexican laborers who can't stay here legally anyway."

As he listened, he wondered how any man in his right mind would spend so much time away from a woman like Claire. Len was sure clearing the way for some other guy to slip through the back door. He asked her if she ever went with him out to his mother's ranch in Yolo.

"He invites me sometimes. But there's nothing for me to do out there except sit on the front porch and watch Mrs. Sutter work. She's nice enough to me, but we don't have a whole lot to talk about."

"I don't know either one of ya very well, but it seems to me that he's a growd-up farm boy, and you're a classy city gal."

She twisted in her chair again and rested her elbows on her knees with her head in her hands. "The real problem with Len and me is that I refuse to sleep with him unless we get married. He says that we have to know if we're compatible in bed before we make things legal. He doesn't want to make another mistake. And I think he's sleeping with somebody here, but I have no proof. There are rumors."

Sisco didn't answer and wondered why she was telling him this when she hardly knew him. Did she just need to get it off her chest? Or did she want to find out if he had other women. He thought about his earlier conversation with Skiddy, who had wanted to know if Claire missed Len this week. Uncomfortable with these questions, he wondered again if he had made a mistake by taking a job in Hayden. He got up to leave.

"Please don't go!" she said as she jumped up and grabbed his arm. "I respect your loyalty to your dead hobo friend ... and to Len. I don't want you to betray any confidences. I just don't want to waste any more time here."

He pulled back from her and sat down, saying that he hadn't had time to know anything about anybody in Hayden. He'd seen Len for a couple of hours on Monday; as far as he knew, he hadn't been at the high or at McFadden's since then. He wanted to be her friend, and

Len's, too, but he wouldn't be a referee in their romance. They had to straighten things out for themselves.

She began to cry and put her hands in front of her face like she was embarrassed. Since there were no more napkins on the tray, Sisco didn't know how to comfort her. He didn't dare pull out his dirty handkerchief, so he sat still in the lawn chair and listened to the heavy breath of the hog stopped at the tower to take on water. The noise gave him time to think what to say next, but Claire beat him to it after the rattler pulled down the tracks.

"I didn't have to end up in Hayden, you know. When I graduated, I was supposed to marry an engineer and move to Seattle where my fiancé was working. I already had a teaching job there. One day during my last semester at Berkeley, I accompanied a friend to a meeting where Len was recruiting teachers to come to the Central Valley. You can guess the rest. It's all my fault."

Sisco stayed quiet and drank more tea. He had to piss but didn't know whether to go into the alley or ask to use the toilet inside. Claire rambled on until she noticed that the pitcher was empty and asked him to carry the tray into the house so she could make more tea.

What he wanted was stronger than tea, but he followed her inside and excused himself to go to the toilet while she puttered in the kitchen. Taking a piss, he looked around the bathroom. There was no sign of a man's presence—no shaving cream, no smelly lotion, no pajamas on the door hook. It didn't look like Len was bedding down there.

He carried the tray with a full pitcher back outside to the table and the lawn chairs. It had started to get dark. As they sat down, Claire said, "I hope you don't mind that I added some brandy. After all, it's Friday afternoon on a long weekend."

"That suits me just fine," he answered.

75

They talked until the mosquitos began to buzz and bite. She invited him inside for another pitcher of brandy iced tea with potato chips and hard-boiled eggs. He described Dust Bowl Kansas and life in a soddie when you couldn't see your hand in front of your face during a storm. She talked about life in Berkeley and sleeping in the same bed with her grandmother, who had spells at all hours of the night. She finally smiled when she said that her folks were opposed to all liquor, and it must be time to bring out the brandy bottle without the tea.

By the time the nine o'clock freight rolled through Hayden, they both were plenty relaxed. Claire excused herself to the bathroom. When she came back, she was wearing the blue satin housecoat and her hair hung loose over her shoulders. She steadied herself as she sat down at the kitchen table. She smelled like jasmine and ginger and had trouble keeping her robe closed in front.

Sisco steadied himself; she was so beautiful and vulnerable at the same time. "Gotta go, Claire," he fibbed. "One of the 'bos will be in on this last rattler. Thanks for the talk … and the tea. Can ya make it okay to the bedroom?"

"Oh, yes, I'm perfectly fine," she answered as she fumbled to tie her robe. "Please don't tell Len how unhappy I am. If he knows, he'll lose interest completely."

"Ya got no worries from me."

Back in the jungle, Sisco searched the crates for food. Potato chips and chicken bombs had only whetted his appetite. He found an old bag of beef jerky and chowed down, letting the salty stuff creep into his empty gut. The brandy had heated him up so that he sweated like the hog on its way south from Roseville. She had pulled into Hayden, slowed down, and crept on through, belching a trail of smelly smoke that made him struggle for breath. He was drunk.

As the caboose snaked past the jungle, a tall, lean figure slipped out of the shadows. It was Memphis Shorty. He grabbed a crate, sat down, and lit up a fag. "The Peach is gone. Hung hisself in an empty boxcar in Red Bluff."

Sisco stood up and went behind the oaks to puke out his guts.

Terry A. Albritton

Ranch

In the fall of '49, the Yankees never should have made it to the World Series because DiMaggio was hurt. But Casey Stengel kept his team in the game and set the New Yorkers up for another run. They had their work cut out for them, though, with the other team. The Dodgers from Brooklyn showed off their newest star—a kid from the Negro leagues. Jackie Robinson already had a reputation as one helluva ballplayer. Mr. Mac invited some of the ranchers to listen to the games with him in the back room of the drugstore. The Series was one of the few times he hung around. Everybody knew his mistress lived over in Clay Station where he spent most of his days—and nights. Mrs. Mac acted as though she was accustomed to this arrangement, but Len told Sisco otherwise. He said that she hoped he'd get tired of this woman just like he had with others before.

After Labor Day, most of the kids at the high came back to school. Some straggled in late from the corn or the pears or the almonds. The heat was so bad in the afternoon that Sutter allowed the students to leave early if they had done their lessons in the morning. He said that the teachers would have to review everything anyway when the crops were picked and the rest of the kids came back.

Over at the primary, Claire tried to give lessons to the first-graders outside in the afternoon. The little guys were supposed to be learning "Run, Jane, run!" and "Look at Dick come!" Instead, they kept asking her for permission to go to the toilet—by way of the swings. When she figured out what they were up to, she gave in and let them play for the rest of the afternoon.

During the third game of the Series, the faucet in Claire's classroom started leaking for the second time. Sisco said he would take the thing apart on Saturday when the children weren't there if Skidmore gave him permission to work on the weekend. Claire reminded him that Len was the boss and could open up on Saturday without anyone's permission. She offered to talk to him.

Sisco hadn't seen much of Len since school started. He wasn't bunking at the drugstore most nights; Sisco wasn't flopping there either, but he knew that no one had been upstairs when he came over from the jungle to clean up in the bathroom before school. They ran into each other at the high but always seemed to be going in different directions. Len looked busy enough and managed a friendly "Howdy" even when he was in a hurry.

On Friday morning after the discussion about the leaky faucet, Len looked for Sisco in the gym. "I've neglected you these past weeks," he said as he leaned against a basketball pole. "Wanted to give you and Skidmore a chance to get acquainted. How're things going?"

"Fine—by me," he answered, resting himself on the push broom used to sweep up the gymnasium floor. "Hasn't he reported to you about me?"

"Not really, but that's good news for you. If he had complaints, he'd be in my office every day. And we'll just keep this faucet business between the two of us because the trustees don't like things open on the weekend. I'll meet you at the primary tomorrow at ten o'clock." He winked and took off across the floor to the opposite door.

On Saturday, Sisco was up with the first blow of a hog. The sky showed white hot in the east to signal a scorcher. With the ranchers fertilizing at all hours, the air smelled like a musty horse blanket. Since it was still early, he made a small fire to brew up some coffee before heading over to the primary. With hot java and a smoke, he sat down on a crate to think. He hadn't seen any of the hobos since Shorty came south to tell him about Peach. He had reported that the other hobos took it pretty hard since they rode with him for years. When it came to the body, the guys weren't sure what to do. Shorty had recalled a preacher in Redding who had tried to save him once at a rescue mission that offered free meals for anybody who repented. So the boys got off there with the extra baggage. They found the reverend, who was pleased to provide Peach with a proper burial even though he wasn't too happy that the corpse had taken his own life. The 'bos told the pastor that the Peach's "wife" had been murdered and that he hung himself out of grief. After the service and the burial, the boys stayed on for a few more handouts and one last flop. Shorty had come back to Hayden when the others caught out for Dunsmuir.

Sisco didn't pretend to understand why Peach had done what he did. He and Shorty chugged a few bottles of dago and tried to figure it all out. The only thing they came up with was that Carlos was Peach's true love and that life didn't matter without him. Neither of them had ever felt that deep about anybody, so how could they know why he killed himself?

Walking over the tracks down E Street to the primary, Sisco wondered how strong you had to feel about somebody to end your own life when that person wasn't there anymore. Had Ma been so crazy in love with Pa that she just went to sleep after he died? She had never seemed happy when he was alive, but how could he tell when the only grown-ups he really knew were his folks? There had been plenty of arguments between them and between Carlos and Peach, but that didn't seem to matter where their love was concerned.

As he reached the primary, he saw that the front door was wide open and Len sat outside on a wooden bench beside the playground. He wore a blue work shirt and Levis, both spotted with white paint. He smoked a Lucky with two or three butts at his feet. His shoes looked to be the same ones he used for school. If he had combed his hair, you sure couldn't tell.

"Morning," said Sisco and took a seat next to him. Refusing one of Sutter's smokes, he took out a pack of his own.

"Feels pretty good to have a little money in your pocket, doesn't it?" Len asked with a nod and a smile.

Sisco took a deep drag and said, "Thanks to you. Mighty obliged."

"You're doing me the favor of keeping Skiddy off my back. Good day for us to do this faucet job. Mr. Skidmore is probably listening to the Series. If the Yanks take the Dodgers today, they could end it tomorrow with another win. You like baseball?"

"Yeah. I might catch some of the game later with Mr. Mac."

"Not much of a baseball fan myself," he said, finishing off the Lucky and lighting up the next one. "Boxing is my sport. Heavyweight title fight next week, in fact. Ezzard Charles defends his belt. I'll see it on television at Caminetti's Appliance."

Sisco shook his head but said nothing. Skiddy had told him that Len was romancing Ed Caminetti's wife, Janine, on the side. She came to the high a few days a week to teach modern dance to the girls in their physical education classes. It was easy to see why he liked her. Tall and blonde with big knockers and curvy hips, Janine wore bright red lipstick and tight clothes. Wherever she went, she turned heads. Truth be told, she didn't walk like a married woman. Her husband looked proud and showed her off like she was his Kewpie doll on display.

Sisco too, had a way with the ladies that had led to a roll in the hay with more than one married woman. He never looked for them in particular, trying hard to follow the second commandment of the Hobo Code: "When in town, always respect the local law and officials, and try to be a gentleman at all times." Somehow, though, there was always a hitched, horny broad who made him promise to pay for a handout afterwards in the barn. He had no quarrel with that since it was her idea, and he was grateful for the meal. It didn't bother him, either, that Len was banging Janine Caminetti, who must have needed something Ed wasn't giving her. What gnawed at him was how the rumors upset Claire and that everyone in Hayden seemed to know the truth except Claire.

Sisco followed Len into the primary and down the hall to the first grade, where he began to work on the faucet. Skiddy had loaned him a small toolbox to keep under the sink so he wouldn't have to carry the heavier one back and forth to the high. As he took apart the pipe, Len went around to open the windows and turn on the big fan at the front of the classroom. Then, he made himself right at home in Claire's chair behind the desk. He settled back, put his feet up, and lit another cigarette. "Always was a sucker for a pretty dame," he said, puffing on his Lucky. "And the little schoolteacher in this room happens to be smart, too. If they're pretty, gals with brains are my Achilles' heel. Take this actress, Helen Douglas, who's in the House of Representatives from California. Now she's declared herself a candidate for the U.S. Senate. She's a beauty—a real corker. Stands up for the downtrodden against the big-money bastards who hijack this state. It takes guts to rattle the power boys—especially if you're a woman."

The smoke from Len's cigarette had drifted his way and gave Sisco an urge to light up himself. But he decided to stay under the sink and work so he could finish and not have to talk.

"All of those greedy sons of bitches want to bang her while they argue with what she says and call her a Commie. She's been in those migrant camps to see squalor firsthand.

When she points it out to them, they say she's a Red because 'who else would care about a bunch of Okies and Spics?'"

Sweating up a storm, Sisco came out from under the sink to look for a smaller wrench and get some air. He felt dizzy and lightheaded. Next thing he knew, Len was ushering him over to the open window.

"Have one of my smokes, and take a breather." He lit the Lucky, handed it over and kept on jawing. "I'm building some little places for the *braceros* who work my mother's ranch. Nothing fancy, but they have running water and indoor toilets. Would you like to go out to see them—meet my mother later in the afternoon?"

His head was spinning. He couldn't understand why Len talked about toilets and running water. He said that he needed to go outside, sit down, and get some air. He felt an arm holding him up and steering him down the steps to the bench by the playground. He put his head between his legs and felt a cold stream of water pouring over his head.

"Don't pass out on me!" Sutter shouted.

"Hey! Ya don't have to drown me, boss! I ain't no sissy. I got my head back now."

They both laughed and had a smoke. Sisco said he was ready to finish the job, stood up, and started toward the building. Just then, a shiny black Caddy pulled into the school parking lot. Skidmore got out and made a beeline for Len still seated on the bench. He never even looked at his helper.

"Afternoon, Chief," greeted Len. "What's the score?"

Skiddy came close to the bench. He was mad and looked ready to throw a punch. His cheeks moved like they were full of meat and potatoes. "What's the idea of leavin' the front door wide open where any kid or varmit can wander in? I drove by here three times this morning, wasn't nobody outside to keep an eye on things."

Len stood up, and Skiddy backed way. As he offered Skidmore a smoke, he answered calmly, "You must have missed me. I've been here the whole time—in and out. Got worried about your assistant here. He almost passed out on me. Practically had to carry him outside."

Sisco nodded his head and said, "That's the God's truth, Mr. Skidmore. Guess I was under the sink too long without water. Len doused me good with this can once he got me outside." He pointed to the watering can next to the bench.

Skiddy's cheeks were still vibrating like he was ready to spit out a mouthful of chaw. While his hands shook, he lit up the Lucky from Len's pack and puffed away until he calmed down.

"You worry too much, Skiddy. I always have my eye on things even when I'm not actually here. You know that! Now, your assistant is going back inside to finish the job, and I'll sit outside to lock up when he comes out. Go on home now to catch the last innings."

As Sisco hightailed it to the building, he caught sight of Len reaching out to shake Skidmore's hand. Skiddy ignored the hand, headed back to his Caddy, and drove off, never looking back.

After the faucet repair was finished, Len suggested that they have some chow at Rosa's Mexican Café.

On their way there, he said, "Don't worry too much about him. Skidmore means well, and he's very protective of the school buildings. One time, the main door at the primary was left ajar; somebody or something went inside and shit all over the entrance hall. He had to clean up the mess. He wasn't very happy, and he's never forgotten."

The restaurant was two buildings down Fourth from McFadden's and across the street from the depot. It was the same greasy spoon where the hobos ate when they got off at Hayden a few years before. It was owned and operated by Rosa and Pepe Lopez. Rosa had hung red, green, and white curtains on the windows; they were always starched and spotless. When Sisco asked her how she kept them so fresh, she explained that she had more than one set so she could change them often. He told her that his ma tried to keep up with nice curtains on the little windows of their soddie, but the dust blew up to soil them as soon as she got them hung.

Rosa herself looked like her starched curtains had come to life. She wore a white blouse with puffy sleeves, a bright skirt of red and green stripes, and a yellow apron with big pockets. A woman in her middle years, she had skin the color of coffee with just enough milk mixed in to keep it smooth. Her long black hair had some white threads; but when she wore it pulled back tight in a knot, you didn't notice.

Len and Sisco sat down at a table near the back. Other customers, mostly Mexicans, ate from huge plates. The heavy, sturdy odors of corn and lard gave the place a smell so good that Sisco could hardly keep from grabbing a *tortilla* from the little brown basket at somebody else's table.

"*Buenas tardes, señores!*" Rosa greeted them like they were family she hadn't seen in a long time. She asked Len about the schools and gave him the results of the Series. She and Pepe had turned on the game so everybody in the café could listen. The Philco radio on a corner table was quiet now that the Yankees had carried off another win.

"We want the Dodgers, but nope! *Los Yanquis* do it again! Pepe like the *moreno* player, Jack Roberson, but he couldn't save the game. Oh! I see you have hunger. What do you like to eat?"

They ordered plates of pork *carnitas,* beans, and rice. Rosa rushed off to the kitchen to tell Pepe what his *gringo amigo* and a new *compañero* wanted to eat. Len smoked while they waited. He already had filled up the little ashtray on the table.

"These people are the salt of the earth," he said as his eyes followed Rosa's every move. "They work hard and expect little in return. I guess you already know that, though, after being on the road with that kid we buried."

"Yeah. Carlos did more than his share, and he put up with the heat in this valley better than any of us when we was workin' the fields."

Len snuffed out another Lucky, broke wind, and looked around to see if anyone had noticed. Then he said, "You think one of your boys did him in?"

"I never figured it to be one of us, though some of the 'bos didn't like him much. Out of respect for Peach, we kept Carlos on the road. He didn't bother nobody. Just wanted to pick up a stake for his folks in Old Mexico."

"That's why I helped you fellas out of your jam. Most of the wetbacks struggle to eat just like the rest of us. And most of them come here to work so they can help their folks south of the border."

Rosa darted out of the kitchen with their plates of hot chow. Steam danced off the refried beans, melting the cheese on top. She set the food on the table with a round basket of *tortillas*. Sisco dug in before she could say, "*Buen provecho, señores.* If you wish more *tortillas,* just call me."

They chowed down like they hadn't eaten for weeks. Midway through their plates, Len asked Sisco if he had mentioned anything to Skidmore about Carlos in the confessional.

"Never talked to him. Not even sure he knows it was me at the Catholic that morning. I looked different then with full whiskers and long hair. It was still pretty dark in there."

"Better to leave it all alone," he said as he finished his food and lit up a Lucky with the last mouthful. "Sad to say, but nobody except you boys and I care about what happened to Carlos."

Sisco figured it was the right time to tell Len that Peach had hanged himself in a boxcar on the way to Dunsmuir.

"Sorry to hear that," he said leaning back in his chair and belching. "I saw how bereaved he was at the river. Kind of envy that degree of love. I've never cared that much about someone else. How do you separate lust from love?" He looked straight across the table like he was stumped and expected an answer.

"Can't really say, to be honest with ya. Only thing I know is that if ya keep goin' back to a gal for somethin' besides a roll in the hay, there's more to it than makin' whoopee."

Len crushed his smoke as Rosa cleared the table and emptied the ashtray. "I think you're on to something, but that assumes you're having some success with the lady. What if you like the dame and respect her, but you're locked out of her bedroom, and you keep going back just to see if you can open the door?"

Sisco pretended he didn't know who the dame was. "I'd still say there's a bigger reason why ya go back even if she won't open the door. Has to be somethin' else, or it wouldn't be worth the trouble. Dames are a dime a dozen in this jerkwater. A man has his pick."

Rosa brought the check, and Len grabbed it up to pay. He left her a good tip, and she thanked him in a loud voice so the other customers would know that the *gringos* liked her service.

They walked to the drugstore. Len said he needed to go upstairs to get some supplies for his mother. With nothing better to do, Sisco sat down on the curb and lit up a smoke. It was fall, and the sun cast an autumn filter over everything, making it look yellow and orange. The royal palms across the tracks and alongside Fourth Street were streaked with gold like a painter had swiped his brush over them. The first rains had come early, and the brown summer grass under the trees had begun to turn green with new life.

His thoughts jumped to Claire. He had no reason to think that she would ever have him; and yet, he couldn't stop thinking about her. There was never any woman as beautiful, as gentle, as honest, as smart. To know that she was untouched by any man made him want her all the more. His mother would have said that Claire had high standards; she wouldn't run off with the neighbor or fool around with an old boyfriend when she was married.

When he came back downstairs, Len carried grocery bags to deliver to his mother. For the second time, he asked Sisco to go along for the ride and to see the *bracero* cabins. Although tired and sleepy, he agreed because he was already beholden to Len, who seemed desperate for his company.

§ § § § §

Len did want company out at the Sutter ranch because he didn't like to spend time there alone with his mother and his older brother. A gnawing anger at them made him uncomfortable and anxious when no one else was around.

At nine years old, he had been sitting upstairs by the attic window reading *Alice in Wonderland*. Frank, his strapping 19-year-old brother, found him alone and started to talk about the white rabbit who led Alice down the hole on her adventure. He said that if Len stood at the window to look out at the rows of tomatoes in the field across the road, he would spot the very hole where Alice and her rabbit disappeared. Curious, Len went to the window with his back turned to his brother. Before he knew it, Frank had pulled down his overalls and forced himself into his younger brother, saying that this was what older guys did to boys to make them "tough." No shame in it, Frank had said. After all, the sheep, cows, and horses did the same thing right out in front of everybody. No reason to tell their mother, either, because she needed Frank to run the ranch and to teach Len how to do things.

When he was high-school age, Len convinced Mrs. Sutter to let him live in Woodland with his married sister, Jessie. The high school there was larger than the one in Yolo and offered better training for a student headed to college. His mother gave her consent, as long as he promised to help Frank on the weekends and during school vacation. After he moved, things got better for Len and worse for other poor young boys. He never told his mother how Frank had hurt him those years, but he felt sure she had to know. He had not forgiven her for letting it happen.

"So, you coming with me, Sisco?"

"Wouldn't mind meetin' your ma."

§ § § §

They headed north on Highway 99 past the neat rows of field corn that came close to the road. Sisco noted that in an automobile, you had no idea how far the row crops stretched out in a perfect pattern like the spokes of a wheel that reached for a place to meet up. Since you couldn't see the end of the rows from the highway, you thought they came together at a spot on the horizon. From the top of a boxcar, though, they never seemed to connect up anywhere and just went on until they stopped.

"You're mighty quiet there, Sisco. Not still worrying about Skidmore, are you?"

"No. I was just thinkin' on the rows of corn, or tomatoes, or pumpkins. When you're on the highway, you're just shore they join up someplace in the distance.

From on top of a rattler, it's different. Ya see that they don't meet at all."

"Yeah," said Len. "It's an optical illusion—kind of like two people's lives. You think they're headed for some point of union, a connection. But like row crops, they never meet. They go on side by side until they stop at some ditch or fence or the edge of a rancher's land. A dead end— parallel lives with everything and nothing in common."

Sisco was never sure that he understood what Sutter meant. He figured that Claire was one of those rows alongside Len's row and many others in front or behind. If those two talked about school issues or went out to eat or dance, they moved together toward what looked to be a happy end. Anything else kept them in separate rows toward a dead end. He had heard their arguments about politics. Claire's folks were Republicans; Len was all Democrat. They couldn't discuss the president or the election for senator next year. Their biggest disagreements had to do with the time Len spent away from Hayden and his job. Claire told him that it was unprofessional to be gone during school hours and that the trustees were bound to catch up with him. Len argued that he was the boss and that they always gave him a new contract because the students and their folks thought he walked on water.

On the way out to Woodland, they stayed quiet for a long time. As they passed the flooded rice fields, Len talked about the Chinese who began to grow rice during the Gold Rush a hundred years before. He said they had a lot to do with the building of California and had worked on the state's railroads and levees. They were strong laborers and good thinkers. He asked if any of them ever rode the rails with the hobos. Sisco's answer was "no" and that "the only Chinamen on the road made tasty chow and sold it for little dough."

Though he talked about Woodland as his home, Len admitted that he was really from Yolo, a jerkwater just off the S.P. line north of Sacramento. The town didn't have much to offer—a one-room school, a post office, a blacksmith shop, a mercantile, and a Methodist church. You could have missed the place if you blinked, and Len didn't seem too anxious to show it off. What he did seem proud of was the land that spread out in green patches and rows of oak trees as far as the eyes could see on all sides. Sprawling fields of alfalfa and field corn and lines of walnut trees helped themselves to the earth right up to the edge of the road.

"The land here is so fertile that you can grow almost anything that tolerates some cold in the winter months. Gold seekers a century ago discovered that the lasting treasure in the Sacramento Valley is the land. Many who didn't strike it rich here—and most of them did not—took up farming, ranching, or commercial ventures."

They zigzagged and crisscrossed on narrow roads until they hit a long, straight stretch. Len slowed down and said they were close to his mother's place. He pointed straight ahead to a white speck on the horizon—the Sutter house. Before heading to the ranch, though, they stopped by the side of the road next to a curious little white church in the middle of a field of headstones.

"Mary's Chapel," Len said, "one of the oldest churches and pioneer cemeteries in California. Many of my people are here—not John Sutter, of course. It would have been too risky to put him here. He had many enemies, and his creditors or grave robbers would have vandalized his site a long time ago."

Sisco was impressed with the place and how peaceful it looked with the tall oak trees giving shade and breeze to the departed who were surrounded by a green carpet of alfalfa.

"Can't help thinkin' on my ma and how easy she'd of rested in a place like this. We had to bury her in a graveyard where most of the deceased had been blown 'way by the dust. Even if I went back to Kansas, I probably couldn't find her marker—just a wooden stake with her name and dates painted on."

As he pulled out the choke to start the Ford, Len said, "I think cemeteries are more for the living than the dead. Don't feel too bad about it. Under the circumstances, I'm sure that you did right by your mother."

Like they were late for a meeting, they ran at full speed to the speck of white on the horizon and a two-story farmhouse circled by a wide porch. On the front steps was a short, thin lady in a plain housedress covered by a brown sweater that looked like it was swallowing her. Len parked next to the porch, got out of the automobile, and walked slowly to the steps. He motioned Sisco to follow him. They climbed the steps together.

"Mother, this is Sisco Griffin, the fella who came off the freights to try a new life in Hayden. He works with Mr. Skidmore and does a helluva job keeping things swept, waxed, and clean."

Sisco reached out his hand to Mrs. Sutter, who shook it with a little squeeze. "Glad to know you, young man. Leonard talked about you before. You look older than I pictured."

He recognized the hardness in Anna Sutter's face. He had seen it in other women during the dust storms, on the whores in Chicago, and in his mother before she died. They all had been through enough hard times to wear that mask of "You can't hurt me anymore 'cause I seen it all before."

Her voice was soft and gentle, her shy smile a last place for her heart to show itself. "Won't you come inside, young man, for a glass of iced tea?"

They followed her through the front door into a small sitting room with a strong smell of cigarette smoke even though all the windows were open and the faded curtains tied back. Four easy chairs with their cushions spilling out cotton sat on a braided rug unraveled at the edges. In one corner was a wooden hutch with shelves of dishes closed in by a smudged glass door. Painted pale yellow, the walls were bare except for framed pictures of daisies, roses and gladioli. The room felt old and tired, like the lady of the house.

"It's too hot in here," said Len in his school principal's voice before they could sit down. "We're going back outside on the porch. And there's no ashtray anymore." He was lighting up a smoke as he headed for the front door.

"Suit yourself, Leonard," said Mrs. Sutter with no particular feeling. "You men have stunk up this room so bad that I can hardly stay in here myself. If you cared as much about this house as you do about the shacks out back, we'd have a decent spot for folks to sit when they come to visit. Your cigarettes have it smelling like one of them trashy big blondie bars in the Delta."

Len laughed and steered Sisco to a wooden chair on the porch. They smoked and waited for the tea served by Anna Sutter with a bowl of sugar and a plate of iced lemon slices. She put the tray on a table between them.

"Much obliged, ma'am. Shore looks good on a day like this."

"Thanks, Mother. I haven't forgotten that I made you a promise about this house when we finish with the wetback places." He stood up and gave her a quick peck on the cheek.

Mrs. Sutter did not look at her son but smiled at Sisco as if she had heard this promise before. "I'll believe it when I see it, Leonard. I gave up a long time ago. Now, go on out to your shacks. I know that's why you brought your friend here, and he's welcome any time." She turned to Sisco with another weak smile and went inside.

They finished the tea and headed out to the Sutter land, which was quite a spread. Acres of alfalfa and corn reached off to the horizon and beyond. Behind the barns was a large mound of dirt circled by a makeshift fence of posts strung together. Len explained that several professional diggers from the university were working on a project there. He said that he and his sisters had grown up playing "Capture the Flag" on that hill of dirt and never suspected that it was an Indian burial ground.

"It took one of the *braceros* to point out how important that mound might be. A half-breed Miwok himself, he said that people from the university would come to take a look. Sure enough, the archeologists were interested and marked it all off so nothing would disturb it before they could dig. My brother, Frank, was pissed as hell that I let them come in here."

Sisco felt something strange from Len like he wanted to make his brother look bad on purpose. He asked if Frank ran the ranch.

"Hardly. Frank's kind of a queer duck. Never wanted to get married and have his own family. Lives by himself out there in that old cook wagon." He pointed to a speck of something in the distance. "Comes to eat with Mother two or three times a week. I hired a foreman, a guy here legally from Old Mexico. He runs things fine and keeps an eye on Frank."

They headed west from the barns and came to five small cottages strung together with common walls like in modern motor courts where tourists in their automobiles stop to spend the night when they go off to see the sights. Each little place had its own door with two cement steps leading up to it. Inside was a whitewashed room with three or four shelves hammered to the wall. To one side was a toilet. A spigot and nozzle hung off the wall for washing up. The floor was covered with brown and white linoleum that Len said would be easy to mop.

"When we're finished, I'll bring in some cots for each cabin," he said with a proud grin on his face. "I know that four or five fellas can bunk here. These places are for the *braceros* who have helped my mother for the past few years. Hard workers who deserve a decent place to sleep."

Sisco wanted to ask him why he hadn't built one big bunkhouse with toilets and sinks like they had at the rescue missions and the Sallies on the road. The Spic workers would have been more at home all together, sharing everything like the 'bos did in the jungle. They could have made an inside cook-up for a kitchen.

"Well, what do you think of my project?" He grinned like he expected a good answer.

"Never seen anything like it for field workers—their own little houses. You got a helluva different idea here!"

Len sat down on the front step of the middle shack. He smoked and looked back and forth at the two places on either side like he didn't quite believe they were really there. Sisco took a seat on the step of the cabin to his right and hoped there'd be something different to talk about. There was when Len asked if he had ever read any books.

Sisco took a drag on his smoke, inhaled, and let the tobacco shoot through his body in a rush. "Yeah. Growin' up in Kansas, I read some. Had to sneak to do it 'cause my pa didn't think I needed more books than the ones for lessons at school. That made me want to read everything I could read in secret. Ma knew. She said that books take ya places you'd never see on the prairie. After she died, I figured she'd want me to see some of those sights, so I caught out on the rattlers.

"In Chicago at the Pickle, I got ahold of their library books—read some Mark Twain, Charles Dickens, even a fella with the first name of Lewis and the last name of Carroll. Always thought his names got turned round backwards. My favorite, though, is Robert Frost and his poems. I memorized 'Death of a Hired Man' to recite in Bughouse Square."

Len stood up and pointed to the Sutter house in the distance. He said that he'd read maybe five hundred books in his attic bedroom upstairs. The one he most remembered was called *The Grapes of Wrath* by John Steinbeck. "Talks about the Okies making their way to California during the Dust Bowl. Could have been some of your Kansas neighbors, I guess. They were treated badly all the way here and even worse when they finally arrived. They had only one decent Hooverville to bunk in, and that one was too small to accommodate everybody. It was Steinbeck's novel that made me realize the gravity of the migrant's situation. So, you know where I got the idea to build these cottages."

"Mighty generous of ya. I know that it gets cold and wet in these parts during the winter."

What Sisco wanted to say was that those little shacks were kind of pretty now because they were new and nobody was tracking dirt and manure inside. After the first big storm, there would be mud everywhere, and the wash-up space would just spread it around. A bunkhouse would have been much easier to keep clean. Still, he had to admire ole Sutter for being fair-minded.

Len wasn't done yet with his story about *Grapes*. He went on to say, "That book by Steinbeck was actually banned in some bookstores and libraries. Hell, the Board of Supervisors in Kern County south of here ordered it removed from the Public Library in Fresno. Can you beat that?"

Nothing surprised Sisco about how people down on their luck were treated. He had seen hard working hobos pushed off trains by the railroad dicks and even by the conductor. In the fields picking grapes with wetbacks, he'd seen labor contractors rough up guys just doing their job— punch and kick them right there in front of everyone. Sometimes the *migra* showed up to cart off guys who had worked all day and never got paid. He sure didn't know any of the Okies in the book, but he knew plenty just like them.

They walked toward the house where Mrs. Sutter was sweeping the porch. Sisco reminded Len of the bags for his mother in the trunk. He shook his head as if they'd slipped his mind and went ahead to unload them, saying that they'd be headed back to Hayden as soon as he took the groceries inside. Sisco figured to leave him alone to say good-bye to his mother and got into the Ford to light a smoke.

Even before he had finished his cigarette, Len was in the driver's seat and they were headed over the country roads back to the main stem. It was all quiet between them, with Sutter probably thinking about his migrant shacks and Sisco remembering his ma and wondering how she would have looked now if she were still alive.

They had turned onto Highway 99 south toward Sacramento before Len broke the silent spell "Well, what do you really think now, Mr. Griffin?"

Surprised at hearing his last name, Sisco sat up in the seat and said, "I think she's a fine woman. You're lucky to have your ma alive and sturdy. When I first met her, I wished my ma was still alive. Then I saw all 'em lines in your mother's face, and I knew that if Ma had lived past the dusters, she woulda looked older than her years, and we'd of had more hard times till the rains came. She woulda worked some two-bit job just so we coulda had food on the table, and ..." He stopped talking because he felt worn out and sad.

With his right hand loose on the steering wheel and his left arm straight out the window to catch the breeze, Len said, "I meant your opinion about the cottages. But since you started on a different subject, I'll say some things about our mothers. I think they both got a raw deal in this life. Could be they married the wrong men, but they couldn't seem to handle life without their husbands. After my father died, my mother had to rely on Frank to run the ranch. He got himself in trouble with the law for … for some things with a neighbor's kid. My mother bailed him out more than once and finally said he had to live apart from her, my sisters, and me. From that time on, she ran the ranch the best she could. She's alive, but she doesn't have much to live for, as you can see."

He was right on that, but he didn't seem to want to make things better for her, either. All of a sudden, Sisco was pissed at Leonard Sutter. His own ma had died in a sod shack on the Kansas plains without even a decent dress to bury her. Here was Len with a good principal's job and money to burn at the 241 Club, but no time to sit and visit with his mother or drive her to a picture show in town on the weekend. But he sure did have time to romance some dance teacher or a big blondie while his mother and Claire waited. Mrs. Sutter wouldn't complain; she'd just go on and get another crease in her face. Claire would put up with him, too, and cry on Sisco's shoulder in the hope that things might change.

They didn't speak again until they had passed through Sacramento and Elk Grove. As they came near Hayden, they saw three bright lights lined up perfectly over Thornton and the Delta. The lights stayed still as if they were strung together.

"All kinda funny bright things over there by the rivers. Saw somethin' like 'em the night I found Carlos' body."

In the dark, Len fumbled for the ashtray on the dash, gave up, and tossed his smoke out the open window. He didn't seem to notice that the sparks blew back inside to burn more holes in the seat covers.

"I saw lights over the Cosumnes and the Mokelumne during the war. People say they show up when somebody dies," said Len.

"Noticed that myself," said Sisco. "Saw some outside on the night my ma passed. I didn't know she was … gone, but I did know she was sick and needed help. Dust had piled up to block the windows and the door. I couldn't get out. Then from nowhere come these lights, and one of the windows opened just 'nough for me to squeeze through."

Nodding his head, Len said, "Some of the Indian elders around here believe that you can see the spirit of a dying person ascend. Of course, you have to possess the special powers of vision those wise fellas have."

They were silent the rest of the way. When they pulled into town, everything was shut down except the Mexican grocery store two doors up from McFadden's. Len told Sisco to wait as he made a beeline for the store. In no time, he came back with two brown bags. He handed one to Sisco. Inside were a jug of wine and a carton of Luckys.

"Just a small token of my appreciation for your company today. When the *bracero* cottages are finished, I'll take you back to see them. Right now, I'm headed over to Claire's. Haven't seen much of her lately, and she gets lonely if I don't stop by once in a while."

Sisco nodded and thanked him for the trip to the Sutter ranch, the hooch and the smokes.

Len had finished with him for now, and was likely certain that Claire would have time for him even though he hadn't talked to her. He placed a high price on his company and never passed up the chance for an audience.

Before they went their separate ways, Len said that the guys inside the grocery were buzzing about a body washed up on the bank of the Cosumnes near the big trestle north of town. He didn't know any particulars and said they'd get more details the next day. He didn't seem worried as he got into the Ford, turned around and headed toward F Street. Sisco figured it was past time for some wine.

Terry A. Albritton

Bubble Lights

The day after Sutter took Sisco to Yolo, the Yankees pulled off the Series in a game with lots of runs, including a homer by DiMaggio. Sisco heard most of the action at the drugstore where he and Mr. Mac sat at the soda fountain and drank a total of fifteen cherry Cokes fortified with some squirts of Jack Daniels. Len wasn't around, but his Ford stayed at the same spot out front where he had left it the night before. He hadn't flopped upstairs, so it was hard for Sisco to believe that he wasn't nearby at Claire's. Truth was that Len could have been anywhere with his automobile as a decoy in front so folks would think he was in his room.

Turns out the body found by the Cosumnes was a farm kid who lived off Franklin Road a mile or so from the river. A Sacramento County sheriff found the boy's fishing rod all neat with a fly ready to cast off. It was laid down along the bank like he had left it there while he went off to check something or to relieve himself. He was a student at the high and good at his studies. No one could explain what had happened to him because he knew how to swim; besides, there wasn't enough water in the river to drown anybody. The big rains hadn't hit yet.

Len went out to the ranch to pay his respects to the boy's family and to ask the father for permission to look at the body before it was cleaned up for the funeral. Although the father gave his okay, the sheriff said, "No!" It was none of his affair to butt into things that were the coroner's business. Skiddy agreed with the Sacramento dick and wanted him to know that he was the honorary deputy police chief in Hayden and could identify the body as well as anybody else. The sheriff said that wouldn't be necessary because family members had already seen the corpse.

Two days later, the Sacramento detective came over to the high to question the townies on their whereabouts during the weekend. When it came time for an alibi on Saturday, Sisco and Len had a good one since Skiddy had seen them both at the primary in the morning. Len explained that they had gone to Woodland in the afternoon and spent the rest of the day and early evening with his mother. He gave the sheriff her telephone number to confirm they had been at her ranch. Sisco wanted to mention the lights over Thornton but decided against it. He didn't want to open a can of worms with dead bodies in it.

All of the teachers at the high were anxious to say what they had been up to on Saturday. Most of them had been tuned in to the Series with their neighbors and families. Some had been at the 241 and had drunk enough hooch that they had to be carried home. Everyone wanted to know why the law was so interested in their whereabouts when it looked like the boy had drowned. Skiddy piped up that he knew why but wasn't supposed to say. When he and the detective from Sacramento asked Sisco if any of his hobo friends had passed through on Friday or Saturday, he said that he didn't think so because he hadn't seen any of them for weeks.

While Len and Skiddy went to the funeral service, Mr. Singleton, the band teacher, was left in charge of the high. Skidmore was mad that classes hadn't been cancelled, but Sutter said that not everybody knew the dead boy and the trustees hadn't authorized him to let the students loose for a day of mourning. Of course, when the time came, everyone "did" know or "thought" they knew the deceased, so almost no one showed up for classes. Many of the kids went to the river to fish, have picnics, skinny dip, and whatever else they did to play hooky.

With so few teachers and students at the high, Sisco decided to polish some of the floors on the lower level where the traffic was heaviest on a regular day. He started with the music room where the tuba and trombone players had returned from the funeral to practice. Since other band members weren't there, they stayed to help him move chairs and instruments outside so he could wax the floors.

It turned out to be a good thing that he did some polishing that day because the rains came down hard in late October and into November and December. The students had to stay inside most of the time, and the Hayden football team played only half of their scheduled games that season because the field was too wet. The band couldn't practice their music and marching outside either.

On Halloween, the kids at the high were restless from being cooped up like chickens. It had rained all night, then let up in the morning, but looked to start pouring at any minute. The grass and sidewalks were full of puddles. Len had scheduled an assembly for second period. Skidmore and Sisco stood by the entrance of the gymnasium with big mops and tried to get the students to wipe off their feet before they went inside. They put burlap sacks on the front steps to soak up as much of the water and mud as possible. They took turns mopping and wringing as the students filed in—some as witches, skeletons, queens, and pirates.

What with Halloween, the rain, and no exercise outside, the inside bunch was wild. Len had already arrived and was pacing the floor to calm things down. When he saw it was no use getting the kids to sit in their chairs, he walked to the master light switch at the back of the gym. He pulled it, and the place went dark. The only light came from the windows on the ceiling. The black sky looked ready to unload at any minute.

The students stopped jabbering and made their way to the seats as Len hurried toward the front and the microphone. "Thank you for sitting down and giving me your attention. You have come to a place of learning, a place of enlightenment that deserves your respect. As soon as you are ready to treat it as such, the lights will return."

When the gym was quiet, he continued with announcements: a reminder of school rules and after-class clubs; a message for parents about the importance of voting the next week. Then, he stopped to pull out a small book and a tiny flashlight from his pocket. The kids gawked to see but stayed quiet as he started to read:

> "Round about the caldron go:
> In the poisonous entrails throw.
> Toad, that under cold stone
> Days and nights has thirty-one
> Sweated venom sleeping got,
> Boil thou first in the charmed pot
> Double, double toil and trouble;
> Fire burn and caldron bubble."

As he spoke, it started to rain. The drops pelted against the windows overhead. Len turned off the flashlight and closed the book. The kids were quiet.

"What I have read to you is a witches' spell from a play called Macbeth. It was written by the greatest author of the English language, William Shakespeare. Macbeth is a man who, with his wife, plots to murder the King of Scotland. In blind ambition, they end up killing almost everyone in the play. Three witches follow the murder spree with the spell you just heard. For anyone who is interested, I will be here at lunchtime with copies of the play to read aloud. I invite you to join me. Now, Mr. Skidmore, will you please turn on the lights so I may excuse the students to their next classes?"

Whether he knew the students would be restless after all the rain and had called on the witches to settle them down or whether he had already planned to read with them at lunch didn't matter because he did the right thing. Sisco had never seen anything like it; he couldn't help admiring how Len had used the book of a play to control a whole gymnasium of rowdy kids. He asked Skidmore what he thought.

"He's used the light switch trick before when the kids wouldn't calm down. Dunno 'bout the rest of it, though. He's been an English teacher and always has some book or other in his pocket. Far as I know, the flashlight's a new gimmick."

§ § § § §

One thing was pretty clear: the students liked and respected their principal. Sisco often heard them talk between classes, saying how he carried assignments to the fields when they had to work on school days; how he loaned money to their folks when times were tight; how he didn't count a student tardy when he was late after doing chores on the ranch in the morning. He looked for every way possible to keep a student enrolled at the high until graduation.

Sisco already knew Len's good points from Claire. When she wasn't mad at him for something, she bragged on how smart he was. She told him that although she couldn't discuss politics with him, she had learned a lot more from listening to him talk than she had ever understood from her folks. When they played canasta with some of the teachers at the high, the subject of a loyalty oath came up often. A man named Tenney had written something called "The Fifth Report" to prove that every important person in California was a Commie and that they were going to take over the country and the world. Claire spoke up to say that she was worried about the situation in Berkeley, where her best friend's father was a professor at Cal. She was certain that he was not a Communist, but he wouldn't sign a paper saying he wasn't. He had been warned that he would be fired if he refused to put his John

Henry on the loyalty oath. The teachers who heard her story couldn't agree about whether he should sign. Len spoke up to say that anybody could say he was loyal to something when he wasn't. A paper meant nothing and should not be necessary to keep a job.

As the Christmas holidays came closer, the children at the primary got ants in their pants waiting for Santa. The big kids at the high had some critter or another in their drawers, too. A week before vacation, Sisco was sweeping up the hall between the front steps and Len's office. Some of the students had brought in a six-foot pine and decorated it with strings of popcorn, flashy tin ornaments, and bright glass balls. It looked mighty pretty and smelled real fresh when you came through the door.

Len developed a thing for that tree. He had watched the boys on ladders as they wove the popcorn strands in and out, over and under the green branches from top to bottom. He had called out directions to the girls who hung ornaments as far up as they could and then handed them off to the guys on the ladders.

When they had gone back to their classes, he pulled Sisco aside to say, "You know, most of these students won't have a tree at home. That's why it means so much to them here. They did a good job, didn't they? But there's something missing. I have an idea how to make this tree more festive and give a big surprise to our kids. I'm going out. I won't be back until after dismissal. Wait for me ... please."

He didn't show up till after dark. By that time, Sisco had swept up the pine needles and dusted and mopped the office area and the hall. He heard Len honk his horn three times and hurried down the steps to find Sutter standing behind his Ford with the trunk open.

"Look what I brought to spruce up the spruce!" he said in an excited voice. He took out a flat box and opened it to show a string of lights that looked like little colored candles. "Bubble lights—the newest thing in holiday decorations. They sit on the branches and percolate like coffee when you plug them in and they get warm. What do you think?"

"I reckon they'll be just fine," answered Sisco, knowing there was a long night ahead. The students would be happy, and Skiddy would be pissed. He hated for the school building to be open after class even with the principal right there.

Sure enough, the next day when the students came in, they stood around gawking at the tree that percolated with bubbling lights on every branch. Many kids went in tardy to their first- period classes. Skiddy could hardly contain himself; he marched Len inside the office, banged the door behind them, and began to blow off steam. Sisco was outside in the hall doing his best to untangle the extension cords from the tree to the outlets.

Skidmore's voice was loud and mad. "You got yourself a set of hard ones, Leonard Sutter, coming here in the middle of the night to put up lights without even the right extensions. Shore hope ya didn't use school money to buy them stupid bubbly things, 'cause if ya did, the trustees gonna hear 'bout it. And ya can bet they'll hear plenty 'bout the fire hazard with them cords runnin' all over creation!"

For a minute, there was no answer. That's how Len handled Skidmore; he let him go on and on, blow his stack until he finished saying his piece. Then he'd come back calm with a short, simple answer and no anger. "It's all for the kids, Skiddy—my Christmas present to them. I'll keep a close watch on the extension cords. Don't worry. Things are under control. This building will not burn down like the first high school did."

Whether he was satisfied or not, Skiddy stormed out of the office so fast that he almost tripped over one of the cords. He said something under his breath. Sisco couldn't hear it but figured it wasn't a cuss word because Skidmore was a good Catholic.

Len followed him out and walked back to where Sisco was untangling the mess from the night before. Clapping him on the back, he said, "Thanks for your help on this. I'll appreciate it if you keep an eye on the tree and the outlets when the lights are plugged in. I'm going to be gone for a few hours. Have to pick up my Christmas present from a leggy blonde I know." He winked.

That was Leonard Sutter for you—real quick to start something and not so fast to finish it. The lights heated up and bubbled. The high didn't burn, and the students got a big kick out of the fancy tree. Some of them helped to take it down before everybody went separate ways for the holidays. Claire drove to Berkeley to be with her folks, and Len took off for Yolo, or someplace, before the dismissal bell on Friday. Skiddy announced to anybody who would listen that he was going to spend a lot of time in prayer for the sinners who drank too much and made whoopee with other men's wives over vacation. Sisco bunked at Mrs. Mac's because it was too wet and cold to bed down in the jungle. He missed the company of his hobo pals and figured they were down around L.A. or San Bernardino where it was warmer.

Then, the bad weather hit hard. It rained for thirty-six hours straight. The Cosumnes and the Mokelumne Rivers rose up to their highest levels in years; the levees were hard-pressed to hold back the water that would have taken out Walnut Grove, Thornton, Rio Vista, Isleton, and maybe even parts of Lodi if it flooded. The farmers put up sandbags on the levees and the rivers. The Mok was swollen up so bad that it looked like it might let loose and cover the land at any moment. Further north by Yuba City and Marysville, the Yuba River had crested, and folks just waited to be flooded out.

On the day before Christmas, the rain let up. The sky was still dark with heavy thunderheads; but by afternoon, the sun had made its way through for the first time in almost a month. Sisco was outside on the sidewalk, listening for the next rattler headed north. He felt her vibrations on his feet before he heard her toot. The old hog, a Baldwin locomotive, panted into Hayden with heavy breath to take on water. She hardly had left the tower, dragging a full load, when he spotted Shorty with his cocky walk headed up Fourth Street. His bindle over his shoulder and his hair and whiskers grown together in a big bush, he looked like a bum if ever there was one. He wore a long black Marshal Earp coat that kept him warm but was a nuisance when he decked or jumped off a train. He had his same old boots; the soles were worn through.

"Well, what do ya know?" greeted Sisco as he held out a mitt to shake. "Just like Santa Claus! Don't see ya 'cept on Christmas."

Memphis laughed and stared at his reformed hobo pal. "Boy, this jerkwater shore civilized you! Look at them duds ya got on!" He pointed to Sisco's red and blue striped flannel that had cost him three dollars at Benson's Mercantile. "And how 'bout that shear up of your gold curls—nothin' left of your wheat crop! Yeah, they damn near made a city fella outta ya!"

Sisco gave him a smoke and steered him to a bench across the street from the drugstore, but it was so wet they couldn't sit down. He didn't want Shorty going into McFadden's with a head and beard full of lice.

"If ya plan to stay in these parts for a few days, ya gotta get deloused, shaved, and washed up."

At first, Shorty argued that he was just passing through to wish his best pal a Merry Christmas. He changed his tune fast when he heard how much it had rained north of Hayden and that everything was wet, slippery and dangerous on the trains. Why should he risk another accident like the one that had crippled his arm? Besides, there was going to be a real feast at Mrs. Mac's the next day, and she always had room for one more.

Shorty stopped his protest and smoked as Sisco led him back to C Street to find Jonah Sturgeon, who had cleaned him up when he first got off the rails and kept him decent through the fall months. Lucky for the fellas that the barber was just closing up shop. At first, he didn't take kindly to delousing a hobo on Christmas Eve afternoon; but with the promise that it would be well worth his while, he agreed. The weather had cut into his trade during the past weeks, and he was happy to have some quick cash.

Jonah steered them out back of the barber shop and into the alley. He wouldn't let Shorty anywhere near the barber chair, the scissors, or the razor used on his regular customers. "Just sit your ass right on that there old oil barrel, and stop your whining. You're lucky that Sisco here is willing to pay holiday rates for this job."

"Nobody told him to," Shorty piped up. "I was just passin' through this lousy jerkwater when he hijacked me here for Christmas."

"The only lousy one in this town is you, young fella, and you ain't even so young. And for your information, I'm throwing away all these tools when we're finished here. One of you guys is gonna have to pay me for them, too, or go down to the mercantile and buy some more. And while I'm working on Shortcake here, you can start to wash all this lousy hair into the gutter and the drain so it gets the hell away from Hayden!"

He turned to Sisco who laughed and got up from his seat on another oil drum. He took the garden hose coiled up on the back step, hooked it up, and began to wash the loose hair falling from Shorty's head and beard into the drainage, which moved fast because of all the rain.

"Ya gonna lye me up, too, Sisco?"

"Damn right! Ya ain't bunkin' in my room till you're decent 'nough for your wedding night. We'll just share a little Christmas cheer down here with Jonah before I take ya upstairs to wash ya up myself."

"You fellas plan to stick around tomorrow?" asked the barber as he took a long swig of the dago, relaxing into the job at hand.

"Thought we'd help Mrs. Mac out with her Christmas dinner. That's why my friend here has to be decent."

"Good idea," said Jonah. "I'm sure she could use your help with them long tables she hauls out every year. Almost too much for her, 'cause the word's been passed about her spread and there's an overflow of eaters. Last year, she ran out of turkey and ham. Had to feed grilled cheese sandwiches and milkshakes to the latecomers. This year, she's got some of the ladies in town cooking birds on account of so many folks out their homes with the floods."

Sisco asked the barber where he and the missus would spend Christmas.

"Going out to Herald to the daughter's if the road ain't flooded. Say, you fellas hear they found the remains of a Spic kid on the bank of the Cosumnes where they was sandbagging the river?"

From his seat on the oil drum, Shorty shot Sisco a bullet stare that he ignored while pretending to hunt for his smokes, which he knew were in his pocket. As he came up with the pack of missing Luckys, he said, "Naw. Hadn't heard a thing 'bout it."

"Well, ya know I ain't heard nothin' till now," piped up Shorty, shaking his head so fast that the barber had to stop the shear up. "Just rolled in here right before I was kidnapped for Christmas."

"So, how'd they know it was a Spic?" Sisco asked as Jonah came around in front of Memphis to survey his work. Shorty looked like he was going to leapfrog off the oil drum so he wouldn't have to meet the barber's eyes.

"Hold still there, young fella. Let me take a look from this angle. Have to be shore it's all even to get ya ready for them pretty lassies that'll show up at Myrtle's for dinner tomorrow."

Satisfied that he was earning his money, Jonah gave an up-down nod with his head and went behind again. "Oh, they knew it was a Spic, all right," he answered. "Buried in one of them big blankets from Old Mexico, like he was a mummy. Been dead a while, I guess. No way to identify him."

"How'd they know if it was a boy or a man, then?" asked Shorty innocently.

Jonah shrugged his shoulders. "What kinda question is that? I guess they saw his prick, or whatever was left of it. I heard that Spics don't have much to start with."

Sisco saw Shorty squirming around like he was uncomfortable and figured it was time to bring out the bills. He reached into the pocket of his overalls and pulled out a fistful of green ones. "Take as much as ya need to buy new scissors, razors, and anything else. And double your pay for the holiday, Jonah. We're much obliged for your services on such short notice."

The sight of so many bills took the barber's attention off the dead body and distracted him from Shorty, who jumped off the oil can to shake off the loose hair. Jonah counted out what he thought was fair with a little more for good measure. He thanked the hobos, saying that he was always at their service, provided they could pay for the extra tools. He wished them a happy holiday and disappeared inside the barber shop.

"Done near left me bald, that guy did," Shorty said when they had climbed the stairs at McFadden's. He took off his duds and started the water in the bath tub. "Ya paid him too much, or should I say that he paid hisself too much. I coulda done the same job with a pair of clippers and a mirror."

From his seat on the toilet, Sisco answered, "Never ya mind. I gotta live in this jerkwater for a while yet, and I don't want any enemies. Besides, you're my family, and it's Christmas!"

In the tub, Shorty stopped his scrub-up and licked his lips like he did when he was getting ready to make a speech. "Nobody's forcin' ya to stay here. There's plenty of pussy in other burgs on the road. These townies know 'bout Carlos, and ya shouldn't trust any of 'em. It's no skin off their noses if ya rot in some calaboose."

Sisco waited for the tub to fill up so he could shut off the spigot. He respected his older pal a lot, but couldn't make him understand that the life they knew on the rails was changing fast. With the diesels, it would be harder and more dangerous to catch out on the trains and to jump off them. Shorty seemed to figure that he'd always be lucky, no matter how old he was or how fast the rattlers traveled.

"Did ya hear what I said?"

"Yeah, I heard. But ya never hear me when I say that I don't wanna be catchin' out on freights for the rest of my life. I'm only twenty-nine. Ya got me by at least fifteen years. This isn't what I wanna be doin' at your age."

Shorty shook his head and looked away. He soaped up a second time and said nothing for a minute. Then he started his "I'm older and know better" speech he had made many times before. "Look, I know ya have your own ideas, like we all did when we was younger. But ya ain't a war veteran and got no education to speak of. You're just gonna have to take whatever ya can get whenever ya can get it."

Sisco lit up a smoke, took a long drag, and handed it to Memphis, saying, "Len and Claire both talked to me 'bout a diploma. They want to help me get one. They say it's never too late and that graduation from high school makes everything easier when ya go after a job."

As he licked his lips furiously, Shorty tried a different line of talk. "What if that janitor fella knows it was you in the church where the body was? What if he shows up tomorrow at this wingding downstairs and tells folks that you killed Carlos?"

"Skiddy ain't invited tomorrow. Mr. Mac thinks he's a busybody who preaches at folks and tells 'em how to live their lives. If, by some chance, he shows up and says somethin', just say that we met a Spic on the road who came into town, took off for a dance at the Catholic and never came back."

"Fine by me, Sisco. It's your deal."

He turned on the spigot full blast to wash off.

Christmas Day was a good time. The hobos enjoyed things as much as anybody. They helped to set up the long tables between the soda fountain and the door. The fountain was closed to customers, but they helped themselves to plenty of cherry and vanilla Cokes while they unfolded the seats for the festivities. Mrs. Mac asked Shorty to wipe off the tables and chairs before spreading on the tablecloths. Sisco went outside to sweep up the sidewalk in front where mud had collected all week since the rain started. Smells of turkey, ham, yams, sweet potatoes, and vegetables from the kitchen kept building up their appetites for the big meal.

Taking a breather, he lit up a smoke and walked to the corner where he could see across the tracks to the Catholic church. The bell had begun to ring for noonday Christmas

Mass. He made out Skidmore's black Caddy parked on the side where he always pulled up. He never missed services and liked to brag that Father Martinez was a good friend. They often shared a meal after services.

Skiddy had kept after him to go to church, but Sisco put him off with one reason or another. He had no quarrel with the Catholics but didn't think he could ever go to Mass without memories of Carlos in the confessional. In spite of his bluff with Shorty, he was worried that Skidmore connected him to the body. Did he think that Sisco should confess to a crime "to get things right with God"? According to the janitor, a confession took away the sin; Father Martinez would forgive anything—as long as you promised to say the proper number of Hail Marys and swore to do better next time.

When Christmas dinner was laid out, it was a feast like you hear about in the old days. The farm folks invited by Mrs. Mac brought in all manner of fresh things grown on their land and preserved—asparagus, string beans, squash, pickles, relish, cucumbers, and tomatoes. The yams and sweet potatoes had been fixed with melted butter and brown sugar, while the mashed Idahos were prepared with butter, sour cream, onions, and chives. There was every kind of pie—cherry, apple, pumpkin, pecan, mincemeat– still warm from the ovens where they had been baked earlier on the ranches or in town. Mrs. Mac had roasted two twenty-five-pound turkeys with dressing and three hams spiced with pineapple, cherries, cloves, and cinnamon. Her stuffing had day-old bread, chopped onion, celery, garlic, dill pickles, and sausage all mixed together with the insides of the big birds. Some neighbor ladies brought in two more turkeys and a big ham.

Shorty didn't want to sit next to folks he didn't know, which included almost all of them. Sisco put him at the end of one long table, seated himself next to him on his right,

117

and waited to see who would take the chair on his left. He hoped it wouldn't be one of those silly hick farm gals who stopped by the fountain to flirt.

Sure enough, Lottie Levino, daughter of the feed store owner, sat her plump, brown-headed body next to Shorty while she giggled the whole time. "Ya shore do look nice today, Mr. Griffin. Merry Christmas! The Macs shore put on a good spread, don't they? Ha, ha!"

Sisco nodded and introduced Lottie to Shorty, who mumbled something about the food. Then, everybody stood up for the blessing said by Mr. Mac, who had come in earlier from somewhere to carve up the birds. The twenty-five or thirty guests were all colorful in their Christmas duds and looked to have big appetites. Mrs. Mac served hot apple cider. Shorty whispered that he wished he could bring out the jug of dago red, but Sisco told him to forget it until later.

A couple of the guests had hooked up a phonograph in the corner to play "White Christmas" and "Jingle Bells" sung by Bing Crosby. Then, somebody brought out a new record by the cowboy Gene Autry. The song was about a reindeer named Rudolph with a red nose that helped Santa find his way to the good kids' houses on Christmas Eve. Everyone began to sing with the tune like they already knew the words. The hobos were glad that the guests belted out the chorus because they didn't have to listen to Lottie who ate, sang, and giggled at the same time.

"Betcha that mouth could do other things," Shorty whispered to Sisco. "Ya could find out later if ya wanted to. Warm her up with some dago. I'll make myself scarce if ya wanna take her upstairs after dinner."

Sisco turned to take a better look at Lottie just to see if there was any possibility she wasn't ugly. The side view on her was pretty good. Her brown hair hung loose and natural on her shoulders, and her nose quirked up a little at the end.

From what he could see, she had a nice set of tits covered up by a bright green sweater that was too big. She was probably not as plump as the sweater made her look; it folded over two or three times around her middle, so it looked like she didn't have a waist.

"Ya know, Shorty, I don't think she needs much warmin' up. I'll be a good sport and give ya first chance on this one. The room upstairs is open. I'll hang 'round down here to help Mrs. Mac with the clean-up."

Shorty wasted no time in his move on Lottie, who had been giggling her way through a piece of pumpkin pie when he pecked her on the cheek and invited her upstairs. Some of the ladies started to clear off the tables, and the men began to pull back the chairs to sit in circles and talk. Sisco said a few words to Mr. Mac before heading into the kitchen to take over the pearl diving from Mrs. Mac, who stood at the sink full of dirty dishes in her stocking feet.

With a big sigh, she said, "This is my favorite time of year, but I have to admit that it plumb wears me out."

She wiped her hands on a dish towel, pulled out a handkerchief from her apron pocket, and soaked up the sweat from her brow. It was still warm in the kitchen even though the ovens had been turned off after dinner.

"Ya work too hard on this, Mrs. Mac," he said as he soaped up a stack of plates.

"I know," she answered, "but there's people here who wouldn't have much Christmas without this meal. And I'm so glad the Robinsons decided to come after all. They said it would be too sad to stay home without their boy on the first holiday after his passing."

Sisco knew she was talking about the family that lost their son in the accident by the river. He had noticed them when they came in with two pies. They sat at the table behind him. "Yeah, I guess this is a hard time for 'em."

119

She bent over to put on her shoes. It was a chore for her to tie the laces with her fingers all gimped up from arthritis. He wanted to help her but decided not to offer. Mrs. Mac had a lot of pride and was always worrying about others.

She looked at him with a red face and said, "Been even harder for them after the body of that Mexican kid was found. Looks like they weren't accidents."

Grabbing two more plates, he asked, "Did they know the Spic kid?"

"Oh, no," she replied. "Far as anyone can tell, nobody in Hayden recognized the Mexican kid. With two bodies, the sheriff is suspicious and plans to call in the F.B.I. after New Year's."

She stood up and handed him a stack of plates from the sideboard.

Sisco's gut felt ready to give a big heave; and for a moment, he wished he could run out of the door to deck the next rattler—whichever way it was headed. If Sutter had been around, he would have hurried to see him, but Len wouldn't be back in town until New Year's Eve when he was supposed to take Claire to a dinner dance at the Vineyard Club in Lodi. Memphis was the only other person he could trust, and he already knew how he felt. Just the same, he made an excuse to check the fountain in case Shorty had come back downstairs. There was no sign of him or Lottie.

It took another hour or so to straighten up the mess in the kitchen. Many of the ranchers and their families had gone home with leftovers, but some stayed to help with the cleanup and to sit down and converse with Mrs. Mac, who had been too busy to visit with her friends. Somebody brought out a bottle of Jack Daniels, a pitcher of water, and tall glasses. Nobody was in much of a mood to drink; they were still too full.

Just as Sisco was ready to excuse himself to go upstairs, Lottie Levino came in the door all mussed up. Her hair was tangled, and her lipstick smeared. She wore a grin from ear to ear. Then she started to giggle. "Sorry to disturb you folks. Have you seen my coat? I left it here at dinner."

Mrs. Mac got up and went behind the soda fountain. "Put it back here, honey, so it wouldn't get lost. Didn't know who it belonged to, but figured they'd come back with how cold it is outside. You just now missed it?"

Lottie squirmed and looked at the floor. "I didn't feel too good after all the food I ate," she giggled. "It was delicious, ya know, but I just stuffed myself. Thought I might throw up, so Mr. Griffin here kindly let me lie down upstairs. Took me a little nap. Ha, ha!"

Mrs. Mac glanced over at Sisco who nodded. Then she turned to Lottie to ask, "How you getting home at this late hour, honey?"

With a big giggle, she answered, "Oh, I'm staying with my cousin over on F Street, here close by. No cause for worry, Mrs. Mac. It's only a few blocks. I'll just walk."

Since it was dark and cold outside, Sisco felt he should offer to walk her to her cousin's a few blocks away. On their way there, they never said a word to each other. Just to be polite, he told her goodnight as she went inside. Then, he walked down F Street to pass Claire's house. He knew that she wouldn't be back until New Year's, but he had hoped that she might return early. The house was dark.

Back at McFadden's in his room, Sisco found Shorty sawing Z's on top of the bed. Next to him on the floor was half a jug of dago. He took two big swigs, put the hooch on the table, and sat down hard as he could on the mattress.

"Wake up, ya old bum! Ya ate my food, drunk my hooch, made whoopee with one of my gals, but ya ain't gonna sleep in my bed!" He bounced up and down.

121

"What the hell?" yelled Shorty and threw Sisco onto the floor before he realized where he was. "Thought I was on a rattler with some jack roller tryin' to stick me," he said.

Recovering fast, the younger hobo got up, and went for the dago. "You're so far in front of me on this that I ain't gonna offer ya more."

"Don't even want any more," replied Shorty as he lit up a fag. "I've had 'nough of everything for today."

"Yeah, I bet! And how was the dessert after the dessert? Did giggle pussy Lottie wear ya out?"

"Ya was right 'out that mouth. Best blow job I had in years! That farm gal must be tearin' 'em up in the fields. Shore have to piss now, though. So get in your bed, like a nice civilized fella, while I go to the toilet."

By the time Shorty came back, Sisco was near to sawing Z's. Just before he fell off to dreamland, he heard a voice in his ear: "I don't think Peach remembered that he did it, but I believe that he killed Carlos."

The Kiss

When the hobos first took Carlos to ride with them, they were hard-pressed to understand his funny accent. They did get that he had a *novia*, a girlfriend, in Old Mexico. In his broken English, he had made it known that they had loved each other in a special way since they were little kids. She promised to wait for his return to their village with money to buy land, pigs, and cattle. Their plans didn't set well with the families because they were cousins.

When he made Carlos his punk, Peach already knew about the girlfriend in Old Mexico, but he wasn't going to give up. Sisco explained to Carlos that he didn't have to do the things the older hobo wanted him to. The Spic just answered, "Is OK! Is OK!" Truth be told, the punk seemed happy enough with their arrangement. Peach let his fellow knights of the road know that Carlos belonged to him and that everybody better keep hands and peckers to themselves. The hobos took him at his word; they knew he did have a temper.

Shorty was sorry he had whispered his suspicion to Sisco on Christmas night when he was still drunk. He knew that Sisco didn't want to suspect Peach of any crime because he had seen and felt the love between the jocker and his punk. Any conversation 'bout Peach's hot temper would get Sisco riled up and defensive. On the day after the big dinner, Shorty decided it was time to leave Hayden and get back on the road before there was more speculation about the body.

In the week between the holidays, the weather turned chill with frost in the mornings. When the sun did come out, it warmed things up a bit; but as soon as it disappeared over the Delta, it got real cold again. During the daylight hours, folks were cleaning up after the big storms and the floods before Christmas. Sisco helped Mrs. Mac with a good scrub-down of the soda fountain and the shelves behind it. Since business was slow, it was easier to pull out the shake and soda glasses, the sundae and banana split dishes stacked behind the counter. He washed them all spanking clean while Mrs. Mac wiped down the shelves and cut new paper to line them. She said that everything got dusty in the summer and fall, so you had to wait until the rains came to settle the dirt. He wanted to tell her that she had no idea what real dust was and that he'd helped his ma wipe things down two or three times a day in Kansas.

One afternoon between Christmas and New Year's, Mrs. Mac had Sisco mopping the floor of the storeroom in the back. He heard her talking with the customers in front when, all of a sudden, there was a big scream. He dropped the mop and hurried to see what the ruckus was. There was Len with Myrtle McFadden in his arms, twirling her around and around like they were on the dance floor. Then, somebody at the soda fountain had the idea to put a record on the phonograph that was still in the corner from the big dinner. Pretty soon, you could hear old gravel-voice Phil Harris belting out "The Old Master Painter" while Len and Mrs. Mac whirled all over the store. Next somebody turned the record over to "Smoke, Smoke, Smoke That Cigarette", which wasn't too good for dancing.

Len steered his partner to a chair and bowed to her like she was some special lady. "Thank you, my lady, for the pleasure of this dance with you," he said and walked over to Sisco. "Happy New Year, Mr. Griffin! Had any real fun since I've been gone?"

"Can't say that I've had the kinda fun you mean," he answered.

"Well, I'm about to get some real excitement. Just stopped in for a change of clothes before I trip the light fantastic with my favorite dance teacher."

He was out the door before anyone could say a thing.

Sisco saw that Len was feeling no pain and smelled of stale booze. His clothes were caked with mud; must have come from Yolo or somewhere outside. He hadn't had a bath or a shave- up for days. He'd be in better shape by the time he saw the dance teacher. He recovered fast when he wasn't totally buzzed.

Much as he respected Len, Sisco felt disgusted with him that day. He had tracked mud on Mrs. Mac's clean floor. Of course he was "her" boy, so she said nothing and went to get the mop.

He thought of Claire and his first day in Hayden. She had been cleaning up after Len the whole time inside her house—coffee on the table, dirt on the floor, ashes on the counter, cigarette butts in the ashtray. She hadn't seemed to mind because she loved him, or thought she did. If she ever married him, she would spend the rest of her life straightening up some kind of mess he made. His mother had done that; she just put up with crazy schemes that cost her money and heartache. In spite of the messes he made, the guy sure had a way with the ladies. He'd joke or dance or flirt with them no matter how old they were, and they'd melt like butter on a hot biscuit.

Two days later, on the last afternoon of the year, Sisco walked down Fourth Street and crossed the tracks into the jungle just to see if any of the hobos had been through after Shorty left the week before. It was still daylight, but cloudy and cold. One of those badass storms looked to be headed toward Hayden from the north, and the wind had kicked up. With rough weather on the way, he didn't expect any visitors to the jungle for a New Year's jug of dago. The place was still a mudhole from all the water before Christmas.

He looked east over the tracks up F Street and spotted Claire's Chevy parked in front of the house. She had come back for her big date. He had missed her and decided to pass by to wish her a "Happy 1950."

At the back door, he knocked hard.

She opened and acted surprised to see him. "Oh! I thought you were Len—although he never knocks. Come in, please! Happy New Year!" She kissed him on the cheek.

Sisco had to catch his breath as he followed her inside. She wore a black sparkly dress that fit tight enough to show off her body in all the right places. It was low between her breasts—just enough to want it lower still. It almost covered her shoulders and looked like it was held up only by the sleeves that went halfway down her arms. Her waist was so small that he figured she must have been wearing one of those new girdles. A full flared-out skirt hid her hips and legs but made her look like a queen. To him, she was a queen, and he tried hard not to stare.

"Ya look real pretty, Claire. I like the 'do' on your hair."

She had pulled her hair back and piled it on top of her head with waves and curls all over. It was so fancy that he figured she must have been to the beauty shop.

"Do you really like it? I'm not sure that I do, but we are going to a formal dance. Have you seen Len?"

In his hurry to cover for Sutter, he let it slip that Len had been in town earlier in the week.

"You mean he's came back since Christmas? Tell me the truth now, Sisco. You are probably the only honest person in town."

"I ain't ... I haven't seen him since right after Christmas, Claire. Honest! He showed up for 'bout fifteen minutes at McFadden's to pick up something. Left fast as he came."

That was a fact—more or less. What he hadn't said was that Len had been back to Hayden the night before and made all kinds of noise climbing the stairs. He had pounded on the door. Sisco hadn't answered or opened it because he was fed up with Sutter's drunk ass carrying on about what a good lay the dance teacher was. He was plenty horny himself after Shorty's story of giggle pussy Lottie. Just thinking about it all with Claire right there in front of him gave him a hard-on.

"I don't understand why he hasn't called me. We are supposed to go to a dinner dance in Lodi. Cocktails started an hour ago."

He wanted to tell her that Len's cocktails had started days ago and that she shouldn't be surprised if he never made it to Lodi with her. She already must have figured as much because she kicked off her silver high heels, turned toward him on the couch, and put her long, stockinged legs on the cushion between them. She was careful to keep her gorgeous gams close together. "Well, let's face it. I've been stood up again! It's no good. This relationship can't continue because it works only one way—his way! I don't think I can stay here much longer."

Her eyes teared up, and the glittery stuff on them began to drip. He didn't have a handkerchief, so he went to the toilet and took a towel off the rack. Back at the couch in the nick of time, he handed it to her just as the eye paint started falling down her cheeks. She tried not to cry, but the tears poured out anyway.

He sat down in the chair next to her side of the couch and put his hand on her arm to squeeze it. "Ya know, Claire, some fellas never settle down. That doesn't mean they're bad folks. It just means they can't content theirselves with one woman. They're ladies like that, too, but I know you're not one of 'em."

She stopped bawling, turned around on the couch, and took his hand. He expected her to squeeze it and let go; but instead, she held on and pulled him closer to her. He looked into her eyes and felt with every bone in his body that she wanted him to kiss her. He let go of her hand and pulled back in the chair. "Claire, do ya have any firewater? Let's have a New Year's toast."

Without a word, she moved off the sofa like some kind of robot following orders. He believed that he could have his way with her after a few drinks, but he needed to think about what he would do before the hooch clouded his brain.

§ § § § §

In the kitchen, Claire tried hard to stop crying. She had messed her face paint and put a run in her stocking. She was furious at Len and wanted to get even with him. She had hoped that he might propose on New Year's so she could just sleep with him and get past that hurdle. She wanted him to take her in an easy, tender way that she would remember forever. She loved him … or, at least, part of him.

Claire had begun to think that she fancied a person who wasn't all real. That magic man was smart, educated, charming—like Len. But he was also gentle, patient, kind—not like him for the most part. Plain and simple, Len was selfish, forceful, and always thinking of what he wanted whether that set well with her or not. She suspected that his marriage had gone bad because of his selfishness.

As much as she didn't want to admit it, the hobo-turned-janitor had an innocence and charm that aroused her. He was savvy about a lot of things but didn't show off his worldly ways. He was handsome and strong like a lumberjack or a cowboy. He was uneducated and a few years younger, but who cared about that if she didn't plan to marry him? She didn't really think about him much except when he came near her. Then, she always felt like she needed to use the bathroom, which she would do now before their New Year's toast.

She came back with a bottle of champagne and two chilled glasses. Sisco opened the bubbly with a big pop that made them both laugh. Then she put on a record—"I Can't Get Started" by Benny Goodman and his orchestra. Claire said that the song had been special for her and Len when they went to the Vineyard Club in Lodi. After he poured the champagne, she proposed a toast even though it wasn't yet midnight. "To 1950! May it be a year of peace in the world and happiness for you and me because we deserve it!"

They clinked glasses and finished the first toast in two or three gulps. She poured another and another and another. He hadn't eaten much that day, and the bubbly went to his head fast. When she insisted they dance, he didn't refuse even though she put on a jitterbug that he had no idea how to do. "Anybody who can do this jitter stuff can deck a rattler," he said and made a move to sit down.

She laughed and put on a slower tune by Harry James, who played a mean trumpet. Sisco's head started to spin, and he whispered to her that he really did have to rest a minute. He stumbled over to the couch while she headed to the kitchen for the next bottle of champagne.

"Ya musta planned a party here tonight with all 'em bubbles," he said as she refilled the glasses.

With more tears in her eyes, she sobbed, "I thought Len might ask me to marry him this evening, and we'd celebrate our engagement here after the dance in Lodi."

Then, the dam broke. He stood up and took her in his arms as gently as he could. She hugged him and held tight. His body tingled like someone had passed electricity through it; he didn't know whether to run or hold on fast.

She pulled away, saying that she had a perfect dance tune for midnight—"Moonlight Serenade." The phonograph started up, and she came to him, throwing her arms around his neck and leading him to the sway of the trombone and the clarinet. She moved closer as he eased his hands onto her waist and below. She was so close that he felt her heart beat. He froze there to keep the moment in his memory forever.

He was the Prince with Cinderella at the royal ball. She floated in his arms as they whirled on the dance floor. Fairy dust moved them with the rhythms of the music as the moon peeked through a window to warn of the bewitching hour. For that instant in time, they were held together by a magic spell that kept other worlds outside.

If she had been any other woman, Sisco knew he would have taken her in the bedroom before the record finished. But he just couldn't do that with Claire—not only because she was Len's woman, but also because she was so virgin pure and like a young woman ready to learn what a man wants. She had no real experience with a man or his body. What's more, Claire had no idea of the explosive spots in her own body and the buttons a man might push to make her feel good like he does. How Sisco wanted to teach her about those places and please her in ways she had never imagined!

He let her hold fast to his neck while he moved his hands up and down her back and her buttocks. She was so thin that he could almost reach each breast with the opposite arm. She seemed to melt right into him. Just as the record ended, the front door opened. Len stumbled in, and Claire stepped back.

"Happy New Year!" he shouted, slamming the door behind him. "What you doing with my woman?" he said as he clapped Sisco on the back. He waited for Claire to come to him; and when she didn't, he made a beeline for the sofa. "What you two drinking anyway?"

"It looks to me like you've already had enough booze," she said. "You're a mess! Another happy date with the principal of Hayden High! Excuse me. I'm going to scramble some eggs."

She padded to the kitchen.

Len shrugged his shoulders and lay down on the couch. Soon he was sawing Z's. He paid no attention to the smell of bacon frying up in the kitchen or the pop-pop of firecrackers exploding by the railroad tracks.

Sisco went to Claire, who stood over the stove cooking breakfast. She had put on a blue and white apron over her dress and wore her fluffy pink slippers. She had been crying again. She looked so beautiful and helpless that he could not hold himself back.

"Happy New Year!" he said as he took the spatula out of her hand and turned off the stove. He lifted her arms, and pulled them around his neck so he could hold and kiss her. She did not push back; he held her closer than they had been during the dance. He moved his lips to her wet mouth and kissed her gently and deep. Her tongue began to rest in the safety of his mouth. He was as hard as he could ever recall. Never letting go of her mouth, he guided her hand to the bulge in his Levis. Through his pants, Claire held on to his pecker while they continued to kiss. Sisco knew there would be an explosion soon and that he had to get to the toilet fast. He pulled back, excused himself, and ran for the bathroom. With the pressure released after months of longing and desire, he wiped himself off. He looked into the mirror to see spots of Claire's face paint on his cheeks. As much as he wanted to leave them there, he washed his face just in case Len woke up.

On his way back to the kitchen, Sisco glanced at the couch where Len snored loudly and comfortably. He didn't want Sutter to know what had happened, but he wondered if it would even matter one way or the other if he found out. Len would probably shrug it all off and ask why they hadn't finished things up in the bedroom.

After New Year's, Claire was different. At first, she hardly spoke to Sisco; then she talked a lot and looked for more reasons to tell Skidmore that she needed some repairs in her classroom. Although she had never mentioned their midnight dance and kiss, he had hopes that he might steal a few more of those same moments after school. But she never gave him a chance, and he figured that she was either ashamed or embarrassed. She had told him once that her folks had never touched or kissed one another in front of her. She wondered how they ever got close enough to make a baby.

Len made himself scarce after the New Year. He spent less time in his office and wasn't bunking much at McFadden's. Skiddy kept asking Sisco if he'd seen him at the 241 Club. Sisco could say honestly that he didn't go there much himself, but that he hadn't run into Len on the few occasions that he had stopped in for a beer. All Claire said was that Len needed to watch his step with the trustees and that he was trying to cut back on the booze he drank in public places.

Around Valentine's Day, it got cold—down to freezing and below. The rain blew in from the Delta side—one of those rare storms in the valley that turns to hailstones and then to snow. The kids at the primary were so excited that they couldn't do their lessons. Some of the youngsters never had seen snow even though they lived practically next door to the Sierra. Since most had worn galoshes that day, they begged their teachers to turn them loose on the playground for a long recess after lunch. The smaller ones tried to make snowballs that fell apart in their hands. Wet and dirty, they were having themselves a fine old time. Sisco went over to the swings, where the first-grade girls giggled and squealed as they pumped back and forth in little flurries.

"Push us! Please push us, Mr. Griffin!" they sang out when they saw him.

He stood behind the swings and took turns pushing each of the three little girls. At the far end of the playground, he spotted Claire with a small boy who had fallen down on the slippery pavement and was bawling his head off. She helped him get up and walked him over to the swings. A red trickle of blood dripped behind him.

"Mr. Griffin, will you please take Paul to the classroom to wash up the 'owie' on his elbow? I'm going to gather up the rest of the class. It's too slick out here."

He looked into her green eyes and saw something he had not seen there before. Hard to say what it was exactly—part sadness and part joy. She was at her happiest there at school with all the kids around her, just like Snow White with her dwarfs. But behind that joy was a sadness in her life because she had not found her Prince Charming in Hayden, and she had given up so much to look for him there. Still, she tried each day to make things right. She showed a sweetness—a thankfulness toward him, and Sisco believed that she did love him in her way because she knew that he would never let her down. He wanted her more than ever.

Once inside the primary, he sat Paul in a chair next to Claire's desk and opened the drawer where she kept the first-aid kit. With a damp paper towel, he put pressure on the bloody scrape. Paul was still sobbing and started screaming when he saw the iodine.

"Look here, son. Look at this giant bandage I'm gonna put on your elbow after the iodine dries. All the other kids will know ya was injured and how brave ya was to get this big band-aid."

Paul quit crying as Sisco talked to him about the dust in Kansas that had been so thick you couldn't even see your hand in front of your face; how folks had to wear masks everywhere; how lots of them got pneumonia from the dust and died. As he talked, some of the kids who had come inside walked over to listen. He decided to make a good story out of it by putting in the thunder rolls of dust as it blackened everything to force folks into their houses, where they might be trapped forever.

"The biggest storm of all came on Black Sunday in April of '35. That was when I ... lost my ma. We was inside with the dust piled so high that there was no air and no way to climb out 'cause the door was blocked."

He choked, wanted to cry, and pushed out a cough to cover it up. The children thought it was all part of the dust story.

Claire was there to rescue him. "Maybe Mr. Griffin will talk to us another day about his experiences riding the freight trains across the United States?"

She nodded at him.

The students clapped their hands and yelled, "Hurray! Yeah! More stories!"

One little guy, Walter Boone, raised his hand and looked afraid. He was a boy who always came to school with a dirty face, torn clothes, and shoes split open on the sides.

"Yes, Walter?" said Claire.

"My daddy says that hobos are bogeymen, and ya gotta watch out for 'em. He says to stay 'way from the train tracks 'cause a tramp might jump ya."

Claire walked over to Walter, put her hand on his shoulder, and spoke to the class. "Mr. Griffin is not a bogeyman. You all know that because he helps us here. In fact, he is not a hobo or a tramp because he has a steady job in one place. He goes to work every day just like your fathers do. There will be no more talk of bogeymen. Now, I think we have just enough time this afternoon to play with the puzzles or to color in our alphabet books."

The youngsters scattered like squirrels to pull out puzzles, alphabet books, and crayons. Claire watched them get settled and then sat down behind her desk. She motioned to Sisco to take the chair next to her where Paul had been. "Sorry about the hobo, bogeyman comment," she apologized. "You know that parents of some of these children come from Dust Bowl states. It wouldn't surprise me if some of their fathers traveled here on the trains. These kids need to know why men and women give up everything familiar to them to go to something new and unknown."

She stopped to blow her nose on a hankie from the top drawer of her desk. Sadness had blotted out the joy in her eyes. What she said next made his heart beat fast. "I was engaged once. Maybe I should have married him. He is a decent, responsible man, but I didn't love him. When he touched me, I felt repulsed. I couldn't imagine having babies with him."

Stumbling over his words, Sisco said, "You are a ... a smart and beautiful lady, Claire." He reached for her hand and was about to say something else when the door flew open, and Skiddy came bursting in like a tornado. He was out of breath, and the legs of his overalls dripped water on the classroom floor.

He went straight to Sisco without saying a word to Claire. "Ya gotta come over to the high right now. Water main broke. I need you and your tools. Like usual, Len's nowhere to be found. I'll wait for ya in the Caddy."

Skidmore was out the door as fast as he came in. Sisco followed with his tool box and got into the automobile. Skiddy had the motor running, and they took off for the high school.

"Must be a bad break for ya to be all wet."

"Happened one time before ya got here. Len shoulda had the pipe replaced, but he never did. No surprise that it broke again."

"Ya don't care much for Len, do ya?"

Skidmore didn't answer until they pulled up in front of the high school and he had turned off the motor. Opening the glove box, he took out a pack of Chesterfields and offered one to Sisco. Funny how, all of a sudden, the water main break wasn't so important. He lit another for himself and said, "I had a lotta respect for Leonard Sutter. When he came here after college, he was the best. What he did with them students in his classes was like nothing we ever seen before … or since. Taught them to read the highbrow books and enjoy it. Made the kids want to go to college so their folks would be proud. Always reminded them that he had come off a ranch hisself and made good. Said they could do the same if they studied hard."

Skiddy finished his smoke, threw it out onto the wet pavement, lit up another one and went on. "Great principal and superintendent during the war and right after. Made sure the kids who worked hard earned a diploma even if they wasn't in class every day. Walked homework assignments out to the fields so the students workin' for their folks could keep up. Things settled down after the armistice. Len spent less time at the high and more time at the 241 Club … and other places."

Sisco interrupted him to bum another smoke. He was having a hard time finding what to do with his hands because the talk made him nervous and he knew that Skidmore wasn't finished yet.

Skiddy must have wanted to tell this story for a long time, like he needed to get things off his chest. "Some mornings when I get here, I find him asleep in the boiler room dressed in the same duds from the day before and smellin' like a brewery. I wake him up so he can at least

136

wash his face, comb his hair, or go home to change before the students come in. Sometimes, it happens two or three times a week. Now, do ya wonder why I don't have the same respect for him that I had before?"

Sisco couldn't look him straight in the eye, but he shook his head and said, "Ya make a lotta sense. I see the good things he's done. Sometimes he listens to me, so I'll try to talk to him. By the way, what happened to Len's wife?"

Skidmore gave a big, tired sigh. The wrinkles on his forehead deepened as his eyes squinted from the smoke. "Joanne was a real looker—the only kind Len ever goes for. She also came outta College of the Pacific and played piano with the best of 'em. Used to come over to tickle the ivories for the kids in the chorus at Christmas and Easter concerts in the gym. Joanne was from old Italian Frisco money and dressed like them high society dames whose pictures ya see in the newspaper. Don't know what happened between her and Len after the war. She just disappeared. One day he told me they was divorced. Never said why."

The rain had started up again with a cold dampness that soaks you fast. They got drenched as they jerry-rigged the busted pipe outside and mopped up the water that seeped onto the floor of the gymnasium. Sisco saw the water problem didn't seem to be as serious as Skiddy made it out to be.

They didn't see Len until the following day when he had scheduled a meeting in the late afternoon for the townies. Sisco went about his business setting up chairs for the meeting in the gym. Nobody had told him what kind of deal it was, and it had appeared mysteriously on the master calendar in Len's office. As he formed up the rows of chairs, he saw Sutter walk in dressed in a gray suit with a black and yellow tie that looked like a fish from the

Klamath River. His hair was neat and slicked back; his shoes had a fresh polish.

"Afternoon," he said in a business-like manner. "Important meeting here later for Mrs. Douglas—candidate for the Senate." He began to count the chairs.

Somewhere in his memory, Sisco recalled talk of a Mrs. Douglas, but he had no notion of why she might have a meeting at the high. He waited until Len finished his count before he asked, "Why is Mrs. Douglas comin' here for a meeting?"

At first, there was no reply. Sutter had started to move chairs from longer to shorter rows. Finally, he said, "I don't expect many to come, so I've shortened the rows. It will look like there are more people here. You can put away half of these. Sorry for your trouble."

He pointed to the chairs pushed off to the side and left the gym through the side door. He hadn't answered Sisco's question, never said a word about the broken water main, and didn't explain where he'd been for the past day and a half when he wasn't at the high.

An hour later, Len came back carrying a stack of papers. He walked up and down between the rows to place a sheet on each seat. He handed one to Sisco. On it was a black and white picture of a gorgeous dame who looked a lot like Claire but older and with shorter hair. Since it was just a head shot, you couldn't see her body. Under the photograph were the words: "Meet Helen Gahagan Douglas, whom thousands proudly embrace as their candidate for United States Senator." Below the picture was a list of her good works, including three terms as a member of the U.S. Congress. She also was a delegate to the United Nations and a member of the Foreign Affairs Committee.

"Looks to me like this lady Douglas has all the right things to get elected," Sisco said after he read the flyer.

"She certainly does. Trouble is that she's a woman and too qualified. Nobody expects a woman to be so smart and experienced. Her opponents are muckrakers."

A "muckraker" sure sounded like a mean SOB; but Sisco didn't want to seem stupid, so he nodded his head and kept quiet.

Len was on a roll now and plenty ready to explain some things. "Mrs. Douglas has a distinguished record in the House of Representatives. Her views differ from those who oppose her. Instead of having a dialogue with her about the real issues, her opponents try to discredit her by saying that she is soft on Communism."

It was nasty business. Len said that powerful conservative groups would do anything to overturn Roosevelt's New Deal and to discredit candidates who spoke up for the poor. He believed that the rich men in Southern California had put out a kind of hit on Mrs. Douglas to make her seem "pink"—a Commie. When Sisco asked if he could stay to meet the candidate and hear her speech, Len told him that she wouldn't come herself, but that she would send someone to represent her and the campaign. He was invited to stay and listen, which he had already planned to do because of the chairs. Skiddy would have a heart attack if the chairs were left out overnight.

When the townies filed into the gym, most of them were still dressed in their work duds. They had come in from the fields or their businesses; some had quit early to make the meeting. Their wives and youngsters came, too. Even a few students from the high showed up and straggled in behind their folks. Sisco counted almost one hundred people, though it looked to be more because of how the chairs were arranged.

Mr. Flynn, who came in to talk about Mrs. Douglas, was a tall, bald, serious man. His clothes were fancy enough, but they were all wrinkled like they'd been folded and carried overnight in a grip. He wore a dark suit with a white shirt and a blue tie. His thick spectacles made his brown eyes big and blurry when you looked straight at him. He didn't sit down the whole time. When Len made a move to introduce him, the man stood as close as he could, like he was afraid to stand up front by himself.

Mr. Flynn read off of a crumpled paper; he went on and on to talk about who Mrs. Douglas was—how she stuck up for farmers, workers, and the people of California when she was in Washington. It was fine to listen to him for a few minutes; but after that, it was hard to pay attention. One of the ranchers in the audience raised his hand and stood up to be seen and heard. The speaker stopped and asked the townie for his question.

"I jus' wanna know if Mrs. Douglas is pinko and if she hangs 'round the Commies in Washington. Ole Tail Gunner Joe McCarthy says that the Reds are everywhere in the State Department."

The gym was quiet. Everybody waited for an answer. Len, who had sat down in an empty chair, was on his feet in a flash. He walked over to Mr. Flynn and nodded that he would give the answer. He started to talk, and everyone listened because they knew him and most of them trusted him, too. He began by saying that he had met Mrs. Douglas and she was a fine, honest person as well as a dedicated wife and mother. She was married to Mr. Melvyn Douglas, a popular actor and supporter of causes that helped workers, especially farmers. The Commie thing had come from her opponents, who figured that she had to be pinko because she stood up for working people. She and many other members of Congress always voted for legislation that favored the middle and lower classes. When he finished, everybody clapped and nodded their heads.

Mr. Flynn stood by but had moved away from the center of the gym. He wiped his brow even though it was cold inside. When Len motioned him to come back and talk, he shook his head and headed farther to the side of gym toward the door.

Len continued, "So, Mr. Flynn came down here from the Capitol to ask you to vote for Mrs. Douglas in the primary election coming up in June. He defers to me now because I have accepted the honor of being a part of her campaign team in Sacramento County."

The crowd gave him a hand. One man got up to say that he'd volunteer after work and on weekends to help out with the campaign. He recalled how Mrs. Douglas had voted in favor of farmers' water rights. A woman in the front row raised her hand to say that it was "about time a lady got elected to the Senate, seeing as how the men had made an awful mess of things." Nobody clapped for that, but the woman in front said she'd help out as much as she could.

As everybody left the gym, only one of the ladies bothered to shake Mr. Flynn's hand. Everybody else ignored him.

Sisco began to fold up and put away the chairs so things would be ready for first-period exercise classes the next day. Len went on talking with Mr. Flynn, who inched his way over to the side door, where he finally escaped.

Len came back to say, "If that moron is typical of the Douglas campaign, then we've got a lot of work ahead of us. Did you notice that he couldn't even handle the Commie question?"

"He shore didn't seem much at home here. Maybe he doesn't think the ranchers are smart 'nough to understand what he has to say. They liked your talk a lot."

Sutter lit up a Lucky. "Many of the voters think the Commie issue is real, but it's not. The problem is that no one seems to be able to get people's minds off of it long enough to focus on what really matters."

Sisco nodded and asked him straight out if Mrs. Douglas was a Red.

"Whoa!" he cried like he was reining in a horse. "So that question made even you have doubts. It's worse than I thought. Just a doubt is enough to lose her a vote. Believe me when I tell you that she absolutely is not."

"So ya met her, Len?"

"Not yet, but I will! You can be sure that by the November election, I'll know her well!"

Sisco had no doubts about that!

May Day

The winter weather of 1950 brought water to flood levels in the Central Valley. Rivers gorged themselves on the rain, spit it out, and filled the Delta so high that it threatened to breach the levees. Some of the hobos who had jumped off at Hayden headed up to Marysville and Yuba City to fill and stack sandbags for the ranchers. As payment, they got two days of square meals and a dry place to flop.

While he was up on the Yuba River, Chicago Blue took a shine to a farm gal who showed him a good time in a tree up over the raging river. Later, he told his fellow knights of the road that doing her on a branch above the high water was almost as fun as banging a dame on a hot shot train.

After the Douglas meeting in the gym, Sisco figured out that Len was gone so much from the high school and the 241 Club because of the campaign. He went to San Francisco a couple of times to the Douglas headquarters before the primary election in June. The first Democrat fella to run against her quit his campaign at the end of March. That guy passed his supporters on to the next candidate named Boddy, who ran the biggest newspaper in Los Angeles. When that happened, Len was happy because he was sure that she could win over Boddy. He said that the hard guy to beat was the Republican candidate, Richard Nixon, who would run against Mrs. Douglas in November.

Although Sisco paid no attention to politics, he watched Len's excitement over the election. One afternoon in April, when the sun came out all day and the youngsters had spring fever, he was washing windows outside the principal's office. High up on a ladder with a view inside, he saw Skidmore come into the office and sit down in a chair from where he could talk to Len while keeping an eye on his helper outside. Len had one of those big city newspapers spread out over his desk. He was reading something out loud while the janitor shook his head back and forth, smoked his cigarette, and never said a word himself. Finally, Skiddy got up, left the office, and came outside, where he told his helper to climb down.

"Why don't you go in there and listen to his nonsense? I'll take over the windows now that you've covered the higher ones. I can't stand any more of this election business. See if ya don't think that he's finally lost a screw."

He picked up the pail of dirty water and walked over to the outside hose.

Curious, Sisco had a notion that whatever was in the newspaper had to do with Mrs. Douglas. Inside the office, there was so much smoke that he had to open the windows he had just washed. "Ya gotta get some air in here," he said.

Len looked up as if he didn't even realize that Skiddy had left and Sisco had come inside. "Oh! Glad to see you! Have a seat. I want to read you something. 'The Congresswoman appears decidedly pink, even pink shading to deep red. She is part of a small minority of Red-hots who intend to use the election to establish a beachhead on which to launch a Communist attack on the United States.'"

Then, as if he were preaching to a big congregation, Len pounded his fist on the desk and shouted, "What do you think of that rubbish? An outright false accusation based on a few of her votes in Congress! These muckrakers have no ethics!"

His blue eyes flashed and dared anyone within earshot to say the wrong thing.

As calmly as he could, Sisco said, "Look! We know she's not pinko. When these guys make up such hair-brained lies, it sounds to me like they're kinda desperate, or even afraid. Ya shouldn't let 'em get to ya so much."

It was all silence in the office, except for Skiddy outside on the lower ladder with his up and down on the windows.

Finally, Len said, "It's like I told you before. All these fellas have to do is create a doubt about her political affiliation. Then, they don't have to discuss the real issues because their readers never get past that doubt. The average Joe never asks important questions about foreign policy, the labor movement, water rights, and land usage in California. The whole discussion turns to the Commie thing. Unfortunately, from what I've seen, Helen's not very adept at refocusing the public on important issues."

Sisco told him that he had a particular way of looking at the situation and that maybe he could help Helen more by writing for the newspaper. He reminded him that the students at the high needed their principal to be present and wide awake at school every day. What he didn't say was that Skidmore acted like the boss when Len wasn't there and that he kept little notes on a pad in his toolbox: "L.S. asleep in the boiler room"; "L.S. gone all day"; " L.S. in dirty duds and smelling like a brewery".

On the day of the newspaper article, Len left the high an hour before the students were dismissed. He told Skiddy that he needed to mail some school business in big envelopes, but he let Sisco know that he was headed to the 241 Club and would park his automobile in front of the post office. He said that he hoped his hobo friend would join him later for a beer or a bourbon.

With no inclination to go to the 241, Sisco headed over to the primary. It was warm for April with spring in the bloom of the almond and cherry trees, the poppies and the daffodils. He looked forward to working outside after a wet, windy winter. The grass was overgrown from all the water; it would soon be dry enough for a good mow. The bushes next to the building were uneven and needed to be

145

trimmed. The hopscotch lines and dodgeball circles on the playground had faded and needed fresh paint; so did the redwood benches outside. He sat down on one of them to have a smoke.

"Have you been a naughty boy? Did your teacher punish you here, Sisco?" Claire had come up behind him and now moved around to the front. Her long brown hair hung loose on her shoulders over the high neck of a white wool sweater. She wore a blue plaid pleated skirt and looked like a high school girl. Her lipstick had faded, but her warm smile made him tingle.

"Claire! Sit down, please! I'm takin' a gander at all the outside work that needs to be done before summer."

She took a seat and moved closer to him. "Where will you go during vacation?"

"Dunsmuir and the Sacramento River to fish with the boys. Just the usual lazy days of summer at the prettiest place ya ever seen."

She was quiet, and then, unexpectedly, she took his hand and held it in her lap. "Do you ever think about settling down, Sisco? Would you ever stay in a place like Hayden?"

"I dunno," he answered and squeezed her hand. "Maybe if somebody like you was here permanent. But ya don't like this jerkwater, do ya?"

She pulled back. "I might like it better if I hadn't been lured here under false pretenses. I was told of the God-fearing citizens who care about their children's educations. No one warned me about the gossip and the small-mindedness."

He let go of her hand and turned to face her. "Look, Claire. I know 'bout small towns. They're all the same. Ya gotta take the good with the bad if you're gonna live in one. Folks have to depend on each other every minute of every day, so 'course they know everybody's business; it's how they survive. They're all related to each other—or darn close to it."

"Well, I don't need them," she sobbed. "I don't want them telling me about a late night rendezvous at the Dew Drop Inn or a secret meeting in the back of the 241 Club."

He didn't know who was telling her what; but they most likely were stories about Len, and at least some of them were true. It wouldn't do to pretend they were all lies.

"Did ya ever think that these folks here care 'nough to wanna protect ya? From what I see, you've earned a lotta respect ... and love from the townies."

She lowered her head and began to cry. Her shoulders shook as she sobbed, "I know, but I just can't face people who pity me."

"Ya face 'em every day, Claire, and teach their youngsters best ya can. That's why the townies 'preciate ya and wanna protect ya. Ya can't blame these folks here for who Len is. He's a wild buck who shouldn't get hitched 'less his missus will share him. One woman, no matter how pretty or smart, will never be 'nough for him."

He felt bad for her but thought she needed to hear the truth. He lit up a cigarette. Claire's hand reached over to take it from him; and when she didn't give it back, he lit up another smoke for himself.

"Forgive me. I know you're right, but I'm not sure that I can come back here. I won't have tenure for another year. Len knows that, so he just plays with my feelings because he's certain that I'll be around in the fall."

Sisco couldn't argue with what she said, so he stayed quiet and close to her. They sat together without conversation until the sun went down and the late afternoon turned cool. The primary teachers had left a long time before, and the last of the kids on the swings had wandered off. He took Claire's hand and walked her around the corner to F Street and her house. At the back door, his eyes pleaded for an invitation inside. She shook her head and gave him a quick peck on the cheek.

He crossed the tracks to see whether any of the hobos had come off the afternoon rattlers. Funny thing was he hadn't heard a single train all day. When he first got off in Hayden, the trains were his clock. They signaled when to wake up, when to report for work and to eat lunch, when to walk to the primary and afterwards back to the high or the drugstore. The blow of the hogs kept him from being late anywhere, he thought. Then one day, Skidmore told him that he needed to get a real timepiece because everything in the schools ran on an exact hour; it was important not to be early or late for anything. Sisco said that he'd think about buying a watch if he decided to come back next year. Skiddy shrugged his shoulders like he didn't care one way or another.

The jungle was empty and overgrown, but he couldn't bring himself to hang around and clean it up. Truth was, he felt like a nap; but if he went back to the drugstore, Mrs. Mac would think he had taken sick and fuss all over him. He wasn't up for that, either. There was only one other place to go, and the closer he came to the 241, the more it felt like a mistake.

As he neared the open door, a familiar voice boomed out to him on the sidewalk. "Hey, Sisco! Just the man I want to see! Come on in and toast the Pink Lady!"

Once inside the club, he saw how far gone Sutter was and knew better than to argue with him. At the bar, he sat down next to Len, who was talking with the gentleman on his other side. Sisco recognized Ezekiel Coker, whose oldest girl was set to get her diploma in June. His youngest was a cute little towhead with braids in Claire's class. Zeke was a strapping man with a big voice and a belly to match. He had dressed like Santa Claus at Christmas for the kids at the primary. You could hear his "Ho, ho, ho!" from one end of the school to the other. He was a drinking buddy of Len's and took his side on everything.

"Yeah, Sutter, I agree with ya. She looks mighty fine for the Senate. I'll vote for her if she doesn't turn out to be a Commie. I like the way this Douglas lady stands up for the farmers. Besides, I think a smart dame can do a good job. Hell, I got all girls, and not one of 'em dumb."

He nodded his head so furiously that he belched loud enough to be heard all over the club. The other guys at the bar gave him a round of applause.

"See there. Zeke Coker knows a good thing when he sees it. No stinking newspaper, especially one from L.A., can fool old Zeke."

Sisco mustered a smile and drank his beer. Then, he caught sight of two men coming through the door and talking in whispers with each other. He knew they were trustees. One of them was Jedediah Morris, who had raised money for new band uniforms. His son played the tuba and stood out because he was over six feet tall and had no uniform until his father collected donations to buy outfits for all the band members. The other was Tremont Sorenson. He seemed like a nice enough guy. Everybody felt sorry for him because his wife had died and he had lost his older son in the war. His younger kid wasn't much help and spent more time with the big blondies on the Delta than he did on the family ranch. He had never earned his diploma. Len had tried to help him, but the guy didn't seem to care about his studies.

As the two trustees walked toward the bar, Sisco moved to give up his stool. He had to piss, anyway. Heading toward the toilet, he noticed somebody alone at a booth in the darkest corner of the club. Though the light was dim, he recognized Skidmore, who didn't drink or hang out at the 241. Skiddy turned his head away when he caught sight of Sisco, who hurried into the john.

149

By the time he came out of the toilet into the smoky room, Jed and Tre had joined Skidmore at the booth. They huddled over the table and talked fast and furiously; nobody had a drink. Len was still up front carrying on with Zeke Coker, who just kept nodding his head. Spread out on the bar in front of them was a newspaper. He figured it was the same one from earlier in the principal's office. He went behind Len and tapped him on the shoulder. "If ya got a minute, I need a private word."

Sutter ignored him at first, so Sisco sat down on the stool where he had been before. Shortly, Zeke got up, shook hands with them both, and left. With no one to listen to him, Len turned around. His eyelids drooped, and his shirt was unbuttoned halfway down his chest. He had taken off his coat and draped it over the bar.

"I think there's a trustee meeting in the back booth, Len. Might be a good idea if you and me went outside to talk private."

Glancing over his shoulder, he shrugged and said, "Those guys can have as many meetings as they want. They have a right to do anything they please."

"Ya know that Skiddy's back there, too?"

"Is he now? Sneaky little bastard! It's after hours, and he can be anywhere he wants with whatever company he chooses. Just so you know, he owes me big time for his job."

He ordered a brandy and downed it in two gulps.

"C'mon, Len! Just step outside with me for a minute. The smoke's bustin' up my eyes!"

Giving the Doc a sign for his next brandy, he picked up his Luckys and the newspaper off the bar and threw the suit coat over his shoulder. "I'll go with you for a minute, but I'm not done in here yet."

It was dark outside, and C Street was empty except for automobiles parked in front of the 241. They sat down on the curb and lit up smokes.

"So, what's the problem now? You afraid of Skidmore? I'll protect you. I saved his ass before, and he knows it."

Hoping to hear more, Sisco answered, "I dunno what you mean."

"Years ago when I had just been promoted to principal, there were some parent complaints. These folks, who were Protestants, accused Skiddy of trying to convince their kids to come to the Catholic church. They said he talked to them during school time about the Catholic faith as the 'only true religion.' So, I met with him alone, and then we met with the parents. I diffused the problem as a misunderstanding—stopped it right there and then. Skidmore knows that I could have reported him to the higher authorities, but I didn't. At that time, the board of trustees was quite a different bunch. If they had known the story, they would have fired his ass in a heartbeat."

Sisco sighed. The whole thing between Sutter and Skidmore vexed him more all the time. "Look here. I have no right to tell ya how to do your job. You're the principal, and a good one—most of the time, far as I can see. Skiddy finds fault with near everythin' ya do. Thinks he can do it better. Ya shouldn't trust him to tell the truth to the trustees.

"But that's not why I needed to conversate in private. I came to tell ya that Claire is serious 'bout leavin' Hayden if certain things don't happen."

Len listened and was quiet; he appeared less drunk than earlier. Snuffing out his smoke on the sidewalk, he lit up the next one and said, "To finish up on Skidmore—he's a busybody. He watches everybody and especially you, Sisco. He knows I won't pay attention to him if it's petty stuff, so he doesn't complain too much to me anymore. If he's found some of the trustees to listen to his bullshit, there's nothing I can do about that.

"Now about Claire. She's an expert teacher and a fine lady. I respect her. But you know the story. There are two types of dames—one kind you screw and the other kind you marry. I've had both. And to be honest, I'd rather stick with the first … for right now. I never promised Claire anything but a job when I brought her here to teach. She knows that. Her reputation is safe because folks know I'm not banging her. I'm making whoopee elsewhere. If she leaves, her honor will be intact, and I'll give her an outstanding recommendation for future employment."

Like always, Len made the hard things sound easy. If you listened to him, you'd think he was doing Claire a favor instead of hurting her feelings. Sisco didn't know how to make him see that, but was spared the trouble by a commotion at the door of the 241. Skiddy, Jed Morris, and Tre Sorenson were having a loud conversation as they left the club. As soon as they saw Len on the curb, they stopped talking and started for their automobiles. Skidmore had parked out of sight because his Caddy was nowhere in front, and he slipped around the corner to Fourth Street.

"Good evening, gents!" shouted Len to no one in particular as Jed and Tre drove off. He stood up, reached out to shake Sisco's hand, and said, "You've become a real friend. How about a nightcap on me?"

"No thanks. I need to hit the hay. Just one thing. If you haven't already told Claire how you feel, I think you should. She's hurtin' pretty bad."

He wasn't sure if his advice had any effect, but things got kind of interesting over the next few weeks. Len called two late afternoon meetings with Claire and Skidmore at the high. Sisco had never seen the three of them huddled together in conversation. As he watered the daffodils next to the building outside the principal's office, he saw them leaned over the desk, laughing and drawing on paper with kiddy crayons like they were grammar school pals making a picture. He wondered how they could get on so well one minute and be mad at each other the next.

He was curious all right, but he was angry, too. He felt like those three joshing in the office used him as a referee whenever they got pissed at one another. Trouble was that the prizefights never got past round one. He was caught between Len and Skiddy, between Len and Claire. They threw jabs and punches while he dodged around in the middle and sent them back to their corners. In the end, there was never a real match, and the referee was more banged up than the boxers.

The meetings in Len's office had to do with a maypole dance. The year before, Claire had taught her first-graders how to wrap the maypole so they could invite their folks to a picnic on May Day. The event was to celebrate the beginning of spring. Now, last year's first-graders were in second grade and wanted to be part of things again this year. Their parents made such a fuss that the second grade teacher begged Claire to include them with her first-graders. Len stepped in with a scheme to please everybody—except Buck Ratcliff, the industrial arts teacher at the high.

The plan was to combine both first-and second-grade classes in the dance, which meant that four more maypoles had to be turned and painted. Sisco was assigned to work with the shop teacher for a week to get the job finished on time. Skiddy said that Len had never mentioned a loan of the janitor's helper when they met in the office. Sisco wasn't too keen on the idea either, since he'd never had any experience with power tools. They chalked things up to one more of Sutter's crazy schemes.

On the Monday they were supposed to start work on the maypoles, Len took Sisco aside and whispered. "Appreciate your help on this. The real reason you're in the shop for a week is to help Buck Ratcliff stay on task. He's not very good at deadlines, and these poles have to be finished by Friday. I know you don't mind a break from Skiddy."

Inside the industrial arts building, the shop teacher's office was at the back behind the six workbenches of power saws, lathes, and other equipment. Buck Ratcliff was seated at a desk too small for his body. He stood up when he saw Len and Sisco come through the door. He looked over six-feet tall, and his ears stuck out on both sides of his head like antlers. His nose could have been an ear that got put in the wrong place. He was bald with a pencil-thin mustache above his upper lip.

Len reached out to shake his hand. "Thanks, Buck, for taking on this project at such short notice. Sisco's here for this week to be sure that your students stay focused on the maypoles. He's had lots of experience with paint and can lend a hand on the finishing touches. He works over at the primary, too, and can impress on your students how important the project is to the first-and-second graders, and their teachers."

Ratcliff looked disgusted; his dark eyes glared at the intruders across from him. His expression said that he wondered why a bum had any business in his classes. "See here, young fella, this is my shop, and you're welcome to visit any time. There's a lot of dangerous equipment in here, and these students have strict instructions about how to handle it. We've never had an accident during school hours, so I don't want you interfering. You're okay here in my office. These kids will have the son-of-a-bitch poles turned and painted by Thursday. Guaranteed!"

Len listened, slapped Sisco on the back, and told him that he'd learn a lot from Buck this week. He promised to check back on Wednesday to see how things were going.

Sisco was so bored on Monday that he thought about telling Ratcliff that he was sick and needed to go back to McFadden's to rest. He sat in the office while the shop hummed and pounded with saws, hammers, lathes, and every other tool known to carpenters. Buck ignored him even when he came back in the office for a smoke. He closed the door, pulled down the window shade, and lit up a Chesterfield, never offering one to his helper or striking up a conversation.

On Tuesday, Sisco was already seated in the industrial arts office when Ratcliff came through the door to say, "Really don't know what Len expects you to do in here all week. Are you here to spy on me?"

"Beats me what I'm here for. All I know is that Claire Lewis over at the primary wants thirty youngsters in first and second grade to wrap up the maypoles in front of their folks for the spring picnic."

Buck closed the door, pulled down the shade, and took a new pack of Chesterfields from his overalls. This time he offered one to Sisco and lit them both. "Known Len Sutter for ten years. He was an English and history teacher when I came. Fella's a natural in the classroom—gets the students to reach beyond their own limits, inspires them. Can't say as much for him as principal. He has too much free time to get caught up in things he shouldn't be meddling in. Hell, this cockeyed plan ain't nothing compared to some of his other crazy ideas!"

Skidmore had said the same thing about Len, and Sisco figured there was truth in it. He knew that the janitor and the shop teacher weren't too friendly with each other. Skiddy had told him to steer clear of Buck because there had been some trouble when another janitor's helper had tinkered with tools after hours, causing an accident. Even if they had problems from before, Ratcliff and Skidmore seemed to agree that Len had been a better teacher than he was a principal.

After that morning in his office, Buck treated Sisco just fine. He even let him come out on the floor where the students worked on the maypoles, which took shape fast. He wanted them sawed up, turned, and ready to paint by Wednesday afternoon or Thursday morning so they could dry on Friday and be ready for the May Day celebration on Monday. He gave Sisco permission to lend a hand since he had a lot of practice with the painting of houses, barns, fences, and even churches. Claire wanted the poles with stripes in different colors like sticks of candy. With each one, a student had to go up a ladder to hold the pole steady while another student on a second ladder with a bucket of paint put on the white coat. The base supports that Len had ordered arrived on Tuesday, so the poles were steadied from below. Once the white paint dried, the green, orange, red, and yellow stripes had to be added. Buck hauled in the big fans from the gym to speed up the drying.

After Monday, the week went by fast. They laughed, told jokes, and poked fun at people in the motion pictures. It turned out that most of the students on the project had seen a new movie at the Hayden Theatre. It had to do with a mule named Francis who talked and had a lot to say about everything. One of the kids said that the mule was supposed to be the President. A different kid piped up with, "Francis has more sense than Harry Truman, who lets Commies run the government."

As they finished up and got ready to rest the new maypoles against the wall of the shop, three eighth-grade boys from the primary came in with the old maypole that needed a fresh coat of paint. Everyone in the shop groaned, and the guys who had been on the ladders started to bray like donkeys. Soon everybody picked up the "hee-haw", "hee-haw" like Francis, the talking mule. At first the students from the primary didn't know what to make of it; but then they joined in with "hee-haws."

At that moment, Len came through the door with a strange look on his face. He ignored the donkey chorus, but motioned Ratcliff and Sisco toward the back office. "You fellas notice any students missing from class this week?"

Buck looked at Sisco for an answer since he had called the roll for the last three days. "Nope. Everyone here. Someone's in the doghouse, huh?"

Len shook his head and lowered his voice. "More serious than that. Another body was found by the river— underwater for a while from its appearance. Some men from the Bureau of Reclamation pulled him out while they were surveying the levee. Took the corpse to Sacramento for identification and examination. I'm heading over there now to help ID the body, Please don't say anything to the students yet."

They nodded to each other, and Len left the office. On his way to the door, he stopped to admire the maypoles drying on the wall. He smiled at the kids and clapped one of the painters on the back in approval. None of them ever would have guessed that he was on an errand to identify a dead body that might be someone they knew.

On Monday, the first of May, the pole wrapping would get underway at noon. It was a good day to welcome spring with a warm sun, a light breeze, and a few feather clouds over the foothills. Early that morning, Skiddy and Sisco swept up the playground with the wide push brooms from the gym. Then, they hooked up the big hose from the industrial arts shop. Buck had loaned it to them with the promise that it would be returned to the high before school started. So, the janitor and his helper showed up at the primary just as the early rattler rolled through Hayden. By the first bell at 8 o'clock, the playground had been hosed down and had begun to dry.

Sisco wheeled the janitor's cart loaded with the hose through the parking lot behind the shop. Len was already waiting there to put the pink, green, yellow, orange, and purple poles in his automobile for the short trip to the primary.

The poles were propped up against the wall with Buck Ratcliff standing next to them like a guard. "Followed your orders to the tee, Len," he said proudly. "Still can't figure how peppermint sticks fit in with May Day, but they do look good enough to eat!"

"And I just followed my orders from the primary teachers. You and the students did a first-class job, Buck, and in record time. We'll figure some way to use these candy canes again at Christmas—maybe a winter wonderland theme or something."

To load up the poles in Len's Ford for the short distance to the primary, they had to open all the windows and fit them in sideways over the seats from front to back. It didn't matter to him that small patches of paint were still damp and rubbed off on the upholstery of his automobile. He made a joke of it, saying that Pluto had stained the inside with horse shit and dog crap, so the paint smelled better and covered up some things.

"I guess you'll have to walk over to the primary. No room in here." As he got into the driver's seat, he motioned Buck and Sisco closer to the Ford. "The corpse is Bub Sorenson, Tre's only living son. He used to disappear for days at a time, and Tre hadn't seen him for almost two weeks. Figured he was shacked up with one of the big blondies over in Walnut Grove. The F.B.I. will be called in. I'm guessing we'll all be interviewed sooner or later."

Buck shook his head and left them to go back inside the shop. They saw that he was plenty choked up about the

Sorenson kid, who had been his student off and on when he did show up for classes at the high. Seems like Bub had liked to work with wood and had earned his only decent marks in shop class.

Alone with Len, Sisco asked, "What are we gonna say 'bout Carlos if the G-man asks us?"

"I think we have to tell the truth—as much as we know of it. You did what Skidmore and I told you to do. Either he or I should have reported Carlos, and we didn't. Technically, we are accessories to the crime and could lose our jobs."

Sisco took out a cigarette for both of them; Len hadn't smoked while they loaded up the poles. "I don't see why ya have to be in this at all. It was Skiddy who shoulda reported the body to the priest or somebody. He loves to tell everybody that he's the assistant big dick here. No one needs to know how we got the body to the river. Hell, for all anyone knows, we coulda ridden Carlos up the tracks on a rattler. He was so small that we coulda loaded him up on a boxcar and rolled him off the trestle into the river."

Len said that he was grateful for Sisco's loyalty, but he should remember that the Gadsten brothers—Tweedledee and Tweedledum—had seen them all in his automobile on the way out of town with the body. They weren't the smartest guys in town, but they were two witnesses who would tell exactly the same story if the gumshoes came to Hayden.

Sisco asked if Len thought the G-men would show up before school let out for the summer.

"Doubtful," he answered, straightening up his soiled tie. "These agents are caught up in looking for Reds under our beds. The only way they'd give priority to a small town crime is if they could link it to a Commie pervert plot. I can't see those stuffed shirts investigating anything out here in the country during the damned 100-degree heat of the summer."

That sounded fine to Sisco because in a month he'd be headed to Dunsmuir to jungle up with the boys on the bank of the river where they'd fish, swap stories, chug dago red, and pass out on the grass under the stars. He had saved up a stake to keep them in mulligan when they weren't frying trout. The only drawback was all those days without Claire. He'd have to count on daydreams to get him through.

The maypole dance and spring picnic were a big success. The five peppermint-striped maypoles got wrapped, unwrapped, and wrapped again right on key. Claire's students looked especially nice; the girls wore long skirts decorated with colored flowers and white blouses with puffed- up sleeves. The boys had on short black pants and white shirts. Mrs. Mac had helped to sew the costumes because some of the parents couldn't afford to make or buy the right attire.

Music was brought in by two men who stood at the edge of the playground pumping on bagpipes. Claire had persuaded them to come over from the Scottish Rite Temple in Lodi. No one wanted to tell her that the bagpipe didn't match the rhythm of the "over and under" music the kids had heard in practice. At first, the children laughed at the funny sounds, but they soon figured out how to sashay in and out to get the poles wrapped and unwrapped.

In Sisco's mind, though, it was Claire who stole the show. She wore a long, sky-blue skirt with yellow daisies sprinkled everywhere. Real wildflowers ran through her hair hanging loose on her shoulders. Her white blouse had long, puffy sleeves and a low, scoop neck that showed off her china-white skin and her full, rounded breasts. She pranced around the children in her white sandals to give directions and to praise the dancers. From the opposite side of the playground, Len took in her every move. He smiled and clapped for the kids each time they finished wrapping or unwrapping the maypoles.

After the May Day celebration, the students and the teachers caught a good case of spring fever. Everybody looked forward to three months of summer vacation.

Sisco didn't see much of Len until after the primary election in early June because he was getting out the vote for the Mrs. Douglas, who had her hands full with Richard Nixon. He wasn't even supposed to run against her in June, but he had put himself on her part of the ballot, too. He kept after her on the Commie issue; it didn't help that some Red newspapers were in her corner. Somehow, she won the primary election even though Tricky Dick Nixon received lots of votes from her party. Len had always said that the fight was on now, and the knockout was coming in November. He planned to spend the summer finding votes for her in Yolo County, where his mother and all his relatives lived.

No sooner had school let out for the summer than there was another war in a place called Korea. The Commies in the northern part invaded the south and took over the capital city. Back in Washington, Give 'em Hell Harry wouldn't say it was a war, but he sent troops and drafted more soldiers. He wanted to look like he wasn't soft on the Reds.

As he thought about whether to come back to Hayden in the fall, Sisco realized that he hadn't given up on Claire as a friend or possibly a lover, or on Len as his boss and a friend. He had decided that if he did return, he wouldn't referee their differences with each other or with Skidmore. He'd let the chips fall where they would, grab any of the spoils that fell his way and always respect the third commandment of the Hobo Code: "Don't take advantage of someone who is in a vulnerable situation, locals or other hobos."

Terry A. Albritton

Mother Mountain

Early one morning in late June, Sisco decked a rattler headed north and found himself a boxcar empty except for a couple of bums sleeping in a corner. He didn't know them, so he moved to the other corner to get some shut-eye. Truth was, he wanted to be as scarce as possible for a few months. With the F.B.I. on the way into town and the draft board on the lookout for soldiers to fight in Korea, he didn't want to be near Hayden or any other jerkwater in the summer. Besides, it was hotter than the devil's workshop in the Central Valley during July and August. He asked Mrs. Mac to save his room and paid her two months' rent in advance. When he kissed her, she cried and gave him a bag of fried chicken. She made him promise to come back to say good-bye even if he decided not to stay on permanently.

He couldn't sleep. Too many things stirred in his head; so he climbed on top after the rattler cleared Roseville, where the railroad dicks got their jollies throwing hobos off trains. The only time they tolerated knights of the road was during the picking season when the clover kickers needed harvest stiffs in their fields. Now was the time for the cherries, tomatoes, and corn, so he figured the detectives had relaxed and traveling would be easier through the harvest.

On top of the boxcar, Sisco felt a peace he hadn't known since last summer before he jumped off a freight at Hayden. From up there, things were predictable. The neat rows of grapevines would release their sweet purple beads to olive-skinned harvesters. The straight lines of arched almond trees full of tiny nuts and the leafy peach trees laden with heavy fruit would give passage to the stick-figure ladder boys. Neat furrows of rice with wavy green stems would allow their treasure to be plucked. Firm, fresh tomatoes hid under tangled vines daring the pickers to tame them into the boxes. All of this he saw without spotting a familiar hat, kerchief, or lamp shade wrap in the fields and orchards.

He thought about Carlos and Peach when they worked the grapes together, talking in a mix of lingos and laughing with communication that none of the hobos understood. He wondered how two guys from places that don't have the same talk could get on so fine. Never mind that Peach was old enough to be Carlos' father. There was a special thing between them, and it didn't matter about their age difference. To think that Peach might have taken out Carlos was impossible. When Carlos died, Peach died, too, because they were connected like twins breathing the same air, sharing the same mind, and loving with the same heart. What Sisco could accept was that Peach had hanged himself to be with Carlos in some other place.

As the rattler ran through the Central Valley past Woodland, Zamora, Williams, and Orland, up through Red Bluff and Redding, where it made stops, his thoughts turned to Hayden and how the townies there had accepted him without really knowing anything about him. Things still could turn bad with two dead locals and Sisco as the outsider. He might be fingered for Carlos' death, although no one seemed to care much about Carlos. If Skidmore knew he was in the confessional that morning, he might just alibi his helper anyway, since he hadn't reported the body like he was supposed to. Skiddy was a strange old geezer, but he seemed to have a good heart, and he gave lots of leeway on the job.

After the rattler pulled out of Redding, Sisco ate four pieces of fried chicken. The other 'bos had sprung it at Red Bluff, so he didn't have to share Mrs. Mac's lunch. He was by himself to enjoy the countryside as the slow freight climbed north into the Cascade Mountains. Rolling hills with scrub bushes and scrawny pines gave way to the peaks in the distance. You left the infernal valley heat with its alfalfa and manure smells to get a whiff of the fir trees. You wanted to bottle up that pure pine scent for the long, hot nights below. As the hog trudged and twisted through the ravines, the icy Upper Sacramento River raced out of the mountains that loomed up in front. The big girl mountain was still hidden among the other peaks. Then, Lady Shasta appeared with an invitation to come closer. White and firm, she tempted and disappeared quickly only to poke her backside up once more—bigger than ever. At Dunsmuir, she was so near and so huge that you could just about touch her. Over to the east, her female part was tucked in between her snowy backside and a second peak—Shastina—likely her offspring. On that side was a bare, rolling plain with stunted pines, black rocks, and wild grasses with yellow and purple flowers. Sisco had had more than one flirtation with that big girl, thinking he'd like to fall into her cracks, get washed by her icy juices, be buried in her crevices, and folded into her womb. You could lose and find yourself in that woman, the mother of all mountains. Nobody knew her secrets, but many believed that she was some kind of goddess.

Mother Mountain looked after the hobos when they jungled up in a sweet place on the north side of town. Not far from the road, it was next to the river, but you had to double back under a bridge to get there. That grassy patch near the pine trees and close to the boulders in the shallows was all they needed. They fished from the bank or waded out to the middle of the river if the water wasn't too high. In that special place at the foot of Mother Shasta, Sisco found Memphis Shorty, Cleveland Jack, and Big Mouth Whitey in the summer of 1950. On his way to the jungle there, he stopped at a mercantile for a new rod, reel, and some flies. He had loaned his gear to Peach in the summer of '49 right before the mess with Carlos. After what happened, he lost track and figured that some tramp was snagging salmon with it up on the Columbia. He didn't care to have it back anyway.

Shorty liked to be in charge of the fishing camp. He said that his order of things brought the 'bos luck with their poles. No one could tell him anything about how to fish because he'd get all bent out of shape and say, "Do you fellas catch 'em when ya follow my rules? If ya do, then just shut up and follow 'em. If ya don't, then get the hell downstream and see how lucky ya are!" None of the regular hobos dared to argue with him, but some of the tramps who didn't know him caught the next rattler out of Dunsmuir after they heard his rules.

When Sisco got to the river, Jack was seated under a tree puffing on a reefer. He didn't expect that he'd get up to greet him because the rule was that nobody walked on the bank while any of the guys were fishing. Something was different this time, though. Shorty stood thirty feet or so downstream from where Whitey held his pole. He usually stood further upstream and behind anybody else, so he had first chance at a trout.

Sisco sat down next to Jack, whose eyelids drooped under his Dodger cap after a good hit of Panama Red. Only after a nudge did Jack realize he had company.

"Well, I'll be goddamned if it isn't a reformed bum come in from his civilized life! I shore thought you'd be spending the summer with your school teacher down in the valley."

"That's what you useless tramps get for not stoppin' by to pick me up." Sisco grabbed the joint and took a hit until the smoke filled his lungs. Then he began to laugh as loud as he could, knowing that Shorty would hear him and get pissed.

Sure enough, Shorty looked over at the river bank and glared his hardest stare.

Sisco waved at him and laughed louder. "Say, Jack. What's he doin' at the second spot downstream? I never seen him give up the top spot 'bove. I don't see any sign of our dinner here on shore."

"Oh, he's trying to prove that he can catch 'em wherever he stands. Old Big Mouth Whitey keeps ragging on him for grabbing the top place. Neither of 'em caught a thing yet."

Jack yawned and stretched his legs like he was going to spread out on the grass.

Sisco felt like dozing off himself. The late afternoon sun with a light breeze in the firs sent invisible waves of pine smell through the air. The rush of the river as it cascaded over the rocks was lullaby enough to put anybody out for a nap. He was ready to lie down on the bank when a shout came from the water where Whitey jumped up and down like he had a live one in his drawers. Sisco poked Jack, and they stood up just in time to see a big trout break the water. For a second, everything turned silver as the sun hit the trout and the river in a flash. Whitey began to gyrate like he was on a wild steer or a bucking bronco. His arms struggled to control the rod while that fish gave him a run for his money. By this time, Shorty had left his spot much against his rule never to move when the other fella was landing a fish. He waded up to the bank, threw his rod on the ground, and made his way out to Whitey, who was almost falling down as he tried to hang on.

"Lemme have her! I'll bring her in!"

It looked like Whitey wanted to hand off the pole to Shorty, but he couldn't seem to let go of it. The pull of the fish and his grip on the rod had his hands glued to it. Shorty had no way of grabbing it, and Whitey would soon be dragged down the river if he didn't get some help.

"Friggin' trout must be eighteen inches long!" shouted Sisco as he and Jack went to the edge of the bank to watch the silver streak break the water over and over.

"She's a big one, all right! And that ole hobo ain't about to let Whitey land her by hisself. Has to have a piece of the action so he can tell everybody it was his catch, too."

Sisco had an idea and shouted to Shorty, "Get behind him! Corn hole him to hang on!"

They started to laugh, never expecting that he would do it. But he did—just grabbed on behind Whitey, practically stuck himself to him, and hung onto the rod to steady it. On the riverbank, Jack and Sisco were so hysterical that they nearly cried.

"Stick it good to him!" Sisco hollered. "Never mind the fish. Give that 'bo a joyride he'll never forget!"

He was so out of his mind watching Shorty pump back and forth, up and down, that he fell onto the grass from weak knees.

As the trout began to give up the fight, hardly breaking the water now, Jack yelled, "You can take your dick out now, Shorty. Don't get too used to that hard-on!"

They came out of the river like two near-drowned dogs. Shorty's hair and beard dripped water like he'd been swimming. He hadn't had much of a shear and shave since Christmas in Hayden.

Whitey always kept himself trimmed up better, but he, too, was wet and exhausted. He had finally turned the rod and the prize fish over to Shorty and was wringing his raw, bleeding hands. He had a big grin on his face. "Don't let no one say it was anybody 'cept Big Mouth Whitey who snagged this fella! And I got the hands to prove it!' He held up his bloody mitts.

"Ya sure do, Whitey!" shouted Jack. "We seen the whole thing from the bank. No doubt who caught that trout.

Ole Shorty here—he snagged something else, and he'll never be the same!"

They all laughed.

"You fellas always poke fun at my rules, but I woulda landed this mother by myself if I'd been in my usual place. I just gave Whitey here a chance today 'cause he ain't caught nothin' big in this river before."

"Well, he caught two big ones today!" whistled Sisco as he held up the trout. She was a beauty as she wriggled on the hook, looking every bit a foot and a half long.

"Guess we have our dinner tonight," said Jack while he secured the line so Shorty could take her off and lay her to rest on the grass.

"Not so fast!" piped up Whitey. "This trout's gotta be some kinda record, and I aim to take her to town for a measure up. Down at the mercantile, they have pictures of the big ones landed hereabouts. This mother could turn out to be a record breaker." He sat down on the grass next to the fish. "And don't forget who snagged her!" he said as he glared at Shorty. Whitey had a long gash on his forearm where the line had cut him. His hand still dripped blood.

"Ya gotta take care of your mitts," Sisco said. "Let me run this rainbow into town in case they want a picture. I'm more civilized than you guys. Ya look like a coupla tramps!"

The other three stared him down like he'd insulted their kinfolk.

"Well, look at whose shit don't stink," said Shorty while he pretended to jack off in his wet overalls. "They've made some kinda civilized bastard outta ya in that valley jerkwater, haven't they?"

Sisco looked at him and then over at Jack and Whitey. "Hey, fellas! I didn't mean anything. Ya know how the townies are—if ya look like a bum, ya get treated like a bum. They'd just as soon hold this fish for theirselves and never say who snagged it. I wanna be sure one of us gets the credit—not one of the townies."

Cleveland Jack walked over to Whitey like he needed to protect him. "Look here. You guys been together longer than I been riding with you. I know you look out for each other just like you look out for me. Sisco, why don't you go along with Shorty and Whitey to be sure they get the fish weighed and a proper picture taken of them both?"

Everything got quiet. The sun had gone west, and the afternoon breeze began to settle the birds so they could find resting places for the night. From the north came the blow of the Shasta Daylight headed south to Redding and below. Within seconds, she'd streak through in a silver orange flash, her passengers riding the cushions out of the mountains into the valley and the Bay Area.

As usual, Shorty had the last word. "Let's not get too sentimental. Whitey and I'll take her into Dunsmuir for the measure up. I'll get us some dago and a bottle of Jack Daniels at the mercantile. You fellas get the fire started so we can cook her up for dinner. There's still some mulligan left from last night. Later on Sisco can tell 'bout his love life in the big city."

They all laughed together as the Daylight roared past. Whitey went off to take a piss before he and Shorty set out for Dunsmuir. Neither one of them was eager to deal with the townies, but they didn't want anyone else getting the credit either.

That night they had themselves quite a fish fry, with a big jug of dago and a bottle of Jack Daniels to wash things down. The fishermen reported that the trout had measured just short of eighteen inches. Some guy from the local newspaper came in to take their pictures while they held the fish between them. He said it would come out in next week's edition, and they could each have a free copy.

Jungled up by the fire, they had another good laugh about the afternoon. Jack poked fun at Whitey as he passed him a reefer. "You looked like you was getting used to that rod up your rear end today."

"Hell, it wasn't me with the hard-on," laughed Whitey. "Can't help it if some old hobo got all lathered up over my ass."

Shorty was feeling no pain after a good supper, plenty of dago and a joint. Spread out on the grass near the fire, he sat up to slug down some firewater. With his tongue tying up the words, he said, "I gotta tell ya boys—that was the biggest, longest hard-on I ever had. Each time we'd pull her in a little more, I added an inch."

"An inch to the fish or to your pecker?" teased Sisco.

They all went into hysterics louder than during the afternoon. Shorty had to stand up to catch his breath because he was laughing so hard. Soon he disappeared behind a pine to puke that rainbow bullet soaked in dago. When he came back, he grabbed his bindle and, without a word, took off to a little patch of grass behind the trees and went to sleep. The others finished up the booze and called it a day, too.

The rest of June and most of July didn't bring much excitement. After the Fourth, the heat picked up, but the 'bos kept cool in the river swimming with the fish when they weren't snagging them. Nothing topped the eighteen-inch trout. At least once a week, Shorty got out the newspaper to show his picture. When other knights of the road passed through, he cornered them to tell the story. Sometimes he talked about the hard-on, and sometimes he didn't. The others never mentioned it if he didn't bring it up first. They always made sure that Whitey got his fair share of credit for hooking the fish in the first place. Shorty took back his spot on the river, but never caught anything to compare to their trout.

The summer of 1950 was slow and lazy. When the thunderheads moved in around Mother Mountain, they let loose up there and sprinkled on the hobos but not as heavy as in years past. Cleveland Jack was certain there were saucer men inside Shasta and that they managed the weather.

"Don't you see them big pink and white saucer clouds above the mountain?" he asked Sisco late one afternoon as they sat by the river. "Are you gonna tell me those ain't from some other place?"

It was true that sometimes at dusk or dawn, pancake-shaped forms hovered around the top of Mount Shasta. Unlike regular clouds that broke up into bits and pieces, they looked whole and seemed to move together. But they were different from what Sisco had seen over the rivers at Hayden. The valley clouds, or whatever they were, formed giant white triangles in the sky.

Jack wanted to hitch a ride over to Shasta City where he could get closer to the saucers. None of the others was convinced that a trip was worth leaving his sweet spot next to the water—especially in the heat. Jack wasn't going to give up, though. A couple of days later, he took a bath in the river, put on his overalls, a flannel shirt that didn't show too much dirt, and his Indians ball cap. "Gotta look more respectable if I wanna hitch over to Shasta," he said as he tried to put a comb to his curly hair. "Sure you fellas won't come with me?" he asked Whitey and Shorty as they cooked up a mulligan with some beef bones begged from the butcher in town.

"Not me," answered Memphis. "And I ain't about to look for your sorry ass if ya don't come back. So don't let the saucer men kidnap ya, 'cause I won't rescue ya in my flying machine!"

"It's a waste of time," laughed Whitey as he dropped some wild carrots into the stew. "Them's just pretty clouds that hang out at the mountain."

Sisco considered hitching with Jack to keep him company. He knew Cleveland better now than when they had first met two years ago on the road. Jack had never talked much about his life in Ohio, but he had said that he had a wife and a son. The missus ran off with some rich fella who took the boy to a fancy place in Chicago where his kinfolk lived. Jack left his job in a Cleveland assembly plant to look for his son, but the trail went cold. He began riding the trains to get away from it all and to forget.

Something told Sisco that Jack needed to be alone with the Mother Mountain and her saucer clouds. He didn't think there was anything to find up there except more respect for their big girl. Cleveland left the jungle before noon, and when he hadn't returned by dark, Sisco started to wonder if he should have gone after all. Peach had done himself in over a punk. What might a guy like Jack do over a wife and a son? He was in search of a reason to keep living, but he might also be looking for a way out of everything.

"Guess ole Jack found the saucer men up there on the mountain," said Shorty as they sat by the fire with their bellies full of mulligan.

"Probably got hung up in town," said Whitey. "Shasta City this time of year has more action than Dunsmuir. Maybe he found a nice gal ready for a quickie. Do him good to get laid. I wonder if saucer men have saucer ladies." He laughed.

Sisco stood up to get a pack of fags from his bindle. At that moment, Jack walked into the jungle. He said nothing; he just sat down on one of the logs next to the fire pit. He took out a smoke and a light while he stared straight ahead into the night and up at the stars. Something was different about him, and they all felt it. Nobody cracked a saucer joke.

"I saw it, fellas," Jack whispered in a soft, steady voice.

"What did ya see?" asked Whitey, trying not to laugh.

"I saw where the saucers go in and come out of the mountain on the east side."

After a minute, Shorty said, "Was ya smokin' some of that Panama weed up there? It's mighty powerful shit."

"I swear on my mother's grave that I wasn't tokin' on nothing. I saw a big opening on the other side just below the snow line."

"And how'd ya know it was a hole for the saucer men?" asked Whitey with a funny grin on his face.

Jack took off his Indians ball cap and ran it across his forehead like he did to catch the sweat. "I saw a saucer go into the mountain, and then, the hole closed up. I swear on my mother's grave that I ain't never seen anything like it, can't believe it, and shore can't explain it."

It sounded like a story made up for kids who wanted to hear about Buck Rogers, but Jack was so serious that nobody laughed.

Shorty spoke up. "Well, I reckon there could be a saucer base up there. Since the end of the war, there's been plenty of reports from New Mexico and Arizona. Makes sense that saucers gotta go someplace to pick up gas and get repairs."

"I don't think saucers run on gasoline," Sisco said. "They don't need gas stations to refuel."

"Okay," said Shorty, who seemed to have decided not to argue for a change. "They still gotta have a spot to rest. Inside Mother Mountain might be as good a place as any."

They talked on, but Jack didn't seem to hear any of it. He sat quietly and looked up at the sparklers so bright that they blended together in patterns of light.

"Wonder why the stars shine brighter up here," asked Whitey, trying to change the subject.

"'Cause they don't have no city lights to interfere with their shine," answered Shorty, who seemed bored with all the saucer talk.

"Don't be too sure," said Jack, as if he knew differently. "One big battery gives energy and light to everything and everybody inside and outside of that mountain."

None of the hobos volunteered to go back with Cleveland onto Shasta; he didn't seem to want company, anyway. One thing was for sure—something had happened to him up there. After that first trip, he was gone for days at a time and never gave more reports of saucers.

"He don't need to tell us nothin'," said Shorty one hot afternoon in late July as they lay on the grass by the river. "Ya gotta remember that he lost everything before, and he's searchin' for something to take its place. He's not really a bum like us."

"We ain't bums either!' piped up Whitey. "Don't we work for our stake? We just don't do it in regular places like other stiffs." He began to roll a reefer.

Shorty picked up on the talk. "So what's your plan, Sisco?" he asked after a big toke of the joy smoke. "Whitey and me is headed up to the apple knockers pretty soon. Why don't ya come with us?"

Sisco took a hit from the reefer. For a minute, it lifted him to a different place and then settled him back down nice and easy on the riverbank while they waited for his answer. "You fellas are my only real friends. Ya know that, don't ya? None of the townies in Hayden come up to you guys."

"What do ya mean by that?" asked Shorty.

"Gotta finish the business I started in the valley. Figure it will be over one way or 'nother by next summer—maybe sooner."

"Your business?" asked Whitey with half a smile.

"Just let me guess," mocked Shorty. "I'm bettin' it's that pretty little school teacher who's pussy-whipped this here hobo. She's made him think he's real special when she ain't got any notion of hitchin' up with him like he thinks she does. He's keepin' his pecker in his pants for a weddin' day that'll never come." Memphis was feeling no pain from the joy smoke.

"It's not just Claire," he said as he sat down between them. "It's something else I gotta figure out for myself. I gotta find out if I can settle down or if I'm a permanent hobo like you guys."

Sisco felt a cool chill from the river as it raced past. He knew what the others were thinking—that he thought himself better than they were because he might settle down in one place. He'd tried to tell them that he had lived a different kind of life before the rails and he liked to come back to a home after a day's work. Shorty and Whitey didn't understand, but he suspected that Jack did. Jack had gone after what he'd lost, hadn't recovered it, and was still in search of a replacement. "Just don't know which kinda life I like better."

Shorty got up and began to pace back and forth. "And what 'bout Carlos? Let's say Peach didn't do him in. Two more bodies found in that jerkwater with the F.B.I. comin' to investigate and all. There's a killer in that burg, and ya gotta be careful they don't try to pin it all on you."

"Sit down, Memphis. You're makin' me nervous. Yeah, there's a killer in Hayden, but they ain't gonna pin anything on me. I have friends in high places."

"You don't know shit 'bout friends in high places!" shouted Shorty as he kept pacing. "They protect their own, and you ain't one of 'em, even if you'd like to be. Wanna settle down? Find some cute little Mexican gal who can cook, keep a neat house, raise your young'uns, and give ya a blow job when you're tired. That school teacher ain't your type!"

Sisco didn't feel like arguing anymore; it was too hot. The air stayed warm even after the sun went down. Shorty brought out a bottle of cheap grape wine to cool off. The 'bos talked about good times together in the past: in the strawberries down Oceanside way when they ate more than they picked, and Memphis had such bad runs that he had to hide in the bushes until he got rid of everything; in the oranges around San Bernardino when the temperature hit 115 degrees, and they all puked until the boss told them to lay off and let the Spics finish the job; in the San Joaquin Valley out east in the grapes when a freak storm from the Sierra hit, and lightning bounced all over so that Whitey's bindle got torched like the burning tumbleweed in the Bible; and up by Red Bluff in the almonds when Sisco fell off a ladder, injuring his leg so bad that the boys had to carry him to a sawbones who bandaged him up and told him to get back on the trains.

As he remembered these times, Sisco wanted to hit the road again. He figured there'd never be better pals in Hayden or anywhere else. Yet, he had a need to call someplace his home. Hayden seemed like as good a spot as any while Claire was there.

"You fellas gotta come in sometime," he said.

"Who says so?" shouted Whitey. "Hell! You'll be back on the rails in no time. Remember, you're the Sisco Kid, and we're your sidekicks!"

The next morning, they were still asleep when Jack showed up. He'd had a shave and a trim to his red bush. He wore a new green sport shirt and some new trousers.

177

"Got me a stake in Dunsmuir, boys," he barked while he set the coffee to boil. "Nice lady runs a boarding house for the Southern Pacific workers. Railroaders from outta town bunk there between trains. I'm the maintenance man, gardener, and part-time cook for a free flop and three square ones every day."

"Well, now," piped up Shorty as he pissed hard against the tree near the fire. "Got us 'nother houseboy here. You and Sisco will be ridin' the cushions together," he laughed.

"And what else ya get for all that work, Cleveland?" teased Whitey.

Jack smiled. "Oh, shit! I dunno. She's clean, runs a decent place. Lost her husband two years ago and been struggling to keep her business goin'. I'll help her out awhile—just till she gets on her feet."

"Shore you will!" said Shorty in his playful voice. "Maybe she can help ya make the acquaintance of some saucer men."

While he poured hot coffee into cans for the hobos, Jack didn't say anything. Then, he sat down on the log next to Sisco. "Says she sees a lotta things up there. Thinks everybody in these parts is protected by the mountain and whoever lives inside."

"Ya don't say!" laughed Whitey. "From now on, we'll know to look for ya in the sky with the saucer men and saucer ladies."

Shorty and Sisco didn't laugh because they saw that Jack was happy—wanted to believe it all and make a new life in Dunsmuir. They were glad for him.

Whitey seemed to watch their reaction and must have decided to keep his mouth shut. Before he left to go north to the apple knockers, he shook Jack's hand and told him he'd always be welcome on the road and in the jungle.

A week or so later, Shorty and Whitey caught a northbound hot shot train to Portland on their way to

Seattle and the apples. Sisco stayed by the river a few weeks more to avoid the valley heat as long as he could. He had told Skidmore to expect him toward the end of August if he was coming back. Truth be told, he was happy to be by himself at the base of Mother Mountain with the smell of pine in the warm air and plenty of rainbow to snag for supper. He went into town to the mercantile for supplies and picked up a big beefsteak that he fried over the fire and ate for two nights.

While in Dunsmuir, he overheard some locals talking about the new handyman at Brennan's Boarding House. They thought that he was a relative of the widow Brennan's deceased husband; a widower himself, he came out from Ohio to help save the business. Sisco figured that was as good a story as any for the townies, who couldn't make a scandal if they didn't know the truth about Cleveland Jack.

Folks at the mercantile were upset because of food prices. They worried about the Korean War and shortages, so they bought up whatever they could, which raised prices. Coffee was up from twenty-five to eighty-one cents a pound. Milk had gone from twelve to nineteen cents a quart. General MacArthur had requested more troops for Korea, and Truman was going to call up 50,000 more men. After hearing the draft talk, Sisco made a beeline back to the river.

At night under the stars, he thought about Claire and wished she were there with him. They'd watch the twinklers in the sky and find paintings in those dancing lights while they made love between the picture shows in the heavens. She would like all that, but she would hate the flies, ants, and mosquitos that enjoy the summer as much as people do. She was a city gal through and through, but he believed that he could show her the beauty of the fields, the trees, and the sky. Patience, tenderness, and love would lead to a reward nothing less than heaven. He would taste her kisses in his mouth like the fruit of a honeydew picked off the vine. Like a rose, Claire had layers of petals that could be plucked off one by one until her heart was laid open and her scent became part of him. It was her core tucked so tight inside that he most wanted to share—maybe because no man had ever known it and maybe because she, herself, didn't know it was there.

G-man

Until that summer, Claire Lewis hadn't been a sentimental person. Her mother and father had raised her to study hard, never complain, and keep her feelings private. To show herself too happy, sad, or angry would let others take advantage. Early in her life, she learned to confide only in the imaginary playmates who followed her up and down the stairs of the house in Berkeley.

Things took a different turn for her in the summer of '50. Claire's best school pal, Marjorie, married her Jewish beau in one of those fancy weddings with high-society guests from the University of California, the Beth Israel temple, and San Francisco. Of course, Claire and her folks went to the ceremony, but her parents refused to attend the reception because liquor would be served there.

On Marge's wedding night, Claire wrestled with the sheets in her bed. She couldn't stop thinking about the newlyweds making love in their classy suite at the Saint Francis Hotel in San Francisco. She had learned everything she knew about "doing it" from Marjorie. When they were sixteen, the best friends spent the night at Marge's house. They played records and read movie magazines until they heard Marjorie's parents close their bedroom door. Leaving the phonograph on, they tiptoed down the hall. The sounds creeping under the door and into the hallway were strange to Claire, and she felt afraid. Only when she heard a soft sigh and a throaty giggle did she start to feel safe. Then came a kind of panting followed by a long gasp. She recalled her grandmother having a spell and rushed down the hall back to her friend's bedroom where the needle on the phonograph zigzagged on the record.

Marjorie explained the noises they had heard in her parents' bedroom. She said they "did it" nearly every night and seemed to enjoy themselves without saying a word.

181

She told Claire about the sweet spot every woman has and even showed her how to touch it right so you could "fly to the moon" by yourself.

Once she learned how to please herself, Claire did it often, especially when she wasn't able to fall asleep. She kept wondering about real love, and she felt lost without Marjorie, who seemed to have it all figured out.

With her best friend married, Claire decided to sign up for a summer session class at the university. She planned to go back to Hayden in September, teach there another year, and look for a job somewhere else. She'd have teacher tenure and forget about Len once and for all.

The class at Cal didn't keep her interest much because of the big ruckus on the campus. Protestors carried signs and marched around to support professors who hadn't signed the loyalty paper. The big shots at the university threatened to fire teachers who refused, calling them reds. Claire tried not to pay attention to the demonstrations, but in her heart she sided with the professors. She couldn't discuss the protest with her parents because they said the marchers were rabble-rousers and Communist sympathizers.

At night in the big bed, she couldn't sleep and felt angry at her mother snoring in the next room. Claire had always resented her mother's deafness because it was the reason her folks had made her sleep with her grandmother, who had regular spells at night. Daddy slept too soundly to wake up, and Mother took off her hearing aid. Claire hated that ugly ear gismo; it squeaked and squawked all day long. She remembered the time she hid the stupid thing, throwing her mother into a panic that brought them both to tears. She felt so ashamed, that she retrieved the hearing aid from the kitchen drawer where she had hidden it.

More mixed up, she tried to sleep but kept thinking of Sisco's strong fingers on her sweet spot and on her breasts.

Had she fallen for a hobo who was just a janitor? Why wasn't she thinking about Len, who had all the right pedigrees?

In July, all hell broke loose. A month after her honeymoon, Marjorie's father shot himself in his office at the university. The big bosses had fired him for being a Commie. Marge and her mother were too devastated to make funeral arrangements, so Claire and Marjorie's new husband took over everything. As hard as it all was for her, Claire's worst time came when she asked Mother about what to wear to the funeral.

"You wear anything dark, Claire. Daddy and I will not be attending. We can't take the chance that someone from the government will be there and think we're Communists like Marjorie's father."

"Mother! You know he wasn't a Communist. Daddy knows! He and the professor had long talks about it on their walks in the rose garden."

"Still, dear, it's too risky for us to be seen there. Daddy has to keep his job, you know."

"You're a hypocrite, Mother. Marge and her parents have been our friends for twenty-five years. No real Christian would stay away because of some phantom F.B.I. agent."

Claire was beside herself; she didn't understand. Her father worked for a private contractor in San Francisco, and no one at his company had been asked to sign a loyalty oath. With tears flowing, she left the house and didn't come back until the next day. She didn't want to go to the funeral by herself, so she called Len in Yolo. He wasn't afraid of any G-man and promised to drive to Berkeley early on the morning of the funeral.

As usual, he was late and feeling no pain when he met Claire at the Jewish temple. They sat in the back row because the place was full. She was just as glad; Len needed a shave and smelled like stale brandy. She couldn't stop crying. He sat close to her with his arm around her shoulders. After the service, he followed her to her Chevy in the parking lot.

"I'm sorry about your professor friend, Claire. I hate to say it, but he wasn't the first, and he won't be the last. These Red baiters are everywhere, and they will stop at nothing."

"Thank you for coming, Len. I wish I could invite you to my parents' house, but I just can't."

Flicking a Lucky onto the sidewalk, he answered, "Just as well. I'm afraid of what I might say that would make things worse for you. I'll catch some Z's in my Ford and head back to Woodland. I'll call you soon."

He gave her a quick smack on the cheek and crossed the street to his automobile.

Claire knew she wouldn't hear from him until the school year started. With all that had happened, she even felt anxious to get back to Hayden. She was mixed up more than ever before in her life; things were happening too fast. She needed the classroom and the innocence of first-graders to help get her bearings.

§ § § § §

Sisco left the mountains on top of an open boxcar. By the time the rattler came into the valley, the heat was bad enough to be the inside of a coal burner on a hungry hog. At Redding, the temperature shot up more, and he ducked inside. In his hurry to leave Dunsmuir, he had forgotten his canteen on the sidewalk where he stopped to talk to Cleveland Jack. One of the 'bos in the boxcar took pity on him and offered him a drink of water. He must have figured him for a scenery bum or a Minnie the Moocher because he made a big speech about not going on the road without a canteen.

Sisco dozed all the way to Roseville and rolled into Hayden just as darkness fell. It was still hot, and his clothes stuck to him as if they were pasted there. He jumped off the rattler next to the jungle; it was deserted and dirty. Piles of tin cans, loose papers, and cigarette butts littered the fire pit and the open spaces between the oak trees. None of the regular hobos would have left such a mess. It seemed likely that the traveling Weary Willies or the local drunks had dirtied up the camp. With the kids out of school all summer, it was possible they'd been playing hobo or smoking where their folks couldn't see them. Nobody had bothered to sweep the trash with the broom in plain sight by the crate of cooking pots. Serious knights of the road honored Rule Number 8 of the Hobo Code: "Always respect nature; do not leave garbage where you are jungling."

When he opened the crate with the mulligan pot, he saw that nothing inside had been disturbed. The pots and spoons were dusty but stacked up neatly like when Shorty was in charge. He figured that no one had made a fire, either, because it was too hot or the local fire chief had given a warning to the jungle buzzards. In the dry months of summer, there was always a danger of brush fires. All the regular 'bos took extra care with the campfire because it was the heart of their lives together.

He hadn't slept soundly for two nights. He threw down his bedroll next to an oak tree, flopped on top of it, and went to sleep. He didn't hear any of the night crawlers going north and south. The next morning as the sun peeked through the branches an early rattler sounded after leaving Lodi headed for Hayden. It was his morning wake-up call to get ready for work at the high.

After two months away at the river, Sisco wanted to be sure that he still had a room over the drugstore. He had missed his landlady and figured she would have news of

Claire and Len. The door to the soda fountain was locked up tight, which didn't seem right. The heat must have kept Mrs. Mac home later than usual. He walked up C Street past the post office and the barber. Nobody was around; even the 241 was closed up. Sunday! The Catholics and everybody would soon be headed to one of the four churches. Skiddy was probably there already to sweep up.

He turned, walked back to Fourth Street and over the tracks to the Catholic church. If he could help it, he never went there. The memory of Carlos in the confessional still had him spooked. The front door was open, but he decided to go around to the side, where he saw Skidmore's Caddy parked in its usual spot. Skiddy was sweeping the sidewalk. He looked up and flashed a big smile.

"Thought you might show up in these parts before long," he said and put out his hand. "Looks like ya lost some pounds with the fish up there on the river. Any luck with them trout?"

"Hell or heck, yeah! One of our 'bos, or two of 'em together, snagged a record fish. Even got their picture in the local rag with the eighteen inches. Plenty decent fishin' for most of the summer."

"Ya don't say," he said, as he moved down the sidewalk with the broom. "I saw Claire a coupla days ago. She wanted to know if I had heard from you."

His heart jumped. So she had come back and was asking about him. He tried to keep his voice steady and casual. "Guess she decided to give it 'nother try here, huh? I thought she planned to look for work in Berkeley?"

Skiddy had reached the end of the sidewalk, but turned around and came back. "Ya know she can't get Len outta her system. So long as he's here and not hitched to somebody else, she'll be back." He started to say more, but stopped when he spotted the priest. "Morning, Father

186

Martinez. Like ya to meet Sisco here. Works with me at the high and the primary."

A handsome priest with dark hair slicked back and coal black eyes reached out to shake Sisco's hand. "Mr. Skidmore has told me about you, son. I had hoped to meet you and to invite you personally to Mass."

"Thanks, Father," he said and took off his Dodger ball cap to shake. "I'm not much for church, but I'd like to try one of your Masses sometime. I was baptized Methodist in Kansas but stopped goin' when I hopped the rails at fifteen. Us 'bos make plenty a stops at the local Sally's on the road. Christian folks there always give us a decent handout and a night's flop."

The priest didn't seem interested in the generous Jesus-loving people at the Salvation Army. With a hand on Sisco's shoulder, he spoke again in a soft, sing-song voice, "You are always welcome here. I serve the Sacred Mass in Hayden on Wednesday and Sunday, but I can come over from Lodi or Stockton if you need to talk any other day. Just let Mr. Skidmore know. Now, if you'll excuse me, I have to prepare the sacraments. The bells, please, Mr. Skidmore. God be with you, my son."

With his talk about Mass and confession, Father Martinez had thrown Sisco a curve ball. Instead of asking more about Claire, he was off on a spur line with thoughts of Skidmore and Father Martinez scheming to get him into the confessional. The priest said Mass in Mexican, so he had to know the Spics who came through on the trains; most of them were Catholics. Skidmore surely would have told him about the body and who found it. It wasn't too late to deck a rattler out of Hayden, but Sisco had to see Claire at least one more time and to let Len know if he decided to leave.

While he thought about these things, he walked over to Fourth Street again and spotted Mrs. Mac on the sidewalk with her mop in front of the drugstore. She was getting ready to do the job that had been his chore every Sunday morning while she went to church. With her back turned to him, he sneaked up behind and said, "Need a hand there, ma'am?"

She dropped the mop and spun around. "My stars!" she squealed, as she gave him a big hug. "How I've missed you! You look mighty healthy—all tan and strong. Musta done you good to be up there by that river. Let me fix you some breakfast, and we can talk." She hurried inside.

Like he'd never been gone, Sisco finished mopping the sidewalk and went into the soda fountain. On the counter at his usual place was a plate of bacon and eggs. He tried not to eat too fast while Mrs. Mac chattered about all the town gossip. She told him about the latest boy to be drafted for Korea, the newest girl to be knocked up, food prices out of control, and a teacher at the primary who up and married some guy from Los Angeles that nobody knew.

He chewed the last of his buttered toast and washed it down with a big swig of coffee. "And, Len?" he asked.

"Oh, you know that old soft-soaper," she replied. "In and out like always. I think he drove over to Woodland on Thursday. He knows that I'm perturbed with him after he brought that hunting dog in here last week. All kinda varmits on its back, dirt everywhere he walked. I told Len to get him out of the store and not to take him upstairs. I know he was mad, so he probably took the mutt back to his mother's place. Even she won't let the hound inside."

"Same old Len," laughed Sisco as he lit up a smoke. "First day I met him a year ago, he had Pluto inside Claire's place—all dirty from the fishing camp. She put up with him, but she didn't like it much."

"Poor Claire," sighed Mrs. Mac. "Never gives up on him. Nobody's ever gonna domesticate old Len. Believe me, I know. Some men never should be married."

Just then, Mr. Mac came into the fountain from the back room. Sisco was surprised to see him at the drugstore because he didn't spend much time there. Everyone knew he had some gal on a ranch in the country. For a man his age, he was a good-looker with silver hair, deep blue eyes, and the kind of body that makes you think of a young buck.

He gave Sisco a big smile and came over by the counter to shake his hand. "Myrtle and I missed ya round here," he said. "Room's been shut up all summer waitin' for ya to roll in. Best go upstairs to open the window."

While Mrs. Mac went to fetch the key, the men made small talk. Mr. Mac was real easygoing, and you couldn't help but like him. Still, he'd caused his wife lots of heartaches, just as Len had brought tears to Claire's eyes many times. Some women always had to wonder who their men were screwing. It was even harder to know who the other women were, because then things got personal and stung even more.

Up early and dressed the next morning, Sisco walked over to the high just as the sun peeked out from the foothills. Nobody was there yet, but he knew that Skiddy would show up soon. The day felt like another scorcher, and he was glad the students wouldn't be back for a week. He sat down on the front steps to smoke. A rattler thundered through Hayden with a long line of rolling stock headed for Roseville. Truckloads of *braceros* lumbered past the high school on their way to the tomato fields. He figured that he would have been one of those poor bastards working all day in 100-degree heat if he hadn't found Carlos' body and gone to town for help. Carlos' death had shown him a new life, which was a hard thing to figure.

A few minutes later, Skiddy pulled up in his Caddy, all waxed and shiny in spite of the dust everywhere else. "Thought you'd be here early," he said as he leaned over to the open window on the passenger side. "Want you to come along with me to meet some fellas for breakfast."

After yesterday at the Catholic church, Sisco realized that something was up. He didn't want any part of it; but being as it was his first day back on the job, he didn't ask any questions or make any excuses. He got into the Caddy. They drove north on Highway 99, then left onto Twin Cities Road. They passed the Cosumnes River where Len had taken the hobos to bury the body. Skidmore headed north again on a long dirt road lined with oak trees and hedges. At the end was a turnaround in front of a two-story house--one of those grand old places with a big porch and long vertical windows. It looked in need of repair and a good paint job. Shingles were loose on the roof, and molding was missing from around the door and windows.

"Tre Sorenson's place," offered Skiddy. "Ya know, the father of the kid they found last spring. Ya shoulda seen this spread before the missus and the older son died. Bub, the younger one, never did a lick of work to help his father."

They pulled in behind three other automobiles. Sisco recognized Buck Ratcliff's Hudson, which he always parked next to the industrial arts shop at the high. The Plymouth was familiar, too; it was parked next to Len's Ford on the days when the trustees met. The third automobile was a shiny black Lincoln with an "E" plate—some kind of official vehicle.

Skidmore led him up the front steps and knocked on the front door. Before anyone answered, they slipped inside. Skiddy motioned him down a hall past a sitting room on the right where the furniture was draped with bed sheets. On the left was a big, empty room. At the end was a large, bright kitchen that looked to be the only part of the first floor where folks lived.

"Morning, Skidmore. Got the coffee brewed up and the eggs ready to fry. How ya like 'em?"

Sorenson held out his hand to shake with Skiddy and then with his assistant. "Glad to see ya back with us, young fella. Your boss here ain't no spring chicken, and ya helped him a lot last year. Come on over to the table, and I'll pour ya a cup of java."

Seated at the round table were Buck Ratcliff, Eldon Venable from the trustees, and another guy who didn't look like a rancher. He wore a dark suit with a long-sleeved white shirt and big gold cuff links. He seemed about to strangle himself with a black tie too tight around his neck. From his build, he could have been a palooka retired from the ring. He mopped his forehead with a handkerchief that had the letters RHJ sewed on. He shook hands with Skidmore and Sisco saying, "Robert Harold Johnson, F.B.I."

Buck appeared to be in charge of the meeting. He told the G-man to make himself at home and to take off his coat if he would be more comfortable. He said that everybody at the table was connected in some way to Hayden High School and had known the dead boys. Sisco squirmed in his chair because he hadn't made the acquaintance of either one. Why had Skiddy brought him? Were they going to try to pin something on him or try to get him to snitch on Len?

El Venable looked nervous, too. He chain-smoked and guzzled coffee like there was no tomorrow. He passed his pack of Chesterfields around the table; they all helped themselves except Skiddy, who was chowing down his eggs. Sisco had skipped the breakfast offer; his stomach wasn't in the mood for headlights.

Tre spoke up. "Ya know my boy was found out here by the river, and it looked like he was choked … to death."

He took a swig of coffee to keep from breaking down. He ran his handkerchief across his eyes and his forehead.

"Sorry for your loss, Mr. Sorenson," said Johnson. "The Bureau is looking into his death and the other victim's, too. Up until now, though, we haven't got any real leads. To be honest, the Bureau is currently focused on the Communist threat."

El Venable piped up. "Out here we don't tolerate no Commies, so ya ain't gonna find Reds under anybody's bed. What's a worry to us is the killer in these parts. I got two sons at home myself."

Johnson took a drink of coffee and snuffed out his smoke in one of the big ashtrays on the table. "I understand your concern, Mr. Venable. I'm aware that you suspect foul play, but our resources are limited right now. If you or anyone else has a lead, we'll investigate it as soon as more manpower is available."

Buck spoke up. "Aren't you fellas supposed to find the leads?"

Johnson lit up a Pall Mall. He had put Venable's Chesterfield in his pocket. "Yes, Mr. Ratcliff, that's our job, all right. But we respect you folks enough to know that we can't just come out here like gangbusters—especially if we don't know who or what we're looking for."

Skidmore had finished his eggs and put in his two bits' worth. "See here, Johnson, I'm the honorary deputy police chief in Hayden. I can tell ya that if we didn't need help in finding leads, we wouldn'ta asked for it."

The G-man mopped his forehead with his already damp handkerchief and waited for someone to say something. When no one did, he asked, "Just what makes you think these were homicides and not drownings?"

"Look here, Johnson," answered Tre in a loud voice. "My boy was as good a swimmer as any in these parts. He was raised on the Sacramento. Bub—Helmut's his real name—did not drown. Those marks on his neck prove it."

Johnson took another sip of his coffee, patted his forehead with a paper napkin from the table, and tried to be polite. "With all due respect, Mr. Sorenson, we do know that your son had a … propensity for imbibing and that he may have had one too many on the day he died."

"If ya mean that he liked to have a few drinks, you're right. But Helmut could hold his liquor good as the next guy, and these fellas here know that. Alcohol don't explain the rope marks round his neck or the bruises on his wrists and ankles."

Johnson loosened his tie a little more, put the gold tie clip in his pocket, and asked for a glass of water. While Tre fetched a pitcher of cold water from the ice box, the G-man said, "Guess I'm a little dehydrated. Been working double shifts on this Commie problem. Can't seem to get a handle on it."

They looked at each other. No one understood why he kept going back to the Reds when two boys had been murdered. Carlos would have made three if anyone had mentioned him, but Sisco had no inclination to do that. It did sound as if he'd been killed in the same way as the two local boys.

After two glasses of water, Johnson said, "So, let's suppose these two cases were homicides. Who in this town would have had a reason to kill them? Is there a motive?"

Tre stumbled through when he answered, "We uh, we, uh, was told by the coroner that the boys had been … cornholed before they died."

"Yes, I know," said Johnson as if he had just heard the weather report. "We've seen those files. Now who's to say that these two boys—no disrespect, you understand, that these two guys weren't queers?"

Tre jumped to his feet and pounded his fist so hard on the oak table that the hot coffee in Skidmore's cup bounced right out on the table.

193

"My son weren't no pervert! We don't have none of 'em criminals in Hayden. If our boys was diddled, then somebody from outside the town done it."

The others nodded to agree but stayed quiet.

"Well, then, gentlemen, do you have a possible suspect? Somebody passing through Hayden on more than one occasion or possibly an individual who lives nearby in one of these valley burgs?"

Sorenson sat down and turned to Sisco. "Ya know 'bout these bums who pass through, don't ya?"

Sisco looked around the table in the hope that someone would vouch for him, but no one seemed too anxious, so he did it for himself. "Mr. Skidmore here has been my boss for the past year. He knows that I stayed in Hayden workin' till late June when I went north to Dunsmuir to fish. I never even met the poor fellas who ..."

Skiddy didn't let him finish. "I can tell ya all that Mr. Griffin here is the best helper I've had in twenty years. He didn't know the boys who died 'cause he was doin' double shifts at the high and the primary while helpin' out Myrtle McFadden at the drugstore, where he stays in a room upstairs. Hasn't been back to bumming since he set foot in Hayden last August."

The G-man shifted in his chair and looked like he wanted to leave, but he didn't know how. He took Venable's Chesterfield out of his pocket and made a big production of getting a light for it from Buck, who cleared his throat again to talk.

"I'd like to vouch for Mr. Griffin myself. He worked with me in the industrial arts shop for a week last spring to make four poles for the May Day celebration at the primary. He was with me when they found Tre's boy in the river. No way could he have been out there that week. We worked day and night on those poles."

194

Sisco gave Buck a nod. He figured that the shop teacher and the head custodian had taken him off the hook, but a glance at Johnson left him uncertain. The G-man looked like a firecracker had gone off under him. He sat straight up in his chair and nearly yelled as he pulled a notebook out of his pocket. "What's this about a May Day celebration?"

The men looked at each other trying to figure him out. Skiddy piped up to explain that the principal of the high had decided to help the primary with their May Day poles because there weren't enough for all the kids in first and second grade to participate in the maypole wrapping. As he talked, Johnson wrote in his notebook with a fury. The faster he scribbled, the more he sweated, but he looked awake for the first time all morning.

"And just who is this principal—a local fella or an outsider?"

"Len Sutter? Oh, he's a local, all right," answered Skiddy. "Grew up in Yolo over by Woodland. Distant relation of John Sutter, the guy from Germany—or someplace over there—who built the sawmill where gold was discovered hundred years ago. Ya couldn't be any more local than Leonard Sutter."

Sisco had never known if he could trust Skidmore, and he still wasn't sure. Now, he began to have doubts about Len. Did he really know Sutter after just a year? Len disappeared often during the day and slept somewhere besides the drugstore most nights. You could never know what he would do when he was drunk. What made him check Carlos in his private parts? Was the dance teacher an excuse for something else?

"Ain't that right?" Skiddy had asked Sisco a question that he hadn't even heard. "Sorry, Mr. Skidmore. I was just recallin' those windows at the primary that I never finished up last spring. What did ya ask me?"

Johnson jumped in. "Now, I find that mighty peculiar, son. Why would you be thinking about windows when we're discussing the principal and his May Day celebration?"

"I stayed over at the high with Mr. Ratcliff to work on the poles when I was s'posed to be washin' windows at the primary. I told Mr. Skidmore that I'd finish 'em up the next week and just plumb forgot."

Skiddy nodded his head and lit his first Camel in the Sorenson kitchen. The others had been smoking one right after another. Tre had perked up three pots of coffee, and the sun had cleared the windows on the eastern side. Johnson pulled out a fresh pack of Pall Malls and passed it around the table. He seemed to think that he finally had a lead for the F.B.I. and was in control.

"So, let me understand this correctly, Mr. Skidmore. Your boss, Leonard Sutter, took Sisco Griffin here off his regular assignment at the primary school to saw and paint May Day poles with Mr. Ratcliff's boys in the shop class at the high school?"

They all nodded their heads, but no one said anything. Skiddy shrugged his shoulders.

"Now, did either of you—Mr. Skidmore or Mr. Ratcliff—find that unusual? To change a janitor's duties for a whole week to work on a May Day celebration?"

Buck got up and walked over to the ice box. He took out the pitcher of cold water and poured himself a glass. "I've worked under Len Sutter for ten years. Things like this are normal for him, especially if he's sweet on some gal at one of the schools."

Johnson pushed back from the table. "Just how does that figure into the May Day celebration?"

"Because the gal he was sweet on then is the primary teacher who organized the maypole dance," explained Buck.

Johnson closed his eyes, crossed his arms over his chest, and bellowed like he was channeling the Lord himself. "So this guy who's the principal comes from an immigrant bunch, isn't married, plays around with dames, and maybe utilizes school personnel and time to promote Commie celebrations for innocent first and second grade children? Have I got it right, gentlemen?"

You could have heard a pin drop on Tre Sorenson's kitchen table. The men looked at each other and then at the G-man, who rocked back and forth on two legs of his chair.

Finally, El Venable spoke up. "Nobody ever said anything about Commie celebrations. We've been having a May Day picnic since the end of the war. The kids and their folks get a big kick out of the dancing and the good eats."

"So you folks don't know that May Day is an official holiday for Reds everywhere? I'm sure that Principal Sutter has known this all along."

"Now, look here, Johnson," said Buck. "Last year was the first time Len Sutter paid any mind to the May Day dance. I'm sure he doesn't give a damn about it one way or the other. Never showed any interest till he got a thing for the pretty first-grade teacher who needed more poles for her dances. She's one of our best school teachers—came to Hayden from Berkeley."

Johnson spilled coffee down the front of his sweaty white shirt as he tried to steady his chair. He looked ready to take off like one of those new rockets they were building to fight the Russians. "That settles it, gents. You have a big problem here, and it's a lot bigger than two dead farm boys. One of your 'best' teachers comes from the most subversive university in the country, and she's hooked up with a pinko principal. My! My! I guarantee you that the Bureau will be back to investigate further in this backwater."

197

Tre Sorenson had the last say. "We got no Commies in Hayden, but we got two of our own boys dead. If ya can't help us find the killer, then ya don't need to come back here for any other reason. I'll see ya to the door."

The other men had enough, too. Like it was a thing they had planned, they stood up to give the G-man his walking papers. Nobody shook his hand. They all waited to sit down until the front door slammed. When Tre came back to the kitchen, he brought an unopened bottle of whiskey with him. He was upset and angry as he perked another pot of coffee. Tears ran down his cheeks, and he turned away from the table so they wouldn't see.

Buck asked the question in everyone's mind as he opened the booze and poured a generous shot into each coffee cup. "What does being a pinko have to do with the murder of two innocent boys?"

On their way back to the high after the meeting at the Sorenson ranch, Skiddy and Sisco didn't talk much. Sisco wondered why the F.B.I. wanted to connect the deceased with a killer the Bureau believed to be a Commie who had called the G-man in the first place. He got no answer from the honorary deputy police chief of Hayden. That seemed like proof itself that Skidmore and Robert Harold Johnson had set things up with the others. Were they hoping to finger somebody in particular, or did they just want serious help from the government? Whatever they had intended, Sisco felt as if the hobos were off the hook and Len had taken their place.

§ § § §

With the 1950 school year underway, most of the townies had Korea on their minds. "Give 'em hell Harry" still called the situation there a police action, but Len said it was supported by the United Nations and paid for by the United

States. General MacArthur was in command of the troops, and everybody knew he meant business.

Len was more interested in the campaign of Helen Douglas. She was flying all over California in a "Helencopter" while Nixon drove up and down the state to make speeches from the top of his Woody station wagon. Len had campaigned all summer in Sacramento County and didn't seem to care that people accused Helen of being a Red. He hadn't made any headway on the farm worker cabins in Yolo because he was on the road campaigning for votes.

When Sisco saw Claire the first time after vacation, he felt the same familiar attraction to her. His head was mush, his arms and legs like electrical current, and his private straining in a silent salute. The teachers at the primary were in meetings until noon and then went to their classrooms to work after lunch. He had waxed the gymnasium floor at the high in the morning and told Skiddy that he planned to check on the primary teachers in the afternoon. Skidmore had been testing the bells at the high and nodded like he didn't care where his assistant went.

It was 100 degrees when he walked into Claire's classroom. He stood at the door to take in the sight of her. She was all tanned, her brown hair streaked with gold from the sun. She looked thinner in a yellow dress with straps that barely hid her brassiere. The tan covered her shoulders and stretched into the valley between her breasts. He imagined her naked with the sun above kissing her. He still wanted her—come hell or high water!

When she saw him at the door, she dropped the package of orange construction paper in her arms and started toward him. Then she stopped, like she thought better of it. Still, she called out, "Oh, Sisco, I'm so glad to see you! I was afraid you weren't coming back."

He walked to her, throwing his arms around her waist before she could back away. He held her close like he did on New Year's Eve, and her body shook with a chill that vibrated through her and into him. She seemed to tense up and heaved a huge breath before the tears came.

While keeping his arms around her, he backed away to see her face. "You are the only reason I'm here, Claire."

He kissed her gently on the lips and kept himself in check. At first, she hesitated; but then, she returned his kiss. It was warm and wet as his tongue slid past her teeth and into her mouth. She pulled away; they were both soaked in sweat.

"Sit down here with me, Sisco. Please!" she said, leading him by the hand to a chair next to her desk. "You look refreshed. Spent a lot of time by the river, I bet."

"Yeah," he answered, trying to think of something smart to say. "Days and nights by the river with the 'bos and the poles."

She sat down next to him and fidgeted with a pencil on her desk. "Away from everything, huh? Nothing to worry about. Wish I'd been able to do the same."

"Ya look mighty rested up," he mumbled because he couldn't come up with anything else and couldn't look her straight in the eye.

"I wish I had stayed here or maybe gone to Tahoe for a month. Nothing good happened in Berkeley."

"Sorry, Claire. Musta been pretty bad for ya to wanna be here and not at your home."

She choked up, but went on. "My best friend forever, Marjorie ... her father was fired from the university because he refused to sign the loyalty oath. He...he...he ... took his own life."

Covering her face with her hands, she broke down in tears.

Sisco pulled a clean handkerchief from his overalls and put it on her lap. He waited until she picked it up before saying, "One of my tramp buddies did the same. I wasn't there myself, but it bothered me plenty. Still does."

She wiped her eyes and blew her nose. "Thanks ... I'll launder your hankie. I got caught off guard today—thought I'd cried myself out this summer."

"There's always more tears. Ya cry 'cause ya need to let go."

"I didn't know how to comfort Marge. And my parents, who were good friends with her father, didn't even attend the funeral. That hurt me more than anything." She sniffled and wiped her eyes.

"I never met your folks, but they raised you, so they gotta be decent people. They musta had a reason ..."

"Oh, yes, they had a reason! They had the same reason everybody else had who stayed away. They were afraid that Hoover's G-men might be there and spot them, find out their names, and have them fired or arrested for being Communists." She shook her head like she still couldn't believe it.

"Was your friend's father a Communist? Is that why he didn't sign the paper?"

As soon as he asked her that question, he was sorry because she was ready to cry again. He wanted to hold her, wipe her tears away, and let his tongue find the warmth of her mouth one more time.

With effort, she answered, "The professor was a German Jew who hated the Nazis. The Communists in Europe opposed Hitler long before we did. They had no quarrel with the Jews. As a U.S. citizen, Marge's father felt that he should be able to sympathize with the Russians, out of gratitude you might say. It's supposed to be a free country. He never joined the party here or did anything disloyal to the United States."

Sisco still didn't understand why her folks hadn't gone to the funeral. He knew that her father worked construction and had nothing to do with the government. One thing didn't seem to connect to the other, just like earlier at the Sorenson meeting. He decided not to tell Claire that the F.B.I. had been investigating in Hayden. It was time to move on to another subject. "Ya seen Len?"

"Another bad thing about the summer. I called Len and asked him to go with me to the funeral. He got there late and had been drinking. The only seats left were in the back. I couldn't stop crying, so we left as soon as the service was over. He never even met Marge or her husband. I'm sure he expected me to invite him to my parents' home, but I couldn't take him there. They hate alcohol, and he probably would have tried to discuss politics with them."

Sisco felt like taking Len's side but held back. Sutter made the drive to Berkeley during the hottest days of summer to take her to the funeral of a guy he didn't know. She hadn't even invited him to her home for a meal or a cool drink of iced tea.

Instead, he said, "That ya respect your folks and their home is a good thing, Claire. Sooner or later, though, if ya love Len and hope to hitch up with him, ya gotta tell your family."

"That's just it. I don't know how I feel about him. Sometimes, I trust him. Other times, I don't. If we were married and there were an emergency with my parents, could I count on him to help and not embarrass me? I'm not sure of his loyalty. How could I be certain he'd be faithful if we were married?"

Her green eyes sparkled with tears that begged him to tell her something she wanted to hear.

He shook his head and said, "Hard to say how a fella might change if he was happily hitched. Gotta remember, Claire, it didn't work out for Len the first time, so who's to say the second time would be any better? One thing's for shore—nobody's gonna force Leonard Sutter into anything."

Terry A. Albritton

Loyalty

Len didn't show himself at the high school until Friday afternoon before the Labor Day weekend. Skidmore told the teachers that their principal had been held up by a family matter in Woodland. When he pulled into the parking lot about 3 o'clock, his automobile was dusty, and so was he. His white shirt was wrinkled and dirty, with the long sleeves rolled up to his elbows like he had been working with his hands. The tips of his fingers were more yellow than ever after so many Lucky Strikes. His teeth had started to color up, too, from the tobacco. As usual, his hair was slicked back and shining. After a summer of campaigning for Mrs. Douglas, his face was tan and sunburned near the hairline. He never wore hats because he said they got in his way and made him sweat more. The gut that he had in June was almost gone by September.

At quitting time that Friday, Len walked over to the homemaker room where Sisco had just finished a waxing of the floor. He burst through the door before he realized the wax was wet. He slipped and fell on his ass.

"Serves ya right, Mr. Sutter! Ain't ya s'posed to set a good example for the kids? No runnin' in the halls and all 'em rules ya got 'round here?"

Paying no attention to the fall, Len got up. "Glad to see you. Got a lot to tell you. I hope you're free next weekend to meet Mrs. Douglas in her Helencopter."

"Well, I'd like to meet her all right," Sisco answered and sat down at one of the homemaker tables. "Been hearin' her on the radio. Even saw somethin' on her in the *Hayden Herald* this week."

Sutter pulled out a pack of cigarettes but didn't light up. "I made sure the local rag covers her. The big newspapers like the *Tribune* and the *Los Angeles Times* haven't given her any coverage to speak of. Not even a picture, and she's such a looker. Wouldn't you think they'd at least show her face on the front page during a major election?"

"Well, it shore ain't a beauty contest 'cause she woulda already won. That fella Nixon looks like a mule. His picture's everywhere—even up north in the Dunsmuir rag."

"He's an ass all right, but he has very clever people working for him. So, what do you say, Sisco? Will you come with me to see Helen?"

At that moment, Skidmore showed up at the open door. He stopped, poked his head inside, said nothing, and walked on past.

Len went on talking like he hadn't seen a thing. "We'll drive down to Modesto early Saturday morning, grab some breakfast along the way, and meet her when she flies in."

Without waiting for an answer, he nodded, smiled, and left Sisco to finish his waxing.

During the first week of classes, there was a power outage at the high. Nothing turned on for a day and a half, so the bells and clocks didn't work. The lights didn't matter so much; but without the fans, things got hot inside. Len ordered the classes on the top floor to go outside on the grass where the janitors had set up chairs from the gymnasium. It was just as hot outside. As the sun moved, the kids moved. They thought it was a hoot to pick up the chairs every half hour to stay clear of the direct light. The closer they came to the building, the better chance they had to make faces or flash other signs to the students on the first floor who were still inside with all the windows open.

To make matters worse, one of the water pipes broke at the primary and flooded two classrooms. The youngsters saw dirty water shooting out of the pipes under the sink and began to shout, "Poo-poo, pee you, pee you!" Of course, the teachers had to take the children out of the flooded rooms and move them with their books and pencils to other classes. With no place to sit, they doubled up with the other kids in their small desks. Nobody could concentrate on lessons because of the blistering heat. The teachers finally gave up and took everybody outside for free play in the school yard.

Since Claire's classroom wasn't hit by the flood, Sisco didn't see her much that first week of school between running back and forth between the high and the primary. When Friday night came and he could get away from Skidmore, he made a beeline for the 241 Club and a draft of cold Schlitz. Len had beaten him there and was sitting at the bar with two brandy old fashioneds in front of him. He looked tuckered out. He had thrown his coat and necktie over a stool and rolled up the long sleeves of his white shirt.

"Sit down, my friend. Let me buy you a drink. After this past week, you deserve to tilt a few."

Sisco sat down on the next bar stool and ordered a beer. "Ya ever seen a first week of school like this past one?"

"Hell, yeah! Not the same kind of problems, but bigger ones on account of the war. In September of '44, we were in danger of losing our funding for the high because we didn't have enough students enrolled. With so many of our boys overseas, I had to search out the ones left at home in the tomatoes, the dairies, and the factories. Had to convince the boys to come in a few times every week to get assignments and return them finished to the teachers. Biggest problem was the parents who needed their younger sons at home to work the farms and ranches."

Sisco winked at him and said, "I heard it different when I first started to work here. Somebody told me that you went back and forth to the fields with homework assignments."

Len laughed as he downed the second brandy on the bar and ordered two more. "Bet it wasn't Skidmore who told you that. He thinks that when I'm not at the high, I'm making whoopee with a dame. He's right—sometimes. But, yes, I made more than a few trips back and forth to the fields, dairies, and ranches during the conflict. Tried to keep the parents off my back while making it possible for the kids to get their diplomas."

"You had to keep the high open, and ya needed your job, too, right?" asked Sisco, as he signaled to the Doc for a second draft.

"Right! Without my job, I could have been drafted, or I might have signed up on my own. I would have gone, but I figured I was more useful here. We didn't know which side would win. I reasoned that whether the Allies or the Axis prevailed, the country would need educated young men and women with critical thinking skills to prevent another war."

"So, what about the Commies, Len? Where do ya put 'em in all this?"

He took a long drag off his smoke and started on one of his speeches. "Communism, with an equal share for everyone, has great appeal to the working poor who get left behind in a system of capitalism like ours. The poor struggle to survive while they watch their bosses become wealthier. Franklin Roosevelt understood the need for everyone to have the essentials—food, shelter, a decent wage. His government programs saved this country from ruin. But, FDR also believed in democracy—freedom of thought, speech and the press. He put limits on Washington programs and encouraged the middle and poorer classes to be educated, creative, and empowered so that the government didn't control their lives. Communist governments, on the other hand, punish and repress individual initiative and private enterprise."

As usual, Sisco understood only part of Len's sermon, but he didn't ask more questions because the 241 had started to fill up and Sutter's voice got louder and louder. He knew that he shouldn't have mentioned politics at the bar, but the subject always seemed to come up anyway. It was time to make himself scarce and hit the hay before Saturday's trip to meet Mrs. Douglas.

§ § § § §

As soon as she had agreed to go with Len to the rally, Claire regretted her decision. She had no desire to meet Mrs. Douglas, who was everything she wanted to be and wasn't—a beautiful actress married to a handsome movie star, an elected Congresswoman admired by people in Washington, and a brave woman courageous enough to say her piece. Her enemies called her The Pink Lady because they thought she had Commie ideas. Claire didn't know what they were, but Len certainly believed in them, too. Wasn't he asking for trouble by speaking out for a candidate suspected of being a Red? Would he be asked to sign a loyalty oath like Marge's father? Maybe all the teachers in Hayden would be forced to sign if they wanted to keep their jobs.

Claire knew that she could not risk her employment by refusing to sign. Mother and Daddy would never forgive her, and her teaching career would be finished. How she wished she had even a little of Helen's courage; how much she wanted Len to respect her like he admired Helen Douglas. If she were honest with herself, Claire had to admit that she was jealous ... and afraid. It was probably a big mistake to go to the rally, but it was a way of showing her gratitude to Len after he went with her to the funeral. Still, she couldn't help her anger at him.

§ § § § §

209

Terry A. Albritton

For a change, Sutter's automobile was clean. The outside was shiny, and the inside decent after a quick cleaning with Clorox. Claire sat in front, her hair light and loose over her shoulders. She looked like Lauren Bacall with that hint of a smile teasing that she was ready to pull a caper on her leading man. She winked at Sisco when he climbed into the back seat.

"Soon as we find out where she'll land, we'll grab some breakfast," said Len as they pulled out of Hayden.

"Don't ya think it's kinda dangerous for her to be flyin' all over the state in a helicopter?" asked Sisco.

"She's way ahead of her time. That's why people like her."

Claire spoke up in an angry voice. "Is that why the Communists and other fools like her, too?"

No one said anything else for the next ten miles. They traveled south on Highway 99, passing vineyards on both sides. The grape pickers worked everywhere to get a jump on the hot September sun, and a musty, sweet smell filled the air and the inside of the Ford.

"See all those poor bastard farmworkers?" said Len in his preacher voice. "Helen's the one initiating and supporting legislation to help them and the small ranchers trying to hold out against agribusiness moving in all over the Central Valley. You know those farm kids, Claire. They're your students from families just trying to survive."

Sisco had begun to think it was a mistake to tag along to the rally. Len hadn't told him that Claire was going with them. She was sure pissed about something, and Len didn't seem to care. He was excited to meet his candidate. It wasn't a good start to the day, and things only got worse when they came into Stockton.

They found the Douglas headquarters for San Joaquin County on a side street. It was a plain office in a shabby building that needed painting. What it did have was a huge

210

front window where a giant poster of Helen Douglas smiled out at the traffic. If you didn't know, you would have thought she was an advertisement for one of those fancy hair lotions or a pearly toothpaste. If you could read, you saw the letters at the bottom—"Douglas for Senator." The front door was wide open.

Len went inside, leaving his passengers in the hot Ford. Claire didn't say a word to Sisco, who kept himself quiet. He figured that he'd been invited as the referee for another prizefight that had started days ago. He wanted to get out of the automobile and head back to Hayden but didn't see a decent way to do it. Through the door, he saw Len and another man staring at a map on the wall. They appeared to be the only ones in the office.

A few minutes, later Len came out and got back into the Ford. "This guy isn't even sure that she's flying in today. They won't let her land in Modesto—safety reasons. A likely excuse! The last he heard she has been cleared to land in Lodi about one o'clock. Piss-poor communication. If the rest of the state looks like San Joaquin County, Helen's campaign is in serious trouble. Let's find some breakfast."

They turned around and started north on Highway 99 the same way they had come. The day had heated up; they rolled down all the windows. Claire moved away from Len and pulled a pink and white bandana out of her purse. She covered up her hair, facing out to the east where a train snaked along the tracks. Like a giant black worm, it wiggled its way through the neat rows of grapevines. Atop the boxcars, traveling hobos headed to Roseville and beyond to pick up their next stake.

They pulled over at a Mexican café full of locals who had ordered coffee and eggs. Len pointed to a table in the back where a noisy ceiling fan didn't do much to cool things down or shoo off the flies. Sisco held out a chair for

Claire under the fan so she could feel a little breeze. Sutter said he'd get coffee and order for them at the counter. He liked to speak Mexican whenever he had the chance. The locals always understood him or pretended they did.

When he came back to the table, he was in good spirits with a cup of coffee and a smoke in his hand. "Yours is coming up," he announced. "The fella at the counter's perking up a fresh pot."

With things so stiff between them, Sisco wondered why he hadn't offered Claire the last of the old pot while he waited for some fresh brew. Over at the jukebox, Len dropped coins into the slot. Sisco excused himself and went to the counter to fetch the fresh coffee. It was black, strong, and smelled like the beans. He knew that Claire would need cream and sugar, so he made another trip after placing her cup on the table. He didn't tell her how many flies circled the sugar on the counter.

"Thank you!" she whispered to him. "You are a real gentleman. Your mother taught you how a lady should be treated. I find it hard to believe that Mrs. Sutter didn't teach her son more manners."

When the cook brought out three plates of eggs over easy with salsa smothering them, Sisco saw the next big problem staring at him from the runny yolks.

As Len dug into his breakfast, Claire raised her voice over the *ranchera* music that blasted from the jukebox. "What is this? Why did you order my eggs over easy? What is this red stuff all over everything?"

"Oh, come on, honey! It's the house specialty—*huevos rancheros*," he laughed and started to eat. "Delicious!"

She looked at Sisco, tears in her eyes, ready to break down right there in the café.

"Lemme see if this guy knows how to scramble 'em up," he said as he headed back to the counter.

By then, a pretty young Spanish girl came out from the back to help the cook with the orders. She had big, full knockers that peeked over a white drawstring blouse. Her dark eyes danced under long black lashes. Natural red lips invited a kiss, and Sisco wanted to take her right there on the spot. She smiled at him like she read his mind.

"I can help you, *señor*?"

"Yeah, ya can!" he answered and sat down at the counter. "My friend over there ordered the wrong thing for his … wife, and I'd like to get her something she likes. Can you make scrambled eggs and leave off the *salsa*? Please!"

"*Si, señor*, coming up right away, as you say! How kind you are to worry on the wife of your friend!"

They both laughed as she turned toward the kitchen. He watched her go with her long, thick black hair tied back and hanging almost to her skirt. Her waist was so tiny that he imagined he could circle her with his arms two or three times. He sure wanted to find out!

At the table again, he pulled up a chair next to Claire. With Len at the toilet, she was by herself. She looked straight at him and said, "She's awfully pretty, isn't she?"

He shrugged his shoulders to pretend that he hadn't noticed anything special about the Spanish girl. "She's OK, I reckon. Says the cook knows how to scramble eggs. Let's see if that's what ya get!"

By that time, Sisco's eggs were cold, but he finished them anyway. A hobo learns to eat anything—hot or cold—because he never knows when or where his next square meal will be.

When he came out of the toilet, Len detoured over to the jukebox and began to pump it with nickels. "Goodnight, Irene" played four times, with some *ranchera* music in between. He came back to the table just as the Spanish doll brought a big plate of scrambled headlights covered in *salsa*.

"*Gracias,*" Sisco said and winked at her.

"Yes, *gracias,*" echoed Len, who took her in his sights for the first time. "*Apreciamos servicio bueno.*" He laughed, expecting her to answer, but she just nodded and smiled at Sisco who wanted her more than ever because she hadn't fallen for Sutter's flirtation.

"I can't eat these either," sniffled Claire with tears in her eyes. "Why do they ruin perfectly good eggs with hot sauce?"

"Actually," answered Len in his principal's voice, "It's not very hot. They probably make it milder for us *gringos*. Technically, it's not hot sauce at all but *salsa*—a mixture of tomatoes, cilantro, green and red chili peppers."

By that time, Claire had had enough. With tears streaming down her cheeks, she pushed back from the table and hurried out of the café toward the Ford. She hadn't eaten a thing.

"Let her go," said Len. "She has no business on this trip anyway. I don't know why she agreed to come in the first place. She probably thought I'd make a pass at the candidate in a political rally. Too bad she doesn't care more about the issues and the danger of a guy like Nixon."

He had eaten Claire's eggs and spilled *salsa* on his white shirt, which was already wet with sweat. He took a paper napkin from the plastic holder on the table to clean it, making the spot darker.

Sisco kept his eye on the waitress, who stood behind the counter and watched him. When she saw the empty plates, she came over to the table to ask if they liked the eggs and wanted anything else. She winked at Sisco and blushed as Len placed a ten-spot on the table.

"My eggs was mighty tasty, and I'm lookin' to try some other things in the afternoon. Ya go on, Len. I'll hang 'round here for a while to see what else is on the menu."

Sisco had had his fill of World War III and didn't want to be cooped up in the back seat for even one more battle.

Sutter got his drift. "Take your time, my friend. I'll drive Claire back to Hayden. If I'm not running late, I'll come pick you up. You can take care of yourself, can't you?" he laughed.

When he was sure that Claire wouldn't rush back into the beanery, Sisco sat down at the far end of the counter. Things were pretty loud with the pound of trumpets and the twang of Spanish guitars while the wetbacks jabbered in their lingo. He ordered a beer and a shot of tequila with lime to get him in the mood for his afternoon meal.

Like every Spanish girl Sisco had ever known, the little beauty from the café was named Maria and had a love of tongue. She wanted deep, wet kisses in her mouth and lots of lapping in other places. She refused to give him head because she said it was *sucio* or dirty. Since they had to make do with a storage shed behind the beanery, he couldn't be as romantic as he had wanted. There was no place to bed down. After some gentle coaxing, he convinced Maria to stroke and hold his member while he fired it half a dozen times into a dark corner of the shed. It sure wasn't the best place to court a lady; but after a long dry spell, it did more than did the trick. Before leaving her, Sisco held Maria tight and promised to look her up real soon.

He hitched a ride back to Hayden and went to sleep on top of his bedroll in the jungle. It was too hot to go to McFadden's; and besides, he didn't want to tell Mrs. Mac where he'd been or about the blow up between Claire and Len. He woke with drops of rain on his face. Black clouds had moved in from the east. Lightning flashes zigzagged their way across the sky, an early fall thunderstorm moving west from the Sierra. As he folded his bedroll, lights approached the jungle. Len's Ford pulled in slowly behind

215

the oak trees on the access road next to the RICO Milk Plant.

"Thought you might be back here by now. Put your roll away, and climb in before you get wet."

It started to rain as Sisco stashed his personal belongings in a crate and got into the automobile. Big drops fell hard on the leaves and bounced off the metal body of the Ford.

Len handed the Kid a flask of hooch. "Might as well wait out the storm here," he said and cranked the window shut on his side. He still wore the white shirt from earlier but had rolled up the sleeves and ditched his necktie. His shoes were covered with dust.

After he lit up a smoke and took a swig of the hooch, Sisco said, "Sorry I missed Mrs. Douglas. I sorta got held up, and then held down, by a certain Spanish *señorita*."

"So, you finally got some, huh? That little waitress had her dark eyes on you the minute she caught you in her sights. What a set of knockers! Big as any melons I've ever seen!"

"Yeah! She was some dish—mighty tasty all the way from the soup and salad right down to the dessert!"

They laughed.

"You didn't miss much. Helen arrived late and landed next to the Lippi vineyards, where a few ranchers and some wetbacks had gathered. Hell, the Mexicans don't even know who she is, and they can't vote anyway! She gave a short speech, shook everybody's hand, and took off because of threatening weather. Like I told you this morning, the whole thing was piss-poor organized. Hell, that idiot at the Stockton headquarters didn't even show up!"

Hammered by the rain, the windshield fogged up; but Len didn't seem to notice as he threw down the whiskey, and whispered in a low voice like he was under a spell.

"She was so pretty with her hair flying in the air kicked up by the helicopter blades. Her skirt blew up over her face as she got out, but she didn't notice how the wetbacks laughed and made fun of the *gringa loca.* Imagine how those damn crooks will eat their words when she's elected senator."

"What's her chances?" asked Sisco, cranking down the window to get some air.

"Pretty decent, I think, if this Commie thing doesn't get out of hand. When Tricky Dick calls her the Pink Lady, she doesn't know how to respond. She's a fighter, but she's not a dirty one like he is."

"So, is she a Commie after all?"

"Come on! You're smarter than that. You and I favor the working class—whether laborers, domestics, or *braceros.* Are we Communists?"

Len was mad. He tossed his cigarette out of the window, where it sizzled for a second in the last of the drizzle. He sat up and fumbled in his pants for another smoke. Then he started off in his principal voice to preach one more lesson about the election.

"Helen represents the working stiff, as you fellas call him. She also has some support from the motion picture industry because of her husband and the Jews. Nixon is backed by the bosses--big land interests, oil and media barons. They have the money, so they have control of the press and the power brokers."

"In other words, Helen stands to lose."

"A lot can happen in the next eight weeks. I'd hate to think that the Douglas campaign is no more efficient in the rest of California than what we saw today in Stockton."

Sisco wanted to change the subject; this political mumbo jumbo would go on and on if he let it. Len never got tired of talking about the messes in Washington and Sacramento, and he repeated the same things over and over.

Sisco wanted to know about Claire. "Did she cheer up by the time you took her home?"

He answered right off the bat and clearly wanted to talk about her. "Claire is one unhappy lady. She wants me to be somebody I'm not. She loves the witty, well-spoken, extroverted parts of me. She loathes the reckless, brash, hard-drinking side, which is just as much who I am. I think our romance is over, if there was ever a romance in the first place."

"Then, what brought her back to Hayden this year? She coulda stayed in Berkeley to teach."

"I'm not sure," he said as he shifted in the seat and looked straight ahead like he saw something on the other side of the windshield. "Claire is dedicated, loyal, and even courageous. Although her parents refused to attend, she went to the funeral of her best friend's father, who hadn't signed the loyalty oath at the university. So, I think when she's committed to someone or something, she takes it to the end."

He thought for a moment and continued. "I never meant to hurt Claire when I recruited her to teach. She told me that she was engaged to be married and planned to stay here for a year to get experience. It all started with a call from her father when he found out I would be in Berkeley to interview recent Cal graduates. His people and some of the old Sutter clan go way back in this area, so he knew who I was."

He seemed to believe that he had done Claire's father a favor by hiring her. Sisco had a hard time with that idea since he knew Len was partial to smart, good-looking dames, especially if he could get them into bed without any promises.

Len appeared to read his mind. "Don't get me wrong. As soon as I met and talked with her, I wanted to lay her. I was still married but separated; she was engaged. There was a strong attraction, and I'd be lying to you if I said I didn't want her from the beginning. But she's also savvy enough not to jump into bed without a commitment."

Sisco had the last word for that moment when he said, "By now, I think she knows that ya don't wanna be tied down."

They sat quietly in the automobile until it got dark. It struck Sisco that Len collected people the way some folks collect model airplanes, trains, and dolls. He used any lure he could find to reel them in, then held on until they gave in, and finally mounted them like the trophy trout on the shelf or the wall. Claire belonged to his collection; so did he. Neither of them wanted to break free because they knew Len had a good heart. He just couldn't help the dark side of himself; and somehow, they felt obliged to protect him from that part.

They went back to Mrs. Mac's, each to his own room. Sutter was soon asleep while Sisco sat up in bed with a jug of wine. He hadn't had enough to drink for sleep to come. He kept thinking about the day—Maria and her knockers, Claire and her anger, Len and his easiness in every situation. The high school principal would have made a good hobo because he was smooth at jumping from place to place, person to person. In the morning, he had been jawboning with Mexicans at the beanery; in the afternoon, he had kept company with a beautiful candidate for the Senate; in the evening, he had shared his brandy and shot the shit with a tramp in the jungle. He could have run for office himself because the words rolled out of his mouth like sweet cream ready to be lapped up by anybody who would listen.

After their palaver in the Ford, Len and Sisco didn't see much of each other outside of work. Between Halloween and Thanksgiving, things grew tense. Sutter called everybody from the two schools to a big meeting in the gymnasium. When the janitors and the cafeteria cooks were told to attend, everybody knew it was some serious business. On a Friday in early November before the election, they all assembled to hear what their principal had to say.

"The Levering Act is now law in California. Every employee of state and local government is required to sign the loyalty oath. You probably know that there have been serious consequences for those who refuse to sign. Your decision is personal, and I will not tell you what to do. I do not believe that anyone here intends to overthrow the U.S. government, although we may disagree with some of its policies. On the other hand, I am certain that some of us stand by our right not to be forced into this by the Red baiters."

The teachers squirmed in their chairs and turned from side to side to look at each other. Claire caught Sisco's eye from where she sat at the end of a row. She frowned and shook her head back and forth. He smiled to reassure her that it would all be fine; but he couldn't convince himself, so he was sure that she didn't believe it either.

Len continued. "I will have the loyalty oath documents in my office. You need to know that the trustees will review the signatures when I turn them over. Personally, this is a sad day for me. As a firm believer in democracy, I never could have imagined that the state and federal governments would resort to a repressive measure like this one."

He looked down at the floor, ran his hand through his hair, and left the gym.

In a place where you could hear the lowest whisper or the quietest movement of a chair, there wasn't the slightest noise. Everyone seemed to wait for the next person to speak up, but nobody did until Skidmore said casually, "Come on, folks. Shake a leg so I can put away the chairs!"

As the rows emptied, he began to collapse the chairs, and his assistant followed. Somehow, it didn't seem right to make all that racket when everybody was serious enough to be in church.

Sisco noticed that Claire was standing alone by the back door. She seemed to be waiting for somebody, even though most of the other teachers had gone. He went to her and asked if she was okay. She answered in a low, throaty whisper that she knew Len wouldn't sign and he'd be fired.

Skiddy was headed in their direction. Sisco wanted her to stop talking, so he interrupted her loudly enough for his boss to hear, "Never mind, Claire. I'll stop by your house on my way back to Mrs. Mac's." She understood, nodded and left the gym.

Skidmore took out a smoke for himself, offered one to his assistant and pulled up two chairs. "Seems pretty bothered by all this, doesn't she?"

"Her best friend's father was fired from the Berkeley university for refusing to sign. Not long after, he did hisself in."

"Seems like that shouldn't be so bad if the guy was a Commie." He took two long drags on his smoke.

"That's just it—he wasn't. He was a Jew, grateful to be here and loyal to this country."

"Then, why didn't he sign?"

"Claire says that he felt like he shouldn't have to sign to keep his job if he wasn't a Red."

Skiddy rubbed his forehead, crossed his arms, and leaned back on two legs of the chair. "Far as I'm concerned, anybody who doesn't sign has something to hide. All of 'em should be fired and run outta town!"

"But what's to stop a real Commie from signin' the paper and then blowin' up the government?"

Skiddy came back down on all four legs, uncrossed his arms, and stood up. "A guy like that is suspicious for other reasons. Him and the other Commie perverts never go to church a day in their lives and are probably running from the vice squad and the G-men at the same time!"

When Skidmore started on the church thing, it was time for Sisco to make his exit. He got up and turned to the pushcarts loaded with chairs. As fast as he could, he wheeled them under the stage, saying that he needed to do something for Mrs. Mac before he dropped in on Claire. Skidmore ignored him and went to the back of the gym to turn off the lights.

§ § § § §

Claire had rushed home and headed straight for the new bottle of brandy. She opened it and mixed an old fashioned in a tall glass with extra liquor and cherry juice. When it was almost gone, she went to the bedroom, changed into her white, sequin-sparkled housecoat and sat down to study herself in the mirror. For a woman over thirty, she knew that she looked pretty good. Her brown hair was still sun-streaked, and no gray had popped up yet. Her face didn't show any wrinkles to speak of, though there were some chicken scratches around her eyes. Standing, she unzipped her robe and held it open to take in her body. Full and straight up, her breasts showed no lines or sag. A few days before she had measured her waist—still twenty-four inches. She thought about the Spanish girl at the restaurant and wondered about her waist measurement. It was obvious that Sisco had taken a shine to her even though he tried hard not to show it.

What if she ended up an old-maid school teacher like Miss Southern or Miss Bennett? Claire knew she was prettier than either of them, but her good looks wouldn't last forever. She wasn't meeting many eligible men these days, and Len had no intention of marrying her. Besides, he was going to be in big trouble before long, and she didn't want any part of that. She couldn't forgive him for putting himself in danger and causing her so much worry.

Then, there was Sisco—ever ready to listen to her and to offer comfort. She liked his firm body pressed against hers and his tongue in her mouth moving every which way. When they danced on New Year's Eve, she felt herself melting into that hard bulge in his pants. She'd held his penis and liked it. He never forced her to give him more than she could. He had what Marjorie called "the technique." There was a knock at the back door—Sisco. Claire zipped her housecoat and let him in. He had come straight from the high and hadn't changed his clothes or combed his curly, yellow hair.

"Came right over, Claire, 'cause ya looked mighty bothered after Len's speech."

"Relax, Sisco, and join me for a drink. The brandy's open, and I have a head start on you."

She put ice into a short glass and led him to the living room, where her tall old fashioned and the bottle were on the coffee table. She poured him some brandy and sat down on the opposite end of the couch. "You know he won't sign it, don't you, Sisco?"

He took a swig of his cocktail and swallowed slowly. "I think I can talk him into it if I have some time alone with him. He needs his job if he plans to finish what he started at his mother's ranch."

She chugged her brandy, leaving two cherries in the bottom of the glass. Pouring herself more, she moved closer to him. "I don't know. He's not a Communist, but he is stubborn. He believes in his right not to sign, like Marjorie's father did. It's just stupid!"

Sisco lit up two Camels from the pack on the table. After handing one to her, he slid to the other end of the couch. "I promise that I'll talk to him, but ya should, too. He respects ya a lot, Claire."

223

"Not like he does Mrs. Douglas! And he doesn't love me, does he? Tell me the truth, please!"

"The straightest answer I can give is that he has never said he does, but he has never said that he doesn't, either."

Sisco didn't like the way things were going. Claire's eyes filled up with tears as she poured herself more brandy and moved close to him. The zipper on her housecoat made its way down between her breasts; his pecker took notice. The more she drank, the more she talked about Len and how scared she was for him. Sisco thought about Maria and wished he had gone to see her after the meeting. He took a deep drag on his smoke and listened to Claire, who continued on and on about the Communists, her friend Marjorie, and her parents. Finally, she finished her drink, sat straight up on the couch and looked at him with a soft, pleading sigh. "I'm ready," she whispered.

"Ready? For what?" he asked, thinking she wanted him to mix her the next drink.

"I'm ready to sleep with you."

He looked at her but could not speak. He knew what she had said, and he couldn't come up with any answer. She was plenty drunk, and it would be easy to take her now. He could never forgive himself if he had his way with her when she was so far gone.

"That is, if you want me, Sisco?"

His voice cracked as he said gently, "There is nothing I want more, but not now when you're angry and upset. With all my heart, I want the time to come 'cause I love ya very much!"

At that moment, the front door opened, and Len walked in. He had been drinking, but he wasn't as drunk as Claire was.

"What's this? My special lady crying?" He sat down next to her on the couch and pulled up the zipper of her housecoat.

"Leave me alone, Len! You show up here when you're loaded and expect to kiss and fondle me because none of your whores are available. If you and I ever had anything, it's finished!"

He put his arm around her, but she moved away. He looked at Sisco for an answer.

"This all started 'cause Claire and I both are afraid that ya won't sign the loyalty oath and the trustees'll get rid of ya."

"What makes you two think that I won't sign?" he asked as he offered Claire his soiled handkerchief.

"Because we know how stubborn you are," she cried, pushing his hand back and wiping her tears on the sleeve of her housecoat.

"You mean I have ethics and believe in democracy—unlike most people?"

"Don't be stupid, Len! You are not a Communist, but you help their cause by not signing."

"And whose cause do I help if I sign? Joe McCarthy and the right wing fools who have us snitching on our family, friends, and neighbors!"

"Never mind, then! Just refuse!" she shouted. "Deprive all those kids of their principal. Just do it! I'll throw you a going-away party!"

Claire was angry and upset in a way that Sisco had never seen. It made him angry at Len, too. As usual, Leonard Sutter had stirred the stew and riled up people who cared the most about him.

"I'm headed back to McFadden's," said Sisco and walked to the door.

Len followed him outside onto the front steps. "Just so you know, I haven't decided yet if I'll sign."

Terry A. Albritton

New Year's Eve

In 1950, the Yanks took the Series again, which didn't surprise anyone. Mrs. Douglas lost the election, which did surprise some folks. By how much she lost shocked even Len, who always said the campaign was managed badly and that the big-shot Democrats like Truman had abandoned her because they were afraid of the Commie thing and had their hands full in Korea. When all the votes were counted, she won only five counties out of fifty-eight. She lost Yolo and Sacramento, where Len had worked hard to get her elected. He was disappointed and didn't talk much about his candidate after her defeat. Sisco and Claire decided that his feelings were hurt because she hadn't paid more attention to him during the campaign.

Winter came to the valley with a fury in the middle of November. The rains were heavy, and the fields flooded everywhere. The governor declared a state of emergency for Sacramento, San Joaquin, and three other counties after nine days of rain. In Hayden, the trustees canceled school for the whole week at Thanksgiving because the guys from the high had to help with sandbags at the rivers. Sisco did his turn. Len, too, was at the Cosumnes, which had risen to flood levels. He didn't stay long, though, because his mother needed him on her ranch. Claire left town for Berkeley to spend the holiday with her folks.

Sisco was at the river for a day and a half before Mrs. Mac asked him to help her at the drugstore. She had invited some kinfolk from Thornton to come for a big Thanksgiving spread. Their house had flooded, and they were bedded down at the primary school there with other families who had to leave their places because of high water on the Mokelumne. Mr. Mac planned to fetch them in his pickup on Thanksgiving morning if there was a break in the weather and he could get through on the road.

Sisco hoped that one of the hobos would show up for turkey and pumpkin pie. Sure enough, on the day before Thanksgiving, Memphis Shorty came rolling in. He needed a good shear and shave to be decent for the feast. Jonah Sturgeon offered to take care of things for holiday rates, so they met him in the alley before breakfast the next day. Jonah had a pair of scissors and a comb wrapped in red and green tissue paper.

"Saved these here tools from last year when you was here. Didn't want to use 'em on anybody else—could be bad for business, ya know." He smiled and winked at them.

As the barber went to work on Shorty, Sisco passed around a flask of redeye that he had kept upstairs. It had stopped raining, but it was so cold that they could see their breath.

"Time to get a break from this weather," he said as he lit up a smoke for Shorty who shivered under the drape over his shoulders.

"Damn straight on that," said the barber while he chopped away. "I hear they can't even come down from Sacramento with Dillard Road flooded. Had to put off the F.B.I. 'cause the fella couldn't get here."

"It's pretty bad," said Sisco, "when ya can't drive twenty-five miles south of the state capitol. Say, what's the G-man comin' here for, anyway?" He tried to sound casual.

"Beats me," Jonah answered, as he stopped shearing to take a swig of the redeye. "Could have to do with the loyalty paper, I guess. I hear they want to talk to Len. You signed it, didn't ya?"

Sisco swallowed hard. "Sure did. Never thought twice on it. Just a piece of paper, ain't it? Lots of school people signed just to keep the government off their backs."

Shorty smiled. He didn't know about the loyalty oath; but, like most of the older hobos, he was patriotic and would have gone to fight if he'd been younger when the war came on. Same as Skidmore, he wouldn't understand why a fella would refuse to sign if he had nothing to hide.

Jonah finished the job and asked the guys if they'd be around to help Myrtle McFadden with the big feast. Sisco nodded and handed the barber a ten spot. Shorty added some green, too, as they took their leave and hightailed it upstairs for a bath. Sisco insisted on washing up first, because he didn't want to inherit any critters from Memphis. Those speedy crawlers can survive soap and water, going to their next life in somebody else's hairy parts.

Like all her holiday shindigs, Mrs. Mac's Thanksgiving was full of food and booze. Besides four turkeys and three hams, she roasted two ducks that her kin had sent over from Thornton. The birds had gone underwater when the Mokulemne crested so fast that they couldn't get out of their pens to swim away. Shorty and Sisco ate more duck than any of the other guests; it tasted juicy and thick with dark meat and fat. They had it pretty much to themselves because nobody else wanted to eat what had once been pets on the Thornton ranch.

After finishing with the pumpkin, apple, and pecan pies, the guests sat around the tables to drink brandy. Mr. Mac talked about how dangerous it was when both rivers crested at the same time. He said that the levees could take only so much. Sisco tried to listen and follow the conversation, but he was itching to get away and go to Maria. Shorty was happy to hear about his new romantic interest and offered to handle the clean-up with Mrs. Mac. He had been in the kitchen with her all morning, chopping celery, onions, walnuts, and the innards for her stuffing, a job she didn't like. By the time dinner was ready, they were fast friends.

Sisco excused himself from the menfolk and went over to where the ladies discussed rising food prices. He whispered in Mrs. Mac's ear that he had an errand to run in Lodi and that he'd be back in a couple of hours. She gave him the keys to her pickup so he wouldn't have to hitch a ride.

Before leaving, he pulled Shorty aside to whisper, "If ya wanna take a nap upstairs, use my bed. Just don't leave any four-legged visitors in the sheets!"

"Hell!" joked his pal. "You'll be so tuckered out when ya get back, ya ain't gonna know what else is in bed with ya!"

As he pulled up to the beanery, Sisco was surprised to hear so much hooting and hollering inside. Since Mexicans don't celebrate Thanksgiving in their country, he figured things would be pretty quiet. Of course, none of the men had to work when all of their bosses were on a turkey holiday. So they were having a fine time with shots of *tequila* and beer. Maria was plenty busy behind the counter. She wore the same white blouse with a low neck and puffed-up sleeves. Her hair was pulled back to show off her coal black eyes and smooth brown skin. She didn't see him until he sat down at the counter. When she caught sight of him, she threw her head back, laughed, and hurried over to take him a draft of some beer from Old Mexico.

"Thees one is in the house!" she smiled. "The next one is in the closet! But you have to wait a while, Seesco. I not leave till Elena come at 4 o'clock." She winked and shook her shoulders.

Sisco wanted to tell her that it was already past 5 o'clock, and Elena might not show up because it was a holiday. But Maria's firm, full breasts stood at attention in front of him while he gave his own secret salute under the counter. He wouldn't be going anywhere soon.

"Oh, I plan to stick around," he said and threw out a five spot. "Just keep the *cerveza* comin', and add in some *tequila* while you're at it."

The fellow next to him heard their conversation and grinned from ear to ear. If he didn't understand what was going on, he sure enjoyed it all anyhow. That's the thing. Them Mexicans always act like they know what you're saying even if they have no idea. This guy aimed to please, so Sisco ordered up a round for him and tried to be sociable while he waited.

It was dark when Elena reported for her shift. Maria took off her apron and signaled him to the back door. Outside, the air was chilled, but the rain had held off. Maria covered her shoulders with a blue and white *rebozo,* which didn't block out the cold. He offered her his heavy jacket with wool lining, but she would not take it. She didn't want to go to the storeroom out back, so Sisco guided her to the front seat of Mrs. Mac's pickup.

She told him that she was from a state named Morelos in Old Mexico. She was the oldest of ten. Her father worked a small farm, and her mother took care of the kids with Maria's help until last year. When the smallest brother turned six and went to school, her folks decided that their oldest should come to California to pick up a stake at her uncle's café. She sent all of her wages and most of the tips back to the family.

As they talked, Maria shivered and moved next to him on the seat. He took off his jacket to cover her shoulders and pushed his body close to hers. Heat was what she needed, and she soon had it from two bodies. At first, everything was slow and gentle; but when she warmed up, Maria was like a wild steer. He rode and tamed her until they both were sweating on that leather seat. When he felt her go limp, he wiped her forehead and her eyes with his handkerchief.

"Did I hurt ya, honey?"

"Oh, no, Seesco! You were *increible!*"

231

He kissed her. "If we had a better place, we could do it again ... and again. But it's late and cold now."

He helped her put on his jacket, and she slid off the front seat behind him. The parking area was empty, and the light on the café sign was off. One small bulb was lit over the back door, which was unlocked. They stepped inside, and Maria took off his jacket. They kissed again, and she wished him *"buenas noches"* as he left.

Between Thanksgiving and the end of December, Sisco spent every weekend and some weekdays with his Mexican sweetheart. Sometimes, he just sat at the counter and watched as she waited on customers. She moved like she wore roller skates. He loved to see her carry five full plates of food and serve them where they belonged. She never dropped or spilled a thing. She had a smile for everyone—and sometimes, a kiss for an old guy who could have been her grandfather. Of course, she gave Sisco his fair share of pecks on the cheek as she walked back and forth from the kitchen.

He always sat at the end of the counter, and it didn't take long for the regulars to catch on that he was Maria's special guy. If she wanted to hide it, she didn't do a very good job as she sneaked over to the last stool to give him special attention. He tried to space his drinks so he wouldn't make a fool of himself. But the closer they came to Christmas, the longer her shift was and the more drafts the home guard bought. Sometimes, he was so drunk by the end of the night that he passed out on the floor in the back of the storeroom. He'd wake up early the next morning with two heavy blankets over him. He'd get up and hitch a ride back to Hayden before Maria or her uncle were in the kitchen.

On the Sunday before Christmas, Sisco arrived back at Mrs. Mac's at sunup. Len was on the sidewalk making a half-assed effort to clean the windows of his Ford. He hardly ever washed the whole automobile; he just dusted off the windshield enough to see the road. That day, he wore a long, black wool coat. It looked new and way too clean to be his.

"Fancy coat ya got on. Get some warmth from it, I bet," Sisco said, offering Len a smoke.

"Claire's Christmas present—a year ago. Probably the last gift she'll ever give me. Don't wear it very often. It hinders me too much."

"You headed to Woodland for the holiday?" asked Sisco who had decided to change the subject.

"Yeah," answered Len as he struggled with a mud clod stuck to a side window.

"Lemme help ya out there. I'll be right back with some rags and a bottle of window cleaner." He ran inside, grabbed his stash of cloth scraps and a half-full bottle of Windex. When he came back outside, Len was seated on the curb smoking a Lucky and looking west beyond the railroad tracks. His coat fell loose beside him on the dirty sidewalk. Sisco circled the Ford and cleaned each window. As he came to the last one on the passenger side, Len seemed to notice what he was doing for the first time.

"Hey, thanks, for the window job. Lots of rain and mud. By the time I come back from Woodland, you'll have to do this all over again."

"Something on your mind? Ya seem kinda troubled this morning."

"Yeah, as a matter of fact, there is. Can't figure why the F.B.I. is taking a second look at Carlos when they had ruled him as a death by drowning." He mashed out his Lucky on the sidewalk and fired up the next one.

Sisco's stomach jumped; his tongue felt trapped behind his teeth. He stuttered, "Ya ... ya think they're onto us? We didn't do anything wrong. Just gave a friend a decent burial."

Sutter sounded pissed. "I know what our part was. I have always believed you and the others. Nothing would have ever come of this if there weren't two more suspicious deaths. Now, Skidmore is in the picture. So far he has protected you, but he can't be trusted under these circumstances. With whispers of a pervert, he may involve you and your pals. His good Christian conscience may be feeling guilty about not reporting the body. Believe me, if it makes him look good and fingers you—or me, for that matter—he will be a real SOB."

Sisco got up and began to pace on the sidewalk. His head was spinning because he saw Len worried for the first time since they met. "I'm not even shore that he knows it was me in the secrets box that morning. He's never said a thing."

Len stood and turned toward him, real anger in his voice now. "That does not, I repeat, does not, mean that he doesn't know. He likes to keep dirt on everyone and to use it to his own advantage. He's got stuff on me that I can't even remember—half of it made up. He runs to the trustees with every little indiscretion on my part. Whether you realize it or not, he has shit on you, and he won't hesitate to use it when it suits his purpose.

"Biggest mistake I ever made was to suggest an honorary title for him. The town fathers bought it hook, line and sinker. I thought it would keep him off my back, but a little authority went to his head."

It was no news that the head janitor had dirt on everybody. When he was first hired, Sisco overheard him shooting the shit with one of the school bus drivers about a lady teacher who had been let go the week before school started. Skidmore discovered that she was banging boys from the high during summer vacation. He called for a meeting with the trustees and the principal. Len said that what folks did out of school on their own time was their own business. Skiddy kept up pressuring the board members to fire her before classes started so there wouldn't be a big scandal. They went along with him and decided it was best to let her go to preserve the reputation of the high and to protect young boys who didn't know better.

As they talked at the curb, the morning warmed up, but Sisco still shivered after a long night at the beanery. He told Len that he needed some shut-eye, wished him a merry Christmas and headed for the stairs.

Sutter nodded and shouted, "Happy whoopee holiday" as he got into the Ford and headed to Woodland.

Even after a hot bath, Sisco couldn't fall asleep. He kept thinking about Skidmore and wondering how he had so much shit on the folks in Hayden. No one seemed to like him; his only friends were a few of the trustees and the priest. Just then the bells at the Catholic church went off; the 11 o'clock Mass would get underway in fifteen minutes. He gave up on any shut-eye and put on some clean clothes to walk over to the tracks.

Skiddy was at the back of the church talking with Father Martinez. He spotted his helper and waved him over to where they were standing. "Morning, son," he greeted, clapping him on the shoulder. "Ya remember our priest, don't ya?"

"Shore do," said Sisco as he reached out to shake the priest's hand. "I don't wanna bust up your talk."

Father Martinez stared at him through thick glasses that made his eyes look huge. "No need to worry, my son. I'm going inside now anyway. Are you here to attend Mass?"

"Oh, no! I'm not … one of ya Catholics," he stuttered. "But I might wanna find out what it takes to get hitched with a Catholic gal."

"I knew ya was up to something," laughed Skiddy. "I just didn't know what!"

235

The priest took Sisco's hand in his and said, "First, you need to become ... be baptized ... a Catholic, my son. I am able to instruct you in the catechism if you attend classes with me. Then, you and your intended have to come to more classes. Is there an immediate urgency? Is your betrothed in a family way?"

Sisco felt a red flush rushing up his neck and onto his face. "Not that I know of, Father," he answered and nodded to Skiddy, who was all ears.

"Why don't you start catechism classes on the first Wednesday after New Year's? We can talk more then. Please excuse me now," said the priest as he walked up the back steps into the church.

The bells at the Catholic church joined in with the chimes at the other three churches, and the noise made it hard to go on talking with Skidmore, which was just as well because Sisco didn't want to give him any more information about Maria. Skiddy was well-connected in Lodi and already could have some dirt on her uncle. Besides, he didn't really want to get married. Or did he?

Waving a merry Christmas to his boss, he walked onto Third Street, where all the congregations were coming and going. He saw Mrs. Mac leave the Episcopal church. She looked surprised to see him coming out of the Catholic church since he had told her that he was raised Methodist. She rushed up to him, but they couldn't hear each other because of the bells. He figured out that she wanted help later on with Christmas decorations at the drugstore. He told her that he'd be glad to give her a hand.

He wondered how long it would take Mrs. Mac to hear that he was looking into marriage with a Catholic gal. That kind of news would spread fast even though he was nobody. He had to tell her something before she heard it from one of the townies. She deserved to know what he had discussed with the priest. He was confused; he couldn't say that he didn't want to marry Maria because he was fond of her in a way that gave him ideas about settling down.

After a couple of hours hanging Christmas balls on the tree, he was ready for a break and some of Mrs. Mac's hot apple cider. She had brewed it up especially for him because he had made such a fuss over it last Christmas. What he liked in her concoction was that she left it more sour than sweet, so the taste of the apples came through real nice. He had a flask of brandy behind the counter to add a little extra kick.

"Ya shore looked nice this morning for church," he said as he sat down on his regular stool. "Mr. Mac oughta see ya dressed up more often."

She stopped stringing popcorn, took off her glasses, and looked at him real serious. "You know that he doesn't fancy me anymore no matter what I wear. Don't feel bad for me because I'm used to it. He's got his life, and I've got mine. As long as he brings me provisions for the store, I let him go his own way. We have a mutual understanding about things."

Feeling kind of uneasy, Sisco gulped down his cider and said, "You're a fine-lookin' woman when ya get all gussied up. Ya still have a waist, and your legs look real good in high heels."

She smiled and put on her glims. "Think careful about the gal you marry. There are always signs of trouble before you tie the knot."

He saw his chance. "I hear ya, Mrs. Mac. I'm lookin' into what it takes to marry a Catholic. Haven't asked her yet, but already it seems like a lot of trouble if ya ain't shore."

She went on talking while she needled through the popcorn. "You're a real good catch for somebody, honey. I'd like to see ya settle down here, but you already know the world is much bigger than Hayden. Think twice before you go into farming or ranching. This way of life will change a great deal in the next twenty years."

He turned things back on her. "Ya oughta find yourself a man, Mrs. Mac. Remember the old saying 'bout what's good for the goose and the gander."

She laughed and blushed. "I've given it some thought," she said. "Not too many opportunities. But if a decent, hardworking man without responsibilities came along, I might consider."

Sisco thought about how dolled-up she had been at Thanksgiving when Shorty was helping her. Ole Memphis stayed put for the long weekend. He and Mrs. Mac had cooked turkey pot pies with leftovers. Shorty said they were just mulligan spooned into a pie crust and baked in the oven. They had talked and laughed a lot when they were together in the kitchen or at the soda fountain. They appeared to be about the same age.

None of the hobos made it into town for Christmas dinner, which was just as well since Sisco passed the day with Maria at the beanery. They ate beef, pork, chicken, and cheese tamales while they drank a fruity thing with a crazy name that he couldn't say. It had bits and pieces of orange, pineapple, and strange stuff that floated around in a big kettle on the stove. He didn't much care for it until he added brandy from his flask. He did like the company of the local Mexicans because they treated him decently, bought him *cerveza* and *tequila*, and tried to practice English with him. He had picked up quite a few Spanish words and figured he could do okay in Old Mexico if he ever decided to go there. It had crossed his mind to try to find Carlos' folks because they sure didn't know what had become of him.

When New Year's rolled around, he was looking forward to a day at the café and a night of firecrackers with Maria. He spent most of the week between the holidays helping Mrs. Mac with her inventory at the drugstore. He was tired of all the talk about the war from the customers. More men and boys had been called up for Korea because the Commies from China came into the fight. He tried hard not to think about the draft but figured the townies had to be wondering why he hadn't signed up. Sisco knew that his 4F from the other war would have kept him out of the infantry, but he felt sure the Army could have found a job for him if he looked up the recruiter.

Then, his world blew up. He borrowed Mrs. Mac's pickup to go to the café for the New Year's party. He packed blankets and pillows into the bed of the truck with the idea of watching the stars and snuggling up with Maria for the night. But when he walked into the beanery in the late afternoon, he sensed that something was wrong. Everybody stopped talking and stared at him with blank eyes. As he looked around for Maria, he saw that her uncle was tending to the customers at the tables where she should have been. He came up to Sisco with tears in his eyes.

"*Mi hijo,* I am so sorry. Maria go back to Mexico early this morning. My sister—her mother—killed in a *horible accidente* yesterday."

"She will be back, won't she?" he choked.

"I not think so, *hijo,* not for a long time. She have to care for her brothers. Who else do it?"

Sisco mumbled something about how sorry he was for the loss of his sister. He didn't think to ask what kind of accident had killed her or if Maria had left any message for him. He walked out of the café into the chilly night and drove back to Hayden like he was under a witch's spell.

Inside the drugstore, Mrs. Mac was doing her best to get rid of the Gadsten twins. Sisco had never known their first names because Len always called them Tweedledee and Tweedledum. They both were a little daft in their heads and hung out most days on the sidewalk in front of the drugstore. Here they were on New Year's Eve hopped up about a dogfight between American and MIG fighter planes over the Yalu River in Korea. Nodding to them, he handed Mrs. Mac her keys. She looked surprised. He waved to her and said that he would explain later.

The night air was clear and cold. The rain had stopped during the week, and the stars sparkled like polished diamonds. He wished that one of the 'bos had been in town, so they could go to the jungle, shoot the shit and get drunk. He lit a smoke and walked down Fourth Street. At the corner, he looked right to see if there might be a fire across the tracks. Nothing. Then he looked left toward Claire's house. Her Chevy was parked in the front; she had come back early from Berkeley. She hadn't planned to spend New Year's in Hayden, and Len hadn't asked her to do so.

Sisco half expected Sutter to be there, but no Ford was parked in the alley. At the back door, he knocked like always and called out so she would know who it was. She opened the door wearing the white sequined robe. Her hair was piled on her head like she'd just had a bath. Waving him inside, she stepped into the bright of the kitchen. She had been crying. He closed the door and locked it behind him. He threw his arms around her and kissed her on the cheek. She smelled of jasmine, and he felt her nipples harden under her robe. His knees wobbled, and his hands shook. He told her that he had to sit down on the couch.

She followed and sat down next to him. "You look like you've seen a ghost. What's the matter? Let me bring you a cocktail."

She brought a bottle of brandy and two glasses. Without a word between them, they finished the first drink. As the liquor warmed him up, Sisco began to talk about Maria. Once he started, he couldn't stop until he saw that his third glass hadn't been touched and Claire had already downed hers.

"I am so very sorry, Sisco. Maybe she'll come back after things settle down with her family."

"She won't come back. She'll do the right thing and take care of her brothers and sisters, just like you'd do if your folks needed ya."

She lit two cigarettes, passing one to him from her mouth. It tasted like her, and his body shivered. He felt worn out and waited for her to say something.

"I don't want to stay with my parents anymore," she muttered while puffing on her cigarette to keep back the tears. "They want to control my life. I am thirty-one-years old, educated, and perfectly capable of making my own decisions."

Relieved to be talking about her, he answered, "It's all 'cause they love ya, Claire. They wanna see ya happy." He wondered if she knew that her father had arranged the job in Hayden but decided not to ask. Knowing that wouldn't make her feel any better.

"I just couldn't be with them in Berkeley tonight on New Year's, trying to act happy and being miserable without even a champagne toast. But I am glad to see you, Sisco. Do you remember our dance from last year?" She finished her brandy and loosened her hair so that it fell to her shoulders.

His tongue was all tied up as he watched her go to the record player. She put on Patti Page singing "The Tennessee Waltz." He went to lock the front door and turn off the overhead light. "Ya know that I will always remember last New Year's, Claire. And ya know where things will go this time … if ya want that."

He took her slowly. From the beginning, she hung onto him with both hands—a tight grip on his arms and back as if she were afraid of falling off a cliff. She was nervous, and at first, she trembled at his touch. He wanted to tell her how many different ways there are to make love but

241

stopped himself and whispered softly in her ear so that she would not be afraid. He kept things slow and easy so that her passion could rise through her hesitation. He did not want to frighten her with his hardness, because it was new and strange to her. He ran his tongue in her mouth, where she had felt him before. When she relaxed enough to let him inside her, he pushed and pulled gently until he knew she was ready. Her nervousness changed to sighs of joy. She gasped for air, and he let himself run wild so they could reach the peak together. She cried softly with pleasure; he took himself out and kissed her all over. He wanted to go again but thought better of it since this was her first time.

"Ya okay, Claire? I didn't hurt ya, did I?"

She wept but managed to answer, "No, Sisco, no. Such tenderness. Thank you."

He excused himself to the toilet so he could come a second time and she could cover up. When he came out, she had torn the sheets off the bed and stood waiting in her robe with a douche bag in hand; she had been ready for this night. He offered to make up the bed with clean linen while she went into the bathroom. Then, the phone rang in the hall. He hurried to answer it just in case it was Claire's mother.

"Sisco, you're there! Happy New Year!" Len's voice sounded clear and strong.

"Happy New Year!" Sisco chimed. "Saw Claire's Chevy out front and stopped by. She's in the toilet. I'll call her."

"No, no, never mind! Just checking up on her. Tried to reach her in Berkeley. Her mother said she had gone back to the valley. You two been drinking? Wish I were there with you for a toast to 1951."

"Oh, yeah!" he said and noticed the nearly empty bottle of brandy on the table. "We've already toasted a few.

I hope that Claire's not sick. She's been in there a long time."

"You know she can't hold her liquor. Let her throw up, and put her to bed. I'll be back in town tomorrow morning."

Sisco promised to tell Claire about the call, and they hung up. He wondered where Len was and why he hadn't asked about Maria since he knew they had plans for New Year's. But Len only half listened if the conversation had nothing to do with him. The call to Claire showed something: either he felt guilty or he still cared for her. He never lost a chance to score with a lady and probably had at least one easy lay lined up for the evening.

What happened that New Year's Eve seemed to Sisco like a fairy tale, one of those experiences that he would hang onto forever because he knew that nothing would ever match it. She didn't love him in the same way he loved her, but he was certain now that she trusted him enough to let go of her fear and guilt for even a few minutes. No one else needed to know what they had shared because it was one of those things that people wouldn't understand anyway. He tucked her into bed with a long kiss and left through the back door into a clear night as a rush of firecrackers lifted off to the heavens before falling back to earth.

Terry A. Albritton

Snitch

On the first day of 1951, Sisco woke up with a start. A man's voice boomed up the stairs and under the door to his room. Shaking off sleep, he went to the window. A long, black Lincoln was parked parallel to the sidewalk, taking up three full spaces—from out of town and most likely a G-man. From below in the drugstore Mrs. Mac's voice jumped up and down like it did when she was excited or nervous.

Although he wanted to sneak out the back, he couldn't leave her in the lurch. He threw on a shirt and went downstairs to the soda fountain. Mrs. Mac had her back to him while she chattered and brewed up a pot of coffee. Her hair had not been brushed, and she wore a house-coat and slippers. The G-man sat sideways on a stool with his hat on the counter. He watched her and then caught sight of Sisco as he came in from the stairs.

Mrs. Mac turned around. "Oh, I'm so glad you're up." Her voice pleaded as she said, "This nice young man has questions I can't answer. Maybe you can help him so I can make some breakfast."

Sisco took his usual seat at the end of the counter. The G-man sat two stools down. They looked at each other and knew they had met before.

"You're the hobo turned janitor, aren't you?" the G-man asked as he swiveled back and forth on the stool. "Two guys who live around here reported that you and some other tramps took off with a body in the back seat of a Ford about a year and half ago. Care to explain?"

Sisco coughed, and Mrs. Mac set a glass of water on the counter.

After a big gulp, he managed to say, "Yeah. One of the guys who rode with us for a spell—a young Spic kid—died. We waited till morning to bury him."

245

With a cold, blue-eyed stare, the G-man eyeballed the janitor's helper. He took a drag on his smoke and let the ashes fall to the floor as Mrs. Mac brought out an ashtray. He rested his cigarette on a corner. "Why didn't you report this dead wetback to the local authorities? You, or somebody, was required to do that."

Sisco put cream and sugar in his coffee even though he took it black. He needed something to do while he thought about an answer. "Look here, Mister. Carlos was just a kid up from Old Mexico to get a stake to send back to his folks over there. Didn't speak our lingo. Never even told us his last name. We didn't know how to get word to his kin or what to tell the law. What was we s'posed to do—lay his body on the rails where he had likely been killed?"

The G-man poured cream from the pitcher into his coffee until it overflowed. Mrs. Mac rushed to clean up the spill. He never said a word to her but turned to Sisco again after he took a long, noisy slurp from the brown, milky stuff that looked like shit. "Do you have some identification, fella? We will need to stay in touch with you."

"Just my birth certificate upstairs."

"You had better grab it *pronto*! We need to know who the guys were that buried the Spic's body. We already have a fix on the automobile and the driver."

Sisco's stomach did another flip-flop aided by the smell of bacon, which had caught in his throat before a single bite. He wanted to say to this bumbling gumshoe that he had no reason to see a birth certificate, but he knew the man had a right to ask for it. He brought the wrinkled-up paper downstairs and handed it over.

"Just how can I be sure this is you?" the G-man asked as he unfolded the paper. "This could belong to anybody. It has no picture on it."

"Well, I reckon you'll have to check it out in Kansas where I was born. Don't it seem strange that I'd carry this piece of paper all over the country while catchin' out on freights if it didn't belong to me?"

"Easy enough to verify," the gumshoe whispered to himself and stuck the paper in his coat pocket. "I'll hang on to it for a spell just to be sure I know where to find you."

"Suit yourself," said Sisco and sat down on his stool, where a big plate of bacon and eggs waited on the counter. He pretended not to mind that the G-man had taken the one paper that connected him to his folks and Kansas. "I got nothin' to hide, and I ain't goin' no place."

After he took the birth certificate, the G-man seemed to forget about the other names he had asked for. He put on his hat, nodded to Mrs. Mac, and left without paying for the coffee. Sisco hightailed it into the storeroom to puke in the downstairs toilet. When he came back to the fountain, Mrs. Mac was sitting on the stool where the agent had been.

"You all right, honey?"

"Yeah. Thanks. I'm fine now that the dick is gone. Do you know what the fuss is?"

"Seems like the Bureau thinks there is a pervert in Hayden. The trustees want a real investigation. Including your hobo pal, there's three young guys dead—maybe murdered."

"No one ever said Carlos was murdered. And, what's a pervert, anyway, Mrs. Mac? Len keeps usin' that word, but I'm not shore what it means."

He pushed back the plate of bacon and eggs, telling her that he and his stomach had been under the weather since yesterday.

She reached into her apron pocket and pulled out a pack of Chesterfields. She hardly ever smoked but now offered him one and took another for herself. "A pervert is a guy who goes after other fellas to have his way with

247

them, if you know what I mean. And Tre Sorenson thinks his boy was done in by a pervert."

Sisco nodded. How many of those perverts had he met in the jungles and on the trains? At least a hundred that he could recall. It was a strange setup; but the boy, or the punk, always went along with things and got something back from the man, or the jocker. Had Peach been a pervert? In his way, he sure did love Carlos. Sisco still didn't believe that he was a killer even though Shorty thought so because of jealousy over some Spanish gal. Shorty had never understood Peach's ways. Even if he had murdered his punk, Peach already was dead before the other two boys died. It made more sense that Carlos ran into a pervert at the dance at the Catholic church.

As he pondered all these things, he saw that Mrs. Mac had started to take down the Christmas tree. Of course, he pitched in and ended up helping at the drugstore all day. They made small talk until Sisco told her about Maria's mother and how he planned to take special classes with Father Martinez. She listened and said that she'd pray for Maria to come back.

By the time they finished clearing up the tree, they both were worn out. Later in the afternoon, Mr. Mac showed up dressed in his Sunday best ... on Monday. He turned on the Rose Bowl in the back room and invited Sisco to listen and join him for a New Year's toast.

"Cal headed for another loss to a Big Ten team. Can't figure out why they play so good during the regular season and lose in the Rose Bowl. Too much bookwork over there in Berkeley, I guess."

He puffed on one smoke after another like he was right there in the stadium. He never noticed that Sisco was paying no attention at all.

When the game was over, with California losing to Michigan by a score of 14 to 6, Mr. Mac got up and turned off the Crosley. "Ain't seen Len around here today but saw his Ford over in the alley behind Claire's early this morning. Shore hope he shits or gets off the pot with her this year. You oughta tell him that. Maybe he'll listen to you. Myrtle has tried, but he's so goddam stubborn. There'll never be a finer woman then Claire Lewis in this town. That's for shore!"

Sisco felt a chill down his back. His stomach began to jitter like a Mexican jumping bean for the third time that day. "Ya know, Mr. Mac, he's my boss, and I can't tell him what to do. I reckon he just doesn't wanna get tied down. If you'll excuse me now, I'm goin' outside to chop up the Christmas tree so you'll have kindling."

He needed to get outside into the fresh air to think. When had Len come to Claire last night and what had they done? She would have been angry because he had spent New Year's somewhere else and with someone else. She had probably asked him to leave, but had she told him what had happened earlier? It was all too much to digest as Sisco seized the ax to chop up the tree.

As he was stacking the kindling behind the drugstore, Len showed up. He was wearing the coat Claire had given him and looked tired. He asked if they could go upstairs to talk in Sisco's room, where there was privacy and an extra chair.

"How was your holiday?" Sutter asked, pulling the chair closer.

After giving Len the details about Maria, Sisco mentioned the G-man and how nasty he had been, never even paying for his coffee.

"So what business does that son-of-a-bitch have here, threatening you two on New Year's Day?" He took a deep drag on his Lucky.

"He didn't threaten us. He said that I should expect to hear from him, and he took my birth certificate."

"He did *what*?" Len stood up. His face began to change from a pale white to a near purple.

"Took 'way my birth certificate so I wouldn't hop a rattler outta here, I guess."

Sutter started to pace back and forth. "He had no damn right to do that! You are not a suspect in any crime. He violated your civil right to possess a document that identifies who you are."

He stamped his foot on the floor and crushed his smoke in the ashtray. Without skipping a beat, he lit up the next one; his lips were folded inward like he was trying to control what might come out of his mouth. "Look! You don't know these people. They work for a boss who hides a lot in his own life and projects his self-hate onto everybody else. He'd have us all believe that folks with leftist leanings—socialists, communists, liberals, democrats—are perverts, queers, crooks, vagrants, and spies. His G-men are indoctrinated to think that they can do anything to anyone in the name of national security. Innocent men and women are losing their jobs, committing suicide, and snitching on family members, colleagues, and friends because they are afraid. I think we should call the ACLU in Sacramento."

As usual, Sisco didn't know what he was saying; but when Sutter explained that they should get a lawyer, he reminded his boss that they had a bigger problem than the birth certificate. He said that the gumshoe was onto the body in Len's Ford and likely would show up at the high soon. When the G-man had questioned him, he had played dumb about how Carlos died.

"What about your hobo pal who went with us to the river—the one who's alive? He knows the truth."

"Don't trouble yourself none 'bout Shorty. They'll never catch up with him. And if they do, he'll act dumber than a door."

Len nodded. "So now we have to worry about Skidmore. If he finds someone to listen to his complaints, he'll become the biggest snitch the F.B.I. has ever met. He dislikes me intensely—jealousy, I think. If he believes he can get to me through you, he'll pull out all the stops."

When Sisco first went to work at the high, Len had insisted that Skiddy was a harmless busybody. Now he was saying that the head janitor could be a real snitch. Something had changed his mind, and Sisco figured that Len's campaigning for the Pink Lady had given Skidmore the fuel he needed for his fire. They agreed to tell the same story about the body and to say nothing about how Carlos had died.

Len stopped his pacing and sat down again in the chair. "I meant what I said to you before. I consider you a loyal friend. I know that you would never do anything to betray me, not intentionally, anyway."

Sisco felt awful. He already had betrayed him, though not in the way that Len meant. He thought about the third commandment of the Hobo Code: "Don't take advantage of someone who is in a vulnerable situation, locals or other hobos." Should he come clean about Claire and deck the next rattler out of Hayden? He was seriously considering that when Len broke out in a big smile.

"What I wanted to tell you when we came upstairs is that I finally scored a home run with Claire."

Sisco froze. His heart sank all the way to his stomach, and he gasped for air. He tried to smile, but his lips shook so much that he just gave up.

"Yeah, it was quite something after all her protests. I guess you liquored her up enough because she was as docile as a lamb—even a little playful. I was already tired after New Year's whoopee with the dance teacher. Claire caught me off guard, but I did my part anyway. And, guess what? Miss Prude wasn't a virgin after all!"

Sisco got up and shook Len's hand because he couldn't think of anything else to do. He said that he needed to use the toilet and then get some shut-eye. Len showed sympathy, saying that he knew his friend had been through a lot with Maria leaving and the F.B.I. threatening him. He said that he, too, needed some sleep and "to give his pecker a rest." He went to his own bedroom, leaving Sisco in the toilet to throw up for the second time that day.

After New Year's, he couldn't get warm. As cold as the weather was, it didn't compare to Kansas or Chicago. Sisco figured that he'd gone soft with life indoors and needed to toughen up with more work. One morning in late January, he passed out while shivering and shaking in the nurse's office at the high. When he came to, he was laid out on Nurse Pettigrew's cot with Len and Skidmore bending over him.

"We sent for Doc Nelson," said Nurse Petty as she leaned into his face far enough for him to see her tits and smell her bad breath. Like always, her nurse's cap was pinned on crooked over her short gray hair. Everybody wondered if she ever looked in the mirror while she got dressed.

"You got fever," announced Skiddy. "Nurse Petty thinks ya might have pneumonia."

"That's a bunch of horse malarkey," said Sisco as he threw off the Army blanket to stand up. His head started to spin, and the room circled around him.

"Oh, no, you don't!" Len piped up and pushed him back onto the cot. "We went through too much to get you here in the first place."

"Lie down, and stay down!" barked Skiddy.

After that, Sisco didn't recall much until the doctor told him to sit up, swallow some pills, and rest. He slept the whole afternoon and woke up when it was dark outside and the overhead light was on in the office. The radio was on, and the broadcaster blared about a troop build-up in Korea and the Russians' plan for World War III. Skidmore sat in Nurse Petty's chair at her desk.

"Came out of it, did ya? I been told to give ya some more medicine. Ya gotta take these every four hours," he ordered as he reached over to the cot with a fistful of pills in one hand and a glass of water in the other.

Sisco sat up slowly, expecting to pass out again. "What's the matter with me?"

"Pneumonia, all right, just like I predicted. Doc Nelson listened to your chest and heard its rumbles in there."

When he didn't get dizzy, Sisco sat up with his legs over the side of the cot to take the medicine and to try to stand.

"Ya gotta stay here for a spell so them pills have time to work. And ya have to rest up at Myrtle's till the doc says you can come back to work."

He turned down the radio after the news report.

Sisco laid back on the cot and covered up with the blanket. He didn't feel hot or cold, so he figured the fever must have broken. Patti Page came on the Crosley with the "Tennessee Waltz," and he wanted Claire with every bone in his body.

Skiddy brought him a second glass of water. "Doc says ya need to drink lots of this and stay clear of the smokes till your lungs empty out. Been wanting to talk more with ya since Christmas. You and the little Spanish gal still plan to hitch up?"

Sisco turned on his side to face Skidmore. He knew he was getting ready to tell a part truth and a part lie. "Yeah. Problem is that she had to go back to Old Mexico to care for her brothers and sisters after their ma died in an accident. She may not be back for a few months. When she gets here, we'll go 'head with things."

Skidmore lit his pipe and puffed to get it going. "Still plan to take them classes?"

"Shore—when I finish with this pneumonia. Gotta have my wits 'bout me to study with Father Martinez."

"Well, you can't go wrong being a Catholic. Everything changes once you're baptized and ya confess your sins. You'll be forgiven for all the things you shouldna' done. Catholic is the one true religion gets ya to Heaven."

Sisco nodded and figured this was Skiddy's way of saying a person could be forgiven for anything if he told the truth to a priest in the confessional. Was this his manner of saying that he suspected *him* of Carlos' murder? Skiddy never said things directly; he always let you wonder and worry about his real intentions.

Skidmore got up and went over to the window, then turned around to face the cot. "Tell me something, son. Do you think that anybody at the high is maybe—a little pinko?"

Sisco thought hard about how to answer without giving an answer. "I never heard anybody talk 'bout messin' with our government. Isn't that what the Commies try to do?"

"I guess ya ain't been here long enough to know for sure. You do know, though, that a few folks at the high never go to church. Them Marxists don't believe in God."

Shrugging his shoulders, Sisco got up and pulled Nurse Petty's chair back behind her desk. He wasn't going any farther with Skiddy on the Red thing because he suspected a trap. He accepted his boss's offer of a lift back to McFadden's so he didn't have to walk in the chilly air. When they turned the corner at C and Fourth Streets, there was the G-man's Lincoln parked at the curb just like on New Year's.

"Looks like your principal has company," Skiddy said without any surprise in his voice. "Want some help up to your room?"

"Naw, thanks. I'm much better. Just hand over the pills. Much obliged to ya ... for everything."

Skidmore handed over the medicine, and they shook hands. Sisco promised to check in at the high after he saw the doctor in a few days. Truth be told, he felt so tired and weak that he wondered if he'd ever get better. He sure didn't want any discussion with Len or the G-man, so he tried to go quietly up the stairs to his room. The hallway was dark except for a faint light under Sutter's door. There were muffled voices on the other side; he slipped into the toilet. Then he sneaked into his room and got into bed with his clothes on. After a short trip to dreamland, he woke up with Len beside the bed shaking him.

"What the hell ...," he cried out. "What's goin' on?"

"Sorry to wake you. I knew you'd want to hear about the G-man."

"Don't ya think it can wait? I'm still under the weather. Oh, never mind! Just turn on the light, and bring me a glass of water."

Len said that he had something better to drink, but Sisco refused the flask and took the water. As he listened to the talk about the G-man, he noticed that Sutter didn't seem too concerned. He said the G-man never mentioned Carlos, though he did want to know more about the dead boys from the high: who their friends were, what kind of marks they had in school, how their folks voted. Len had told him that he had no idea how their folks voted because it was a free country and ballots were secret. Then the F.B.I. agent asked him how he had voted in the last election. Len said that it was none of the government's business.

"The guy finally got around to asking me if I knew anyone in Hayden who had been in trouble with the law and had supported Mrs. Douglas. I practically tore the son-of-a-bitch a new asshole. I told him that was the most ridiculous effort to tie together two things that had nothing to do with each other. Of course, that's a favorite tactic of Red baiters."

"Is that *all* you said, Len?"

He looked at Sisco with a smirk, indicating he was pleased with himself. "I said that his question was like my asking him if he knew a whore whose son was a G-man."

"Ya didn't really say that?"

Of course, he had said it. And the F.B.I. would have him more in their sights from now on, and Skidmore would be reporting in with any old piece of dirt or dust.

The cold spell in Hayden continued. Everybody sneezed and coughed. Teachers were sick right and left because the kids brought their germs to school and spread them like crumbs. Sisco got over the pneumonia and didn't want any second helpings of it. He steered clear of every teacher who even pulled out a handkerchief, and that included Claire, who had a bad cold in the first week of February. She kept inviting him to stop by, and he wanted to go but held himself back. He made every excuse in the book until one afternoon when she cornered him on the playground.

"Oh, Sisco! I have a new refrigerator to show you. It's almost as tall as I am with no wasted space. You can even stand bottles up on the inside of the door!"

He couldn't figure what all the fuss was. The last thing he wanted to do was put himself in front of an open icebox and get cold when he had struggled to stay warm.

"Thanks, but I'll pass on the invite, Claire. I'm still trying to shake off this pneumonia thing."

After everything that had happened on New Year's, he felt funny calling on her. He wondered why she hadn't even bothered to visit him when he was so sick. As he tried to make sense of it all, he figured there were some things about Claire he'd never understand. Had she set him up in her bed so that Sutter would know someone else had her first? Was that her way of making Len jealous? He didn't want to believe he had been used. After all, hadn't she told him before that she wanted *him*?

§ § § § §

Claire, too, had tried to make sense of things on New Year's. She recalled every moment of her first time with a man. She had loved it all—the closeness of his body, the tenderness of his words, the moistness of his kisses, the gentleness of his moves as he brought them together for the joy at the top. Marge had been right. You fly to the moon when you do it with a guy who cares to take his time.

The simple truth was that after her first experience, Claire had wanted more of the same. She hadn't expected Sisco to clean up so fast after they finished. He was thoughtful enough to change the soiled linen and leave, but she had wanted him to stay so they could make love again. When he tucked her in with a loving kiss, she felt grateful, relaxed, and happy. They had hardly spoken, but words hadn't seemed necessary.

She had dozed off and awakened with Len next to her in bed. His breath reeked of brandy and cigarettes. His hardness pressed against her leg, and before she could stop him, he was inside her. As she tried to get free of him, he came and pulled out before she could say anything.

"That wasn't so bad, was it, Claire? You've done this before, but don't worry. It's our secret."

She sat up in bed with her nightgown twisted around her. Between her legs, she felt his sticky, wet mess. "How could I ever have thought about marrying *you*? My eyes are finally open. I know who you really are!"

257

"I tried to tell you, honey, but you didn't listen. Maybe that's because you weren't exactly honest with me. Far as I'm concerned, there's no harm done."

She got out of bed and went to the bathroom door. "That's your opinion, Leonard Sutter. When I come out, I expect you to be *gone!*"

From inside the toilet, she heard the front door slam. She didn't know whether to scream or cry, but she felt something good inside: she had made him angry. He had taken advantage and tried to turn things back onto her. She had won the day, though, because *he* hadn't been her first. A kind, decent, uneducated hobo had shown her what making love was really about, and he likely had saved her from a big mistake.

Claire thought she now knew why Len hadn't stayed married. What *he* wanted always came first. As long as it made him feel good, nothing else mattered. No woman could stay happily married to a man who put himself before his wife and his children. Hadn't Sisco and others in Hayden told her as much? Still, she felt ashamed of how things had happened. Maybe she was to blame after drinking too much brandy and enjoying herself so much with her hobo. Had she become a wanton woman like the girls her mother ranted and raved against? She had never done these things while in Berkeley. Still confused, she promised herself one more time that she would leave Hayden at the end of the year even if she had to go back to the house where she was raised.

§ § § § §

With Valentine's Day less than a week off, Sisco wanted to tell Claire that he loved her whether or not she felt the same. If he bought her one of those fancy lace cards at the mercantile, the whole town would know, and the buzz would start. It didn't help that the youngsters at the primary were so excited. The teachers planned parties in their classrooms with the students making valentines for their families and friends. Then, he had the idea to make a card himself right there in front of everybody without saying it was for her. He asked Claire if he could join her class at the art tables to do a few cards for special people. He explained that his family was too poor in Kansas to buy or make valentine cards, and he wanted to see what he had missed. She invited him to come around the primary on Valentine's Day after lunch.

On that morning of the fourteenth, Sisco made sure not to get dirty at the high. He told Skidmore that he had a project over at the primary in the afternoon. The crumb boss didn't seem interested and gave him the go-head. Skiddy had never questioned how his assistant used work time.

After the youngsters in her class had finished their lunches, Claire laid red and white paper with crayons, scissors, and paste on the tables. As a surprise, she brought out packets of paper doilies bought in Lodi. She said that each child would have only one doily for a special valentine and to plan carefully how to use it. She announced that Mr. Griffin would make cards, too, and asked who wanted him to sit at their table. All of the students raised their hands. That made Sisco feel real good, and he promised to sit for a while at each of the four tables.

Claire showed the youngsters how to fold a piece of paper in half and cut from one corner to the other to make a heart shape. They had practiced before with newsprint paper and began to cut out red construction paper hearts of all sizes. One little fella named Joe Engle decided that hearts could be white, too. He cut out three white hearts to paste on red paper.

"Hey, Joey," snapped Harley Conner, "that ain't right. Ya gotta make 'em red 'cause they got blood all over."

259

Joe Engle shook his yellow hair back and forth. "Be quiet, Harley! I know folks who's had attacks and lost all their blood. I'll make white hearts if I want to."

Claire settled things by telling the kids they could cut the paper however they wanted, as long as they didn't waste it. "Remember, children, it's the thought that counts. You're making cards for people you love, so put your best effort into it."

She winked at Sisco.

He was seated between Debbie Stewart and Mildred Payne, two of the sharpest tacks in the class.

Debbie leaned over to him and whispered in his ear, "Don't tell anybody, Mr. Griffin, but I think Miss Lewis gots a red heart for you." She put her hand over her chest and added, "I got a red heart, too, but I'm not tellin' who my special valentine is."

On the other side of him, Mildred saw Debbie with her hand over her heart and heard what she said. "She don't fool anybody, Mr. Griffin. We all know she likes Joey. I hope he gives her one of his pretty white hearts."

The afternoon was full of who liked whom and which classmates would get whose special valentines. Sisco thought back to Kansas when he was in grammar school. How different things were with all eight grades in one room! There was never any art paper; there weren't even scratch scraps to do sums. He didn't remember any talking about love, boyfriends, or girlfriends. From time to time, he heard that "so and so" was sweet on somebody. None of it had made any sense to a little guy trying to read his primer when his father didn't even want him to be in school.

He wished that the afternoon with Claire and her students could have lasted forever. The young kids made him laugh out loud with their comments about the grown-ups at the school.

"Don't ya see that Miss Lansing colors on her eyes every day? She uses a different Crayola to match her dress."

"Hey, that's nothing. Miss Anderson puts a big piece of Scotch tape on her forehead every morning before school. Says it helps her think better, but my ma says it's to keep her chicken scratches from gettin' bigger."

"I think Mr. Sutter and Miss Brown are gonna make a baby. They have to get married first."

"Bet ya guys didn't know that Mr. Chester picks his nose and eats his buggers when he drives the school bus!"

He tried not to laugh too hard and put his head down to work on the valentines, so the first graders wouldn't get too crazy with their stories. Some of the stories were true; he, himself, had seen the paint over Gladys Lansing's eyes and the adhesive tape on Twila Anderson's forehead. The youngsters carried on like he wasn't there, and Claire seemed to forget, too. Watching her out of the corner of his eye, he couldn't help think that she would be a mighty fine mother if she ever married. It would be a shame if she ended up like one of those old maid teachers at the primary.

When they had finished their valentines, the children watched him work on his. They all wanted to know who his cards were for. He said that one would go to Mrs. Mac, who was like his second mother. Another was for Mr. Sutter, who was his boss and a friend. The third would go to his girlfriend, Maria, who had gone back to Old Mexico to take care of her brothers and sisters because their mother had died. He whispered that he planned to marry her when she came back.

One little boy named Jimbo Lockhart spoke up. He had lost his front teeth and sounded funny when he talked. "Maybe you thoud pick thombody elth for the lath valentine in cath she doethn't get back in time."

The other students chimed in. Susie McDermott, one of Mrs. Mac's nieces, blurted out, "My aunt says you're really sweet on Miss Lewis. Why don't you give it to her?"

The children at his table began to clap and shout, "Miss Lewis! Miss Lewis!"

Claire had been in the supply closet to get more construction paper and came out with a puzzled look on her face. Sisco felt his cheeks turn as red as the hearts on his valentine cards. He kept his head down as he wrote something inside. She walked over to the table, and the youngsters got crazier.

"What's going on, Mr. Griffin?"

He wanted to explain, but the children made such a racket that he decided to give her the valentine, so it would be done and the class would quiet down. He stood up, handed the card to her, and kissed her on the cheek. He hadn't been able to help himself. All hell broke loose, but that wasn't the end of it. Claire seemed to get caught up in the thing and leaned over to give him a quick peck on his cheek. Now the kids went *loco*; they got on their feet, clapping and yelling, "Again! Again!"

It was a high old time until Skiddy appeared at the door. Sisco caught sight of him first and made a sign to Claire, who went back to her desk with a big smile on her face. Skidmore looked like he was going to crack a smile himself but, instead, went on down the hall to the second grade classroom. Sisco helped the youngsters clear up the scraps of paper and doilies and put the jars of paste back in the closet. Soon, the room was tidy enough for them to exchange cards, eat cupcakes, and drink red Kool-Aid.

After dismissal, Claire and Sisco finished cleaning up. They wondered how long it would take for the good folks of Hayden to find out that the hobo janitor had kissed Miss Lewis and she had kissed him back, even if they were only pecks on the cheek. Had Skidmore seen them? They didn't

The Last Real Hobo

think he had, but he'd hear about it soon from the children. As he told Claire what the students had said about the other teachers and the bus driver, Sisco had to restrain himself from taking her in his arms right there in the first grade classroom. Every part of his body ached to hold her, but she pushed him back, saying that Principal Jamieson might walk in at any moment as she did every day after school.

When Claire didn't invite him to her house, he went back to the high to check in with Skidmore. As he neared the janitor's closet, he heard voices from inside. The door was partway open, but the overhead light was off. He walked in and nearly bumped into Skiddy and Walter Gray from the trustees. They were seated on stools and never moved when they saw him. Sisco made excuses and left as fast as had come. He headed back to the office and found Len at his desk with an open bottle of brandy on top in plain sight.

"Whoa!"Sisco shouted. "Something awful good or terrible bad musta happened for ya to be drinkin' out in the open at school. Did they close the 241 for Valentine's Day?"

"Help yourself," Sutter answered, pointing to the bottle. "Old Walt was here this afternoon to make some pretty serious demands."

"Yeah. Ran into him with Skiddy in the closet—near fell on top of 'em in there with the light off."

He took a long swig of brandy. "Those two geezers are up to no good. The trustees have a hairbrained idea that someone at the high is the pervert who drilled those boys. Walt asked me to turn over the personnel files and identify the political party affiliation of every employee here."

"What did ya tell him, Len?"

"Refused, of course, even though I know that legally the board is entitled to access. If they order me to give them

263

up and I deny their request, they'll take legal action and fire me along the way."

Sisco thought about Claire. "Will they look at the primary teachers, too?"

"They're after a pervert—a man. No fellas at the primary, except you and Skidmore. I'm next to certain that we don't have any perverts at the high, either. But when these guys get a bug up their asses, no pun intended, they're worse than foxes in a henhouse. They'll just keep going till they make some poor fella into a pervert."

Behind him, the radio finished playing "There's Been a Change in Me" by Eddy Arnold. The 5 o'clock news came on; Len turned it up and took a chug of brandy. The announcer said that the Rosenbergs had pleaded innocent to treason against the United States. He said that if they were found guilty after a trial, they would die in the gas chamber.

"There's an example of a snitch," Len muttered as he switched the station to some music. "To save his own skin, this guy, Greenglass, fingers his sister and brother-in-law. If they're executed, their two small sons will be orphans."

To Sisco, who had lost both of his folks, it sounded very cruel to lose a ma and pa because of politics. "Are they Commies, Len?"

"Can't tell. Nothing is clear about them yet. What I *do* know is that the government wants to make an example of as many people as it can whether innocent or guilty. And if I hand over those files, then I become a snitch even though I don't finger anybody. The trustees will make something out of nothing and the F.B.I. will make an arrest to satisfy Tre Sorenson."

The loyalty oath thing kept gnawing at Sisco, but he decided not to mention it while Len was so worried about the snitch thing. To ease the situation a little, he talked about the valentine party and how the kids had convinced him to give Maria's card to Claire so they could see him kiss her.

Len smiled and seemed to enjoy the story. "Children are great matchmakers, aren't they? When I go over to the primary, they ask me if I've come to visit my girlfriend. She's a different teacher every time!"

After Valentine's Day, things seemed to quiet down at the high, and Sisco didn't see much of Sutter outside of school. On the Friday before Easter vacation, Len announced that he planned to finish up the *bracero* cottages during the break. He invited Sisco to come with him to Yolo and give him a hand. He thought they could sleep in one of the little cabins just to try it out. Of course, he promised plenty of wine, brandy, and his mother's home-cooked chow.

Polite as he could, Sisco refused the invitation, saying that he had promised to help Mrs. Mac with her spring cleaning. Truth be told, he wanted an excuse not to go to Yolo and bunk inside one of those chicken coops with no air. The other reason was that he hoped Claire would stay in Hayden for a few days so they could have some time together without any snoops or snitches hovering around like vultures.

On the last day of school before vacation, Claire told him that she had been feeling sick and needed to rest in Berkeley. Her mother had promised to brew up homemade chicken and split pea soups. She left early on Saturday morning to drive home.

Sisco was disappointed but pitched in with Mrs. Mac to finish the cleaning in three days thanks to the weather, which stayed cool and clear. You could tell that spring was in the air. Students from the high who came into the soda fountain showed off their light-colored duds and talked in loud voices about who wanted to keep company with whom. He tried to ignore their chatter, but they all knew him and wanted his opinion on which fella or gal would be a likely beau or belle. He insisted that he was no expert on such things because he had never gone to high school or had dates for dances and parties.

Late in the afternoon on the Saturday before Easter, he was upstairs sweeping his room when Len stumbled down the hall. He stopped at the open door like he wasn't sure where he was. Something was certainly wrong. He took a step back, looked at Sisco, came into the room and sat down on the bed. He wore his usual dirty white shirt with mud-caked jeans. The flask of brandy hung out of his pocket.

"What in the hell hit ya?"

"I think I'm about to get hit hard!" he said. "Walt Gray from the trustees called me at my mother's to say that I have to hand over those files or be arrested. They set up a closed board meeting on April twelfth."

Sisco couldn't stop himself when he blurted out, "Did ya sign the loyalty oath, Len? Tell me the truth."

With that sly grin, he answered, "Thought about that one a long time. After everybody else, but I finally *did!* Gave it to Skiddy to deliver personally to old Walt or Sorenson."

Sisco's stomach jumped and fell. He swallowed hard to keep himself from screaming. "Why in hell did ya do that?"

"Hey!" Sutter shot back. "You and Claire convinced me. Why are you—?

"No! No, Len! Why did ya give it to *Skidmore* to hand over?"

He looked puzzled. "Well, because he spends more time with the trustees than I do—than anybody. I figured he'd be the fastest way to get it to them since it was late."

Sisco went to look out over Fourth Street. "Gotta get some air in here," he choked as he lifted the window.

"My flask is empty," said Len as he tossed it onto the bed. "Think you can get us a bottle? I'm buying."

"Yeah, I'll get us 'nother one. It's on my dollar, so ya just lie down on my bunk to rest till I get back. Before I go, though, I want ya to listen to me ... for your own good. Come Monday morning, ask Skiddy 'bout the loyalty oath. Be shore he handed it over to Walt or one of the trustees. I gotta bad feeling."

Len had turned quiet; his brain was working now. "Do ya think I'm being set up?"

"Whatever's happening, Len, ya shoulda never trusted Skidmore with that paper. Ya set yourself up, worryin' so much on the other employees. Start thinkin' on your future!"

He spread out on the bed and closed his eyes. In a whisper, he mumbled, "Couldn't forgive myself if I were a snitch and somebody lost a job because of me."

When he began to snore, Sisco slipped out the door with no intention of buying more firewater. He felt sure they'd both drink plenty before the end of the school year.

Terry A. Albritton

Revelation

Sisco flopped in the jungle that night to give Sutter a chance to sleep off the booze. The next day was Easter Sunday, so there wouldn't be any brandy for sale in Hayden. Of course, Len always had his own stash somewhere. Still, Sisco hoped he'd take a day off so his head would be clear on Monday to corner Skidmore about the loyalty oath.

The church bells for Easter services began ringing as usual. Sisco climbed out of his bedroll and started to clean up the jungle. Since none of the regular guys had been there for weeks, the place was full of trash left by kids playing hobo without anybody to run them off. Late in the afternoon, he spotted Claire's Chevy parked on F Street. He ached to be alone with her but figured that Len would show up sooner or later—if he wasn't already there. Out of his mind to see her, Sisco walked over the tracks into the alley and up to the back door. With no sign of Len's Ford, he thought he might be able to steal at least one kiss.

After a few knocks, Claire opened up. She was wearing her pink terrycloth bathrobe, which didn't flatter her figure. She had hacked off her hair, and it barely touched her shoulders. She had been crying

"Come in, Sisco," she said with a quick peck on the cheek and a move backward before he could catch her in his arms. "I need to talk to you. Please sit down."

She motioned him to the kitchen table while she started the water for some hot tea.

He wasn't partial to that drink and wished she had offered him something stronger. His stomach had begun to jump, so he lit up a smoke to calm down. "That's funny, Claire. I need to talk to you, too. How was your vacation?"

"They're going to fire him, aren't they?" she asked as if she hadn't heard his question.

After a good drag on his smoke, Sisco answered, "I dunno. I just found out yesterday that he signed the loyalty oath but *after* the rest of us. He gave it to Skidmore to deliver to the trustees instead of takin' it hisself to Gray or Sorenson. He doesn't wanna face 'em with the personnel files. Sooner or later, he's gotta hand those over."

She got up to pour hot water into the teapot and came back with cups and saucers. "Just try some. It will calm your nerves."

He wanted to be polite and drink a little, even though it looked like dirty water. Sugar and milk didn't make it much better.

She sat down and went on. "Well, whatever happens with the loyalty oath, Mr. Skidmore is not to be trusted. How can an intelligent man like Len turn over such an important document to the school custodian, who is just an uneducated farmer?"

"I 'spose ya could say the same 'bout me, Claire. Some folks might think I'm tryin' to be better than I am."

She shook her head and patted him on the arm. "Don't be ridiculous! You aspire to better yourself. Skidmore aspires to destroy others. Len has been a fool to trust him with anything except janitorial duties."

He had to agree that Sutter trusted Skiddy too much, but he wasn't sure about who was the greater destroyer of lives. When he asked her just what she meant, she shrugged her shoulders and poured him more tea. "There's nothing specific, and Len chalks it all up to an eccentric widower whose only interests are the school and the town. Since Len pays little attention to his complaints, Skidmore runs to the trustees with everything. They listen to him because he's an insider. He gossips a lot with them and always seems to know who Leonard Sutter is fooling around with, especially the married women. He even hints at these affairs to me—for my own protection, of course. And let's be honest, there's more than one husband in Hayden who would like to get even." She began to cry.

So now, Sisco was sure that she knew about Len's womanizing; he felt how difficult it was for her to admit it. He handed her a paper napkin from the plastic holder on the table and said, "Try not to worry on the loyalty oath. I'll sneak a look in Skiddy's toolbox, where he keeps his treasures. If it's not there, I'll ask him straight out. Len promised that he would, too."

She reached for a second napkin to blow her nose. He poured her more tea but couldn't bring himself to drink any more and was getting ready to ask for some brandy when she dropped the A-bomb on him.

"Sisco, I'm pregnant."

He froze to the chair. He wanted to move his arms, but they were like dead weights on top of the table. He couldn't make his hand reach for anything—a smoke, a napkin, the tea cup—*anything*—to break up the air and make it move again. In his head, he told himself to get a grip on things and to be careful what he said and how he said it. "Claire, whatever you ... want ...."

It was no use. He didn't have the words to comfort her. He knew she could lose her job unless she got married fast or left town. How would it look if she married a hobo? It was unthinkable. Her folks would never accept him. Where would they live? The only person who wouldn't judge or gossip was Len, and he ought to be the guy most pissed off.

"Whatever ya want," he whispered. "How can I help? Whatever ya want to do, Claire."

She couldn't stop her sobs; but through her tears, she managed to mutter, "It's too late to do anything ... except ... go on and hope that I don't have to resign."

What that said to him was that if she thought she had a choice, she would end it. Sisco recalled the whores in Chicago with their particular doctors who took care of things when one of them was knocked up. Claire was no prostitute, and she had no doctor to turn to for help.

"So," he said, "with that outta the question, what else is there?"

As he watched her sob and shake, he hurt hard in his stomach while hoping he could keep the pain there without crying in front of her. "I'm so sorry! For all the gold in the world, I wouldn't have ya go through this on account of what we did."

She raised up one hand to stop him and used the other to wipe her tears. "It's not your fault, Sisco. I ... I wanted it as much as you did."

"That shore ain't true! I wanted ya more than I ever wanted any woman. I loved ya from the first day, Claire. For a year and a half, I figured ya was outta my reach and I'd have to settle for ya as a friend. When I got the go-ahead on New Year's, I thought I was in heaven or some kinda dream."

With that, she seemed to catch her breath. The napkin holder on the table was empty, and the wet balls of paper had piled up beside her. She struggled to tell him something and poured them both more tea.

He sat quietly to listen.

"No way, no way to know ... whose baby this is." She choked. "Len and I ... we did it, too, on New Year's. Should never have let it happen—so sorry!" She started bawling and went to the bedroom for a box of Kleenex.

He froze again. Somewhere in his head, he knew what she said. Len had told him as much, but he hadn't taken him seriously. Sutter was always bragging about some gal here or there. It just didn't seem possible that Claire had let him have her like that. How much Sisco wanted to believe that he was the one she wanted now. Len didn't deserve Claire because he didn't appreciate her.

All he could say was, "Does he know?"

She shook her head but didn't speak. Unable to hold back any longer, he stood up and went behind her chair. With his hands on her shoulders, he began to rub. She bent over the table and buried her head in her arms. Through her housecoat, he felt her tremble. Finally, he embraced her from behind the chair and kissed the back of her neck.

When she stopped weeping, he handed her a tissue and sat down next to her. "Claire, look at me, please!"

She lifted her head slowly and sat up. Her green eyes were red and her cheeks puffy. On her forehead, the hair was stuck to her skin, and he gently pulled it back. Even then, she was the most beautiful woman he had ever seen. He told her to sit tight while he retrieved the brandy and two old fashioned glasses. He poured double shots for them both.

"My stomach has been real upset. I don't know if ..." she said, raising her glass.

He smiled. "I don't think a little brandy right now will hurt anything ... or anybody. This is a toast to the three—or four—of us and our friendship to the end."

They let the brandy settle their nerves.

"I'll help ya in any way I can. If ya want to get hitched, we will." He choked on the words and hoped she didn't take it wrong. He would have married her in a second, but he wasn't at all sure that would be good for either of them.

She answered calmly that she had a plan. "Thank you for caring enough to do the right thing, Sisco. What's right may not be the best solution. I'll finish the school year, resign, and go back to Berkeley. My parents will have to get used to their daughter, the whore!" She burst into tears again.

He handed her more Kleenex and pleaded, "Lemme help ya. Please! Money, a move, whatever ya want or need!"

She shook her head, got up and went straight for the toilet. Even through her bathrobe, he saw that her shape was changing—a little bump up front, bigger tits. It wouldn't be long before the townies whispered that she was showing, and Len needed to do the honorable thing. No one would even think about the hobo janitor who could never have a chance with a woman like Claire.

One way or another, Len would find out. Maybe he did suspect; he was no fool in the ways of the world. He was a show-off and a loudmouth, but he never set out to hurt anyone because he had suffered bad things. Drinking one night in Len's room, Sisco had asked him how he knew to look at Carlos' body the way he did. He answered that when he was a boy, his crazy brother, Frank, had sneaked up and corn holed him from behind. It had torn him up so bad that he missed school for a week. He never let his ma know what had happened but begged her to send him to live with a sister and brother-in-law in Woodland so he could go to school there.

Before leaving Claire, Sisco told her that Len deserved to know the whole story—even the part about New Year's. It might lead to the end of their friendship, but he didn't think so. Len had his faults, but he was loyal and fair. He had never given her any hope for a life with him, so he'd have to forgive her if she made it with another man, even if the other guy was a friend. Unsure on the way to tell Len, she promised to think about it and let him know as soon as she could get up her nerve.

That night in the jungle, Sisco couldn't sleep. His head was full of questions. How he wished Ole Memphis were around to talk to. Shorty never had complicated answers or solutions to problems, but he always made sense. Maybe that was what came from being on the road so long. You had to make quick decisions to survive; you couldn't get into anything too deeply. Sisco wondered if he had left some gal knocked up before Claire. He could never know, and it was better that way—at least for him. Until Claire, there hadn't been a woman who mattered enough for him to think about settling down.

Back at school the first week after Easter vacation, Skidmore hit his assistant with the spring window washing. Sisco was so worried about Claire that he almost forgot about the loyalty oath. He had no chance to ask Skiddy or to sneak a look in his toolbox. By Friday afternoon, he had most of the windows washed at the high and was headed to the primary, where he hadn't gone all week. As he was about to leave after lunch, Skiddy stopped him on the front steps.

"Just so you know, there ain't gonna be a maypole dance or a spring picnic this year."

He answered that he hadn't given it a thought, which was the truth. Skidmore stood on the top step and waited for him to ask for more detail, but Sisco just waved it off, saying that he needed to get busy on the windows at the primary. It didn't feel right to mention the oath out in public with students and teachers walking by.

On the ladder at the primary with his back to the sun, he felt like the up-and-down motion of his arms on the windows was rocking him to sleep. He still wasn't sleeping much at night. He decided to get down before he fell off the ladder when Claire's voice startled him from below.

Her voice sounded anxious as she whispered to him. "The trustees are coming here this afternoon after school for a meeting. Mr. Skidmore is invited."

Sisco was surprised. He knew there was a meeting next week at the high, but no one had mentioned a sit-down at the primary. There was no time to finish the window washing or the outside sweeping. Had Skiddy wanted to discuss the meeting earlier at the high? Why hadn't Len said anything?

"Would you like to stop by my house later, Sisco, so you don't run into them here?"

He told her that he certainly would but that he needed to go back to check on something at the high first. He winked, hoping she'd understand what the purpose of his errand was. She said that she'd have a bottle of brandy ready later in the afternoon.

He walked back to the high by way of the fairgrounds, so he didn't meet up with Skidmore or any of the trustees headed to the primary in their automobiles. He figured that Len had to be part of the meeting and did want to run into him. Sometimes, Sutter took the back route through the Sacramento County fairgrounds if he was trying not to be seen leaving work to visit his woman or to hoist a few at the 241 Club. On that day, the fairgrounds were deserted and overgrown with weeds; there was no sign of anybody.

At the high, he found all of the doors unlocked in the front. That meant that Skiddy planned to return after the meeting or that he expected Len to lock up. Nobody was in the office, although a few students still hung around on the steps. It was spring. You could tell by the way the girls were giggling while the boys flirted to get close to them whenever they could. No one paid attention to Sisco; the students were used to his coming and going.

He headed to the gymnasium and the closet behind the stage where the cleaning supplies were kept. He knew that door would be locked; Skidmore never left it open because "somebody might help hisself to wax, cleanser, or brushes." Poor as some of the kids were, Sisco didn't think they were going to snipe supplies. Len always said Skiddy never wasted, missed, or lost anything he was given.

He unlocked the closet and flipped on the light. It was cold inside, as he walked to the shelf in the back where Skiddy kept his toolbox. It wasn't there. He figured that

Skidmore must have taken it with him to the primary. That meant he wasn't coming back after the meeting. He decided to check the other doors that should have been locked before he left. It still seemed strange that the front hall and the main office were open. Maybe he planned to blame Sutter for not securing the doors. Sisco recalled the story about the open front door at the primary and the shit inside.

Next, he went to the boiler room behind the gym. It was unlocked and quiet. There should have been noise from the water heating up for the showers of the baseball and track teams. He turned on the lights and couldn't believe his eyes. There on the floor next to the boiler was Skiddy's toolbox—open. He picked it up to set it on the table under the hanging light bulb. The tools were out of their places as if he had been at work on some project that he had to leave real fast. Then, Sisco remembered that the boiler needed a new regulator and Skidmore was trying to fix it himself, even though Len wanted to order a new one and call a plumber to install it. The top tray of the toolbox was full of wrenches, screwdrivers, washers, nuts, and nails. He lifted it carefully so as not to rearrange anything. On the bottom, things looked disturbed, too; the heavier wrenches, a hammer, and nails were all mixed up.

There was no paper on the top or the bottom. Whatever had made him think that Skidmore would hide the loyalty oath in the toolbox if he planned to keep it from the trustees? Maybe he had handed it over to Walt or Sorenson, or just thrown it away. While he thought about this, Sisco tried to arrange things on the bottom like they had been as best he could remember. Something caught his eye. It was Carlos' rosary that Peach had missed at the river. He was sure because of the tiny turquoise stones in the cross. Suddenly, something moved behind him, and he turned. Skiddy stood at the door.

"Why is Carlos' rosary in your toolbox?" He felt his face flush.

"You oughta know, boy. It fell on the floor when ya stuck the wetback's body in the confessional or maybe when ya hauled it out."

"If ya knowed it was me in the Catholic, why didn't ya hand it over when I went to work here?"

"Didn't want to embarrass ya. Thought I might need it for a day like this when I found ya trying to steal my tools. Always knew ya couldn't be trusted. No bum is a good bum."

"And what about Len's loyalty oath paper? Ya never gave that over, either, did ya?" Sisco looked him straight in the eyes; Skidmore took a step backwards.

"Ain't none of your affair what happened to it. Len's finished here, anyway, and so are you!" He moved to the other side of the table and began to organize the tools.

Sisco reached into his pocket for the keys to the high. He was going to toss them but changed his mind. Skiddy couldn't fire him, and he wasn't handing over the keys to anybody until Len or a trustee ordered him to. "I shore wanted to believe the best when ya gave me a chance to work here. I was wrong, and the others who told me different was right. All your blabber 'bout being a good Catholic is just bullshit!"

Skidmore picked up one of the wrenches and held it high as though he were going to heave it across the table. His lips quivered as he said, "See this? This is how I've made my living—good, clean, hard work. Breakin' my back every day with no thanks or nothing. Dandies like Len Sutter come in here with their big-shot ideas and get away with everything when they hail from the same dirt as me. You know what he's like ... how he's jilted Claire and many others. He uses the job to play around with pretty teachers and break their hearts."

"That may be true, Skiddy, but it's no reason to fire him. Ya gotta know how much the kids and their folks respect him."

"They'd think different if they knowed he's a Commie pervert!" He went back to the toolbox.

"He's not! And, ya damn well know it!" Sisco's blood was boiling now.

"Well, at the least, he's a pinko pervert. The guy never went to church a Sunday in his life—not even to get married. And I don't know nothing about the loyalty oath."

That did it. Sisco went around the table and punched Skidmore square in the jaw. The blow sent him backwards, but he caught himself before he hit the floor. Blood rushed from his nose; he looked dazed, but managed to utter, "It's Len's word against mine. Who do ya think the trustees will believe?"

Sisco was so pissed off that he didn't remember how he walked back to the jungle. When he got close to the tracks, he did hear the blow of a hog near Lodi. He wanted to catch out on her, never look back, head straight to Dunsmuir, locate Cleveland Jack, and find a place to flop until it warmed up and the others got there. If he left now, he never would have to face Skidmore again. Claire and Len would be two people from the past like everybody else in his life. He would never know about the baby or what happened to Len's job. Mrs. Mac would cry and wonder why he had left Hayden without even a good-bye. She would clean out his things and give them to the next hobo who came through.

He just couldn't do it, not now. He couldn't leave without tidying up his bindle. He had left Kansas because his folks were dead. He had highballed it out of Chicago because he was finished with the bums, jackrollers, yeggmen, panhandlers, and pimps. Nobody there meant anything. But he couldn't do the same with this little farm town because, for the first time as a grown-up, he felt like he had real kin, folks that he needed and who needed him.

The hog from Lodi stopped at the tower, took on water, and picked up steam as she left Hayden. Sisco didn't deck her. As the rattler picked up speed, he recalled that Claire had invited him to stop by after his errand at the high. If he had gone straight to her house, he never would have found the rosary. As it was, he felt confused about what it meant that Skidmore kept Carlos' cross. Most likely, it was just one more Catholic trinket to get him to heaven.

Still, he wanted to tell Claire what had happened that afternoon. As he put on his jacket and stepped out of the shadow of the tower, an automobile raced over the tracks to the Catholic church. Skiddy in his Caddy went straight for the parking area and his usual place. He walked toward the back and disappeared through the gate.

Sisco waited to see if he would come out. When he didn't, he figured there was someone else inside. He walked across the street, slipped into the churchyard, and hid behind the hedge next to the chapel. He waited, and soon the back door opened. Skiddy and Father Martinez appeared and stood at the top of the steps. They were so close to him that he was afraid they would hear him breathing.

"Be calm, Skidmore. Have faith in the Lord's mission for you. The bum hit you on school premises. If Sutter won't take action, you know the trustees will."

Skiddy blew his nose and coughed. "Len's the principal till the end of the year. He can do a lot more damage."

They walked down the steps, onto the sidewalk, and toward the street; they were too far away for him to hear them whisper. Then, they backtracked closer to the steps.

Sisco made himself flush against the church and hoped it was too dark to see him behind the hedge.

"… unless you call him tomorrow and tell him you have new information about the murders."

For a minute, Skiddy didn't answer. When he did open his mouth, he spoke slowly like he was seriously pondering things. "Nothing … nothing to show that he's connected to the other two, only the Spic kid."

They whispered some more, but Sisco didn't hear much because there was a loud ringing sound in his ears. It came from inside his head this time, even though it sounded like the bells of the churches when they were all chiming at once. He had heard the same thing when he realized that his ma was dead and he was trapped by the dust. Fear and anger mixed together sounded blasts in his head. The thought that Skiddy and the priest might try to pin any murder on Len made him crazed with fury. He already felt guilty about the body; the hobos had put Sutter in over his head with the townies. And Tweedledee and Tweedledum were witnesses. If the trustees placed Len in their sights as a Commie, they might try to make him a pervert so the case would stick.

Sisco stayed hidden and shivered in the cool spring evening. Skiddy drove off, and the priest went back inside the church. Sisco hurried over the tracks and down Fourth Street to the drugstore. He decided not to worry Claire about what he had found in the toolbox or what he saw and heard in the churchyard. In her condition, she needed to stay free of other problems, especially if they concerned Len. She had enough of her own shit to deal with.

The next morning, he went to the high as if nothing had happened. Len's car wasn't there yet, but the Caddy was parked in its regular spot. Inside the building, the attendance clerk was tending to tardies and absences, with the door to Sutter's office closed behind her. He headed to the janitor's closet, where Skidmore was fooling with a part for the boiler.

"Morning, Mr. Skidmore," he said as casually as possible.

"Come back to turn in your keys, have ya?" Skiddy asked without looking up. He had a bandage on his nose.

"Before anything else, it seems to me that you and I need to conversate some things with the principal."

"You already talked to him?"

"Naw. He's got bigger things on his mind than the problem 'tween you and me. Ya know he'll wanna hear both sides. He *is* a fair fella, in spite of what ya may think."

"Suit yourself. He ain't here yet. Musta had a hard night." He laughed and went back to the boiler piece.

Right on cue, Len showed up at the door. He looked neat and clean, with an ironed white shirt and a dark blue suit. For once, his tie was straight. It was the one Claire had given him for his birthday. With circles, triangles, and rectangles all joined together, she said that it would hide spilled food and liquor.

"Good morning, gentlemen," he greeted them, calm and cool. "I apologize for such late notice, but I'm calling an assembly before lunch. Will you please set up the chairs in the gym?" He didn't wait for an answer and hurried out as fast as he'd come in.

"I'll pull out the chairs," Sisco offered, glad for an excuse to go to a different part of the building before the assembly. On his way to the gym, he steered clear of everybody, including Len. He swept up the gymnasium floor even though it wasn't dirty. Since the P.E. classes were outside playing softball games, he took his time pushing the big broom back and forth over the floor. Then, he wheeled the carts out from under the stage and began to form the rows.

He was almost finished when Skiddy came in from the back and called to him. "We're gonna see Len in his office after the assembly. He knows the score."

Sisco ignored him and kept on with the chairs. In fact, he was looking forward to a meeting so Len could hear Skidmore lie about the loyalty oath. Sutter would soon find out what he had discovered on the bottom of the toolbox. Skidmore would have to explain why he had Carlos' rosary.

When the students filed in at fourth period, they were hungry and loud. The girls wore their soft summer dresses, and the boys tried to see as much as they could of their tits underneath the yellow, pink, and blue fabrics. They stood in front of the gals who were sitting down and pretended to be interested in their chatter while they peaked down the cracks far as possible. Sisco knew what the guys were up to because he had done the same himself.

Len stepped up to the microphone. His fancy tie was still in the right place with his white shirt tucked in and his suit coat buttoned at the waist. The students liked to call him "Harry James" when he got dressed up; they said he looked like the famous trumpet player and band leader. Skiddy had once said that the dance teacher was Len's "Betty Grable" and that Claire never had a real chance with him because of her brown hair. It was well known that Sutter was partial to blondes.

When the kids quieted down, he began to speak. His voice was calm and strong. "Good morning, students of Hayden High. I realize that it's near your lunchtime. I will not keep you here past fourth period. In fact, you will be dismissed early for a longer lunch if we get through the assembly faster."

Here, he had to stop while the kids hooted and hollered. He waited for them to calm down and then continued, "As we go our separate ways for summer, there are some things you should know, if you don't already.

"One, for those young men headed to college, I applaud you. I strongly encourage you to take the Draft Deferment Test. If your scores are high enough, you will be able to finish your education without being drafted.

"Two, mark my words. Within the next month, President Truman will sign a bill extending the draft until 1955. This bill lowers the draft age to eighteen and a half.

"Three, the importance of a high school education cannot be overstated. Whether a guy or a gal, you are better equipped for the future. I intend to say this again at our commencement exercises, but I want next year's sophomores, juniors, and seniors to hear it today. You will not hear this vital message from me as your principal after June fifteenth. I am not returning to Hayden High in September for the 1951-52 school year."

The gym was silent. Students moved forward in their chairs like they thought there was more to come. And, there was.

"Yesterday, I received notice that the trustees do not plan to renew my contract. I tell you this because of my loyalty to you and to your parents, who have entrusted me with your education. I take this opportunity to thank you and your folks for your confidence and support. I wish you all the best of luck in your future. Godspeed! You are excused for lunch ten minutes early!"

Only a few students got up to leave. Len was mobbed. Girls hugged him and cried; the boys shoved each other to shake his hand.

Sisco watched Skiddy on the other side of the gym next to the wall. He looked bored as he leaned on a pushcart. When more students left for lunch, he started to fold chairs and stack them. Sisco followed, and a few guys stopped to give them a hand.

Donald Martin, who was a junior, pulled him aside. "Hey, Mr. Griffin, can't you talk Mr. Sutter into staying on another year? I want his name on my diploma. He's such a swell guy!"

"Don't think he's leavin' on his own, Don. The trustees are forcin' him out."

"You can bet my dad will talk to Mr. Sorenson or Walt Gray. He likes Mr. Sutter a lot."

Skidmore and Sisco did not have a meeting with Len that afternoon. They couldn't get close to him with all the phone calls and visits from parents. A reporter from the *Hayden Herald* showed up right after school let out. She had graduated in the first class with Len as the principal. Before that, she had been a student in his English class. She wanted an interview and waited in the attendance office with Sisco while two local ranchers talked behind the principal's closed door.

"Mr. Sutter gave me my start in journalism," she said, shaking her red hair turned frizzy from a bad permanent. "I plan to write a strong editorial in his support. He always said that 'the power of the pen is greater than any weapon.' We'll see if that works for him now."

285

Terry A. Albritton

Graduation

Claire told Sisco that he was right—she had to tell Len about the baby. She tried not to expect any kindness from him. He showed more goodness to people he barely knew than to family or friends. He had risked everything to help the hobos and had spent hours and money on the *braceros* while neglecting his mother and her ranch. Len didn't let you get close to him so that he didn't have to get close to you. The thought of a baby, his own offspring, would threaten his freedom, and he would hang onto that no matter what.

When it came to New Year's, Claire blamed Len and herself. He had taken advantage of her, but she hadn't stopped him, at least not soon enough. Mother and Daddy had blamed her, too, saying that she lost her way when she stopped attending church. They never asked who the father was. They assumed that it was Len and that he would marry her. When she told them that she had no plan to marry him, they insisted that she move back to Berkeley to "get right with God."

She hadn't dared to mention Sisco to her folks. They would never understand that a hobo might be the father of her baby. He had been so sincere in his concern for her, offering to marry her or to help in any way she wanted. Most important, he had taken responsibility for what happened on New Year's. Claire did not blame him because she had ached everywhere for a man to take her on that "trip to the moon" that Marge had talked about. With Sisco, it had been swell. She cared for him in a special way. He was a decent, patient man, but she did not see him as her husband.

Claire had made her decision, and she felt determined and strong enough to follow through on it without the help of any man except her father. She didn't expect Len to

287

question or argue with her. Still, she couldn't help but wish that he would ask her to marry him just so she'd have the satisfaction of saying "No!" He was such a handsome, smart, smooth man … and so reckless. Angry as she was at him, she was afraid that bad things were in his future at the high.

§ § § § §

On the last Friday in May, Claire and Len sat at her kitchen table. It was warm, and she had opened all the windows. The smell of night jasmine sneaked through the screens; the crickets were singing as the hogs blew through town. Sutter smoked nonstop but hadn't poured himself any brandy— yet. Claire, however, had a good head start on him.

"I have to tell you something important, Len. In spite of what you believe, some harm *was* done on New Year's Eve. I'm pregnant."

He mashed his cigarette in the ashtray without a word. After he lit up a new smoke, he said, "Are you sure about that?"

She got up from the table, turned sideways toward him, lifted her blouse, and pulled her pedal pushers down partway. "What do *you* think this bump is?"

He stood up and went to the cupboard for an old fashioned glass. Filling it with brandy, he said in a calm voice, "We can get married. You can resign and go live with my mother in Yolo. She's raised five kids, and she will be a big help."

Her fist came down so hard on the table that he flinched. "You'd send me off to your mother so you could go on cavorting with the dance teacher and anyone else who strikes your fancy. You'd escape the whole scandal and go right on doing what you have always done to get instant gratification for your *needs*. No, thank you!"

"Well, I sure as hell won't live in Berkeley where your folks can run and ruin our lives."

"No one knows more about ruining lives than you do, Leonard Sutter. I don't want you anywhere near this baby and don't even think about firing me or asking me to resign because this unwed pregnant teacher will make a scandal with the trustees that sends you out of town on the next freight train."

Without another word, he got up, leaving a half glass of brandy on the table. He headed to the back door and almost collided with Sisco, who was standing on the top step getting ready to knock. In his hand was a copy of the *Hayden Herald*.

"Did ya see this? The whole front page is 'bout the trustees playin' politics to get rid of ya." He was all excited and stepped inside, thinking that Len had come to open the door for him.

"I was just on my way out, but I'll have a drink with you."

While Len fixed another brandy and added some more to his, Sisco sat down at the table next to Claire. He knew that something was amiss by the angry look on her face. He had seen that same face on the day they went to Stockton for the Douglas rally. She was definitely pissed, and he decided not to say anything to her.

Taking a big swig of his brandy, he asked Len, "So, who called for this meeting to let ya defend yourself? The paper says that you're a 'true patriot who signed the loyalty oath which mysteriously disappeared.'"

With that foxy grin that showed up when he had done some mischief, Sutter answered, "*Who* do you think suggested the meeting?"

Sisco glanced at Claire, who continued to frown and stare straight ahead so as not to look at either one of them.

"Guess I coulda figured that one out myself. What will this meeting get ya, anyway?"

"The thing is we've got to do this before the end of the school year and the trustees' final official meeting. All I want them to say is that they will renew the contract, and I'll promise to leave before school in September. That gives me the summer months to secure another position somewhere with a clean slate."

Claire got up and began to pace back and forth between the table and the sink. Both ashtrays were full of butts, and she wouldn't throw them away until she was sure they were all out. She had a fear of fire; and in her condition, it seemed to get worse. Her empty glass of brandy sat on the sideboard next to the sink, where she stood to crush out each smoke until she knew it was dead.

"Just what do you think this local crowd can do to help you, Len?" she asked as she lit a Camel for herself from one of the smoldering Luckys. "They'll tell you what they think you want to hear and go back to milking their cows. Whatever ranchers come to your meeting won't stand up to the trustees. Hell, they *are* the trustees! Don't be so naïve!"

As she stood by the sink, Sisco saw that her tummy stuck out over her pedal pushers. At school, she had begun to wear loose-fitted blouses with skirts. While some of the townies had started to gossip, others remarked that she had just put on a few pounds. No one said anything disrespectful; everybody wanted to believe in her moral character. Just the same, Sisco heard whispers. If someone asked him anything, he played dumb. As far as he could tell, Len was doing the same.

"Hell, if you really want to fight this thing," she went on, "you need an ACLU attorney. You shouldn't try to defend yourself. This Hayden bunch is fickle, even when they like you. What's on their minds now are their men called off again to a war where our soldiers are freezing to death. *You* are not their main concern because you are *replaceable.* Their husbands, sons and brothers are not."

Sisco had never heard Claire swear before. It was a clear signal to him how upset she was and that she'd had enough brandy to speak her mind loud and clear. He wondered what else was bothering her because she was upset before they even started to discuss Len's meeting. While at the sink, she had refilled her glass.

Len didn't say anything at first; he just got up and went to the icebox for more ice. On the way, he snuffed out his smoke in the full ashtray next to her.

Don't do that!" she screamed. "Now I can't throw these away."

He looked at her curiously and put the whole ashtray under water in the sink. "With all of the big issues we have to deal with, Claire, can't you get past this without losing your temper?"

"Don't patronize me, Leonard Sutter! You have created this mess along with others that no lawyer can resolve. If you plan to fight, you need legal representation. Why are you so stubborn?" She went back to the table and sat down.

Sutter followed. "Anything legal would drag on through the summer and beyond. Whatever the outcome, I would be disgraced. Skiddy would lie again about the loyalty oath, and it's his word against mine. With the Douglas campaign in my past, they'll brand me a red for sure. No! What I want is a town meeting to convince three of the five trustees that I'm worthy of a new contract, which I'll tear up as soon as I find another job."

"Suit yourself," Claire said and went to put her glass and another full ashtray in the sink. "I'm going to bed, and I don't want company. Leave all of the butts in the ashtray so you don't set the house on fire."

She strode through the kitchen into the bedroom and closed the door. She had not spoken a word to Sisco, but he did not think she was pissed at him.

Len got up to announce in his principal voice, "I think we'll continue this discussion at another time so Claire can get some rest."

Sisco said that he was headed back to the jungle and that they could talk privately there. He wanted to talk about Claire and Skiddy, but Sutter had other ideas. He was headed to the 241, where he hoped to meet a trustee or two over a few drinks. He was so caught up in his own schemes that he didn't have time to listen to anybody else. If he somehow managed to wiggle out of the mess with the board, he would have to leave Hayden to find a new job. If Skiddy tried to pin a murder on him, he'd be in another jam unless he got out of town quickly. People were already speculating that he was the baby's father.

Sisco felt certain that Claire would never talk and that she'd go it by herself—an unmarried schoolteacher knocked up by some ne'er-do-well who was too much of a coward to take responsibility for their child.

Lying on his back in the jungle under the stars, Sisco tried to think about the morning he had found Carlos. His mind wasn't clear about some things. Had the church stayed open all night after the dance? Was the priest in the church while the dance was going on? Did Skiddy show up on Saturday night to be sure nobody made a big mess? Had Carlos been killed in the secrets box, or had he been moved there? When had he lost his rosary, or when had it been torn off him?

Since he couldn't sleep anyway, he got up and walked across the tracks to the Catholic church. A cool Delta breeze had blown in from the river. The only sound was some noisy pigeons flopping for the night in the bell tower. Everything else was quiet as he went up the front steps. The door opened easily. It was dark inside except for a light bulb hanging over the altar. Without knowing why, he walked toward it.

"Have you come for confession, my son?" The priest was close behind him.

"Oh!" he said, struggling to catch his breath. "You scared me, Father. I didn't think anybody was here."

"You have not come to confess, then?"

The priest sounded relieved.

Sisco tried to think of a reason to be inside the church. "I ... I just wanted to pray a little here. It seems that God hears ya better if you're at one of his churches."

"You would learn many things if you took my classes. Unfortunately, I cannot spend any time with you now because I am hearing a confession."

"I never came for your classes, Father, 'cause my gal went back to Old Mexico after her mother died. When she comes back, I do plan to take 'em."

Sisco turned to vamoose and saw movement in the confessional. Headed to the back of the church, he felt the priest close behind him, pushing in front to open the door and usher him out.

"Peace be with you, my son," he muttered.

It was good to be outside. The Catholic church gave him the creeps, and so did Father Martinez.

On the other side of the tracks, a small fire was burning. An evening rattler had come through from the south while he was inside. He hoped the 'bo who had jumped off was one of his fellow travelers and not some jungle buzzard looking to raid the grub box. He was hungry himself and wanted some good company to go with it.

Even before he saw Shorty behind the tree, he called out in a loud voice, "Hope you're heating up some cannon shells."

"Seen ya been here," Shorty answered as he came out to the fire with two cans of beans. "Looked like ya took off in a hurry somewhere."

"Yeah. Got to thinkin' on Carlos and other strange things 'round here. Went back over to the Catholic."

"You'd be better off if ya forgot about Carlos. Like I said before, the fellas and I are pretty sure it was a love spat gone bad. Peach couldn't handle Carlos dancin' with a Spic gal ... or something like that."

Sisco sat down on a crate near the fire while Shorty threw the cannon shells into a pot. He lit up a smoke and said, "If that's what happened, why did Peach get crazy to find Carlos? He was *loco*, out of his mind, when we went searchin' for him down by the depot. Naw, Memphis, I can't 'gree with ya. Think for a minute. What if Carlos just went to confess his sin of keepin' company with a jocker, and the Spic priest took that to be a 'go-head' for hisself? Carlos was caught off guard, struggled, and well ..."

"Ya caught *me* off guard with that idea, Sisco. Something else happen round here since Christmas?"

"Something's goin' on right now at the Catholic. Somebody's in the secrets box, and Father Martinez practically booted me outta the front door. He ain't even s'pose to be here today."

"Oh, c'mon! Nothing strange about a priest needing privacy for a confession. Your 'magination's got the best of ya, Kid. You been in this jerkwater too long!"

"O.K. What if I told ya that I found Carlos's turquoise rosary in the bottom of Skidmore's toolbox?"

Shorty stopped cooking and lit a smoke. "Now, I would find that kinda interesting. Let's think on how it mighta got there. Most likely it fell off somewhere in the church when the yegg, or whoever it was, roughed up Carlos. Being a good Catholic crumb boss, Skidmore picked it up and kept it till somebody showed up to claim it. All 'em Catholics have rosaries."

"Not rosaries like *that*. Carlos told me how much he loved those little blue stones from Old Mexico. Said his ma gave it to him for good luck when he caught out north."

Shorty went on with his ideas. "Or the priest mighta' found it before Mass, picked it up, and gave it to Skidmore to hang on to till the owner came along to claim it."

Sisco began to pace back and forth next to the fire pit. What his pal said made sense from somebody who didn't know Skiddy or Father Martinez. He had a sick feeling in his stomach, recalling the galway's voice behind him in the church. Father Martinez knew that he hadn't come to confess; he clearly didn't want Sisco to be there.

"Hang on a minute, Shorty. Let's s'pose that's not the way it happened. If Peach was innocent, who else coulda done in his punk?"

At first, there was no answer. Shorty just spooned up the beans into a couple of cans so they could get some food in their guts and go on talking. "These cannon shells ain't much of a sit-down. Guess you're used to better chow on the other side of the tracks."

Sisco nodded and shoveled the hot beans into his mouth.

"Lookee here," said Shorty. "Who's the only two with keys and access to the Catholic? They's thick as thieves from what you tell me. Jockers? It don't take much brains to figure out what kinda racket they could run with the church as their place of business."

Sisco stopped eating. "Skiddy knows it was me in the Catholic that morning with the body. I was never shore 'cause I hadn't been shaved or sheared up yet. The bastard 'cused me of being a yeggman when he found me in his toolbox lookin' for Len's loyalty oath that disappeared. He said that *I* let the rosary drop off the body."

Shaking his head like he could hardly believe what he heard, Shorty went to the cooking crate to pull out a full jug of dago. He said that he didn't care what booze hoister had left it there because they needed a drink or two right now, and he'd replace it later. He opened it and let Sisco take the first big swig.

"You should know one more thing. There's talk of a pervert in town. Ya know ... a fella who's a jocker?"

"I damn well know what a pervert is! Why the hell you still in this burg? Get back on the trains where ya belong and hightail it outta here! Let's vamoose on the next hot shot!"

He was right. Sisco knew he was in deep water and way over his head now. But he had unfinished business in Hayden that would haunt him the rest of his life if he didn't settle it. He had to do right by Claire because he loved her and would lose her soon enough anyway. He needed to help Len, too. Sutter was a decent man in spite of himself, and he had treated a traveling hobo like somebody special.

"I'm gonna hit the road soon as school's out. Skiddy can't fire me while Len's still the principal. I need to finish what I started."

Shorty took a big swig of the dago and coughed like he was going to say something important. "Well, I reckon I better clean myself up in town and ride it out here with you. I don't trust them townies—their noses too far up each other's asses. I don't want 'em framin' you for Carlos when ya risked a lot to do the right thing."

Sisco wanted to tell him that he didn't need to hang around Hayden on his account, but he couldn't. Truth be told, he wanted him to stay to help see things through. Shorty still didn't know about Claire; but the minute he laid eyes on her, he'd be asking questions.

The next morning, Shorty woke Sisco before the sun hit the jungle. He had made a small fire and brewed up some coffee. They drank a can together and talked about plans by the river and reelin' in a bigger trout than the one the 'bos had snagged last summer. After more coffee, Shorty said he was headed into Hayden to visit old man Sturgeon at the barbershop. He knew he would have to pay well to be deloused and cleaned up, but there'd be no snooping in town until he did. Sisco fished a ten spot out of his bindle. The least he could do was to pay for his best friend's shave and haircut.

Later that day, Sisco found a spruced-up Shorty in the drugstore shooting the shit with Mrs. Mac. Neither one of them seemed to notice when he walked in and sat down on his regular stool at the counter. They were deep in conversation about the roof that Mr. Mac had promised to repair and never got around to starting. Shorty said that he had some experience on a roof, which was much easier to ride than a moving freight train. He offered to take a look at the holes and patch them as best he could.

When Mrs. Mac went into the storeroom for paper napkins and ice cream cones, Shorty sneaked over to Sisco and whispered, "Ya gotta keep your distance from me so I can snoop and not be connected to you."

"*You* gotta keep your distance from me! I live and work here, remember?"

They agreed that Shorty would flop in the jungle unless it rained. If it did, he could creep upstairs and bunk on the floor next to the bed like he had before.

After the newspaper article and pressure from the townies, the trustees gave permission for Len to hold his public meeting. They wouldn't allow it until after graduation. The meeting got put off to the last Wednesday of Len's contract, with his final day on Friday. Sutter figured that gave him time to work his charm on three of the five board members. He felt confident that the Hayden parents with kids at the high already were lobbying hard to keep him as principal.

Sisco was so pissed at Skiddy that he didn't know if he could hang on until the end without delivering a knockout punch. He steered clear of him as much as possible. It got easier near the close of classes because the primary teachers needed more help than the teachers at the high. They had to box up paper, crayons, paste, blocks, and all of their personal stuff to store in the deep, dark, cool closets where the summer heat didn't fade, melt, or bleach them. While he helped every teacher, Sisco always seemed to wind up in Claire's room. It was obvious now that she was expecting, even though she still wasn't dressing in the baggy maternity smocks that pregnant women wore.

One afternoon after the kids had gone home, he sat with her to sort puzzle pieces. When he asked her how she was feeling, she tried to hold back the tears. "I'm sorry, Claire. Ya don't have to be brave with me. It's not good for ya to keep everything inside."

To get hold of herself, she went to the class toilet and returned with paper towels. She came back with red, puffy eyes but no more tears.

"The doctor in Lodi says everything is normal. He hears the baby's heartbeat, and I feel lots of movement."

"I'm mighty happy to hear all that," he said and took her hand. "I just wish you'd let me help ya with something—anything!"

"Thank you, Sisco. You are the most thoughtful man I've ever met. I don't know which one of you is the baby's father, but I hope with all my heart that it is *you*!"

He swallowed hard and said, "I would marry ya today, Claire, if I thought that's what you really wanted. I know ya can't take a hobo home to your folks in Berkeley. But after the baby comes, we could live somewhere else. I'd go anyplace to be with you and the baby."

"It's not that you couldn't come home to Berkeley. It's just that you wouldn't be comfortable there. And right now, I don't know if I'd be comfortable anywhere else."

"And Len?"

"Len doesn't belong in Berkeley, either. He could never settle permanently in a city even though he thinks he can get by anyplace. He is happy here and would have stayed in Hayden forever if this mess with the trustees hadn't come up."

Before they could continue their conversation, one of the primary teachers came looking for Sisco to help her move some boxes. He told Claire not to lift anything heavy and that he would be back soon to lend a hand with the packing. He still didn't know if she had told Len that she wasn't sure about the baby's father.

As the end of the school year approached, things moved fast. Students at the high were all excited about graduation. Skidmore ordered Sisco to find time to wax the gym, knowing that it would be rough with commencement practice every morning and afternoon. He messed with Len, too, by bothering him on all sorts of problems with the public address system, the fans, the lights, the boiler, the chairs and every other difficulty he could think of to keep his attention off other things.

Len was in charge of the graduation speeches given by the top two students in the senior class. He had his hands full. The boy with the best grades was a Japanese kid named Joe Fushida. He and his parents had come back from an internment camp to farm when the war was over. A Chinese girl named Ling-Ling Chen also had top marks. She hailed from Locke, a small town on the Delta built by people who had worked on the railroad and the levees in early California. The trustees tried to prevent them from being the speakers, but Len stood his ground. He reminded the board that the top students always were named as the graduation speakers. To change the tradition would make that honor a contest of favoritism. He told the trustees that they could do whatever they wanted when he was gone.

At the last minute, Joe Fushida backed out, saying he was too scared to give a speech. That cleared the way for the next student with the highest marks. Sven Nelson's boy, Lars, took Joe's place, which made things easier for Len. Lars didn't need much coaching, but Ling-Ling needed a lot of help. She was hard to understand until you figured out that every time a "w" came up in a word, it sounded like an "r."

"Re roud like to relcome you to this special day of our graduation from Hayden High."

Since Len had been trained in public speaking, he knew what exercises to practice with Ling-Ling so that she could pronounce the "w." Every afternoon during the last two weeks of school, he took her and Lars to the gym to practice their speeches with the microphone. He was patient with them both, but took extra time and care with Ling-Ling. She was so short that she had to stand on a box to reach the mic already adjusted to the lowest position. She looked like a Chinese doll in a store display on top of that crate. Her feet were so tiny that you couldn't help but stare and wonder how she found shoes small enough to fit.

As she climbed on top of the box to speak, Len pulled up a chair in front of her like he was in the audience. "Now, wait until you have the attention of the folks in front of you. When they see you at the mic, they'll quiet down. You may have to wait a few minutes so everyone in the back realizes you're up here. If there's too much noise, I'll get them in order."

He gave Ling-Ling a chance to hear her own voice over the mic and then went on. "Look around from side to side, and try your best not to stare at the floor because your voice will be muffled. Keep telling yourself to slow down and enunciate clearly as if there were deaf people in the audience, which there will be." He winked at Sisco, who stood nearby.

The closer they came to graduation, the better she got. The day before commencement, she and Lars rehearsed in the gym while some students decorated the walls with red streamers and senior pictures. Len had instructed the kids to go about their business so that the speakers could practice with other people in the gym. He wanted Ling-Ling and Lars to be comfortable for the real thing.

Commencement day was hot. Len ordered the big fans set up on the sides of the gym, with the two largest ones pointed toward the seniors in their white caps and gowns. There would be forty-nine graduates all slicked up and walking like they had a nest of eggs on their heads. The girls had a hard enough time with their high heels and their dolled-up hairdos; Sisco wondered how Ling-Ling would get up on the box for her speech and get down after.

At 2 o'clock on graduation afternoon, the gym was abuzz as parents, relatives, and friends filed in to watch the students receive their diplomas. All the windows were wide open, with the fans on high. Len instructed Sisco to turn them down to medium when things got underway because they made too much noise on high. As it was, the crepe paper decorations flapped all over the place. The president of the senior class begged him to turn off the fans so the streamers and pictures would stay on the walls. Sisco told him that he had to get Mr. Sutter's permission first. Of course, Len said "no" with the gym already like an oven.

By 3 o'clock, when things got underway, most of the decorations had held to the walls, and no one seemed to notice the fans. Claire and Shorty arrived late and sat in the back row by the open door. She was already warm when she sat down and began to fan herself with the graduation program. Shorty tried to help her out with the breeze from his program. After the flag salute, the Episcopal galway said a prayer. When Len took over as principal, he began a custom of inviting a different priest or minister to open and close the commencement. Father Martinez had done the honors for the class of 1950; this year, he was nowhere in sight.

After Sisco saluted Claire and Shorty in the back row, he made his way along the side of the gym to the front. The graduates stood up to sing songs that sounded like they belonged in church. Ling-Ling was in the front row. More than ever, she looked like a china doll with her red cheeks and her short black hair tucked under the graduation cap. He caught her eye and winked at her. She smiled back at him and then looked straight ahead. Len had told him that he scouted all over creation for a graduation costume small enough to fit her. Sisco tried to stay close when she was on the box just in case she needed him.

Lars Nelson gave his speech about some date the class of 1951 had with the future. It sounded like one of those boring speeches the President might give to get elected. When he finished, the audience clapped loud. Len stepped forward to shake his hand and to introduce Ling-Ling as the student with the best grade point average in the senior class. He said that she did so well because she studied hard to make her family proud. That was Sisco's cue to carry the crate over to the mic. Ling-Ling came up behind him, and he reached out to take her hand and help her up. She steadied herself on the box, looked from side to side, and waited to have attention from the audience.

"We would like to welcome you to this special day of our graduation from Hayden High." Her voice rang loud and clear. Every word with a "w" sounded like a word with a "w." Sisco knew her speech by heart, and it sounded almost perfect to him. At the end, everyone clapped as loud as they had for the Nelson boy. Ling-Ling's family in the audience stood up and bowed to her in honor of their daughter, sister, niece, cousin. They smiled from ear to ear; two of the older ladies wept.

What happened next was a surprise. When the other folks in the audience saw Ling-Ling's family on their feet, they stood up, too. Pretty soon, everyone was standing and clapping. Ling-Ling was crying, and Len walked over to the mic for pictures while she stood on the box. When the audience began to sit down, he helped her off the crate. With her feet on the floor, she bowed to him, and he shook her hand. The folks went wild a second time. Sisco saw his chance to move the box before the diploma part of the ceremony.

Len stepped up to the microphone. The papers for his speech stuck out of his coat pocket. He never needed to read what he wrote and most likely changed things as he went along. That made his talks more natural and easier to listen to.

"What you have seen, acknowledged, and appreciated here today is the soul and spirit of the class of 1951. These students are hardworking, dedicated, and focused on a future world of different races, faiths, and political affiliations. What we of the older generations have not learned, these young men and women of the younger generations will teach us. They are, as you have seen, open to and appreciative of diversity. In my seventeen years at Hayden High, I have tried to emphasize the importance of learning across all cultures. As I look at Lars, Ling-Ling, and their outstanding classmates, I am proud of their academic achievements. Even more, however, I am proud of the human beings they have become—individuals committed to cross cultural understanding and the importance of universal education. With immense pride, I present the class of 1951 to Mr. Homer Russell, chairman of the board of trustees."

Everybody stood to clap—this time to honor all of the graduates. Then came the long line, with Homer Russell handing each senior a diploma after Len called the student's name. It took more time than it should have taken because Len had a private word or two with each student when he shook hands. He knew every graduate, and he must have felt some sadness that he was seeing some of the kids for the last time.

While the students received their diplomas, Sisco eased his way back to check on Claire and Shorty, who had been spending a lot of time helping her pack up school supplies. Sisco had asked him to give her a hand because the graduation practices had kept him busy at the high.

Shorty had finally mentioned the baby one evening in the jungle after dark; he had heard gossip about Claire, Len, Sisco, and every other man who could have been the daddy.

"Ya ain't gonna tell me that kid is yours, are ya? I know you've had a hard-on for her since the day we buried Carlos."

"Maybe yes. Maybe no," answered Sisco as he passed the jug of dago and lit up a smoke.

"What the hell does that mean?"

"It means that we made it on New Year's Eve, and somebody else made it, too, on the same night."

"Well, I'll be horse-whipped and hog-tied," he cackled. "And the other fella is Sutter, right?"

"Right."

"Whoa! What a party you guys had! Did ya watch each other?"

"C'mon, Shorty! Ya know me better than that. Hell, ya know Claire better than that! When I left her, she was passed out in clean sheets I put on the bed. Later that night, Len came in after spendin' New Year's somewhere else. She begged me for it, Memphis. For a year, she begged me for it, and I feel so damn bad for her now 'cause she won't let me help with *anything*!"

After he heard the story, old Shorty finished most of the dago. Then, he rolled a fag, shook his head and said, "Now I know ya gotta get the hell outta here. Let *him* marry her! He can support her and the kid. Ya ain't cut out for this, Sisco!"

"She doesn't wanna hitch up with me. And I don't think she wants to marry Len, either. I don't know how he feels or what his plans are. He hasn't said a word to me."

Shorty stood up and coughed like he did when getting ready to say something important. "Soon as school's out, you're gonna deck the first rattler headed north if I have to deck you first to get ya on board!"

After that little palaver in the jungle, Shorty paid even more attention to Claire. He packed up most of the things in her house, so she'd be ready to go to Berkeley when classes finished. He told Sisco that he didn't want any excuses to stay in Hayden. He said that he felt real sorry for Claire because she was the most innocent broad he'd ever met.

Shorty also had picked up his shine for Mrs. Mac. After he repaired the roof, he spent almost every evening downstairs in the drugstore with her. She cooked his favorite dishes: fried chicken, mashed potatoes with gravy, green beans, and apple pie. The two of them got on real fine. She had a new hairdo and laughed with him more than Sisco had ever known her to with anyone else.

"She's not bad for an old gal," Shorty said after the commencement as they put away the chairs. "All her parts still work anyway—just a little rusty from being in storage."

Skiddy had disappeared from the gym before the last prayer by the Episcopal preacher. Sisco was surprised that he didn't stick around to shoot the shit with the trustees and the townies. It most likely didn't sit well with him that the graduation had come off without a hitch and there wouldn't be complaints about Len. He must have noticed Shorty next to Claire and figured he'd help out with the chairs. By that time, everybody knew that he was Sisco's hobo pal working on Mrs. Mac's roof and helping Miss Lewis with her move.

"The only reason I'm lendin' ya a hand here is that I need your bed for an hour or so. Private reasons, and there won't be no crumbs left afterwards," said Shorty.

Sisco laughed the loudest he had in years. "So now we know just how far some home-cooked mongee goes! Help yourself to my bed, but don't get caught or we'll both be in the hoosegow tonight!"

"The only hobo ever gets caught is *you!*" he whispered and was out the door.

Sisco locked up the gym and walked back to the office. It was near dark, and lights were on with the front doors wide open. Len looked busy; he had pulled all of the drawers out of his desk and stacked them on top. He stuffed everything into a big duffle bag like a soldier on his way to war. He had two smokes lit up in the ashtray and a bottle of booze next to the drawers. He had thrown his tie and coat over a chair and rolled up his sleeves.

"Ya gave a good talk," Sisco said and sat down to light up a smoke. "And how 'bout Ling-Ling? Didn't she make ya proud?"

Nodding his head, Sutter handed over the bottle of hooch. Sisco asked if he needed help packing up his shit.

"No, thanks. I don't need help because I'm throwing away most of these documents when I get back to Woodland. Don't want any of it around here for the vultures." He never looked up from the pile of papers.

"Seems like you've pretty much decided to leave even if they give ya a new contract."

"It's my fault," he answered and sat down in his chair. "I never should have trusted that son-of-a-bitch. I was so fed up with the loyalty oath thing. Skidmore knew it, too. When I finally signed, I practically threw it at him to deliver to the trustees. I'm sure he told them. In my meeting with them, they questioned my loyalty to the country and accused me of working on the Douglas campaign during school hours. They called my moral character into question, accusing me of carrying on with a married dame whose husband is a booster of the athletic program at the high. They said that teachers had reported me asleep in the boiler room during the day. You and I both know that Skidmore is the only person, besides you, who goes in there during classes."

The case against Sutter seemed strong, even if some of it wasn't true. He had been careless in the way he handled the loyalty oath, how he worked on Mrs. Douglas' campaign, and the school time he used to romance the dance teacher. Sisco had never seen him asleep in the boiler room, but Skiddy had written notes of the dates when he had found him there. Like so many things, it was Skidmore's word against Len's. Sutter said that the back-door deal with three of the trustees had fallen apart because they were confused and couldn't be counted on to vote for a new contract. "In the end, my friend, they are good old Hayden boys who don't trust me even though I'm one of them—admittedly from up the highway. This whole business with the murdered kids has them scared, and they want to rebuild the fortress so nobody from the outside gets in. It's time for me to leave—for you, too, I think. Wish I could stick around to help you get your birth certificate back, but I think we both better vamoose. I can't do much to protect you anymore."

Sisco replied that Shorty had been able to get a copy of his birth certificate from the county where he was born which sounded like a good idea. Then Sisco asked about the meeting with the townies and the board arranged for the following week.

"Oh, we'll have the meeting, all right, even if no one comes. I have a few choice words to say to the good citizens of Hayden. I want my formal resignation recorded here by the newspaper. It may serve to vindicate me in the future."

Sisco promised that he and Memphis Shorty would be there. The hobos would see things through to the end.

Reckoning

Skiddy and Len both had predicted that almost nobody would show up for the meeting after graduation. They were right. Sisco and Shorty set up the chairs to fill half the gymnasium. There were extras on the cart in case the crowd got too big. In the end, only three rows filled up. It looked like the meeting would be a waste of time.

All the trustees were there behind a table and faced toward the townies in the chairs. Len showed up just as the thing was supposed to begin. When he came into the gym, he stopped to talk to everyone who stood around and waited for him to get things started. He looked happy enough and never let on if he was disappointed at the small crowd. The trustees finally sat down. He ignored them.

Like almost every day in the summer, that Wednesday afternoon at the end of June was stifling hot. The 'bos had hooked up the big fans just like they did for commencement. The old fans made a lot of noise, and it was going to be hard to hear. When Sisco asked Skidmore for the keys to bring out the mic, he answered that it wouldn't be needed because there were so few people in the audience. If they really wanted to hear, they could sit closer to the front. Shorty suggested they move all the fans toward the back of the gym and point them forward. The air would cool things down, but most of the noise would be at the rear. That's what they decided to do before things got started.

Claire and Mrs. Mac came in through the side door. Claire wore a short-sleeved, loose yellow sundress with a scoop neck. Her breasts pushed up over the top, and Sisco tried hard not to think about how much he still wanted her. It wasn't right to covet her body now, though, because she was with child, and those tits were full of milk for the baby.

309

Mrs. Mac was all dolled up in a green dress with pink flowers and white high-heeled shoes. She looked ready for church, which was the only special place she ever went. Since Shorty had been in town, she wore fancy clothes almost every day. Now, she gave him a quick look and a wave before leading Claire to a seat in the front row.

The big meeting was supposed to start at 3 o'clock, but nobody seemed anxious to get underway. Tre Sorenson sat in front at the table and chatted with the other trustees while he watched Len out of the corner of his eye. He kept taking out his pocket watch to look at the time like he wanted things to begin. Len was not in any hurry; he was principal for two more days, and he was doing things his way.

Shorty came up from the back when Sisco gave him the high sign that the breeze from the fans was right. He walked to the front row to sit down next to Mrs. Mac in a chair she must have saved for him. More ranchers and townies wandered in with handkerchiefs in hand to mop the sweat from their faces. They sat down in the last row, where the air from the fans was at their backs. Sisco counted thirty-two folks, not including a few who stood along the sides of the gym. That's where Skiddy posted himself like he usually did when there was a meeting. Today, he wasn't dressed for work in his overalls. He wore a pale blue sport shirt, dark slacks, and his dress shoes. A toothpick hung out of his mouth like he had just eaten.

Len finally took a seat in the front row, which gave Homer Russell, chairman of the trustees, his chance to call for order and the salute to the flag. Next, he prayed to ask a blessing from the Almighty for "these reasonable and faithful men dedicated to the will of the Lord and the best interests of the citizens of Hayden." He sat down, squirmed in his seat and looked uncomfortable as he admitted that he didn't know why a meeting had been called but that he was certain Mr. Sutter would clear things up soon. He went on to thank Len for his "seventeen years of outstanding service to the students of Hayden High School." He kept glancing over to the side of the gym where Skidmore had begun to pace in front of the door. Russell acted like he didn't know what to do next, so he tried his hand at some jokes that nobody found funny.

An old rancher in dirty overalls stood up to say his piece. "Homer, why don't ya let Sutter have a few words? He's the one we come to hear."

Russell nodded in Len's direction and motioned him up to the table where the trustees were seated. Still looking confused, he sat down with other board members.

Len faced the audience to speak. He began by thanking everybody for their support throughout his time at the high. With a few steps closer to the front row, he said that the good citizens of Hayden knew the trustees did not plan to renew his contract for next year. He promised to abide by that decision so that the education of their sons and daughters would not be interrupted. To fight the board's decision would mean a long legal battle, and he would not paralyze their kids' education with a big scandal that might divide the community. He vowed never to jeopardize any student's opportunity to learn.

The folks in the audience were all abuzz. Rancher Wilson stood up next to his chair. "We're with ya, Sutter! Go ahead and fight 'em!"

Others chimed in, "Yeah! Don't let 'em force you out!"

Len raised his hand to signal that he wanted to continue. He said that he appreciated their encouragement but that a legal battle would be long, expensive, nasty, and full of untruths. In good conscience, he could not put the town through all that. He did, however, want to talk to them about loyalty.

"Say your piece, Sutter," piped up another rancher. "Afterwards, we'll hear from them." He pointed to the table.

Len went on. "I want to talk about the loyalty oath specifically, which I signed and sent on to the trustees. In principle, I do not agree with the requirement that all public officials sign in order to retain their employment. But, wouldn't you—any of you—sign a paper to keep your pay?"

People looked around at each other and nodded.

"Republican, Democrat, Socialist, Communist—whatever party affiliation—a person signs to hang onto a job. My point is that signing is no sure way to measure a person's loyalty to the government of the United States of America. On the other hand, most of us who signed are loyal Americans. Most of you know that I did not serve in the armed forces during the war. You also know that I kept the school going—fully accredited and patriotic. Some of the gents and ladies in the audience helped out with our bandage campaign. Others volunteered here in this gymnasium to assemble care kits of toiletries to send overseas. Many who are not here today joined me on the bus trip to the USO in San Francisco, where we welcomed home wounded soldiers, sailors, and marines from Europe and the Pacific. Some also remember that I personally wrote to our Hayden boys who enlisted as seniors when the Japanese bombed Pearl. I made certain that as many as possible finished their last year through correspondence to earn a diploma."

Here, he stopped to wait for a question or a comment. No one said anything; the folks seemed to be stuck to their seats. Len went on to say that he knew some of the trustees were against his activism on behalf of Helen Douglas and her support of popular causes. He said that everyone in the audience was aware of his efforts on behalf of the farmworkers and the *braceros*. There had never been a secret about that since they, like the people of Hayden, were poor, hardworking, and honest. He was sure that he, Leonard Sutter, had been hired by the board because he was one of them and understood the Hayden community.

With that, he turned to face the table and the board members. None of the five looked at him; they stared over to the side of the gym where Skiddy continued to pace by the door.

Finally, Olaf Gustafson met Len's glance and spoke up. "I ... we know you done a lot for this school, Len. It's just time for you to move on. That's all."

"Are you saying that I am a Commie, Olaf? That's basically the reason you guys gave me when we had our meeting. I want you to set the record straight here and now in front of everybody." He nodded at the frizzy-haired reporter in the front row.

Then something unexpected happened. Claire raised her hand and stood up before Homer Russell recognized her. She turned her back to the trustees to face the audience. "Mr. Russell and other members of the board know me, my teaching record, and my association with Len Sutter. He is not a Communist. I watched him sign the loyalty oath and advised him to deliver it directly to the trustees. Instead, he foolishly entrusted it to Mr. Skidmore. Let me say what is not being said here. Mr. Skidmore has engaged in mean-spirited gossip and lies about his boss. He has a personal vendetta against him in spite of Mr. Sutter's unwavering trust and the fact that Len hired him as head custodian and protected his job when members of the Hayden community wanted him fired. If you are concerned about loyalty, then you should question Mr. Skidmore about *his*!"

She sat down. There wasn't a sound in the gym. Skiddy disappeared out the door, and Len seemed

313

paralyzed in his chair. The trustees looked back-and-forth at each other with worried faces.

The reporter from the newspaper had stopped pushing her pencil. She was on her feet and facing toward Claire at the other end of the front row. "Miss Lewis, are you saying that board members and Mr. Skidmore have conspired to accuse Mr. Sutter falsely of being a Communist, so they have a reason not to renew his contract?"

Claire pulled herself up once more and spoke in a loud, strong voice. "I cannot say who is in collusion with whom. What I do know is that Mr. Sutter's loyalty has been questioned, and he has been falsely accused of Red sympathies."

Now, Walt Gray stood up. Until then, he had remained quiet, but you could tell by the way the other trustees looked at him that he was calling the shots at the table. With a shaky voice, he said, "The board never said that Leonard Sutter is a Communist. What was said is that he has been into some shady activities—on school time. You folks elected us to maintain high standards of professional and personal conduct. There are other issues that cannot be discussed here 'cause they ain't decent and an innocent person or two might be hurt if we did."

To everyone's surprise, Claire got out of her seat one more time to shout back. "What is indecent, Mr. Gray and members of the school board, is that you rely on a custodian for false information and innuendo to make your decisions. If you were more involved in the schools and spent more time in the classrooms like you're supposed to do, you'd know what's really going on and the extent of Mr. Sutter's commitment. Until your secret meeting last week to which Mr. Skidmore was invited and Mr. Sutter was *not*, I had not seen any one of you at the primary school all year. You are the ones who should be terminated!"

314

She sat down, and Mrs. Mac put an arm around her shoulder. The rest of the audience was buzzing. Len looked straight at the trustee table and stared down the board members.

Then Farmer Wilson was on his feet to speak. "If this whole deal is just fireworks between Sutter and Skidmore, it seems to me that the trustees oughta think 'bout another contract for Len."

Homer Russell fingered his mustache like he was looking for something hidden in the hairs. The other four members conferred with each other, and for a moment, it looked like Len might have pulled things off.

Then Homer spoke up. "As chairman of the board of trustees, I want to assure you folks that we do not question Mr. Sutter's loyalty to this school district or its students. Our final decision on the contract will be made at a closed meeting tomorrow. I repeat that the meeting is *closed* because the matter is delicate."

That created more confusion, and the audience broke out in whispers. The reporter with the frizzy hair jumped out of her chair and shouted, "Mr. Chairman, will you please elaborate? The citizens of this town deserve an explanation!"

"Yeah! Yeah!" shouted some of the ranchers.

Homer Russell was lost. He didn't know what to answer, so he asked if Mr. Skidmore was in the gym. Everyone looked over to the side where they had seen Skiddy earlier. He wasn't there.

"Well, then," said Russell with one hand still in his mustache, "since no one has anything else to add, I guess we can adjourn."

Folks grumbled in their chairs but didn't get up to leave. There was a ruckus at the side door. In walked Skiddy with the G-man behind him. Russell found his "chairman of the board voice" and directed the audience to stay seated because there would be some answers now.

The G-man wore the same suit and cowboy boots he had on when he was invited to the Sorenson ranch. With heavy, hard steps that echoed all through the gym, he walked to the front where he handed his cowboy hat to Olaf. They did not shake hands. The G-man coughed and looked over at Skiddy, who slinked his way along the side of the gym and gave a nod to start.

"Ladies and gentlemen, I have been invited here by certain members of the board of trustees and by Mr. Skidmore, who has assisted my agency with sensitive information. I represent the Federal Bureau of Investigation, or as you know it, the F.B.I."

Loud gasps came from the audience. The good folks of Hayden looked back-and-forth at each other. Skiddy stayed on the side but moved closer to the front. He worked a toothpick all over his mouth like he was going to chew it up and swallow it.

"For some time now, the bureau has been investigating Mr. Leonard Sutter's loyalties. You know about his political activities with the Pink Lady because he used a school building for a meeting in her support. He has done other things that you may not fully understand, like having a big celebration on May first last year. That date is the International Labor Day of the Communist Party. And you do know that kids were the main attraction, a subtle way to begin the indoctrination of innocent children."

Claire rested her head on Mrs. Mac's shoulder while others in the audience moved and shifted. Len turned around to see the reactions of the townies. Some folks looked at him, and others looked away.

No one said or did anything as the G-man continued, "Mr. Sutter used school resources and personnel to make elaborate May Day poles for a celebration that glorifies the

Communist Party. Furthermore, he selected a student from China—a Communist country—to deliver the commencement address in a class of *real* Americans who had excellent marks. He has been an open supporter and friend of the Japs before, during, and after a war in which those people attacked Pearl Harbor and fought against us."

There were whispers and murmurs from the audience. All heads turned toward Len, who looked straight at the G-man. Skiddy slinked closer to the chairs and sat down in an empty one on the end of the second row to hear better. Sisco feared the worst was yet to come.

"Although Mr. Sutter signed the loyalty oath, he did so reluctantly and after the deadline given by the trustees. Now, however, the bureau is investigating him on other possible criminal charges."

Len jumped to his feet. He walked up to the G-man like he was going to take a swing but stopped short. "You son-of-a-bitch! I am not a criminal, and you know it! So do the people of Hayden. If you are about to accuse me of a crime, I have the right to legal counsel immediately—in private! You represent the most despicable of Hoover's Nazi police. How dare you accuse me of criminal activity? I am a greater patriot and defender of the Constitution than you or your comrades ever will be!"

From the audience came a clap or two as folks shifted again in their chairs. In their restless movements and their worried faces, Sisco saw their fear. They didn't know what to do.

"You requested this meeting, Mr. Sutter," said the G-man in a calm voice. "None of these allegations was to be public, but the trustees had to defend their actions once you brought things before the townspeople."

"Just exactly what are you accusing me of? I have nothing to hide from you or anybody in this town." He lit up a smoke, which he never did in a meeting with students or their parents.

The agent crossed his arms and leaned back against the table like he was having the time of his life. "No one is accusing you of anything, Mr. Sutter. The bureau is investigating any knowledge or role you may have in the disappearance of two Hayden High School students."

A hush and then a group gasp lifted from the audience. Everyone stood up. Sisco did the same to see if Claire was on her feet. She was standing, but her left arm was hooked through Mrs. Mac's elbow for support.

As he picked up his cowboy hat off the table, the G-man peered into the audience and nodded his head. "You're dead right, Sutter! You *do* need legal counsel, and the sooner the better for you! Don't think about leaving town either!"

He started for the side door where Skiddy followed behind him.

"Hang on, Mister! You're fingering the wrong guy!"

The F.B.I. agent stopped short and turned around to face Shorty, who was on his feet in the front row.

"Who are you? And why are you speaking up now?"

Quick to answer, Shorty replied, "I'm just a hobo in town to help out a friend here. A tramp we knew on the road strangled and ... uh ... took advantage of a Spic kid off the rails here a year and a half ago. We buried him by the river."

Still standing, the folks in the audience made a sound together like they were taking their last breath. Sisco knew it was too late to stop Shorty. He figured they all were going to end up in the hoosegow.

Shorty went on. "This guy is a jocker—likes young kids in high school. He's strong as an ox 'cause he was raised up on a peach farm in Georgia. Ain't seen him much since that thing happened 'cause he ain't someone we wanna travel with anymore. Ya oughta take a look at him for your dead boys."

The gumshoe went back to the table and shouted at Olaf to ask why the trustees hadn't told him about the pervert in Hayden. The board members shot blanks at each other and shrugged their shoulders.

"Can't say any of us knew about this before," answered Olaf. "Why don't ya ask this tramp if he ever reported the crime to the local police?"

"Ya could ask me yourself," piped up Shorty. "And the answer would be no, 'cause whoever listens to or believes a bum? Besides, he was just a dead Spic. We never even knowed his last name."

People sat down again; it looked like there was more to come. The reporter scribbled like crazy on her notepad. Tomorrow's story would be the biggest scoop Hayden had seen in years.

"Does anybody else know 'bout this wetback's body?" asked the F.B.I. agent.

"I'm the one who found him, sir," choked Sisco. "In the confession box at the Catholic on Sunday morning right before Mr. Skidmore came in to get ready for Mass. He told me … his exact words was … 'Get rid of the body!'"

Once more, the folks in the audience were on their feet. The whole congregation turned to stare at Skiddy.

Looking back and forth between the two hobos, the G-man asked, "Either one of you know how to locate this pervert tramp from Georgia?"

Sisco shook his head and nodded at Shorty, who was Johnny on-the-spot with an answer.

"Naw, we shore don't. We heard he went north but ain't seen him since. He coulda come back through here without us knowing. Us hobos sneak in and out pretty good."

With hat in hand a second time, the F.B.I. agent heaved a sigh and said, "There may be more here to investigate, but I don't have the time to look into all this small town intrigue."

"What about Mr. Sutter?" shouted Homer Russell, who needed somebody to tell him what to do.

"You people have to decide. The bureau doesn't get involved in local politics."

With the trustees trailing after him, the G-man left through the side door. As he tried to follow, Skiddy was cornered by Farmer Wilson, who put a hand on his shoulder and wasn't turning loose. Len was tied up with Miss Frizzy Hair and others who supported him. Sisco felt good that he had said what he did about that morning in the confessional. He had told the truth as far as it went. The bureau dick hadn't seemed to remember their conversation on New Year's at the drugstore. Sisco wondered if he recalled the birth certificate he had taken. The G-man didn't seem to be taking this investigation too seriously.

When most of the folks had gone, Claire stood up to leave. Mrs. Mac was by her side, and Shorty held her arm as they headed to the door. Sisco figured he'd see her later at the house; Len would stop by, too, if he wasn't tanked up at the 241.

"That weasel plumb skidded outta all this, didn't he?" said Shorty when he came back to help put away the chairs. "Unless these jerkwaters pretend they didn't hear what you said 'bout gettin' rid of the body, they'll put him on the hot seat now."

"I dunno what they'll do. I just hope we'll be gone by the time they figure it all out. He ain't gonna follow us. Shore pisses me off though that the bull dick still has my birth certificate, but I ain't gonna look him up to get it back. Say, pal, ya really pulled a rabbit outta the hat today at the meeting."

"Don't know what you're talkin' 'bout, Sisco," he answered as he wiped his forehead with an old red bandana from his pocket. "Bad enough I accused a dead man who can't defend hisself, but I know what I know."

Shorty sure did know that Peach had caught the Westbound before the other boys were done in. The fact that he would always blame Peach for Carlos' death gave him the story that saved Sutter and Sisco—for the moment. Len believed there needed to be only a doubt in people's minds. After all the good that folks had said about him that afternoon, the thing that helped him most was Shorty's story. Now the F.B.I. would have to interview Skidmore in a different way than they had so far, and Len might take a chance on leaving Hayden. It was clear that the trustees wanted him gone.

Sisco went by Claire's house. It was dark; she didn't answer either the front or back door. With her Chevy parked next to the sidewalk, she had to be inside. When he couldn't rouse her, he figured that she needed to rest after what had happened earlier. She had helped to point the finger at Skiddy, too, and he was proud of how she spoke up to defend Len.

He crossed the tracks to the jungle, where he found Shorty cooking a mulligan. "What ya got in it?" he asked.

"Few pataturs, celery, onion, and carrots," answered the old hobo without looking up.

Sisco went behind the oaks to pull out a jug of dago. He had bought it in the morning so there'd be some hooch to celebrate if the meeting turned out O.K. He wasn't certain just *how* the meeting had turned out, and he hoped that Shorty would give his opinion about it.

"I'll wager we both could use a few swigs of firewater after today," Sisco said as he took big gulps before passing the jug to Shorty, who didn't say a word until he had chugged down the grape juice and set it half-empty on the ground.

"What in tarnation is wrong with you, Sisco? Why are ya protectin' that sidewinder Skidmore?"

"Hey, you're the one who said he mighta found the cross on the floor of the Catholic."

"Yeah, I did say that before all this shit this afternoon. But, hell, you know him better. Ya had to realize what a snake he is after working next to him for two years."

Sisco shook his head. "Just tried to stay outta things. That's all."

"Goddamned pussy-whipped is what you are! Ya been too busy trying to bed the school teacher. Goddamned townies always get ya into trouble!" He turned to stir the mulligan.

Sisco waited for him to cool off and take a few more swigs of the dago. He lit them both a smoke and said, "Look. I got in over my head. I fess up to that. You're older and smarter. Ya decided way back when to stay on the road long as ya could. I dunno if that's what I want. Just had to try something else before I made up my mind."

After a few good drags on his smoke, Shorty said, "Ya ain't gonna marry Claire even if this baby is yours. Ya ain't gonna save Len even if they investigate Skidmore. Those G-bastards are after Sutter for one thing or another -- not you."

Just then, the 'bos heard an automobile behind them on the road next to the milk plant, and within minutes, Len stepped out from the trees.

"Evening, fellas. I saw your smoke from over on Fourth. Thought I'd stop by."

"C'mon in," said Sisco. "Dago's 'most gone, but ya can have what's left."

"Thanks, but I've got some booze. Happy to share it with you fellas." He pulled the familiar flask of brandy out of his pants pocket, took a drink, and passed it to Sisco, who drank a little to be sociable.

"I came here to thank you both for supporting me today."

"Pleased to help out. We owed ya one," said Shorty, offering Len one of his rolled smokes. "Shore stirred 'em up over there, didn't we? I think some of 'em old geezers was ready to have a heart attack."

"We turned their world upside down, and they're not used to that. But they'll set it up right again. Once I'm gone, things will get back to how they were. These folks don't care about the Commie thing and they don't want the F.B.I. meddling in their business if the Bureau can't solve the murders."

"If ya ask me," Sisco chimed in, "It's the son-of-a-bitch G-man who upset it all."

Everything went quiet except the crickets singing in their full night voices. The mosquitos had stayed away so far because of the Delta breeze. Somewhere nearby, the night jasmine was in bloom, and the air was sweet. Sisco thought of Claire—how she smelled when they danced close. His stomach lurched to know that they'd never be that way again.

As he served up the mulligan, Shorty had to say one more time that he liked Peach for Carlos' murder. He wasn't sure about the farm kids, who could have been killed by almost anybody in town. What he did figure was that the boys had to know and trust whoever did them in. That guy, or guys, wasn't a hobo or a tramp.

Sisco added, "Pretty damn clever of you to finger Peach for the rancher kids. Like Len says, all ya have to do is create a doubt. I'll wager there's something strange, though, between Father Martinez and Skiddy. Always thought it was the Catholic stuff with Skidmore as the crumb boss and all. Then, one night I was outside the church in the back and overheard 'em whisperin'. Couldn't make out all of it, but they wanted to pin Carlos on you, Len. Once they found a way to do that, they coulda invented some shit 'bout the boys from the high. Skiddy has 'nough dirt to make up all kinda stories."

A rattler sounded as she came up from Lodi. They stopped their talking and ate mulligan as the hog took on water. It wouldn't be long before the hobos caught out for Dunsmuir. While he looked forward to fishing on the river, Sisco had a different feel in his stomach this year. He wasn't excited or eager to see Lady Shasta like the summer before. He didn't even look forward to seeing Cleveland Jack and shooting the shit about the saucer men. When he left Hayden, he would lose both Claire and Len, who had been the closest family since his own folks.

After the hogger picked up speed and the rattler was almost gone, Shorty said, "So either them two assholes is real jockers or they're hell-bent to get ya outta here, Sutter."

"Or it's both," said Sisco.

"Look, fellas, they're not after me because I know or care about where they stick their dicks. They're after me because I tried to change some things in Hayden, tried to open up their minds and bring them forward in their thinking. I'm just too liberal for them and the Commie deal has them confused and afraid. These folks here damn well know that I didn't corn hole or murder their kids. And I think it all might go away if I just married Claire, which I am not going to do. There's easier pickin's, but this community is just not having it anymore."

Sisco choked on a carrot in the mulligan and coughed to clear it.

Shorty picked up on things fast.

"Did ya even ask her, Sutter?"

Len put down his can of stew and lit up a Lucky. "Before all this latest mess with the trustees, I told her we could get married so the kid would be legit. I said we could play house here or in Woodland at my mother's ranch. I made it clear that I would not live in Berkeley near her folks."

"And she didn't go for any of it, did she?" asked Sisco.

"None of it. You know as well as I do that Claire has not been happy here. She's not comfortable in a small town, and she misses her parents. They will help her provide the best home possible for the child. Hang on a minute while I get something in the Ford."

Len disappeared behind the trees, and Shorty walked over to Sisco to whisper, "Does he know 'bout you?"

Sisco shrugged his shoulders and whispered back, "Never mentioned a thing."

When he came back, Len had a long yellow envelope. He handed it to Sisco and said, "Right now, I can't offer Claire or the baby anything except money. The trustees will fire me to restore order in Hayden, so I will be on my way somewhere after I see my mother. There's $5,000 in the envelope. Please give it to Claire and tell her that I am sorry for everything, and that I wish her, and the baby, the best."

Sisco was speechless as he took the envelope. He tried to say something but mumbled his words and turned around so they wouldn't see his tears. Shorty covered things up by asking Len where he was headed.

"Like to see Old Mexico. Go south to the border, buy a bus ticket and travel with the natives over to visit the Indian ruins. Always wanted to see the Pyramids. Thought I might pick up a pretty Spanish gal as my tour guide." He laughed nervously.

Sisco wanted to laugh, but he didn't see much that was funny. His stomach was flip-flopping all over the place

325

again. He knew that he'd never set eyes on Len after today. He recalled Claire saying that Len always left his messes behind for somebody else to clean up. Here he was doing that one more time; and he, himself, was fixing to do the same thing in a day or two. He vowed that in the future, he would never settle in with a woman unless he planned to stay around and take care of her.

"Ya gotta do what ya gotta do, Len. Ole Shorty and me are headed north in a few days. We'll hang 'round long 'nough to help Claire pack up her automobile. I'll give her the envelope and your message."

They shook hands. Truthfully, Sisco didn't know how to say good-bye because he didn't practice much. When you rode the rails, you just left whenever a rattler came by headed in the right direction. He did thank Sutter for the job at the high and said that, far as he could tell, Len was a good principal and ought to be able to find another position. They didn't mention Claire anymore, and Len drove off with a wave and a toot of his horn.

§ § § § §

Sisco tried to help Claire pack up, but he didn't go very fast because he wanted every possible minute with her. Shorty did most of the work just to be sure it got done. Claire's father had hired a truck from one of his construction jobs to carry the big stuff to Berkeley. He drove his Pontiac, which was packed full, too. The last of everything went into her Chevy. As they finished the job, Sisco gave Claire the envelope.

"In the end, he's just a coward, isn't he?' she asked him.

"Maybe," he answered. "I think he 'shamed on it all. Figured he'd do ya a favor by gettin' the hell out."

"I hope I've learned my lesson," she said and stuffed the unopened envelope in the glove box of her automobile.

When it was time to say good-bye to her, Sisco wanted to run away. She must have felt the same because all they could do was hold hands and hug each other. Sisco swore the baby inside her moved like a critter in a cage trying to spring free. With her father watching from the Pontiac, he didn't dare kiss her the way he wanted to. Claire had told her father that he was the school custodian and a good friend. But Shorty had jawboned with Mr. Lewis while they were packing up, so it was pretty certain that her father realized they were hobos. If Mr. Lewis had any idea that Sisco might be the father of his grandchild, he would have shot both tramps on the spot.

Sisco promised to keep track of Claire and the baby, but he never did. The only thing he ever gave her to remember him by was the valentine heart card from the first grade class. He had printed his name inside and drawn a simple hobo sign below. It was the cat sketched on the fence behind her house in the alley —"kind lady lives here."

§ § § § §

In the end, a real hobo just keeps rolling on the rails until he no longer can. If he's not killed on the trains, he takes final cover in one of those old folks' homes or in a cheap boardinghouse where he sits on the front porch and waits for the Westbound to carry him to his only real destination. Kid Sisco wasn't a Rambling Rudy Phillips; he never made a reputation as somebody special in tramp lore. But he remained true to the Hobo Code of the Road, staying loyal to his friends on and off the rattlers. He may have left his heart with a lady in a jerkwater, but he left his soul with the hobos on the rails.

Glossary

Alkee - To get drunk.

Apple knocker - One who shakes the branches or hits apples with a stick to get them, as opposed to climbing the tree or a ladder.

Bindle - A roll of bedding and other possessions carried by a hobo on the road.

Bindle stiff - A hobo who carries a bindle.

Blanket stiff - A West Coast term for bindle stiff.

Blinds - The platform outside the door of a car facing the coal car or engine tender.

Bo - short for "hobo"; an itinerant worker.

Boil up - To boil clothes to clean them and kill bugs.

Boomer - A seasonal, temporary or migratory worker.

Bone polisher - Mean dog.

Booze hoister - Heavy drinker

Bull - Detective or any law officer.

Bum - Lazy, non-travelling vagrant.

Cannon shells - Canned beans

Clover kicker - Farmer

Croaker, sawbones - Doctor

Crumb boss - Janitor or porter for the bunkhouse.

Crummy - Lice infested (in the early days cabooses were often lousy).

Dago red - Cheap red wine.

ESPEE - Southern Pacific Railroad (SP)

Fags - Smokes

Galway - Priest

Glim - A match or light.

Glims - Spectacles, eyeglasses

Headlights - Eggs

Hog - Locomotive

Hogger - Locomotive engineer

Jackroller - One who robs other hobos or tramps.

Jerkwater - A small town.

Jocker - A tramp who has boys do his begging.

Jungle - A hobo camp (usually near the tracks and water).

Jungle buzzard - One who eats food left in jungles or begs from hobos.

Kelly stick - A device used while boiling up (usually a tin can with punched holes and nailed on a stick to agitate wash water).

Lousy Anna - Louisiana

Makins - Bull Durham or other rolling tobacco.

Mongee - Food

Mulligan - A stew of whatever is available.

Punk - A young boy who travels with a jocker.

Rattler – A fast-moving train made up mostly of empty cars, so it rattles.

San Berdo - San Bernadino

Scenery bum - A young tramp on the move for pleasure.

Stake - Money saved up for the future.

Stew bum - A drunk, broken down hobo.

Take the Westbound - To die.

Town clown - Town policeman or constable.

Tramp - A vagrant who lives by begging and never works.

The Author

A third generation Californian, Terry A. Albritton grew up in the Central Valley and in the Bay Area. With degrees in Spanish and political science from UC Berkeley, she has bilingual credentials and has taught in Bolivia, Panama, and California.

Her fascination with diverse cultures inspired her prize winning short story, "The Grief Lump," about a West Indian woman in the Canal Zone at the time of the U.S. Panama Treaties of 1979. She collaborated with a Peruvian cosmologist, Anton Ponce de Leon, to translate into English his book, *Y el anciano hablo*. The translation, *The Wisdom of the Ancient One,* was published by Blue Star Communications. During her travels to Mexico over a twenty-year period, she studied with an indigenous investigator, Felipe Alvarado Peralta, and helped to facilitate publication of his four monographs on the legendary Mesoamerican figure, Quetzalcoatl.

For twenty-four years, Terry worked with communities impacted by HIV/AIDS in San Diego and the border area. She returned to the Central Valley in 2013 to complete a full-length novel, *The Last Real Hobo*. Historical fiction, it is based in part on her family history in the Sacramento area. She resides in the rural community upon which the setting of the novel is drawn. She is active in the local historical society while continuing to teach part-time.

TULEBURG PRESS

Seeking to provide a "voice" for the Northern San Joaquin Valley, Tuleburg Press was founded in 2013 by faculty and staff affiliated with San Joaquin Delta College, the University of the Pacific, and the University of California, Merced, along with other members of local writing communities.

Its purpose is to publish works of literary merit and educational value, relevant to life in California's Central Valley, that would not necessarily attract the interest and support of conventional commercial publishers.

Tuleburg Press is a tax-exempt 501 (c) (3) nonprofit organization.

Made in the USA
San Bernardino, CA
11 July 2020